59

W9-CPW-977

RAVE REVIEWS
THE FRAILTY OF FLESH!

"The talented Ruttan turns a spotlight on the gritty reality of law enforcement . . . and the result is truly convoluted and disturbing."
—*RT Book Reviews*

"*The Frailty of Flesh* tore me asunder. Rarely has a novel of such art and skill reduced me to a wreck. . . . It's a kick in the head that is underwrit with sheer compassion."
—Ken Bruen, Shamus Award–winning
Author of *The Guards*

"Brave, dark and utterly convincing, *The Frailty of Flesh* is guaranteed to break the hardest of hearts. An absorbing read."
—Allan Guthrie, Theakston Award–winning
Author of *Hard Man*

"*The Frailty of Flesh* is not only one of the best procedural thrillers I've read in a long time . . . but the ending knocked me right out of my seat. Ruttan captures the nature of crime in a way few thriller writers ever manage . . . this is vivid, impressive, gut-wrenching stuff."
—Russel D. McLean, Crime Scene Scotland,
Author of *The Good Son*

WHAT BURNS WITHIN

"Ruttan manages to keep multiple leads and seconds on the same page admirably: she doesn't drop too many clues in their laps or allow the tension to flag. . . . The straight proceduralism from Ruttan serves the story well through the rewarding climax."
—*Publishers Weekly*

"Well worth adding to any mystery collection."
—*Library Journal*

"One absolute wallop of a novel. . . . A totally mesmerizing narrative and a plot that literally burns off the page."
—Ken Bruen, Shamus Award–winning
Author of *The Guards*

"A taut, crackling read with switch-blade pacing."
—Rick Mofina, Bestselling Author of *A Perfect Grave*

MORE PRAISE FOR SANDRA RUTTAN!

"Ruttan has a spellbinding style."
— *New York Times* Bestselling Author Clive Cussler

"Ruttan's deft touch intrigues and satisfies, making her a powerful new force in the mystery field."
— JT Ellison, Author of *All the Pretty Girls*

"A well executed procedural with a plot that twists and turns like a bad tempered rattlesnake."
— Russel D. McLean, Crime Scene Scotland

"Ruttan clearly has the potential to be a very successful author. . . . Lots of talent which I expect will be realized!"
— Maddy Van Hertbruggen, Mystery News

"Ruttan has made one big mistake in my eyes; she waited too long to bring her writing to us. She is talented in the way that a natural musician is talented, making all the notes seem effortless. Characters that feel very real, and a wonderful sense of timing, Ruttan brings it all and leaves it on the page. Lucky us. And unlucky me, because now I have to wait for the next one. . . ."
— Jon Jordan, *Crimespree Magazine*

"Sandra Ruttan writes with a machine gun rhythm that pulls you through every unexpected twist and dark turn."
— Bill Cameron, Author of *Lost Dog*

FINDING THE BODY

Nolan walked toward the disturbed dirt and then stopped, still as a statue. From where Ashlyn stood she couldn't see anything and when she glanced at the rangers the older man had turned his gaze toward the ground. The younger man glanced at her, then his partner, then looked away. The only one who didn't avert his gaze was Rick. His expression betrayed nothing but his eyes were black as a moonless night and had the force of a magnetic pull that kept her staring back at him for a moment before she looked away.

After a glance at the officer who'd escorted them to the scene, who was also focused on the ground, Ashlyn moved beside Nolan.

God.

She was glad she had her back to the men so that they couldn't see the look on her face. . . .

Other *Leisure* books by Sandra Ruttan:

THE FRAILTY OF FLESH
WHAT BURNS WITHIN

SANDRA RUTTAN

Lullaby for the Nameless

LEISURE BOOKS   NEW YORK CITY

For my mom, Ann.

A LEISURE BOOK®

December 2009

Published by

Dorchester Publishing Co., Inc.
200 Madison Avenue
New York, NY 10016

Copyright © 2009 by Sandra Ruttan

All rights reserved. No part of this book may be reproduced or transmitted in any form or by any electronic or mechanical means, including photocopying, recording or by any information storage and retrieval system, without the written permission of the publisher, except where permitted by law.

ISBN 10: 0-8439-6286-0
ISBN 13: 978-0-8439-6286-4
E-ISBN: 978-1-4285-0778-4

The name "Leisure Books" and the stylized "L" with design are trademarks of Dorchester Publishing Co., Inc.

Printed in the United States of America.

10 9 8 7 6 5 4 3 2

If you purchased this book without a cover you should be aware that this book is stolen property. It was reported as "unsold and destroyed" to the publisher and neither the author nor the publisher has received any payment for this "stripped book."

Visit us online at www.dorchesterpub.com.

ACKNOWLEDGMENTS

Lullaby for the Nameless is the title of a song by Philip Fogarty. Ken Bruen gave me the CD a few years ago, and I asked Mr. Fogarty then if I could use the title for a book. It fit this one perfectly, so my thanks to Mr. Bruen for putting the music in my hands, and to Mr. Fogarty for the inspiration.

My thanks to my agent extraordinaire, Allan Guthrie, who has always pushed me to be a better writer, first as a friend and now as my "boss."

I realize that if I try to name everyone I'd like to thank, I'll miss someone, but there are a few specific people who should be mentioned.

Damon, Jay and the team at BSC Review, who have supported me personally and with Spinetingler.

Russel D. McLean, Daniel Hatadi, Patti Abbott, Stephen Blackmoore, Patrick Shawn Bagley, Chris Holm, Steve Allan, James Oswald, Stuart MacBride, Anne Frasier, Sean Chercover, Angie Johnson-Schmit, MG Tarquini, David Terrenoire, JD Rhoades, Amra Pajalic, John McFetridge, Peter Rozovsky, Linda L. Richards, Duane Swierczynski, Cornelia Read, Brett Battles, Rob Gregory Browne and so many more . . . The online community I've enjoyed over the years.

Jon and Ruth Jordan and the *Crimespree Magazine* family.

4MA, for the great discussions, the community spirit and the genuine love of books that is the foundation of the list.

My editor, Don D'Auria, and the team at Dorchester, for all the support and for loving the books.

Brian, for every little thing, and all the big things too.

And my thanks to all the others, you know who you are, who have contributed to my journey.

Lullaby for
the Nameless

Eighteen months ago

They say your life flashes before your eyes when you think you're about to die, and for Jenny, it was the words of her mother that screamed in her head. She couldn't shake the memories from her childhood . . .

When will you ever learn? Don't you ever use your head?

That's what Jenny expected her mother to say when she got home. That's what her ma always said when Jenny got in trouble. An exaggerated sigh, the flare of the nostrils, hands on the hip and one of those familiar lines would accompany a smack upside the head.

Maybe that'll knock some sense into ya.

What would follow the smack if her ma was really mad.

The summer before Jenny turned seven she'd snuck out of the house, to Old Mrs. Wilson's property, and made her way to the garden to pick berries.

Mrs. Wilson had a face that looked like an apple going bad. For someone as old as she was, she could still move, though, and when Mrs. Wilson had seen Jenny, she'd darted back up the porch steps, yanked the screen door open and grabbed a broom before Jenny even thought to turn and run.

"Just wait till I get my hands on you," Old Mrs. Wilson shouted as she scurried down the steps.

Jenny turned and ran as fast as her scrawny chicken legs would carry her.

"Your little red head will burn in hell! That's what happens to bad girls like you!"

Jenny was only six years old, but by then she knew from experience that it was better to tell her ma she'd done something bad and get a talking to or be sent to her room without supper than to take the chance that her ma would find out later. If she waited for Old Mrs. Wilson to call her ma, she'd get the strap.

When she'd confessed her crimes, her ma had sat still on the faded brown couch.

"Are you mad?" Jenny had asked.

"What did you pick?"

"Strawberries."

"Good."

Silence followed, and Jenny wasn't sure if Ma was waiting to decide how to punish her or just how much trouble Jenny was in. When Ma didn't say anything for what felt like a really long time, Jenny, still staring at her shoes, asked, "Is hell bad?"

"I'd rather burn in hell than freeze in heaven," her ma had said as she pulled herself up off the sofa. "Let's have a snack."

Jenny never even got scolded that day. It was like the idea of being together in hell had made her mother like her a little more. They'd cleaned the strawberries and Ma even let her have a bit of chocolate syrup on top, and they'd sat outside on the back steps and ate their snack together.

It had been the best day of her life.

Don't you ever think? When will you ever learn?

Jenny's ma hadn't asked those questions that summer day, and the next spring she gave up asking those questions altogether, right around the time Bobby Hobbs threw Jenny's slingshot out onto the frozen lake. Jenny was seven years old then, and she'd snuck out of the house when she was supposed to be cleaning her room and keeping out of trouble while her ma worked.

She'd been playing her own game in the woods, near the shore, shooting at trees. When she heard voices, Jenny hid the slingshot behind her back.

"Look, Eddie—it's Scruffy!" Bobby said when he came into the clearing and saw her. Bobby and Eddie were a few grades ahead of her, but they always called her by the name her classmates had for her at school.

She hated being called Scruffy.

"Oooh, Scruffy's out. Maybe we should tell her ma," Eddie said.

"My ma's working," Jenny told him. Her ma didn't like Eddie much, and she didn't want her ma to know she'd been talking to him.

"My mom says your ma works on her back," Bobby said. He elbowed Eddie, and they laughed. Jenny wasn't sure what they were talking about, but that didn't matter. They lost interest in her mother quickly.

"Watcha hiding?" Bobby asked.

"Nothing." Jenny took a step back.

"Aw, come on, what is it? You scared we're gonna cut your Barbie's hair off?"

Bobby and Eddie both laughed. Jenny looked to her right. She was a fast runner. She could probably make it—after all, she'd outrun Old Mrs. Wilson—but Bobby must have figured out what she was thinking.

"Get her!" Bobby said. Jenny started to run, but it was too late. Eddie grabbed her shoulders, and Bobby yanked her arm.

"A slingshot." He pulled it out of Jenny's hand.

"Give it back," she said as she kicked Eddie in the leg. Eddie let go of her. Eddie followed Bobby around and did whatever Bobby told him to do, but even she could push him around if he was on his own. Just a low-down piece of Indian trash—that's what her ma always said about Eddie Campbell. He had a big nose and giant glasses and clothes with more holes in them than hers had.

"You can have it back," Bobby said as he pulled his

arm back and threw the slingshot out onto the ice, "if you go get it."

"She's too much of a scaredy-cat to walk out there," Eddie said

"Am not!" She folded her arms across her body defiantly.

"Sure you are," Bobby said as he elbowed Eddie in the ribs. "You're just a girl. A scared little girl."

"Am not!"

"Are too," Eddie Campbell had said. Jenny thought he was a loser, a kid who pretended to be tough but really wasn't, but she still didn't want him making fun of her.

"Shut up!"

"She'd rather be home playing with dolls." Eddie said as Bobby nudged him in the ribs again.

"Betcha don't like slingshots anyway," Bobby said.

"Do too. I'll use it on you, Bobby Hobbs! I'm gonna shoot you in the butt with a rock."

Bobby laughed. "How you gonna do that when it's out on the lake, stupid?"

She pulled herself up to her full height and crossed her arms. "I'm gonna go get it."

"You're too chicken."

"Am not."

"Are too. That's what Eddie tells me. He told me you said you'd let him touch your privates and then got scared."

"She's a chicken," Eddie said.

"Big fat stupid liar," she yelled as her hands landed on her boney hips. The next thing she knew she was marching across the ice, stomping her feet as she got closer to the slingshot.

She was near the end of the dock before she heard the crack.

They hadn't been standing by the beach the dock stretched out from. Instead, they'd been at a bend that faced the dock from the side. The water was deep by the rock cut where they'd been standing, and she'd forgotten that along the shore, the ice was starting to break apart.

It was spring.

The split-second hesitation was all the boys needed, though. "Bawk bawk baaawwwwwk. Scruffy is a chicken. Scruffy is a chicken."

The singsong way they chanted made her cheeks burn. She stepped forward and looked down.

Each milligram of water had felt like a frozen pin poking into her skin as she plunged through the ice into the lake.

She didn't know how to swim.

She was going to die.

She wasn't thinking about being wet from head to toe. She wasn't thinking about the weight of her boots pulling her down or the way her hair was starting to turn hard as it stuck to her forehead. She wasn't even thinking about Bobby and Eddie, laughing at her from the shore.

She was thinking about the fact that she was cold.

As she felt herself slipping farther down into the water, what scared Jenny wasn't that she was going to die; it was the fact that she was so cold, she couldn't possibly be on her way to hell.

She'd never see her mother again. *I don't know anyone in heaven!* That's what had been going through her mind as everything went black.

The darkness that reached out from behind her eyes and swallowed her was soothing. Everything was quiet, and she had no sense of time passing or her body being lifted from the lake, wrapped in a blanket and transported to the hospital. Blissful oblivion, until the moment a speck of light dropped into the black pool that covered her eyes. The ripples of light spread out from the point of impact, slowly pushing back the mask of darkness that had enveloped her, and with the light came color and sound as the hospital room came into focus.

"Were you born without a brain?" was the first thing her mother barked at Jenny when she opened her eyes. She didn't remember what had happened and she didn't ask, but her ma told her Mr. Zimmerman had been at the dock and managed to pull her out of the lake.

The boys. The teasing. Her marching across the ice . . .

"Ma . . . Singsot?"

"What?"

"Did," Jenny pushed the words out, "he find my slingshot?"

"Forget the damn slingshot. Why do I waste my time carin' about a kid who'll jump off a cliff when her friends tell her to? If you're gonna do somethin' stupid and get yourself killed, why don't you do it soon and save me the goddamn cost of feedin' and clothin' you, huh?"

Not long after that, back when she still thought Ma loved her, she'd dropped a plate in the kitchen. It had shattered into a hundred pieces and as she swept it up she'd said, "Maybe one day I'll learn, if you keep reminding me."

Her way of apologizing before she got into trouble.

"What good's it, wastin' words on a lost cause?" her ma had said.

That was the moment when Jenny knew she was hopeless. Even her mother thought so, and if her ma had given up on her, she wouldn't have much chance with anyone else. She was on her own. She'd been that way since she was eleven, though it felt more like she'd been that way her whole life.

When she was seven and thought she was going to die, she hadn't called out for help or waved her arms around or tried to crawl out on the ice or prayed to God.

She wasn't praying now either.

Jenny couldn't see properly. It wasn't a soothing calm

of darkness she was swathed in this time. Instead, it felt like a heavy blanket that you can't breathe through, that you try to push off but can't unravel yourself from.

It wasn't like being wrapped in a sheet of black this time. It was more like having a thousand fireflies flitting in front of your face. The lights swirled and blurred, but as hard as she tried, she couldn't focus.

Breathe, breathe, breathe.

She couldn't get enough air into her lungs.

When she'd felt the blow on the back of her head and tasted the blood in her mouth, she hadn't found blissful oblivion this time. She could still hear voices, but she couldn't make out the words. Rough hands on her skin lifted her and pulled her and pushed her down, and she could feel the way her body bounced off a rough carpet, followed by an incessant hum.

She was moving but not being carried. By what and to where she could only guess.

That was the closest she came to a sense of calm. The fireflies had gone away. There was a dull ache in the back of her head, and she knew her body wanted to move, but she couldn't make it.

When the hum and sway stopped, Jenny heard a crunching sound, and then a slow, steady creak and the sting of cool air jabbing into her was matched by a brightness that pushed its way through the black.

Everything beyond the light was shadow.

Sandpaper paws yanked her upward and hauled her toward the circle of white. Her feet smacked something hard, and she heard the *shhhhhhh* of them as she was dragged.

The ground. Her feet must be rubbing against the ground as the rough hands pulled her.

Car. She must have been in a car.

Where would they take her? Did it even matter? She couldn't see properly, and she'd been around long enough to know that traitors didn't get second chances.

It didn't even matter if you were innocent. A hesitation was a sign of weakness when it came to discipline.

Jenny pushed harder to try to clear her head of the whorls of light and darkness obscuring her vision with hazy impressions as the hands released her and she crumpled into a heap.

A blur of brown. A tree? No, she wasn't outside. It wasn't a bumpy patch of cold earth beneath her but something hard. Level. A hard floor. Something else rose in front of her. A chair leg. And another.

Where was she?

"Never did like me much, did ya, Scruffy?"

A leering blob with a halo of fireflies circling around it. Jenny tried to blink, squint, but her eyes weren't working properly.

"Jesus, how much packing tape did you use on her face?" A different voice, still familiar.

"Let's get on with this." The gravelly voice that matched the coarse skin squeezing her arms.

"Still don't see why we're doin' this here." Nervous. Anxious. Familiar. Not as deep or strong as the others and filled with fear.

"It's the only place she's seen 'em." The first voice. The one who'd called her Scruffy. "If it's gone and she's gone, it's a dead end."

"Come on, guys. We gotta get outta here." The gravelly voice again, also familiar. "Whatever this is about, figure out who wears the pants."

Rough hands pulled her up again, and she could feel the hot breath on her skin, the smell of eggs filling her nostrils. "Do it," the person holding her said.

She could hear footsteps moving away.

Then she was free of the tight grip and for a moment almost felt as though she was floating. Something was wrong with her legs. She'd figured out that much when she felt herself falling, feet sliding out one way as her head bounced against the hardness.

When it hit the floor the second time she felt the pool of wetness. Warm. Sticky. Rippling out in her distorted line of sight, like a dark pool of paint spilled on the floor.

The *glug-glug-glug* of more liquid pouring against something hard seemed to surround her for a moment before everything went silent. In the distance a door slammed, then another door that was quieter.

The car door. Outside. They were leaving?

No. A *thud-thud-thud* grew louder, and she could feel the hardness under her ear quiver with each step.

He didn't say anything this time. She heard a sound she knew better than her mother's voice, better than anything. Come Easter or Thanksgiving there was never enough money for a chocolate bunny or a pumpkin pie, but Ma would scrimp every last cent to make sure she still had her pack a day.

The strike of a match.

Followed by a *whoosh*, and as the *tump-tump-tump* against the floor faded, a wave of reddish-orange light danced before her, accompanied by the acrid smell of smoke.

The heat surged through her as the wave grew and burned above her and behind her, the crackling encircling her as the fire zipped along the gasoline trail.

When will you ever learn? Don't you ever use your head?

Tears pricked at the corners of her eyes.

Jenny tried to wriggle toward the gap in the dancing light, but even as she inched her body forward, she could feel the wall of warmth drawing closer as it prepared to drag her from one hell to another.

PART ONE

CHAPTER ONE

As he released his breath, a cloud of white rose slowly in front of him, followed by a sharp pang as the icy air rushed into his mouth and chilled his lungs.

It was a good pain, the kind that told you what you needed to know to survive. Summer sun could lull you into complacency, make you drowsy and wrap you in a warm blanket that would help put you to sleep while it roasted your skin, but breathing in the sharp cold of the early morning air felt like how he imagined having a form of sadistic acupuncture performed on the back of your throat would feel.

A hundred reminders that it was not yet spring, that the weather could turn in the blink of an eye.

That the mountain winters could be cruel and unforgiving.

No snow had fallen this April, which was both a blessing and a curse. In snow, they might find tracks, but the officers scouring the wilderness in search of Hank Jeffers risked leaving trails of their own, possibly alerting him to their positions.

Hank Kurtis Jeffers: armed and considered extremely dangerous.

And out there somewhere. While other officers formed roadblocks and followed up on alleged sightings in places as far away as Calgary and Seattle, Constable Craig Nolan found himself on foot, searching the bush in the outskirts of Kelowna, carrying a shotgun, only a few miles from the scene of the crime.

Trying to forget what little he remembered about Jeffers. Thinking about the last manhunt he'd been on.

The search for Lisa Harrington.

That memory connected to others that he'd rather remained buried, so the reminder of the cold, of his current assignment, was welcome. Not just because it kept him alert, but because it helped keep his mind off other things.

He let out a deep breath. It was going on four months now, but if he closed his eyes, he'd swear he traveled through time and space and was right back to that moment, when it wasn't too late to undo the damage . . .

The futility of a case wasn't new to him. When he'd been shot and his partner killed, the senselessness hadn't weighed on him as heavily as it usually did. Ash had gotten him through it.

And when they finally called off the search for Lisa and the blame game began, it was Ash who compounded the hollowness growing within him.

Lisa Harrington. Maybe it was to fill some gaping hole within her, maybe because she thought the pure love of a child would save her from her own destructive behavior, or maybe just for the welfare checks and baby bonuses and tax breaks she could manipulate from the system. For reasons he could only guess at and might never fully understand, Lisa had abducted a child, raised her, then murdered her. That much he was certain of, even if it hadn't been proven in a court of law, even if Lisa had never confessed.

He'd been guilty of letting his own prejudices cloud his judgment, of inferring emotions because of labels. A mother always loves her child . . . right?

As though he hadn't been in this job long enough to know that you couldn't make those kinds of assumptions. As though his own mother didn't prove otherwise.

In the process of getting involved with that old case

and reviewing the investigation, he'd allowed himself to doubt the kind of man his father was. Craig's doubts created new wounds and ripped old ones open. He'd been left carrying demons of guilt he wasn't sure he could ever exorcise.

He couldn't hope for the forgiveness of others when he couldn't forgive himself.

Now, for the second day in a row, he joined the search for Hank Jeffers. A man who'd allegedly murdered his estranged wife and three children.

Something else Craig couldn't forgive himself for.

If he'd seen it coming, if he'd looked harder years ago, he might have found a way stop it . . . If only he'd known what the man was really capable of.

Maybe he didn't want to get to the point where he could understand these people. Maybe understanding them would humanize them, when it was easier to think of them as monsters.

And maybe he didn't want to understand them because if he could, it would mean he wasn't so different from them, that he wasn't better than them.

Or maybe he didn't want to understand because that would provide excuses for his mother. Maybe he would begin to understand her. He might find his grip on his hatred slipping as he started to see things through her eyes.

Just a useless sack of shit, a waste of skin.

He stopped cold and choked on his breath.

"Y'okay?"

Craig forced a cough. He didn't trust himself to speak. It had been so long since he'd heard the voice that had cut through his thoughts that he'd almost convinced himself he'd forgotten it.

Almost.

Another part of his past he wished he could exorcise permanently.

This job had taken him close to his childhood home,

where his mother still lived—what had undoubtedly caused the resurrection of the voice he'd just heard—and that was bad enough. Worse still, this case had dredged up memories about the failed manhunt for Lisa Harrington. And it had taken him closer to the assignment he was on when he'd first met Tain and Ash, both geographically and emotionally. With men being pulled from detachments and reassigned to help with the manhunt, it was possible to cross paths with someone else he'd worked with during that investigation.

It had been hard enough facing Tain and Ash again at first. What was it, eight or nine months ago now? He'd concealed it well, the same way he'd buried all the ghosts deep within himself.

He'd almost believed he was bottomless until the day came when there were too many for him to hold at bay.

Ever since he'd been given his orders and had climbed into his Rodeo to make the drive from the last temporary assignment he'd been on, farther north, he'd been trying to push thoughts of Lisa Harrington, Ashlyn and everything that had happened since he'd first worked with her and Tain from of his mind.

Trying. Failing.

"You don't look so good."

Craig forced himself to focus on the man speaking to him. "I'm fine. Fighting off a bit of a spring cold."

Constable Stanley MacDougall—known as Mac—grinned. "Spring? Never pegged you as an optimist."

"Okay, chalk it up to too much fresh air."

"Yeah, man, I know what you're sayin'." Mac slapped Craig on the shoulder twice and then moved out in front, into the lead. "How this sonofabitch is surviving out here without freezin' his balls off is beyond me."

"We don't even know he's out here."

"You haven't heard?"

Craig had heard and knew exactly what Mac was referring to. "Excrement doesn't mean much, not that close to the road. If you had a nickel for every time someone pulled over and answered the call of nature, you'd be golfing in Hawaii right now."

The grin slipped from Mac's face in a heartbeat, and he looked totally serious, as though he was Craig's dad and had just caught him sneaking in after curfew. "I would not. Get it right. I'd be on a beach with a hot babe in Mexico." The grin was back in place. "Maybe two hot babes."

How long had it been since he'd had a partner who would crack jokes with him, even on a serious case? Not since he'd been reunited with Tain and Ash.

He knew some guys had to keep the laughs rolling. It was how they coped. Grinning ear to ear, taking every opportunity for a cheap joke in public while they were crying their eyes out behind closed doors later or losing themselves in a bottle. That was Mac. Craig knew morbid humor was typical with medical examiners and anyone who worked homicide, but there was a line that Mac kept crossing, and it told Craig that Mac wasn't handling it well.

He was trying too hard to make it seem like he was in control.

" . . . takes a shit in the woods without toilet paper when it's still freezing out half the time, and it wasn't that far from town. That's all I'm sayin'."

"You have a point." He'd missed part of what Mac had said, but he'd read the reports. There were possible explanations for finding feces in the woods this time of year, but a lot of reasons to be suspicious too.

Especially that close to town.

He fought to keep his shoulders from rising with the shiver of his body. An icy finger had just traced a path down his spine, and he stopped walking and stood still, trying to listen.

It took Mac at least a minute to realize Craig wasn't following him, and when he turned back to look at Craig, all hints of amusement were gone.

"You hear something?"

His heart, thudding in his chest.

The sound of the last words his father had said to him before he'd left.

The sound of Ash's voice, her smile never more than a heartbeat away if he allowed himself to close his eyes . . .

The reason he wasn't sleeping.

Had he heard something else? All there was now was the softest trickle of wind through the branches. Without leaves to rustle it was barely noticeable. The woods were still.

Too still.

"Just . . . a feeling."

Mac stared at him for a moment, then cracked a grin. "Ah, you're one of those. A modern man, in touch with his feelings."

"This is serious. You shouldn't be shooting your mouth off. If he's out there, he'll hear you and know exactly where you are."

Mac held up his hands in mock surrender, but he was still grinning like a Cheshire cat. "Geez, I heard you had a bit of a short fuse, Nol—"

Thhhwap. The crack cut through the calm, and the bullet tore into the bark on a nearby tree, sending bits of wood flying into Craig's face. He spun around and dropped to the ground as he swore under his breath, which was coming hard and fast. He wiped his eyes with his left hand, then tightened his grip on his gun. He was ready; he just had to find the target. He scanned the trees. Nothing. No movement between the branches, no sign of color to hint at the location of the shooter.

"Y'okay?" Mac's voice, just a whisper.

Craig glanced to his left. Mac had taken cover behind a large stump. The woods were so still the soft whisper could be heard effortlessly.

"See anything?" Craig asked.

Mac was scanning the woods behind them, where they'd come from, but after a moment he turned toward

Craig. He wasn't smiling as he shook his head. "Nah, man. I—"

Thhhhhwap. Craig jumped at the crack of the bullet as it lodged into the stump in front of Mac. He barely registered that Mac was okay as he turned and looked over the area.

Still nothing.

Ssssssthhhhwap. Bark flew off the side of a tree about ten feet in front of Craig. It sounded like it had been shot from farther away, and from what he could tell had come from a different angle.

Two shooters? Or one shooter who was on the move?

"This sonofabitch's really startin' to piss me off," Mac muttered. In the distance they heard the flap of wings followed by another cry of protest from the branches above them.

Whoever it was, they were running.

As Craig's breaths slowed, he pulled out his cell phone. Mac got up and moved to take cover behind a large pine close to the tree the last bullet had struck.

Mac turned back just as Craig closed his phone, scanned the woods and made a quick move to a tree near Mac's position. He stayed low just in case the shooter was circling around. Once he was at the tree, he turned and scanned the area to his left and behind him.

Nothing.

"They're pulling in other teams from the east and west, hoping to cut him off." Craig nodded in the direction the shots had been fired from. "We're to go north."

Crouched low, taking slow, controlled breaths, Craig and Mac moved through the woods with shotguns in hand. In the seconds when Craig stopped and stood still, his visual surveys revealed no sign of the shooter.

Craig pulled out his cell phone. One of the other things he hated about working in the woods in the mountains. Walk a few feet and you were suddenly cut off from the world.

No signal.

No sign of anything but trees and some rock.

Nothing but stillness. The more ground they covered, the more uneasy Craig felt. Other officers should be out there, patrolling their assigned areas, but there was no evidence of anyone responding. He didn't even hear another team approaching. Half of him cursed the decision to operate with radios on silent mode, despite the fact that he knew that decision had been made to ensure Jeffers couldn't track their positions.

All it would take was a half second for someone to call in on a radio and he'd know where you were if he was close by.

You'd be distracted, and he'd have the advantage.

It made sense to work without radios, but the unpredictability of cell-phone use in the area meant they were flying blind, and the risk of friendly fire was foremost in Craig's mind. Moving forward on preset routes when they were given assignments was one thing; they shouldn't be intersecting other teams.

Now, they were doubling back and heading toward areas at least two other teams had been ordered to search.

They would hesitate before firing, just to make sure it wasn't one of their own. Jeffers wouldn't.

As Craig ran forward, he bent down low, swung the shotgun over his shoulder and pulled himself up over a rock ledge that was about ten feet tall. When he reached the top, he advanced slowly, ready to pull back in case someone took a shot at him right away, but the woods on the other side of the rock were as empty as the ones behind him. He turned back and signaled for Mac to follow.

"You thinkin' what I'm thinkin'?" Mac asked as he cleared the ledge and leaned up against the tree closest to Craig's position, trying to control his quick and heavy breaths.

In the distance to his right, he heard the rustle of

branches and something thumping against the ground, moving fast.

Followed by heavy footfalls. Two distinct sounds.

Mac's brow wrinkled. "Person or animal?"

It took Craig a moment to place it. The sound was like a distant memory his mind was trying to bring into focus, from his training. "Both. Canine unit."

Said just as the dog came into sight, heading due north. Craig barely managed to signal the RCMP officer who jumped out of the bush onto the path in front of them. The man paused long enough to hold up his hand before turning and running again.

Indicating they should hold back

"What the hell? They don't really expect us to let them take charge, do they?"

Craig nodded. It had been a while since he'd worked with a canine team—a year and a half or so—but he still remembered the speed at which they covered ground. There was no way Craig and Mac could beat a trained police dog to the suspect, and if they got too close, they risked interfering with the dog and his handler.

Craig scanned the area before he moved closer to Mac's position. "While we do what, exactly?" Mac sputtered the words, flecks of saliva flying from his lips as he stared at Craig. "Give me one good reason why we shouldn't say 'to hell with it' and go after this useless sack of shit?"

"You mean, one good reason other than getting written up for insubordination and having that stuck in your record?"

"Wouldn't'a thought that would stop you," Mac muttered.

Craig didn't even try to suppress the wry smile he felt tugging at his mouth. "Maybe not, but all we'd do is get in their way. He can't be more than a mile from our position. If anyone's going to catch him when he's on the move and we're closing in on him, it's the dogs."

Mac breathed in and out rapidly, then drew a longer breath and slumped back against the tree, the breaths coming sharp and fast again. "Somethin' 'bout this isn't right."

Something? Nothing about this was right. A man who'd allegedly murdered his estranged wife and three children and was on the run had apparently shot at them. Assuming it was him, was he desperate or suicidal? He'd fired from behind them, which meant they'd either moved past his position without spotting him, or he was following them.

Neither was a particularly comforting thought.

If they'd missed him, why draw unnecessary attention to himself? Even if he'd killed both of them, Jeffers had to know there'd be more cops in the area. Why not just slip off silently while he had the chance?

And if it wasn't Jeffers, then who was it?

What really bugged Craig was the quiet. Other than the moment the canine team had been in view and the sound from Mac's ragged breaths, the air was unnaturally calm. It was like the hush over the earth in the middle of the night in winter, when the blanket of darkness brought with it a stillness that nothing dared to break. Not even the forest animals went about their business, Craig realized. Other than the sound of that one bird flapping its wings and crying out, there was no sign of life in the woods around them, and that wasn't normal.

He glanced at Mac as he felt his cell phone vibrate and reached for it. Out of the dead zone. The voice on the other end was talking before he'd had a chance to finish answering the phone.

Craig closed it again without saying a word.

"Well?" Mac's breaths had leveled out finally.

He offered nothing more than a jerk of his head and started to run through the woods, not bothering to stop and take cover. It wasn't long before there was a hum in the air, voices in the distance. He couldn't make out what they were saying, but he knew it was the canine team. After another few minutes, his own quick breaths prickled his throat with a burning cold, and then a handful of men gathered in a small clearing came into view, two holding dogs back from whatever the others had gathered around.

Déjà vu.

He slowed his pace automatically. All they'd said was that they'd found something, to get there right away. All but one of the men had their backs to Craig, effectively blocking his view of whatever it was they were looking at on the ground.

The man standing in profile met Craig's gaze for a moment. Native, with a piercing gaze that made you feel he could see right through you.

Just like Tain.

He walked around the group to the end opposite the Native officer and knelt down, the blood rushing out of his face. Perhaps it was his way of avoiding what was lying in front of him, but for some reason all he could think of was that the RCMP wanted you to call them First Nations or Aboriginals now.

Aboriginals. For some reason, that made him think of Australia, and as he tried to focus, he thought about the absurd way the mind formed connections, how in the most extreme situations you could find yourself thinking about being politically correct instead of thinking about the fact that you were kneeling in front of a body in the woods.

Maybe it was a way of distancing yourself from the situation. The mind's way of coping.

It was a moment before one of the men standing above him spoke. "Is this what he's hiding?"

Craig shook his head even before he fully processed the question. "Death wasn't recent, but the body hasn't been here long." He'd seen enough bodies in the woods to know that much. There was no evidence of animal activity from what he could see, which suggested she'd been moved recently.

Not to mention the fact that they'd been patrolling the woods for a few days now, and teams had passed through the area without seeing a body.

"How do we know he didn't kill her, and that's why he went off the deep end and murdered his family? Maybe they found out about it." Another voice Craig didn't recognize.

"Came back out here to relive some past glory?" The first voice again.

"With how cold it's been, she could have been out here for weeks. Temperature throws off the process of decomposition." One of the new members of the team. One who didn't know what ground they'd already covered.

"This area's been searched. She wasn't here before." The second voice.

Craig took a deep breath, one that he hoped would help settle his stomach and clear his head. "We don't know anything. Right now, we don't jump to any conclusions. We have a new investigation to deal with."

"You're Nolan."

It wasn't a question. Craig glanced at the man who'd spoken. He sounded like he'd swallowed broken glass, and he had a burly build topped off with a face that had more bumps and lines than a stucco ceiling. Whoever the man was, he'd put in a lot of years on the job, but he still looked like he could hold his own in a bar brawl.

Craig nodded.

"From what I hear, you're no stranger to digging up bodies in the woods."

He felt his neck burn and his jaw clench as he lifted his gaze to look at the man who'd spoken. Instead, Craig found himself staring into the dark eyes of the Native officer, who remained silent but had a stare with the force of a magnetic pull.

The RCMP could be as PC as they wanted, but you couldn't undo the mental programming that came with years of using labels by suddenly changing the official terms. Craig pushed aside a fleeting thought about whether that was part of the reason it was so hard to eliminate racism and prejudice.

"Hey, he's my partner on this assignment, and in case you guys have forgotten, we were shot at. Some guy with a gun is still runnin' around in the woods," Mac said, "while we stand here talking about ancient history."

"Su-som-someone has to call this in and d-deal with the scene." Another voice Craig didn't recognize. Timid. Apologetically stating a fact.

"So why not you?" Mac spat the words out.

"I, uh, if-if I'm ordered to, I-I'll d-do it."

"For Christ's sake, did they let you out of training before your balls dropped?"

The raspy voice returned. "Takes more balls to follow orders than it does to shoot off your mouth, MacDougall."

Craig forced a serious look as he stood and held up his hand to keep Mac from unleashing the retort forming on his lips.

"We call it in, and the sergeant decides who stays." He looked at the thickset man who'd spoken with authority. The one who'd seemed ready to drop the case in Craig's lap. "Agreed?"

For a moment, the small black eyes stared back, and then the man nodded and pulled out his phone.

Craig looked down at the partially exposed grave where the body lay.

Could it be . . . ?

Craig pushed the thought from that old case out of his mind. Based on what he could see of the body, the size, there was no way to know anything for certain. She could be much older than the girl he was thinking of, the one they'd never found. Craig shut his eyes for a moment and when he opened them he forced himself to focus on the body they'd recovered; she'd been partially wrapped in strips of what looked like canvas bags, so there was no way to know. One of the differences, but he knew the routine. Similarities to other cases in the area would raise flags, and although the murders were technically closed, the case had never been completely solved. If she was connected to it, she would have been kept somewhere else for a while and moved recently. Craig realized he didn't even cover a mental checklist before forming conclusions, but then he'd seen bodies like this before.

His . . . experience.

Another part of his past he wished had stayed buried.

CHAPTER TWO

"It's okay to admit when something's bothering you."

"And you'd be the poster boy for the modern man who opens up about his feelings?"

Tain ignored that. "So something is bothering you?"

Ashlyn pushed the door open and didn't slow her pace as she marched outside to the car. "Just your prying."

The zing in her words, color in her cheeks, the way she tossed her head defiantly as she spoke . . . They'd both just come off a week's holiday, and the time away had done her good. She looked better than she had in months. Wherever she'd gone, whatever she'd done, it seemed to have worked for her.

When he reached the car, he opened his door and

was about to get in when he looked up and saw Ashlyn staring at him. Her eyes narrowed and a hand landed on her hip. "Don't play innocent with me," she said.

"I wouldn't dream of it." He sat down and pulled the door shut.

"Tain . . ." Spoken with a bit of a growl in her voice as she got in the car and slid the key into the ignition. "Do you know something you aren't telling me?"

"Why would you think that?"

"Ah." Emphasized by the slam of her door. Ashlyn nodded as she put the car in reverse and began backing out of the spot.

"What's that supposed to mean?"

"Isn't it typical for guys to avoid questions they don't want to answer?"

"I don't know, Ash. I thought it was typical of *anyone*."

"Which tells me what I need to know." She put the car in drive and pulled out onto the road.

"No, it doesn't. Maybe I feel I'm sending you mixed signals, and if I can figure out how I've given you the wrong impression, I can make sure it doesn't happen again."

The sideways glance she gave him said it all, and he silently cursed her instincts.

"You know, Ash, there was a time I could lie to you effortlessly."

"And you miss the good old days?"

"You know I don't."

"So what aren't you telling me?"

"Look . . ." How could he tell her he had a bad feeling? "All we know is that we were asked to investigate something suspicious in a Dumpster. They weren't more specific about what they found."

Although they had been specific in their request for Tain and Ashlyn to take the call, which was probably the reason he felt on edge.

Ashlyn paused. "You've got a bad feeling about it."

Said matter-of-factly, without a hint of emotion. As though the weight of each word had been carefully measured so that he wouldn't have any reason to think she was worried.

"You know how it is, Ash. You never know what you'll find on one of these calls."

For assaults or murders, they had some sense of the situation before they arrived. Carefully prepared masks were in place before they set foot out of the car at the scene.

When they didn't know what they were responding to, they had no idea the emotional toll the call might take on them. It wasn't just the absence of information that gnawed at him, though. It was pure gut instinct telling him that something wasn't right about this one.

A feeling that only intensified when they pulled into the alley. The uniformed officers were standing where they'd taped off the scene near the Dumpster to keep anyone else from approaching, and both were an unhealthy green-tinged shade. Sergeant Steve Daly and Staff Sergeant Bill Gliddon stood outside the perimeter. Steve's posture was rigid, a tightness in his shoulders that Tain was familiar with.

"Well, it could be worse," Ashlyn said as she parked the car. "We didn't rank an inspector." They got out of the car and closed the doors.

She offered only the slightest nod at the two senior officers observing the scene and didn't wait for Tain to take the lead.

He ducked under the tape after her and got his first good look at the Dumpster. Greasy food wrappers, Tim Hortons coffee cups and God knew what else that had been strewn across the body. Didn't conceal it, though.

Something suspicious. Yeah, right.

"Placed on top," Ashlyn said.

"Facedown, arms extended to her sides." He stepped closer and looked at the right hand. "Ligature marks on this wrist."

A mangled piece of cardboard covered the body's knees. "There's a stain between her legs that could be dried blood, but not enough on this side to suggest she bled out and no obvious cause of death from this angle." Ashlyn paused. "Could be more concealed by the cardboard."

"She looks young. Late teens, maybe? Hair hasn't lost its sheen." Tain looked down at her hand, and for half a second he was seeing a different one.

That arm twisted around so that the palm was up.

He blinked. Other than that detail, they were almost identical. He blinked again, snapping his focus back to what was in front of him, away from what was seared into his memory. "Nails have been cut short. No polish."

Ashlyn walked to the side of the Dumpster. "Feet were bound . . ." She hesitated before lifting her gaze and looking him in the eye. "Looks like they were bound together initially, but that she was recently retied. There are fresh wounds that don't match up and rub marks on the inside of her legs."

"No track marks on the arms, skin looks smooth, and she looks like she was slim but not unhealthy. If this was a working girl, she's new to the scene. Body's too clean from what I can see," Tain said.

"Doesn't feel right for a pro," Ashlyn said quietly. She pulled a pair of gloves from her pocket and lifted the cardboard. "Old—" Her breath caught in her throat. "Old-fashioned white nightgown that looks like it would reach down to the ankles."

White nightgown that goes down to the ankles. Tain swallowed.

Ashlyn looked up and past him toward their senior officers before meeting his gaze, the wideness of her eyes betraying the fact that the same thought had crossed her mind, and that she was locking down her emotions . . .

The scene was stirring the same memories in her that it had awakened in him.

Tain averted his eyes as he moved around to the back of the Dumpster. "The trash isn't as deep on this side."

"It'll still have to be bagged and tagged and sorted through."

"Ah, to be in uniform again, stuck on garbage detail," he said as he walked around the side of the Dumpster to where she stood.

"You know, we've done this before. We're all qualified to collect evidence."

"And deprive the guys who specialize in this sort of thing the chance to prove their worth?"

The left corner of her mouth rose just a touch. "Willing to share the glory?"

"If it keeps me from wading through a Dumpster full of trash, then yes, I'm a giver."

"Good thing." Ashlyn's eyes narrowed, and he looked up to follow her gaze.

Someone had already called in a team.

The leader held up a hand silently and the rest of the crew hung back as he approached Tain and Ashlyn. "Constable Johnson," he said.

"Tain and Hart," Tain said with a quick nod at his partner. "Who brought you in?"

Despite the rapidly receding hairline, Tain guessed Johnson was in his early thirties. Piercing blue eyes betrayed a keen mind. Something about the way Johnson had approached alone, as though he knew this one wasn't quite by the book, the way his eyes hardened when he heard Tain's question and paused noticeably before answering pegged Johnson as a career-minded yes-man.

"Look, all I know is, I have my orders." Johnson glanced at Ashlyn. "Is this going to be a problem?"

Tain gestured at the Dumpster. "It's all yours."

"Just the evidence processing, Tain. It's still your case." Johnson hesitated. He stared at Tain, as though he might receive some signal of approval, acceptance of the intrusion.

Tain knew what Johnson read in his face: nothing. After a moment, Johnson nodded at Ashlyn, returned to his team and gave them their instructions. Tain and Ashlyn stepped back wordlessly and watched as the bag-n-taggers began the tedious process of photographing and labeling the contents of the Dumpster.

"They're leaving no wrapper unturned." Ashlyn murmured the words low enough that only Tain could hear.

"From what I've seen so far, she doesn't fit the description of any recent runaways I've seen reports on, but the way they're handling the scene makes you wonder." Tain frowned. "Senior officers, a team called in before we even get to the scene . . ."

"Called to investigate 'something suspicious.'" Ashlyn's voice wasn't just laced with sarcasm; it was drowning in it. "Bet that's not what they told Johnson's crew when they called them out."

"Maybe it's not who she is but what she is," Tain said.

Ashlyn's mouth opened and then she spoke. "You mean . . . because of how she's dressed? They see some superficial similarities to an old case and think it's time to test us, see how we'll do?"

Tain shrugged. "Wouldn't be the first time."

"It's possible Johnson's just nervous because there are senior officers here, and he doesn't know anything more than we do."

"Except whoever called them in didn't wait for us."

"A fact I doubt he's going to give up now."

Before Tain could respond, Johnson called them over.

"We've cleared away enough on this side for you to see her face," he said. With a gloved hand, Johnson carefully brushed the hair back.

Tain heard the sharp intake of breath and for a second he wasn't sure whether it had come from himself or Ashlyn. She moved in front of him, started to reach out for the side of the Dumpster, then stopped herself. "Is that . . . ?"

Tain's mouth went dry. "Millie Harper."

CHAPTER THREE

There were some moments no amount of training could prepare you for. Tain didn't like attending autopsies at the coroner's office. He didn't like it when the victim was a child, and he didn't like it when it was an elderly person. He didn't like seeing someone closer to his own age.

He didn't like seeing anyone that way. He understood it was necessary, and he did his job to the best of his ability, but he didn't have to like it.

This time, it was more than just not liking it. He felt ill as he looked over at the body of a girl he'd known.

Tain heard the sharp intake of breath from his partner, but from the corner of his eye, he could also see the face of stone, how she was putting on a tough exterior to keep her emotions buried beneath the surface. He knew her too well.

The autopsy bay was more crowded than usual, in part because of the presence of Constable Johnson and one of his colleagues. It had been Ashlyn who'd given the tiniest shake of her head, warning Tain to keep his distance and shut his mouth all in one motion. She was right; it was futile. Whoever had ordered Johnson to the scene that morning, all Tain knew was that it hadn't been Steve. He couldn't let the politics of the investigation get in the way.

There was too much at stake.

They'd faced tough examinations before, but this was different, and as they watched Dr. Burke perform his tasks, what kept going through Tain's mind was the respectful detachment with which Burke handled the body. Despite the doctor's care, Tain had to fight the urge to push everyone aside and cover Millie's body.

He found himself choking on his breath as he watched the scalpel slice through her skin, and for a moment actually felt relieved that someone had called Johnson's team to the scene. There'd been no time at the Dumpster to steel themselves against the shock of discovery when they'd realized whose body was lying there.

As the autopsy progressed, Tain felt the case coming into focus. The initial shock had subsided, and now he could process the ramifications of the investigation in a way he hadn't consciously done since he'd talked to Steve.

Everyone would be watching.

Tain glanced up at Johnson, found the man's narrowed gaze fixed firmly on him.

They already were.

Anyone with half a brain could have figured out the old woman, known as Lulu, was two parts crazy to one part hungover and one part starved. Their witness mashed as much sandwich as possible into her mouth and tried to chew it fast, as though afraid the desk might swallow it before she had a chance to eat it herself.

"We were called out of an autopsy for this?" Ashlyn said as they looked through the glass into the room where their witness sat.

"She's halfway through her second sandwich," Sims said as he handed Ashlyn a plate. "She already asked for more."

Tain watched Ashlyn arch an eyebrow as she glanced down at the tuna sandwich she'd been handed. When she looked up, all she did was shake her head.

He opened the door and stepped inside the room.

"How mech?" Mumbled through a mouthful of tuna salad so thick that the overflow was spilling down her chin. The woman hadn't even waited for them to sit down.

Ashlyn had given him one of those you've-got-to-be-kidding-me looks as Lulu jumped up and grabbed the sandwich from the plate Ash was carrying and started cramming it in her mouth. Ashlyn pulled out a chair, forced the irritation from her expression and said, "Excuse me?"

Wide, unblinking eyes stared back as Lulu shoveled another mouthful of sandwich in and chewed. She had a narrow nose that was more like a beak, her skin a dim yellow color, clothes that only a bag lady would wear. "Ye know. Fer witnessin' for ya."

"What did you see?" Ashlyn asked. The grip she had on her pen had tightened. Another day and time and the scenario might have been amusing. As it was, Tain sympathized with his partner's lack of patience.

"Well, the cop. Saw him. I did," Lula said between bites. "'Course he said he'd tell yas himself, no need for me to talk, but he had that diff'rent uniform." The woman worked on the last bite of the sandwich and after a big gulp, wiped her mouth with her shirtsleeve. "Why'd it take so long fer ya to git out there when dat other one was there so quick?"

"First officers on the scene will assess the situation and call for backup if needed, or hand the case over to a different department. If we're already out working a case, it can take a while to get there," Ashlyn said. "Did you see anything or anyone before the first cop arrived?"

"I saw whatever else ya needed me to see, love." The scrawny, wrinkled face nodded solemnly, as though she believed her offer to help make a case was of the utmost importance instead of a complete waste of their time.

Ashlyn stood so abruptly the chair behind her clattered to the floor. "I've heard enough."

She was halfway out the door by the time Tain stood. Lulu continued prattling away as he turned and followed Ashlyn in the hall, but he didn't hear any of it.

"You know, I've heard stories about Loopy Lulu ever since I transferred here. I almost can't believe it took this long to have the pleasure."

The color in Ashlyn's cheeks deepened, then started to fade. "Nice you can have such a good sense of humor about it. To think we got called out of an autopsy for this—"

He held up his hand. "It's not worth it. What's done is done. Let's just get back to the coroner's office." Tain turned toward her as they started walking down the hall. "When the time is right, we'll kick Carter's ass for this."

Ashlyn blew out a breath. "Good. I'd do it myself, but I think he'd enjoy it too much."

Tain had managed to suppress the smile before she glanced at him. Little moments like that gave him hope that his partner was truly back.

She'd been through hell, and the loss she'd suffered had taken its toll.

As Ashlyn started the car, Tain's phone rang. He held up his hand to gesture for her to stop and then closed his phone.

"They're pretty much finished. Burke's sending over a transcript of the process."

Ashlyn smacked her hand against the steering wheel. "What a waste of time." They sat in silence for a moment, keeping their thoughts to themselves until Ashlyn asked, "What's next?"

As he opened his mouth to respond, Tain's phone rang again. He flipped it open, listened to the response, then hung up.

"Back inside. We've been summoned."

A white-hot rage settled in Ashlyn's face, and then she yanked the keys out of the ignition and shoved the door open. He hurried out of the car and stepped in front of her, blocking the sidewalk.

"Get out of my way."

"Not until you calm down."

"This is bullshit, Tain. We're nothing but puppets. Called out from an autopsy for . . . for a hoax? A complete joke? We aren't even running the case. If we don't close this—"

"I know."

Ashlyn folded her arms across her chest and looked him in the eye. "I'm sick of them manipulating investigations, playing politics instead of just letting us do our jobs."

"Just . . ." He looked at her reddened cheeks, her clenched jaw. "Just don't let your anger get the better of you. Don't let it cloud your judgment."

Her eyes widened. "*You're* lecturing *me* about controlling my temper?"

"Ash—"

She clenched her fists, then closed her eyes and lifted her hands to cover her face. When she took her hands away, he could see that some of the color had faded a touch. She breathed in and out before she spoke again, the edge gone from her tone, her voice calm. "I don't want this case, Tain."

He took a step closer, reached out, squeezed her arm and lowered his voice. "I need you with me on this."

She opened her eyes and looked at him. "We've been set up."

A drop of his hand and quick turn put him on the sidewalk, walking toward the front door.

Ashlyn followed. "We're being set up to fail."

He opened the door to the building, voice lowered again by necessity. "Do you really think Steve would do that to us?"

His way of avoiding her assessment, sidestepping the question. He couldn't shake the feeling that she'd sifted through the events of the day, the facts they had, and put her finger on the same conclusion he kept coming back to.

One he refused to believe. Why set them up? Why set them up to fail?

The problem was, he couldn't come up with another solution that fit the facts. When he put together all the information they had, it looked like they'd been handed the case for show, that the investigation was being handled by whoever had called Johnson's team in, and that Johnson knew it.

They'd be getting evidence secondhand until the case was solved or shelved. There might be evidence they wouldn't get at all.

The door to Sergeant Steve Daly's office was open and he must have been watching for them because as soon as Tain could see inside the room he saw Steve stand up and gesture for them to come inside.

"It's a bit premature for an update, sir," Ashlyn said. "The—"

"I didn't call you in for an update." Steve pointed at the chairs on the other side of his desk across from his own. "Please have a seat."

From the corner of his eye, Tain could see Ashlyn's quick glance and hesitation. He forced himself to sit down and was relieved when she also complied without comment.

Steve had gotten a new clock, one that had an audible tick that marked off the seconds. Tain hadn't noticed it before and he didn't see it on the shelf closest to Steve's desk or on the wall. Best guess: it was on the new shelf behind the chairs he and Ashlyn sat in.

The monotony of the clock was finally broken by Steve's words. "I know the past few months have been hard." Steve glanced at Ashlyn, who stared back steadily. "You caught a couple of tough cases, and with the inter-departmental politics . . . What happened wasn't your fault."

Steve paused and shifted his gaze to Tain. For a second Steve looked at him, mouth open, as though hoping for a response. When Tain remained silent, Steve drew a breath, looked at his desk a moment, then lifted his head and cleared his throat.

"I wanted to talk to you about this case. About reassigning it."

"What?"

Steve raised his hand calmly and gestured for Ashlyn to let him speak. "Under the circumstances, I think it would be best to—"

"And what circumstances would those be, exactly?" Ashlyn asked.

Tain touched his partner lightly on the arm. Her face had reddened, but she kept her gaze lowered instead of looking at him directly. Once he was sure she'd stay silent, he turned to look at Steve. "Respectfully, this is bullshit. You guys called us out there. You asked for us."

"I know." Steve looked down at his desk, gaze on the open folder in front of him. A photo of Millie Harper's body after it had been turned was sitting on top, staring back up at him.

Tain got up, yanked the folder off the desk and held up the photo, tapping it with his index finger. "She's the reason we were called out, without details, and before we even have a chance to get started, you're pulling us off." He tossed the file down in front of Steve and leaned down, hands clenching the edge of the desk. "I feel like I spend more time being jerked around than working."

"Look, I can appreciate you're frustrated, and that's the only reason I'm tolerating your behavior," Steve said as he glared back at Tain. "I am your senior officer. You may not like my orders, but you do have to follow them."

"Then I'd like to speak to your commanding officer." Ashlyn's voice cut through the tension on Steve's face, and he flinched as he turned to look at her.

"Listen to me, Ash—"

"No, Steve, you listen. We spent months being jerked

around after your temporary transfer. When you came back, we thought that was over. You guys picked up the phone today, you assigned us a case without giving us any details, and you started handling it before we even got to the scene."

Steve's brow furrowed. "We didn't handle anything."

"Then explain why we were called out to investigate something 'suspicious.' Explain why a team had already been called out to process the evidence. I mean, all you had to do was take one look at what was in the Dumpster—"

There was the tiniest gasp as Ashlyn's breath caught in her throat. Tain was familiar with her way of stopping the tremor of emotion that sometimes crept into her words, but so was Steve.

He pointed at her. "That's why I want you off this case."

"*You* want us off the case? You, or your superiors?"

"Ash." Tain kept his voice low as he turned to look at his partner. There was a tension in her body he hadn't seen in months, evident in the stiffness of her neck, the clenched hands, the color in her cheeks that hadn't dissipated.

"I want you off the case."

Tain watched as his partner's face darkened. The first wave to hit was anger.

"Ashlyn—"

She held up her hand to silence Steve and opened her mouth to speak, but stopped before Tain could make sense of what she was going to say. The anger was followed by what he interpreted as disbelief and shock as her skin turned white, and she seemed to shrink half an inch. It took only a second for her to pull the door open, and she stomped out of the room before Tain had a chance to keep her from leaving.

Silence followed, and it was a moment before Steve spoke. "That's why I don't want you on this case."

"Then that's a pretty lousy excuse, Steve. You pushed her. You pushed *us*. You called us out there, and all we were told was that something suspicious had been found in a Dumpster. I think it would be pretty obvious even to some high-ranking bureaucrat who didn't want to get his hands dirty that it was a body."

"Look—"

"You were at the crime scene. You asked for us. You think we don't know why? You knew."

Steve leaned back in his chair and covered his face with his hands for a moment. "But I didn't know it was her."

Spoken so softly that for a second Tain wasn't sure if he'd imagined Steve's words.

"What?"

When Steve looked up, Tain saw a muddled mix of sadness and frustration in Steve's eyes and what he interpreted as a measure of desperation. The way Steve's eyebrows rose made Tain feel as though his senior officer was pleading with him to understand, and the way the corners of Steve's eyes sagged made Steve look as though he'd aged years.

Steve looked Tain straight in the eye as he spoke. "I didn't know it was Millie Harper."

"Then . . . why? Why call us out there? And why take us off now?"

A half smile flickered across Steve's face as he leaned back and gave his head one small shake. "I wasn't going to take you off."

"But you said—"

"I said I wanted you off."

"You implied—"

"Tain, it was . . . I was playing a hunch. Call it my way of toying with you if you want to. Hell, maybe I've felt like a mouse being dangled by its tail in front of a starved cat for so long I can't help myself anymore. You guys got called out there because of the superficial similarities to that old case. It wasn't my decision, and I'm not going to defend it."

"Good, because I'm getting pretty sick of feeling like I spend more time fighting with people in this office than I spend doing my job. We're both fed up with it. You think we need therapy, you send us to a shrink and stop playing bullshit mind games with us."

Steve's hands were folded in front of his face and for a half second Tain almost wondered if he was praying with his eyes open, but then Steve nodded. "You're right. And you're right about the fact that I pushed Ashlyn, and I shouldn't have."

"You can tell her that yourself."

Tain turned and started walking toward the door when he heard the creak of the chair. From the corner of his eye, he saw Steve stand up.

"But look at how she responded." There was silence, and Steve didn't continue speaking until Tain turned to look at him. "We didn't know it was Millie. All we knew was that it was superficially similar."

A test for both of them. Steve could claim he was concerned about Ashlyn, but Tain knew better. He was under as much scrutiny as his partner over this call.

"We didn't want the press catching wind of it. Not since they found a body in the woods near Kelowna earlier."

"Isn't that where the manhunt is? The multiple murderer?"

"That's what the press is saying."

"And what about the RCMP?"

"Details are thin. It's just, first a body in the woods, and now a body in a Dumpster . . . I was worried about Ashlyn before I knew it was Millie."

Tain was beginning to see where Steve was going and what was really bothering them. The reason they'd been given limited details when they were called out. "There may have been some loose ends, but we closed the file. Campbell's dead. Hobbs is in prison."

"And I want him to stay there." Steve reached up with

both hands and scratched his head before he gave up on the pretense and dropped his arms to his sides.

This was about more than the connection Tain and Ashlyn had to Millie Harper and what he hoped were the coincidental similarities between her death and others they'd investigated before. For Steve, it was personal in a different way. Old cases and old wounds. The implications of Millie's death had brought back painful memories for Sergeant Daly, and he was projecting his own fears onto Tain and Ashlyn.

"Then you should keep us on this case. Millie didn't die like the others. There's no reason to think it's the same killer."

"But the nightgown, the dumping of the body . . . the fact that she'd been tied up?"

"Circumstantial at best." Tain knew they'd have to look at the other cases. It was standard procedure. But he had no doubt about Hobbs's guilt and the role Campbell had played. "We know the history inside and out. We both knew Millie. We don't have to be brought up to speed. The only person who knows this case as well as we do . . ." Tain paused as he considered what to say about Craig and his prolonged absence. "He's not here. We are. You'll be behind from the beginning if you take us off the case now."

Steve stared at Tain for a moment, then nodded. "I know. But are you sure she can handle it?"

A question Tain wasn't prepared to ask himself, never mind answer to Steve.

"Either you have confidence in us to do our jobs, or you don't. You can't have a list of conditions over what kinds of cases your officers handle. You either trust them with everything, or you trust them with nothing."

With that he turned and walked away.

CHAPTER FOUR

The woman who stood behind the desk barely glanced up as Craig and Mac entered. She continued riffling through stacks of papers as she spoke.

"I hear you have a habit of finding bodies in the woods, Nolan."

He could feel the burn creeping up the back of his neck as his mouth opened, but he pulled back the words.

Sergeant Linda Yeager looked up then. "From what I've been told, you nearly lost your head while you were out there. Did someone leave out the part about you actually losing your tongue?"

"No, Sergeant." Craig never could figure out if ranking female officers wanted to be called ma'am. Past experience had taught him that no matter what protocol was, using the label was more likely to offend than not.

She stared at him for a moment, sharp green eyes set on a weathered face, blonde hair that was giving way to gray tightly pulled back into a bun. Give her a meter stick and she could pass for Craig's high school calculus teacher, a conclusion that didn't make him more comfortable.

The heat was spreading to his cheeks.

Yeager's sly smile was making him uneasy. Something about the cynical twist of her mouth, the way her eyes pinched just a touch . . . It was like Yeager could see his discomfort, the desire to squirm, and she enjoyed twisting the screws just a bit.

Then the moment passed, and she went back to sifting through papers. After she worked her way through part of a small stack, she extracted a pink slip, skimmed the message, pulled open a drawer and placed the paper inside. She set her hands on her desk and looked up again, first scrutinizing Mac before she glanced at Craig as she nodded.

A woman brushed past Craig as she handed the sergeant a file.

"We've exhausted tips in Calgary and on Vancouver Island, and have a few more officers arriving tomorrow morning." Yeager studied the contents of the folder she'd been handed. "Ballistics has been digging bullets out of trees. Too much damage to make a conclusive match, but it looks like it could be the same type of ammunition used in the murders."

One of the things about the killing of the Jeffers family that didn't make sense. Why use a rifle? If you're going to murder your wife and children and then run, not even try to feign innocence, why not kill them in the house where the bodies could be concealed?

The killer had wanted them to be found. Quickly.

Yeager ignored her ringing phone, closed the folder and looked up. "If the evidence is correct, we're closing in on Hank Jeffers. I don't think I've ever been happier to have my men shot at."

"Glad we could be of service," Mac muttered.

"And I'm glad he didn't have better aim this morning because we need you to work the body."

It was what Craig had expected when they were called in, but the words had the effect of having a bucket of cold water dumped on him in the middle of winter. He felt the shiver surge down his spine and through his arms as all the heat in his face disappeared.

Yeager stared at him with another look that suggested she could read his mind. "Do you have a problem with this?"

"I do."

Craig almost jumped at Mac's voice as Yeager shifted her gaze to Craig's partner. It wasn't that he hadn't expected Mac's opposition; it was that he hadn't expected Mac to actually voice his objections to his commanding officer.

Which told him that he'd misread his partner.

Which wasn't exactly a comforting thought.

The sound of her phone ringing didn't even make her blink.

"Respectfully"—Mac failed to soften the cynical edge in his tone—"we should stay on Jeffers. We need to find this guy fast, and—"

Yeager held up her hand. "And *we* will. *You* will ID the body in the woods, find out how she got there and arrest her killer."

"Assuming he isn't already in jail."

Yeager's head snapped so fast, Craig heard her neck crack as she turned to look at him. Her phone rang again, but she didn't seem to notice. "That wouldn't explain how the body got in the woods today, though, would it?"

Before she could continue or Craig could respond, Mac cut in.

"Which is exactly why we shouldn't be on this case. He worked that serial killer thing a couple years back."

"Which is exactly why he is leading this investigation," Yeager snapped. "In case you haven't noticed, Constable MacDougall, we're stretched a bit thin these days, dealing with a manhunt for a multiple murderer." Her phone rang again, and again she ignored it. "I can't make it two feet from my desk before there's another call, from Edmonton, Moose Jaw, Prince Rupert or Head-Smashed-In Buffalo Jump, of all places, without someone reporting another sighting. I've got to stay on top of every one and follow up, even if they're bogus calls from ninety-year-old great-grandmothers who can't see their own hands in front of their faces without Coke-bottle glasses. I don't have time for pissing contests or for you second-guessing my decisions, and I don't have time for someone to get caught up to speed on that serial murder investigation. I don't even have time to review all the details about that old case myself right now. I need someone who knows it, and one of those people just happened to be in the woods today when we recovered a body. Call it fate, destiny or whatever you want. I'm not going to look this gift horse in the mouth. Nolan is in charge of this investigation, you're his partner, I'm your sergeant and I've given you an order. I expect you to shut up and do your job. Understood?"

Mac offered a curt nod and after a split-second hesitation, Yeager turned her attention back to Craig.

"I just meant that if the killer's Jeffers, you might get him first," Craig said. He could feel Mac's disbelieving stare, but he kept his focus straight ahead, on the sergeant.

"For now it's just the two of you. I expect you both"— she shifted her glance to Mac for a moment—"to keep that quiet. We're prepared to pull resources as needed *if* they're needed, but we don't want to look like we're jumping to any conclusions about this case before we even start investigating, and we sure as hell don't need the media shit storm it'll stir up if the press catches wind of it. Work fast and be thorough, and before you come back and tell me this is part of an old investigation, a loose string that should have been tied up more than a year ago, you make damn sure you're right, because there'll be hell to pay if we're wrong."

Those green eyes prying into Craig's, boring a hole in his skull. Trying to impress upon him the importance of this investigation, of getting it right.

As though he needed the explanation.

As though he didn't understand exactly what was at stake.

He nodded. "Yes, Sergeant. We're on it."

"Good." She passed him a folder. "They're expecting you back out at the scene."

"Of all the goddamn useless ways to waste our time."

Mac muttered the words as Craig drove back to the woods where the body had been found. He'd muttered a number of things since leaving the sergeant's office, and Craig had resisted the urge to turn on the radio to block the sound of Mac's words. It would be a response, which was what Mac was after.

Craig could hide behind the excuse of duty, of following orders, to explain his cooperation with the sergeant in her office, but now that he was alone with his partner, he knew saying anything would put him on a side.

"You got nothin' to say about this?"

"No point complaining," Craig said as he pulled his Rodeo over to the side of the road, near the other emergency vehicles. "It isn't going to make me feel better, and it isn't going to change anything."

The manhunt had tapped their resources, all the way down to the need to use officers' personal vehicles. Craig hadn't drawn the short straw—he'd volunteered to use his. It had four-wheel drive and was built to handle the terrain. Plus, it meant he held the keys.

Ashlyn had told him once, when they'd first worked together, that he had control issues. Close his eyes and he could imagine her watching him, shaking her head, her dark hair contrasted against her creamy skin, saying, "Some things never change."

He got out of the vehicle and grabbed the gear he needed.

Mac took the lead as they headed into the woods. "You want to work this case?"

By Craig's estimation, even parking where they did, they had about a mile to hike through the woods. He'd already had fifteen minutes of Mac's bitching on the drive over. "What difference does it make?"

"You aren't the guy sergeants get stuck with on a case. You're the guy they ask for. If you'd said no, Eager Yeager woulda listened."

"You're wrong. Maybe I used to be."

"So you proved you aren't perfect. You've still got an old man with rank. I'm sure if you called him—"

Craig grabbed Mac's arm and pointed at him. "She made the right decision."

Instead of jerking his arm free, Mac stopped in his tracks and turned around. "You're okay with this? You really don't have a problem being pulled off the manhunt for . . . this?"

"I'm at one with the universe."

"Bullshit, Nolan." Mac pulled his arm from Craig's grasp. "You've been wound tighter than a homophobe in a gay bar the whole time I've been working with you."

"All of what? Three days?" Craig pushed past Mac and started walking. He heard footsteps behind him.

"You shouldn't be on this case, Nolan. It already doesn't look good. If it goes bad, they'll hang you."

Craig kept walking. The universe may have deliberately set him up, but the RCMP hadn't. They hadn't taken shots at Craig and Mac so that they could set a series of events in motion that would ultimately lead them to the spot in the woods where a partially exposed body lay.

The RCMP may have had its share of scandals and blunders over the years like any other police department, but they hadn't conspired to hang Craig with this case. Call it God, fate or a cruel joke the universe was playing. Call it whatever you want, it had just happened. The fact that it had happened to Craig wasn't something he was particularly happy about, but even he had to admit that if he'd been in Yeager's shoes, he would have done the same thing.

Mac's blatant disapproval wasn't going to make it any easier, but maybe if Mac got it through his thick skull that Craig wasn't going to back down, he'd just shut up and do his job.

Craig felt a smile tug at the corner of his mouth, thought back to what Mac had said to him only hours earlier, before someone started shooting at them in the forest.

He'd never pegged himself for an optimist either.

CHAPTER FIVE

"I've already made a few calls," Ashlyn said as she marched across the room, yanked the top drawer of the filing cabinet open, riffled through a few folders, pulled one out and slammed the drawer shut. She was halfway back to her desk, gaze fixed on the pages in front of her, before Tain even had a chance to respond. "There are a lot of gaps. Seems she didn't stay in the system for long. We're going to have to piece together the past few years, which won't be easy, given Millie's history."

"Didn't she have an aunt or a cousin still living?" Tain said, instinct kicking in, the words out before he had a chance to recall them. He hadn't seen Ashlyn this energized in months. He glanced at her desk, already cluttered with checklists, a few other folders and old notebooks.

While he'd been talking to Steve she'd been busy.

Ashlyn snapped her fingers and set the file on her desk as she spun around to look at Tain. "You're right. A cousin. If we can find her, she might be able to—"

"Whoa." Tain held up his hand. "Are you okay?"

Ashlyn's eyes narrowed the tiniest bit. What Tain thought of as her look of mild annoyance. It was always fleeting, an instinctive motion comparable to swatting at a fly, but it hinted at what was going on beneath the surface. "Why wouldn't I be?"

A defensive response. One that suggested more than slight irritation.

"Ash." He reached out and squeezed her arm. "You got pretty worked up in there."

"I'm just tired of all the crap. I want to get to work."

"But this case? You said yourself—"

She held up her hand. "We're on it. And if anything was going to convince me it's the right thing, it's the bosses trying to pull us off." Ashlyn slid out of his hold, sat down at her desk and automatically got busy leafing through the papers in front of her.

Mechanical actions. Lacking her usual thoughtful scrutiny of the details.

"That wasn't what Steve was doing."

"Really? You could have fooled me."

Tain sat down across from her. "He was pushing your buttons to see how you'd respond."

She glanced up at him. "Don't they ever get tired of playing games?"

"Look, you—"

"Do you trust me with this?"

"I wouldn't have fought with him if I didn't."

She stared back at him for a moment, appearing to consider his words. "Then why are we even having this conversation?"

"I just want to make sure you're okay."

"How do I look?"

"Ash." The growl in his voice sounded harsh to his own ears, which wasn't what he'd intended. He tried to soften his tone. "This isn't going to be easy."

"If I was looking for an easy job, I made a big mistake joining the RCMP."

Knowing what he meant, choosing to avoid it.

When he saw the woman who was clearly in charge at the scene, Craig suddenly felt old. She looked as though she'd barely graduated from high school, although that wasn't to suggest a lack of maturity, just that she looked young. Her olive skin was framed nicely by dark, curly hair that was swept back off her face into a loose bun. As she snapped on gloves, she barely afforded Craig and Mac a quick glance.

"Are you the ones who found the body?" she asked.

"Constables Nolan and MacDougall," Craig said, with a quick gesture to indicate who was who.

"Not exactly an answer to my question," the woman said briskly as she bent down beside the remains Craig had found earlier that day.

Craig knelt on the other side of the body. "There was a team of us out here, searching the area."

"Must be your lucky day."

"Excuse me?"

"You drew the short straw and got pulled off the manhunt."

Craig paused. "I suppose that's one way of looking at it."

"Boys chasing a suspect around in the woods with guns or a partially decayed frozen body that actually smells better than it looks." She glanced at him. "There's nothing sexy about this."

"I'm here to do my job." He heard the defensive edge in his words, despite his efforts to extricate it.

The woman looked up at him silently, then glanced at MacDougall before turning back to Craig. "You got any experience dealing with a partially decomposed body?"

"She looks good, considering how long she's been dead."

"And how long is that, exactly?"

The heat rushed straight up into his face. "What I meant was—"

"I'm Dr. Winters," the woman said coolly. "And I believe I'll be the judge of how long she's been dead, how long she's been lying here and what kind of shape she's in. Unless, of course, you're just being modest. Perhaps you have more experience than I do and don't want me to be intimidated by the fact that you're really a forensic anthropologist."

She stared at him and after a moment said, "Well?"

"Well what?"

"Are you?"

"No."

There was a tiny tinge of color in her cheeks as she glanced back down at the body. "Now that we've cleared that up, I must admit from what I've seen so far, she does appear to be in good shape."

The doctor looked at him for a second. Was the hint of a smile on her lips or was it his imagination?

"You didn't answer the other question."

Question? Craig scrambled to remember what she'd asked, then nodded. "Sorry. Yes. I've dealt with decomps before." He didn't add that it was on a case he'd rather forget, a case that could tie directly to the body in front of them.

Behind him, Mac cleared his throat. Craig didn't avert his gaze, but the doctor looked up and a shadow flicked across her face before she turned back to Craig.

"Then you know we've got a lot of work ahead of us, and this won't be pleasant."

He looked down at the body again and nodded. There was a lot of work ahead of them, not just in the next few hours but in the coming days, and he suspected the only thing about the case he'd find pleasant would be closing it.

Chapter Six

Craig rolled the driver's side window down as he pulled out onto the road. It was an archaic motion, one most people had forgotten performing, but he'd been unwilling to give up the '91 Rodeo that he'd had rebuilt when he'd purchased it years before. It wasn't the most fuel-efficient vehicle—something that he'd been reminded of constantly in recent months of winter and mountain driving—but it was sturdy and reliable.

Part of him felt that the problem with new vehicles was that there was so much more wiring, it only increased the probability that something would go wrong. Maybe that was the problem with people. So many options, so many choices, opening doors to darkness they might not otherwise have conceived without the twenty-four-hour news cycle and easy access to accounts of barbarity both old and new, foreign and domestic.

His eyes burned in protest of every set of headlights in the oncoming traffic while his body shivered from the cold air. He guessed it was near freezing, if not below, but he needed the cold to help him keep his eyes open. It was almost 11:30 p.m., and his stomach had long since given up complaining about the lack of food and abundance of coffee, a substance he wasn't terribly fond of but occasionally drank when necessary to stay awake and alert.

He'd started drinking it a few months earlier, when he'd left the Lower Mainland on temporary reassignment.

One temporary reassignment after another.

The good thing about constantly being shuffled from one team to another, usually because of an emergency, was that he was continually forced to adapt to a new environment, deal with new people. He was living life on the high end of the learning curve, which required him to devote his energy and attention to the here and now.

No time or energy to think about yesterday and tomorrow, or so he told himself.

If things ever leveled out, he might be forced to remember what had happened, to process it and come to terms with it and consider what he was going to do when the dust settled.

Deal with his guilt.

He had to double-check the number on the motel room before he put the key in the lock, and when he opened the door, there was no feeling of familiarity that greeted him or sense of being home. Just the vague awareness that this room was like so many others he'd slept in over the past few months. Swap out the generic painting on the wall, the color of the bedspread, give or take an extra blanket on the shelf above the open closet and all the temporary accommodations blended together in his mind.

It stood out in stark contrast to the memory of his own living room in Port Moody, swathed in the glow of firelight and the glimmer of the fiber-optic Christmas tree in the corner. Close his eyes and he could almost feel the warmth of Ashlyn's presence, the touch of her skin on his arm, the way his chest tightened when he saw her walk into a room, so aware of how much she meant to him, so afraid it was nothing more than a house of cards that would be blown apart by a sudden breeze.

It's no wonder your daddy didn't stick around. How could anyone love a loser like you?

He pushed the memories from his mind, pulled off his boots and tossed them on the lino near the entrance.

The muscles in his back protested as he straightened up. Hot shower or bed?

He tossed his jacket over a chair, crossed the room, turned on the small bedside lamp and put his gun and cell phone on the nightstand next to the book he'd been trying to read. From there it was a short walk around the bed to the bathroom, where he avoided his reflection in the mirror as he brushed his teeth.

It was a safe guess that he looked as rough as he felt.

The act of pulling off his shirt as he walked back to the bed was instinctive, and he followed it by tossing his pants over the chair nearby, the one with last night's clothes still hanging over it.

Back to the bathroom to shower. The cold would wake him up, and he didn't want to spend another night looking at the ceiling, counting sheep. Or, if he was being honest with himself, counting bottles. Followed by counting mistakes. His attempts to try to forget coming full circle with the laundry list of sins he carried with him, the things he couldn't let go.

His weapons of choice for beating himself up over and over again.

He turned the tap to hot and watched the steam cloud his image from the mirror. If only it could cloud his memories as easily.

When he returned to the main room, he paused beside the bed. He pulled back the comforter and sat on the clean sheets as he stared at the nightstand.

The drawer slid open silently, and he reached inside and lifted the bottle. There was still about a third of the whiskey left, and he held the neck for a moment, watching the light shimmer on the liquid as it sloshed inside.

He set the bottle on the nightstand, turned off the light and lay down. The cushion of the mattress should have signaled the opportunity for desired rest, but although he closed his eyes and tried to clear his mind of the memories bubbling just beneath the surface, sleep denied him. He lingered in the semiconscious state, with a heightened awareness of the room around him, despite the dark. One thing about this motel he hated; it was in a wind tunnel, and when the gusts gained strength it sounded the way he imagined a thousand screaming banshees would, and yet it wasn't enough to drown out the other noises.

Every creak as someone shifted in the bed in the room above him, every time someone in the room beside him flicked channels during the commercial breaks, every beat of his heart . . . It all echoed in his ears, despite the way the wind wailed.

Until replaced by a deafening quiet.

The stillness was unnatural and unsettling. Craig's consciousness began to pull itself through the fog as his muscles tensed.

Sweat trickled down his back as he sat up and threw the covers off, fighting the cloud that still hovered over his brain. Where was he? What was he doing here?

As he connected with the answers, his breathing slowed and the muscles in his shoulders relaxed, but he still felt the twisting in his gut, the way the hair on the back of his neck stood on end.

Even through the thick motel curtains he could tell it was unusually dark outside his room. At some point over the past few months he'd grown accustomed to the dim glow of motel lights slipping under the door or sometimes through the far side of the window if the drape wasn't pulled over all the way. This night, there was nothing but blackness, and he blinked a few times to reassure himself that he really did have his eyes open, despite feeling the familiar burning from fatigue.

He reached for his gun, fingers finding the recognizable metal in the darkness as he swung his legs out of the bed.

That was when his brain figured out what was wrong

with this picture, and he glanced back toward the television.

The lights that stayed on twenty-four seven were off, on all the electronic appliances.

Craig set the gun back down, picked up his cell phone and flipped it open.

4:49 a.m.

He groaned as he shut the phone and tossed it back down beside his gun. How was it possible to feel as though his head had barely hit the pillow when it was almost time to get up?

The wind had knocked out the power, to the motel at least. If the outage was more widespread, it could make for a busy day, with the possibility of getting pulled off the investigation to direct traffic if the lights were out.

Not something Craig usually had to do, but like Sergeant Yeager had said only hours before, they were stretched pretty thin.

He thought about the bone-chilling cold of the night before and wondered if the sound he'd attributed to heartbeats had really been the distant drumming of rain against the roof two floors above him.

Rain that could have turned to ice, taking down power lines, causing days of disruption as crews tried to clear roads, make repairs and the police were needed to follow up on stranded motorists or recluses without power or supplies who might need to be dug out. Chaos disrupting the order of their investigations.

Craig scratched his head as he swung his legs back up on top of the bed, lay down and forced his eyes shut.

It was wishful thinking, and he knew it.

The low moan of the wind returned, and with it he felt himself drifting into a restless sleep.

Part of his brain still wondered how he was going to handle the problem with Mac and part tried not to think about Ashlyn's silhouette in the moonlight or the feeling of her breath on his skin.

* * *

Tain sat on the edge of the bed, head in his hands. It was almost five a.m., and the team could only afford a few hours of sleep before they met at the station.

He lay down against the comforter, knowing he should take the time to get undressed, but not daring to let his body fully relax into a sound sleep. This was another part of working a case that nobody could train you for, how to sleep when your mind was still processing the details, turning over all the information, trying to home in on the things that didn't sit right and figure out why they were bothering you.

Usually for the first day or two, the adrenaline compensated for the exhaustion, but this day had taken an emotional toll.

He felt the burst of anger when he thought about what had happened in Steve's office. There weren't many people Tain claimed to trust, but Steve had earned his respect over time. Tain could speak freely without fear of unreasonable rebuke, and he'd been able to tell himself that as an RCMP officer, he might still be able to do some good.

Lately he'd found himself thinking he couldn't, that he'd be better off walking away. The politics, the bureaucracy that contaminated the process . . .

What he couldn't walk away from was Ashlyn. In the past few months, she'd had to deal with the reality of being a victim herself. First she'd had a physical confrontation with Byron Smythe, a shady lawyer who put profits ahead of people and threatened to jeopardize a murder investigation. It wasn't a stretch to hold him responsible for the deaths of three more people; Smythe may not have pulled the trigger, but his interference kept critical information from them. Tain knew Ashlyn blamed Smythe, at least in part.

The other person she blamed was Officer Parker, a cop from the Port Moody Police Department who'd seemed to feel the job was about power instead of about serving the public, the kind of guy who liked to throw his weight around when it suited him and fell down on the job when it really mattered. When Ashlyn had been assaulted in the home she'd shared with Craig and Officer Parker had been charged it hadn't come as a surprise to Tain, but the evidence was thin. Ashlyn had never gotten a good look at the person who put her in the hospital.

Who caused her miscarriage.

Parker had been suspended, and there were rumors that even if he was cleared he wouldn't get his job back. Port Moody had brought in the RCMP because they needed their resources on a high-profile murder of a four-year-old boy just days before Christmas, and they'd ended up on the wrong end of a scandal when it was revealed that one victim was murdered while police officers who were supposed to be watching him slept in their car outside. Ashlyn had filed complaints about Parker during the investigation, and when the ax fell Parker had blamed her.

They'd had to go to court to testify, and they were still waiting for a verdict. Ashlyn didn't need to say anything. Every time her phone rang he could see it in her eyes. She needed closure, but he feared she might not get it, and in recent weeks both Smythe and Parker had tried to smear Ashlyn in the press.

Smythe being so generous he'd offered to defend Parker pro bono.

So generous, or just hell-bent on getting even with Ashlyn after the confrontation they'd had at the mall, a confrontation that had gotten physical.

He wondered how Ashlyn would cope if Parker got off, about the timing of facing the forthcoming verdict while working the murder of a girl they knew. A girl they knew from the first case they'd worked together, a case they'd both rather forget. Had it been harder to see Millie's body in the Dumpster, or to see Ashlyn trying to pretend everything was okay?

It wasn't a hard question to answer.

In the months since her attack, Ashlyn had closed herself off, had buried her pain and her grief and tried to shield it from everyone, including him, and as much as he wanted to offer her the dignity of respect, of confidence that she'd pull through, the more time passed, the more he worried.

Perhaps the end of the trial would allow her to begin the healing process, even if Parker got off.

Not if. When. He'd seen the evidence himself, and it was purely circumstantial. Smythe had even thrown himself in as another potential suspect with as much motive as Parker for hurting Ashlyn, casting more doubt on a case that was dubious at best.

He tried to push his concerns about Ashlyn from the forefront of his mind and forced himself to think about the case. Although the manner and timing was a shock, if he thought about it, Millie's death wasn't much of a surprise. Victims often had a hard time pulling their lives together.

And he didn't know many people who'd survived what Millie had and gone on to lead a normal life.

The truth was that the greater tragedy might lie in the fact that their investigation would prove Millie had made something of herself. Possibly found peace.

Happiness seemed too much to hope for.

He was glad they'd surveyed the body and made observations before they knew it was her. They'd both said the body was too clean for a working girl, didn't feel right for a pro.

Which meant maybe Millie hadn't been on the streets. Maybe she hadn't deserved this.

No. Nobody deserved to be murdered and discarded in a Dumpster. What he meant was that maybe Millie hadn't been involved in something that led to her death.

An innocent victim who'd simply been in the wrong place at the wrong time, not someone leading a high-risk lifestyle that would increase the chances something bad would happen to her.

Tain rubbed his forehead. That was what was really hard to take. In the coming days, they'd pull Millie's life apart again and either face the heartache of knowing the hell of everything she'd suffered since they'd seen her last, or knowing she'd been strong enough to pull herself through it and come out on the other side, only to fall victim to some other lunatic.

Some other lunatic.

Campbell was dead, and Hobbs was still in prison. He'd made the call when Ashlyn went to get food, waiting until the second she disappeared down the hall before he picked up the phone.

Making sure this didn't connect to the first case he'd worked with Ashlyn.

Making sure it couldn't.

He knew nobody deserved to be murdered and discarded in a Dumpster, but thinking about Hobbs, thinking about the feeling of bone crushing beneath his bare hands . . .

It was almost enough to make him smile.

PART TWO
THE PAST

CHAPTER SEVEN

Three years earlier

Jenny staggered back from the force of the blow, tasted the blood in her mouth, felt the edge of the dresser digging into her lower back as she hit it and reached out with her hands to steady herself. She'd worked her way up to a small room, in the old house across from the Inn. Bobby liked having her accessible but not in the same space, which was why she had the basement suite. Thin slats of light slipped in through the small windows, and her door led out to a basement exit. The only times the door to the stairs that went to the upper levels of the house was open was when Bobby was busy with her downstairs.

At night, she could hear the scratching sounds of rodents scurrying across the concrete floor on the other side of the wall, which was really just a sheet of paneling. The drafty basement smelled of mold and damp, and in the winter it was never warm, but it was a step up from the place in the woods, the shack where she hid out so that she didn't have to sell herself on her mother's terms.

"B-but I thought—"

He sat on the edge of the bed and laughed as he stuck one leg into his jeans, followed by the other. Once his feet were through, he stood. "You thought what? This would make me happy?" He pulled the jeans up and yanked on the zipper.

"It's . . . it's . . ."

"Scruffy, ya think it worked for your ma when she got knocked up with you? Who's your dad, anyway? You even know?"

Jenny felt the tears pricking at the corners of her eyes, but she fought to hold them back as she sank to her knees, hands clasped in front of her chest. "That's not . . . that's not . . . I didn't . . . It just happened. Honest."

Begging him to change his mind. Begging him to believe her.

"Whatever. I'm done with this. Ain't no way I want some screamin' brat around. You'll love it more than you love me, and I always told ya I don't want kids, didn't I?"

"Don't go. Please don't go. Please." She could hear the whine in her voice and hated herself for it, but just the thought of him leaving made her feel like a trunk had been dropped on her chest. What would she do without Bobby? She wouldn't even have a job.

A job. She looked down at her stomach, which in time would swell. She wouldn't be able to fit into the places she currently could, wouldn't be able to thieve for Bobby or spy on drops or anything. Shit. If he was cutting her loose she had . . . nothing. Jenny choked the words out through the sobs that shook her body. "Please, I'll never love anyone more than you, I swear. I promise you, Bobby, I promise. I'll prove it to you. I'll do anything."

He stopped with his hand on the door and turned back to look at her.

"Anything, Scruffy-love?"

She nodded as the tears streamed down her face, and he took a step back toward her, tilted her chin up so that her neck was bent almost all the way back. He looked down into her eyes.

"Okay, Scruffy-love. There might just be a way for you to prove it to me." He smiled down at her, and it was a cold smile. She could see that, and inside she felt her heart sinking as the fear of what he'd demand started to rise within her, but instead of backing away she leaned forward and wrapped her arms around his legs and held him there.

"I'll do anything. Anything you want."

He'd had her body, and ever since she'd started working for him on his side businesses, he'd owned her soul. What more could he possibly ask of her? Whatever he wanted, it couldn't be that bad, she told herself over and over again, until she almost believed it.

CHAPTER EIGHT

Eighteen months ago

When Constable Ashlyn Hart had thought about introducing herself to her new colleagues, she'd tried to work out a number of possible scenarios in her mind. Every attempt to anticipate all possible responses had been made, down to quizzing friends and talking to her mentor from The Depot, the training academy for Royal Canadian Mounted Police officers. She couldn't gain much personal information from anyone who'd worked in the area or might know her new colleagues because she'd been ordered not to disclose the details of her transfer until after she'd joined the team, a fact that piqued her curiosity even more, but she knew she needed to hit the ground running and integrating into the team successfully would be crucial. She'd done what she could to prepare by trying to plan for the various responses she might face when she arrived for her new assignment.

Sidestepping any issues quickly would be critical, so sleep had been exchanged for considering what it would be like working with a new partner, speculating what the Interior of British Columbia was like in the fall, whether her partner would have a family.

The other thing she'd found herself worrying about was how well they'd get along. She'd done one short stint in plainclothes, more by default than anything, because the local people had an issue with strict regulations and the uniform served as an obstacle when it came to building trust. The assignment was at a detachment so far in the sticks that she'd found herself handling nuisance complaints about property lines and curbside parking on the small stretch of dirt road that they called a main street. The weeks she'd spent there in the spring had basically amounted to clerical duty and refereeing. In truth, she was a rookie, and as a rookie plainclothes officer, the only thing she expected was to be paired up with someone older, with a lot more experience. Playing the statistics, it was likely she'd be working with a male partner, and if she had a male partner who was married, it could cause some tension for them in their personal life. It was even possible she'd find herself working with someone who had a problem with women on the force.

It was also possible that she'd be working with someone who would assume she was just a young kid, pushed up the ladder because of her gender, that she wasn't up to the job.

She'd devoured all the newspaper articles about the team that she could find, but there wasn't much information, and she was working off the assumption that she wasn't the only new person being transferred in.

A lot of possibilities had gone through Ashlyn's mind as she'd made the trip to BC's Interior. The one thing that hadn't occurred to her was that she might find the station locked with no sign of anyone around.

Ashlyn turned. The crisp morning air had a surprisingly strong smell of smoke. She wondered if wood-burning fireplaces were that common in the area. Would she have a wood stove in her temporary accommodations? She didn't even know where she'd be living.

The transfer had been that abrupt. Nighthawk Crossing didn't have a large RCMP detachment, but a few bad headlines had put the small town on the provincial map for all the wrong reasons, and it had become a focal point for politicians who wanted to give people the idea they were actually serious about doing something about crime.

Accused serial killer Robert Pickton had been on trial since January, and the press hadn't been content to cover the courtroom drama. They'd been eager to remind residents that the police had failed the women Pickton was accused of murdering, that prejudice against sex-trade workers and the homeless was rampant in society. The number of missing women bore witness to a pervasive indifference, but while most citizens were comfortable living with their prejudices they were also willing to assert that the people paid to serve and protect should not allow their own biases to cloud their judgment or dictate how they handled their jobs.

In other words, the police should care, even if the rest of society didn't. That was the convenient thing to say when the eyes of the world were looking down their noses at a police force that had allowed a pig farmer to murder forty-nine women before being caught.

Pointing out he'd only *allegedly* murdered forty-nine women didn't help much.

With the police, it was possible to understand. Call after call, arrest after arrest—they did what they could to get women off the streets. And court date after court date, they watched the women walk back out onto the street after serving a minimal time behind bars or having their bail paid by their pimp.

The truth was, if one of those windblown citizens had been mugged for so much as twenty bucks or harassed by a squeegee guy on East Hastings they would have begrudged the lack of police response because of reassigned manpower dealing with the serial-killer case. As long as the police were still there to take the call when an upstanding tax-paying citizen had his mailbox covered with graffiti, they shouldn't embarrass the nation with their prejudices, although that was the condition inferred silently. Nobody wanted to be the one to actually say it. It would confirm the bias—the belief that some victims were more important than others—wasn't a police prejudice. The police worked on the scale of priorities within the limits of the manpower and resources they had available and the political pressure they were under. It was people who decided some victims were more important than others.

Reporters had been quick to capitalize on the story, and when interest in Pickton's victims began to fade, they pointed to the stalled investigations of unsolved missing-persons cases and the disappearances of several teenagers in the Interior, in the Similkameen Valley. More accusations of police negligence followed. The first girl had disappeared more than eighteen months earlier, while the most recent girl to disappear had already been missing for a few weeks before her mother had reported her disappearance. During the months between, nine other girls had vanished. The fallout from the finger-pointing had prompted officials to form a task force, and under normal circumstances that would have taken some wind out of the critics' sails.

Not this time. Instead, the mudslinging had intensified. Native girls had been disappearing in the area for over a year and a half and nothing had been done. It had taken missing *white* girls from decent middle-class families to get the attention of politicians. Until then, the various officers investigating individual cases hadn't even been considering a connection between the missing Native girls and missing white girls.

Oddly enough, as many people seemed to be upset

by the use of the term Native as by the lack of action from the police. The problem with changing the language to be politically correct was that you couldn't change what had been ingrained in the minds of people for decades, said with no offense intended but now taken as an insult. Ashlyn had never wrapped her head around the term Aboriginal, and First Nations sounded so general, so vague.

So . . . sanitized. "Black" was offensive, and now "Native" wasn't the preferred label. She wondered when someone would decide "White" should be banned. Perhaps she'd have to start calling herself a European-Canadian.

Bickering over semantics aside, the RCMP was being forced to look over every unsolved missing-persons case in the area over the last five years that could be connected to the missing girls.

Ashlyn paced back and forth on the sidewalk by the entrance. Some members of the team were at least a few weeks ahead of her. The task force had been created in August, and she knew some of the men had worked in Nighthawk Crossing and the surrounding area prior to being reassigned, but for some reason she was being transferred in now, and with only thirty-six hours' advance notice, there hadn't been much time to get a handle on what was going on.

A glance at her watch told her she was ten minutes late. Shit . . . Had she set her clock back when she'd crossed the border from Alberta? Maybe she was actually early. She'd been a bit behind schedule. The Trans-Canada Highway cut through the center of Calgary, and an accident at the intersection with Center Street had forced drivers to weave through residential areas, trying to make their way around the mess. Canada's fourth-largest city desperately needed a ring road, but politics had stalled the process. Billions in oil revenue pumped into the local economy annually, but there wasn't enough money to build the highway. Wasn't that always the way?

She'd still found time to stop at the candy store in Banff and stock up on treats for her nieces and nephews and her cousin's daughter.

Those things were clear in her mind, but what had happened when she'd continued west and crossed the border wasn't.

She drew in a breath and let it out slowly. The way it pricked her throat was a reminder that summer was in its twilight. When she'd gotten out of her car, she would have described it as a crisp morning, but as she stood on the sidewalk, wondering if she hadn't set her watch back, she changed her mind. It was chilly.

She pulled out her cell phone to solve the mystery, then adjusted the time on her watch. Early.

Instead of returning to her car to warm up, Ashlyn started to walk around the building. The station was small, not designed for task forces and long-term investigations that required plainclothes officers. It didn't take long to make her way around to the back.

When she reached the back of the building, a quick scan of the area took in the back door of the station and a handful of vehicles filling up most of the staff parking.

Ashlyn frowned and turned to look at the back door again. It wasn't flush against the frame, and as she stepped closer, she could see what appeared to be a dark plastic bag that had been caught in the bottom. She crouched down and looked at the bag, which she guessed must contain a ream's worth of paper, if not more. Ashlyn ran her hand along the edge of the door and looked in.

It wasn't closed.

Someone had dropped the bag, probably without realizing it, and failed to secure the back door.

They must have left in a hurry. A bundle of five hundred sheets of paper had some weight to it. How could anyone not notice?

Ashlyn grabbed the bag and tugged on it, but failed to dislodge it from the door. She paused.

Her top priority should be closing the door to secure the station, but she had an opportunity to get inside. Part of her disliked the idea of literally sneaking in the back door.

She thought about the locked front door and glanced around the parking lot again. There were too many vehicles on site for the station to be empty, so she pressed her head up against the side of the door.

No voices, no cough, no hum of a photocopier at work or footsteps down the hall. She jumped when she heard a phone ring in the distance. It rang half a dozen times before it stopped. No one had answered it.

After one final glance around, Ashlyn pulled the door open, wedged herself in the opening and picked up the bag. As she looked up into the station, she listened to the silence.

Close the door, go back to her car and wait? Although she was early, she had no idea how long she might sit there, and without access to the station, she also didn't have access to the temporary accommodations she was being provided with, so she had nowhere else to go.

The door was open. She could go inside. Ashlyn glanced at the bundle in her hand. How could a trained officer drop a bag filled with papers and not notice it?

She'd assumed they were dropped when someone was leaving. What if someone had dropped them on their way in? She thought about the unanswered phone.

They could be in the bathroom or, worse, in need of medical assistance. Only one thing was certain. Something wasn't right.

Ashlyn stepped inside. The back door opened to what amounted to a large closet that the hall went through, before turning. It was still possible someone was there who hadn't heard her at the front door.

After a deep breath and quick glance at the fully shut door behind her, Ashlyn walked through the entry area and turned to go down the hall.

"Who the hell are you, and just what the hell do you think you're doing?"

Said as the file she was reading was snatched out of her hands with so much force the chair she was sitting in wobbled. She'd been leaning back, the front legs off the ground, her feet propped up by the bottom desk drawer, which had already been pulled out. Had it not been for her presence of mind and ability to grab the corner of the desk beside her, Ashlyn doubted she would have stayed upright.

The hands that had grabbed the papers reached for her then, and she was yanked up out of the chair before she had a chance to say anything. "You have any idea what kind of trouble you're in?"

"I—"

Native. First Nations. What was she supposed to call him? Whatever the label, the man reeked with the acrid smell of smoke, though it wasn't from cigarettes. It was like a heavily condensed version of what she'd smelled in the air outside earlier.

Not what she'd call conventionally good-looking, but he had magnetic eyes, hair long enough to pull back in a ponytail and was made of lean muscle. She could tell from the grip he had on her.

He looked down at the papers she'd tossed on the desk.

They were the ones she'd found wedged in the back door. After a quick search of the station, Ashlyn had concluded it was empty. The only thing she was sure of was which room the sergeant worked from and which room was being used for the investigation, because a hastily scrawled sign with the name of her team had been stuck against the door with sticky tack. Inside, there were more desks than the room—which was shaped like a backwards capital L—had been designed to hold. Three were pushed up against one another at the far end of the room, with two facing each other in the center.

She'd scanned the desks. Other than the usual assortment of family photos and a picture of a pretty girl on the desk marked *Nolan*, there hadn't been much on the surface to take note of. The bulletin boards weren't much better. Nothing had been left out, available for her perusal, and she was reluctant to leaf through closed folders on desks or files in drawers. After gleaning all she could from the few exposed scraps of paper lying around, Ashlyn had sat down at the one lonely desk closest to the entrance, tucked up against an extra corner where the room narrowed, presumably for a closet or storage space for the room beside this one. The desk shared space with a fax machine, while a portable metal shelf beside it held a printer. She'd sat down and pulled out the bag of papers she'd found.

Jackpot. Copied documents detailing the investigation.

In her initial excitement over having something concrete to study while she waited, she hadn't even stopped to consider the obvious, and now, as she stared into the dark eyes of the man who held her by her shoulders, she realized just how bad it looked.

"I—"

"Tain, where the hell do you get—"

As the voice cut in from the hallway, the man dropped his hold on Ashlyn's left shoulder and spun, pulling her beside him by the right arm.

"Not now, Nolan."

Nolan looked at Ashlyn, and his brow furrowed. "What's going on?"

"I—" Ashlyn started again.

Tain cut her off. "If you've got nothing better to do, you can get lost while I have a little chat with our visitor. I found her snooping around my desk."

"Don't worry. I doubt she found anything of importance there." Said with more than a liberal sprinkling of sarcasm.

The fingers dug into Ashlyn's arm. "Coming from someone who wouldn't know a lead if it slapped him in the face."

Nolan had dirty blond hair, eyes as blue as the summer sky and didn't look much older than Ashlyn was. Now that she thought about it, the man who was still digging his fingers into her arm probably only had a few years on her as well.

Nolan's mouth twisted with a wry smile. Ashlyn detected the smell of smoke on him as well, almost unnoticed because of her proximity to the man called Tain.

"You're still pissed off because the sergeant won't go for a search warrant. In case you've forgotten, you need a little thing called evidence," Nolan said.

"Take your shots now. You can read about them in the newspaper tomorrow."

The smile slipped from Nolan's face. "She's a reporter?"

"Can you think of another reason she'd sneak into a police station and snoop around?" Tain had Ashlyn's arm in a vise and didn't loosen his grip. "Guess she's about to get a jailhouse exclusive."

Nolan sighed and ran his fingers through his hair, then shrugged. "Drop her at the front desk. We don't have time to waste with this crap."

"Who the hell died and made you my boss, Nolan?"

Nolan's voice had started off with the tone of lecturing parent but quickly filled with an acidic bite. He straightened up, adding half an inch to his height. "The sergeant gave you an order, Tain."

"Yeah? And he sent you in here to check up on me?"

"In case you've forgotten, I've got the lead on this."

"One thing you're in charge of and you think you're king of the world. Run off to your little meeting, Nolan. I'm doing you a favor. You don't even want me on this."

Nolan's shoulders stiffened. "The sergeant gave us an order, Tain, or I wouldn't waste my time or breath."

"Good."

"Good?"

"You're catching on. You used to be too stupid to admit when you were in over your head."

Nolan took a step forward, jaw clenched as he pointed at the man who still had Ashlyn in his grip. "And apparently just stupid enough to think one of these days you might get it into your head to do your damn job. If you aren't going to be part of this team, there's the door." Nolan pointed to the back entrance.

Tain laughed. "Is that the best you can do? Get out of my face."

Ashlyn was still constrained by the grip Tain had on her, but she felt a tension in the man that was a direct response to Nolan's approach. For half a second, she thought Tain was going to hit him. But instead of lashing out physically, he grew still. Initially, Tain had given Nolan his halfhearted attention, but now he was staring at the man with the same intensity she'd felt when he'd yanked her to her feet.

Nolan hesitated as he stared back. Then he looked down at the desk.

"What's this?" he asked as he reached for the pile of copied papers Ashlyn had been reading.

"None of your goddamn business." Tain slammed his hand down on top of the stack of sheets.

"Nolan, don't you—"

Another voice, from the hall. This one was familiar, and Ashlyn placed it immediately.

Sergeant Mike Sullivan stepped into the room and

around Nolan. In one hand he held a folder, but it dropped a little as his focus shifted from the papers inside to the people in the room. There was no color in his cheeks, no hint of a smile or lift of his eyebrows to indicate any surprise or annoyance at the scene in front of him.

"Constable Tain."

"Sir."

"Would you care to explain why you're manhandling Constable Hart?"

Ashlyn felt the grip loosen, although Tain didn't let go.

"Sir?"

"Constable Ashlyn Hart, the newest member of our team." Sullivan stepped forward and extended his hand, forcing Tain to release her arm. "I'm sorry I wasn't here to meet you this morning. A local hotel caught fire yesterday evening, and we were out there all night."

Which explained the smell of smoke.

Sullivan glanced at Nolan and Tain. "I trust they've made you feel right at home."

Not an ounce of sincerity in his words.

Ashlyn offered a slight smile. "It's good to be here, sir."

"Since you've already met your partner, I'll let him show you around. After he wraps up the meeting, that is." Sullivan glanced at his watch, looked up at Nolan, then turned and started walking out the door. "She can have Winters's old desk, Nolan.

"Oh, and Tain? I'd like a full report on the meeting on my desk this afternoon."

The sergeant disappeared around the corner, far enough away to not hear Tain's muttered "Yes, sir" response.

Nolan almost smiled before he turned on his heel and marched out of the room without another word to Tain or his new partner.

The Native wasn't quite so forgiving. He yanked the top drawer of his desk open, grabbed the papers Ashlyn had been reading and dropped them inside before slamming it shut. "I ever catch you snooping around my desk again, I'll deal with you myself."

"I—"

"Meeting's down the hall, second door on the right." He spat the words with such force Ashlyn felt her own cheeks color as she took a step toward the door, then another. She turned to go down the hall and glanced back at Tain. He was locking the desk drawer he'd put the copied reports in.

Ashlyn took a deep breath. Only a few hours into her new assignment and a couple things were already crystal clear: two members of the team were at each other's throats, and at least one of them wasn't too happy with her either.

One thing was certain: she'd never imagined this was how her introduction to her new colleagues would go.

CHAPTER NINE

Eighteen months ago

The man called Nolan didn't even pause when Ashlyn entered the room.

Her own hesitation lasted only a second before she sat in a chair near the door.

Someone entered behind her, and that caused Nolan's eyes to narrow. Ashlyn turned her head. Whatever was between Nolan and Tain, it wasn't thinly veiled loathing. It was open contempt.

Tain leaned against the wall, not claiming one of the

few remaining chairs. They were pushed in tight, a long table in what would have been an interview room, the usual desk and chairs removed. Nolan stood at the other end, and three men sat at the desk, two on Ashlyn's left, one on her right.

They all looked older than Nolan, but she knew none had more than fifteen years on her from what she could remember from the newspaper accounts. Two closing in on forty, with the third in his early thirties.

"We lost a lot of time with the fire. Not much further ahead than we were when you left us last night." Spoken by a man on the far side of the table, to her right. Ashlyn put him as the oldest of the bunch, a rapidly receding hairline with thinning straw hair that probably masked the advancing gray. What had lost its color fell away first, the remaining strands looking tired, defeated, as though seeing the end of their fallen comrades had convinced them of the inevitable.

"Not further ahead at all," the man across from him said as he tapped a pile of message slips in front of him. "Two dozen new calls came in during our shift. Probably cranks and crazies, just wastin' our time, but . . ."

"We have to follow up on all of them, Aiken," Nolan said. "Hopefully there won't be a fire, snowstorm or other act of God that interferes with the case today."

The muttered words came from the back, where Tain stood. "More like act of man where the fire's concerned."

"You know what I mean," Nolan snapped back. He looked around the room. "Questions?"

Ashlyn paused. "Are—"

"Okay, we'll see you guys tonight, let you know what progress we've made," Nolan said.

After a moment of awkward silence, there were half-hearted mutters of agreement as the three men seated closest to Nolan stood and moved toward the door. Ashlyn wasn't sure if she should stay seated or stand up and step out into the hallway. She was too busy thinking about the way Nolan had shut her down. There was just enough room to move around her, and in her hesitation she noted Tain stood stone still, leaning against the wall, so she stayed seated at the table.

"Oh, yeah, latest addition to our team," Nolan said. "Constable, uh . . ." Nolan snapped his fingers a couple times.

"Ashlyn Hart," she said as she turned in her chair, toward the three men, who hadn't reached the end of the table where she sat yet.

"That's Oliver, Campbell and Aiken," Nolan said. "They're pulling second shift right now."

She nodded and took the opportunity to respond as the second officer on her left side started to walk around her.

"I was going to ask, who are we coordinating with from the tribal police?"

The entire room fell silent.

"Hart, we'll discuss this later." Nolan pushed the words out between clenched teeth, looking almost as angry as he had only moments earlier, when he'd been arguing with Tain.

"She's been on this team all of five minutes and already she's questioning how things are being run and whether we've screwed up this investigation?" The words came from one of the men behind her as he slammed his fist against the table.

She jumped, instantly wishing she hadn't shown a physical response.

"Calm down, Campbell. I didn't hear her accuse anyone of incompetence," Nolan said in a low growl. "Did I, Hart?"

"No. I—" She glanced at the Native officer who still leaned against the wall, his expression a blank slate that didn't betray any of his thoughts as he stared back at her.

She turned around. The older members of the other team hovered near the door. Campbell was right behind her.

"You don't understand the first thing about policing out here. Some of us, we've got to be able to live in this town after the rest of you are gone. You want to push your way onto the Reserves, really offend the locals? Let me tell you something. Those goddamn Indians only care about using this as another excuse to beat up on white people and throw a pity party for themselves. If you think they actually give a damn about this investigation you can think again."

"What did you say?" Tain stepped toward them. Ashlyn could see him move from the corner of her eye.

"Stay out of this, Red." Campbell straightened as he turned his focus on Tain.

"Okay, enough." The men waiting by the door stepped in, keeping their faces toward Tain as they edged between him and Campbell. One of them—Aiken—turned and grabbed Campbell by the arm. He pulled back, but after a second tug, he murmured something too low for even Ashlyn to hear. Campbell relented.

The three men exited the room and walked off without another word.

Ashlyn wondered if Tain got along with anyone. Wondered why she hadn't been able to get an answer to her question. Wondered why it had made Nolan so angry. Wondered if there was a third shift. Wondered if and when more manpower would arrive.

Wondered what she'd done to piss off the karmic gods who'd stuck her on a shift with Tain and with Nolan as a partner.

"It's eight to eight. Long days or nights, but this is all we've got to work with." Nolan looked up past Ashlyn and to her right. "Tain, someone needs to—"

"Yeah, later."

As he turned and marched out the door, Ashlyn let her gaze settle on the table in front of her. When she glanced at Nolan, his jaw was clenched, cheeks simmering with what she decided could only be called a cool burn. Nolan had a strange way of looking stone cold and enraged at the same time. He stared past her at the empty doorway, rapping the knuckle of his index finger against the table a couple of times before he reached down, grabbed the stack of messages and the notebook in front of him, and started to walk toward the door.

He was behind her and halfway out the door before she realized he intended to keep walking and leave her there. It was possible he was deliberately ignoring her because he was angry about her question, but it was also possible it was an oversight, innocent forgetfulness caused by distraction over his conflict with Tain. To be fair, she didn't want to jump to any conclusions.

Although she had a hunch she knew which one it was.

Ashlyn got up and followed him down the hall, back to the room with the desks. Nolan went for one in the center. A desk was pushed up against it on the other side, holding nothing but a telephone, notepad, pen, and nameplate that said *Winters*.

Her desk now.

The three other desks in the main body of the room were grouped together, two pushed up against each other, with the third one pushed up against the two ends to form a rectangle. From where she stood she could make out the names. From where she'd be sitting Oliver was to her left, Campbell to her right and Aiken's back was to hers.

Tain's desk isolated on the other side, nearest the door, farthest from the other desks.

Nolan closed the gap between the door and his desk, tossed the stack of slips down and riffled through the loose papers scattered over the surface. As he skimmed them, he added some to the pile, then pulled his desk drawer open and tossed half a dozen or so inside.

Some of the papers were ones she'd skimmed when

she'd looked around earlier. Others were new ones that had come in during the short time she'd left the room for the meeting marking the shift change.

Eight to eight, but a quick glance at the clock on the wall said it was 10:57.

Ashlyn walked around to her desk, which faced Nolan's, but didn't pull the chair back. He hadn't, so she doubted they'd be there for long.

Nolan glanced up from the slip in his hand, gaze darting back to take in the last few words before he looked up again. As he folded the paper and stuffed it in his pocket he said, "Something that needs to be followed up on."

"Okay," she said, body turning to walk back to the door automatically.

He took a step backward and held up his hand, then stepped forward, picked up the pile of slips he'd just tossed down and held them out to her.

"There are names and numbers on all of these. Follow up, see if there's any substance to them. I, uh . . . I just need to check on something. I'll be out for a bit."

Ashlyn took the papers from him and watched as he grabbed the jacket off the back of his chair and put it on while he walked to the hallway. She pulled her chair out and sat down across from Nolan's empty desk and jumped at the sound of the back door slamming shut.

The man leaning back in a chair at the corner table of the bar grinned when he looked up, which emphasized the jagged scar that curved up his right cheek.

His smile also showed off the broken front tooth he sported. Fresh since the last time Tain had seen him.

"I cud smell ya the minute ya walked in the door, man."

"Someone burned down Blind Creek Inn."

Kurdy Jeffers's jaw dropped, but his eyes betrayed the shock as false. "You don't say. Guess that means I won't be workin' tonight."

He hadn't eased up on the sarcasm. Kurdy worked odd jobs at the hotel. In a town like Nighthawk Crossing, it was a safe bet everyone but the recluses who lived on the outskirts and only ventured into town once a month had already heard about the fire, but the attitude still pissed Tain off.

Kurdy lifted the shot glass to his lips, but Tain knocked it from his hand just as his mouth opened. Alcohol spilled onto his skin and the table as the glass crashed against the floor.

There was a split-second lull in the hum around what locals considered a town bar. It was the kind of place that served what was supposed to pass for food, but the cook spent more time smoking on the back step than burning anything on the grill. This place paid rent selling booze, with no rule you had to eat to take a table. Tain glared at a couple of the closest patrons, big guys he knew were most likely to cause trouble just for the hell of it. He guessed they figured he was in no mood to screw around with. They turned back to their drinks, and he fixed his gaze on the man still seated in front of him.

Kurdy's brow was creased, his top lip curled up into a snarl as he wiped his mouth with his sleeve.

"Places you work at have a bad habit of burning down."

The man, whom Tain thought of as half weasel, half slimeball, showed off his freshly cracked tooth again as he lifted a hand in a half shrug and then set it back on the table. "Wish I had dem odds playin' 649."

"You don't strike me as the type to buy lottery tickets, Kurdy."

"Man's gotta have his dreams."

Tain leaned down closer. "Yeah? What's yours? A big boat? Cottage on the coast, someplace without long winters and months of snow? No, wait. You used to be a bit of a hunter, a good tracker, from what I heard. You'd like a cabin in the woods with a fair bit of land? Or are your tastes a bit simpler? Say, some high-priced stimulation? Oh, no, wait. I remember now. You like something younger. Maybe with no price tag at all."

Kurdy jumped to his feet. "You get the hell outta my face."

"Strike a nerve, Kurdy?"

The man shoved Tain hard. If it wasn't for the fact that he was of a slim build, no more than five-seven with pencil-thin arms, Tain might have had to step back to regain his balance.

As it was, he didn't even flinch.

He grabbed Kurdy by the shirt and pinned him against the wall, the bar again going quiet. Kurdy looked over Tain's shoulder, then pressed back against the wall. "You got no fuckin' right."

"You seem awfully nervous for someone who's innocent."

"Maybe 'cos you got me backed in a corner an' shoved up against a wall."

Skittish eyes darted to and fro as though he was hoping someone would morph out of the floorboards and come to his rescue.

He tightened his hold and pushed Kurdy harder. "You better watch yourself, 'cos I'm keeping an eye on you. Next girl that goes missing . . ."

"What? You gonna drag me out back and scalp me, Red?"

Tain pushed Kurdy up until he felt the full weight of him lifted in the air. "I find out you've been up to your old tricks, I'll see to it your cell mate'll do things to you that'll make you cry for your mommy."

"Guess they haff ta pull in losers like you on somethin' like this. Nobody else gives two shits about your kind."

"Is that what you count on, Kurdy? Think nobody'll mind if you snatch a couple Native girls off the streets?"

Kurdy snorted. "Yer only pissed 'cos it's a coupl'a red

niggers. You'd never get this worked up 'bout a white girl." A sly smile spread across his face. "But den agin, I heard somethin' about you. Maybe you would."

"Maybe I should ask your wife about your hobbies."

The man in his grasp tried to swing with both arms, and Tain struggled to keep his hold.

"You stay the hell away from her," Kurdy hissed, eyes wide.

"Tain." The voice came from beside him, not the man pinned against the wall in front of him. "Let him go."

Slip his hand to the left and he could wrap it around Kurdy's throat.

"I said let him go!" He knew that voice.

Kurdy's gaze flickered from Tain's face to the person to Tain's right, and he showed off his broken tooth again.

The drop against the floor wasn't enough to hurt him, but it shook the smirk off his face for a second. Tain stepped back.

Kurdy lifted his hand and looked like he might shake a fist, then pointed at the person beside Tain. "You keep him the hell away from me or I'll make a complaint."

Nolan stepped forward and grabbed Kurdy by the shirt. "You want to go running to our boss, say you don't like the way you've been treated? That you think we should be nicer to guys who rape kids?"

Kurdy swallowed. "I didn't know she was fourteen."

"So you say." Nolan let go of the shirt as he gave him a small shove. "Thing is, I don't believe you, and I don't think your wife will either."

Kurdy seemed to have decided arguing was pointless. He marched toward the door, stopping only when the bartender got in his way and demanded he pay his tab.

"So help me, Tain, next time he threatens to make a complaint about you, I should offer to drive him to the station myself."

"Save it. You chase your leads, and I'll chase mine." Tain started to walk away, but Nolan stepped in front of him.

"I'm warning you, Tain, the sergeant will only put up with so much of this."

"Go run and tell on me if you need to, Nolan. Just get out of my way."

Tain brushed past him, but Nolan wasn't about to be left behind. When they'd exited the bar, Nolan continued, "Don't think the color of your skin and local politics are going to save your ass if you're harassing people. I'll go to Sullivan myself if I have to."

"I expect as much from a sorry excuse of an officer like you," Tain said as he spun around. "You stay the hell away from me."

"Don't you even care about those missing girls?"

"More than you do."

"Yeah? Prove it! Stop jeopardizing this investigation. You keep running off, doing your own thing, not checking in with anyone, threatening people for no reason."

"I have my reasons."

"Yeah? How about filling the rest of us in? Sharing your alleged leads? If you've got something on Kurdy, put it on the table so we can get surveillance, bring him in for questioning. You running off trying to save the day on your own is holding us back."

"Yeah?" Tain shifted his gaze deliberately to Craig Nolan's left, then right. "And where's the little chick the sergeant told you to partner with?" He looked Nolan in the eye. "Waiting in the car? Or did you ditch her at the office first chance you got? Don't you lecture me about playin' it solo. Not after what happened to Winters. I'm under no delusions about who isn't watching my back, Nolan. Not unless you think you can put a knife in it, that is."

He spun on his heel and walked away. Somehow, Nolan had known where he was going, what he was doing.

Tain knew Nolan had been keeping an eye on him, but he also knew he'd left the station well ahead of the ambitious officer. There was no way Nolan could have followed him.

And that left a few possibilities. Nolan's instincts could have been better than Tain wanted to give him credit for, or he might have gotten lucky.

Or he had a source.

Tain yanked the car door open and slammed the key into the ignition as he formed a mental list of everyone he'd seen in the bar, anyone who'd noticed him when he went in. It had been the usual crowd of underemployed or hired by the job, off-the-books types who practically lined up outside waiting for the doors to open.

Luck wasn't something he believed in, but the idea that Nolan could read him or had someone tipping him off made his gut twist.

He was going to have to watch his back, more than he already was.

CHAPTER TEN

Eighteen months ago

It was 2:45 p.m. when Ashlyn pushed what was left of her sandwich aside and tossed the latest message on Craig's desk.

Complete with follow-up details attached. She'd done the legwork on every call that had come in since her partner had left, as well as the messages he'd tossed in front of her. Some of the callers had been identified as cranks, people who tried to be helpful by calling the police with what turned out to be useless information. Sue

Sanders claimed she'd seen Mary Donard at the local diner when she was on her way to a ten a.m. appointment with Dr. Daniels on the fifteenth. Sue couldn't remember which month, but she knew for a fact that it was the fifteenth, and if Ashlyn would stop being so lazy and call the doctor's office, they'd tell her themselves.

It turned out the only appointment she'd had with the doctor in recent years was on the seventeenth of December 2002, but between Ashlyn and the receptionist, Sue Sanders wasn't playing with a full deck.

Ashlyn didn't call Mrs. Sanders back to let her know what conclusion she'd reached about her tip.

Doubt was cast on another potential lead when she'd called the helpful citizen, only to discover he had no memory of calling the police at all. A third had called from a long-term nursing facility. Staff confirmed the patient in question had been a resident for two years and hadn't been off the property in more than four months and therefore couldn't possibly have seen a missing girl at a church dance two weeks ago.

For the very few she couldn't refute or substantiate, Ashlyn had outlined a course of action for further investigation. In most cases it involved reassigning personnel to conduct interviews.

Part of her was tempted to reassign herself and get out of the building. The lack of windows in the room where the desks were located was starting to bother her. As important as chasing leads was, she wanted to see the town and get a sense of the local area. The one night she'd spent in a motel on the outskirts of Nighthawk Crossing hadn't offered her much of an introduction; after all the miles she'd driven, she'd been too tired to do more than order room service and fall asleep early.

Instead, Ashlyn got up and stretched toward the ceiling, then braced her hands on the edge of the desk and extended her right leg, then left. When she straightened up again, she reached up from the side, first from one side, then the other. Her attempt to loosen the kink that had developed in her back during the long drive failed, but it still felt good to stand.

As she glanced at Tain's desk, she thought back to the files she'd been reading that morning. That was the meat of the investigation. Although she hadn't read it all, she'd skimmed through enough to know that the files on each of the missing girls whose disappearances were believed to be connected had been included, as well as all the leads that they'd followed up on, tips that had been eliminated, avenues of investigation that had been exhausted.

She wanted to see those files again.

Ashlyn replayed the scene from the morning and was fairly certain Tain had taken the key with him. Short of picking the lock, there was no way she was going to get a chance to see the copied documents.

The palm of her hand smacked against her forehead. Of course. They were copies. The originals had to be around somewhere, and as a member of the team, she had access. She didn't need someone's permission to review information pertinent to the case she'd been assigned.

When she'd looked around the desks earlier, she'd limited her survey to things clearly out in plain sight.

She'd almost forgotten the filing cabinets in the corner.

No matter how hard she'd tried to prepare herself for this transfer, Ashlyn realized she'd expected it to be different. In the past, a colleague had always shown her around, at least pointed out where things were kept. Other than the one prolonged assignment in plainclothes—a technicality, really, an exception made to help the locals feel more at ease with the police because of a history of problems in an area primarily populated by Aboriginals—she'd spent most of her time in smaller communities, where she'd worn a uniform and driven a patrol car.

The job had required her to get out and make contact with people.

This assignment was different. A long-term investigation that involved different tactics than the ones community policing emphasized. When she'd been reassigned, she'd been told she'd be working plainclothes for this assignment and that part of the reason they were sending in outsiders was to get a fresh perspective, as well as to show the community how seriously they were taking the investigation.

It was hard to know what to think about the team and what they were dealing with. So far, they had eleven cases that seemed to be connected, and the trail was already cold. They didn't know if this was a murder investigation or if the girls had been lured into prostitution and were living on the streets in Vancouver, a fact that compounded their problems. Every possible sighting from Victoria to Halifax, from Edmonton to Vegas had to be considered.

This wasn't meant to be a short-term investigation, where they got in and got out fast. Despite that, she'd been told this was a temporary transfer.

It didn't make sense.

She thought about her fleeting introductions to the other half of the team. Two of the men were at least ten to fifteen years older than she was, with more experience, but she'd read about those members of the team from old newspaper articles before she'd packed her bags. There hadn't been any photographs, but the article had mentioned the three officers and Winters, who had been the oldest member listed, in his midforties. She hadn't met him yet. She looked at the nameplate on the desk that was now hers and realized she didn't even know if he was still working the case, but the fact that she'd been given his desk made that doubtful.

What she remembered from the articles was that all had worked in the Interior of the province or in the north, for the bulk of their careers. They'd all worked for local detachments for several months prior to being re-assigned officially. Only Winters had worked in larger urban areas, including Vancouver.

The youngest of the three older officers—Ashlyn guessed Campbell had at least half a dozen years on her, although his age hadn't been stated—was a hometown boy, who'd grown up in Nighthawk Crossing and spent his entire career in the Similkameen Valley, and if what he'd said that morning was any indication, he didn't like outsiders meddling in local affairs. He'd been defensive and hostile, and she never had gotten an answer to her question.

There was no indication any had worked in a city that had a population of 100,000. That fact alone didn't mean that they were unskilled or incapable of being effective on this task force, but she thought back to her own train-ing, to the common philosophies about the differences between small-town policing and city casework.

The differences between community men and career men. Not that officers who focused on community polic-ing didn't have careers, but major advancement often came through high-profile cases, and that meant work-ing in urban areas where the job was divided by the na-ture of the crimes instead of the town boundary lines.

Nolan and Tain hadn't been mentioned, although the article had concluded with the fact that other officers were being reassigned. Ashlyn wondered about the date and whether their transfers had been withheld from the article or really happened after.

Considering the pressure the RCMP had been under to demonstrate they took the investigations seriously, wouldn't they want to emphasize the number of officers assigned? She hadn't found any articles about additional staff once they'd been named.

She thought about Campbell's attitude that morning. Perhaps the truth was in the extreme reaction, that there was concern about how the local people would feel if the investigation was being run by outsiders.

Did that somehow suggest the local officers weren't capable of serving their communities? Was that why they'd picked a rookie, along with a handful of officers who'd focused on community policing?

She had expected to work with the tribal police, especially considering the number of missing Aboriginal girls and the high number of Native Peoples residing in the area.

Now that she considered the situation, she realized she'd expected more Native officers to be assigned.

One other thing she hadn't expected: to be the only woman.

Three officers who'd built careers on community policing shared one shift, and they were the three who had the most experience. By comparison, the combination of herself, Tain and Nolan on one shift was even more baffling. There was no doubt she was the youngest of the three, but not by much, and she'd pursued her career in law enforcement as soon as she'd completed her degree. Tain and Nolan had both only been with the RCMP for a few years, and there was nothing in the newspaper reports that indicated experience with a case like this one because they hadn't even been mentioned.

For a moment, she wondered if she would ever get a chance to sneak a look at their personnel files, then dismissed that thought with a mental note to do a little digging on Nolan and Tain later. Her job was to focus on the investigation, and everything she was looking for was in the filing cabinets. She started to pull out the details of the casework to date, but changed her mind and took out the information that had been collected on each of the missing girls instead.

The files contained the usual information: last known

address, next of kin, age, height, eye color. Each had a photo attached to the upper left corner of the folder and a report of the girl's disappearance.

From there, the files varied dramatically.

Some reports had been filed by mothers. In one case, a sibling had called the police, and another girl's absence had been noted by her aunt.

Another investigation had been initiated by a statement from a volunteer in a soup kitchen who'd eventually wondered what had happened to one of the regulars.

The length of time that elapsed before the reports were made also varied. The mother of one of the girls made the report a month after her daughter had disappeared. Kacey Young, who appeared to be the first girl to disappear, had been reported missing by her sister after two weeks. It only took the man from the soup kitchen ten days to pick up a phone, and the aunt had contacted police after one week.

Another file had been initiated when the girl didn't start school in the fall. A diligent teacher had attempted to contact the parents, and when their letter was returned, they contacted the tribal council. They'd conducted their own investigation and determined that the girl, whose parents had been killed in a car accident earlier in the summer, hadn't been seen since near the end of August.

They hadn't contacted the RCMP until three weeks after news of the task force was made public, which meant Wendy George had been missing for nearly thirteen months, and the report had come in only a few days before Ashlyn had been reassigned.

The George file was the thinnest one they had, with nothing more than the statement. Ashlyn read it over a second time, noting that Constable Campbell had taken the initiating report.

She set that folder to her left and went through the

other files one by one. The report in the Young case had been made to Constable Tain. Constable Aiken had spoken to the aunt, who'd filed her report almost eighteen months ago. Oliver had been the initial contact on three other cases that dated back almost a year. The girls had all gone missing over a two-week period from November 5 to November 19.

Winters, the officer she hadn't met and may have replaced, had taken the statements for two other girls, and while Tain had opened the file on the most recent girl to disappear, Winters had done the follow-up.

The girl's mother had waited six weeks to tell police. Winters had done some digging: Wanda Johnson worked from home. More specifically, from the bedroom. Jenny had a habit of running off and had been picked up as a juvenile on one solicitation charge already.

Campbell, Aiken, Oliver and Tain had all been involved with at least one case prior to being reassigned to the task force. Was Ashlyn the only member of the team who hadn't had some earlier involvement in the investigation?

She riffled through the reports one more time.

Nolan had taken one report, filed in Penticton, for a girl who'd gone missing eight months earlier.

Sergeant Sullivan had opened the file on the first missing Caucasian girl himself. Millie Harper had gone missing just days before Wendy George had last been seen.

Ashlyn pulled the desk drawers open one by one, but they were all empty. She thought back to her introduction to Tain, and wondered what his response would be if he found her going through the cupboards under the printer.

She could snoop around and take the chance, or she could try to find someone she could ask. The risk was that she'd run into the sergeant. If asked where Nolan was, she wouldn't have an answer, but the bigger question would be whether she was prepared to cover for him.

If reprimanded, Nolan might accuse her of deliberately informing their commanding officer that he'd left her behind. He'd jump to conclusions first and, if she was lucky, listen to explanations later. Considering the tension between Nolan and Tain, it was hardly surprising that Nolan wouldn't feel like slipping into tour-guide mode so he could give her an introduction to the case and the town.

That would allow Tain to slip off his radar. Whatever Nolan was doing at the moment, the one thing she was convinced of was that it involved keeping an eye on the third member of their team.

Even if she took Tain out of the equation, Nolan's reluctance to work with her could have been caused by a number of things. The picture on his desk could be his girlfriend, and he might be nervous about her reaction to him working closely with a woman his own age. He may have worked with a woman before and had problems.

He may also be a chauvinistic jerk, although at the moment she was more likely to award that title to Tain. There'd been enough of a warm smile lurking behind Nolan's eyes for split seconds for her to think better of him.

Or maybe she'd imagined it, even wished she'd seen it.

A remnant of the strong smell of smoke that had clung to Nolan and Tain still lingered in the air, and she thought about the reference to a large fire in the town. It was possible the events of the morning had thrown them off, that Nolan had prior meetings set up, things he had to take care of personally, and he didn't have time to show a new partner around, but she just couldn't make herself believe it.

In the distance, the back door slammed shut. She hoped it wasn't Tain.

As she stood, Nolan marched into the room. He appeared to do a double take when he saw her move and stopped.

"I was just—"

Nolan looked at the files on her desk. It took him less than two seconds to close the gap and grab the top folder.

"What the hell are you doing?" He didn't give her a chance to answer. "I left you with a very specific job to do. Do you have a problem following orders?"

She felt the color in her cheeks. "No, I—"

"For once, can't someone on this team just do what they're told?" he muttered as he turned and started moving toward his desk.

"I did."

He spun around. "Excuse me?"

Cheeks still burning, Ashlyn reached over and pointed at the pile of papers she'd left for him. "Every message you gave me and all the calls that have come in since." She watched as he picked up the first sheet, skimmed it, then leafed through the stack.

He looked up and for a second, the tension he'd carried in his face was gone. "I'm . . . I'm sorry. I shouldn't have accused you like that. It's just . . ." His voice trailed off.

She knew he wasn't going to explain.

"I thought it would be helpful to familiarize myself with the case. I didn't get a chance to read all the copies before Tain took them earlier."

His eyes narrowed. "What copies?"

Something about the way his mouth settled into a hard line and the ruddy shade his face turned made her wonder if it was the mention of Tain's name or something more that had struck a chord with Nolan.

She opened her mouth, still trying to work out a response, when Nolan's phone rang. He grabbed the handset, reached for a pen, then stopped. The color in his cheeks evaporated, and he looked up at her with a softness in his eyes that hinted at sadness.

Nolan hung up the phone. "Grab your coat."

She was about to ask where they were going but thought better of it. As she pulled her jacket on, she noticed the solemn gaze, the way all the tension in Nolan shifted. Before, his shoulders had pinched and the lines in his face were hard.

Now his face had softened and sagged, which made him look as though he'd aged a few years in the past few minutes. Even his shoulders had dropped, although his hands were balled into loose fists.

He looked up. "They found a body."

There hadn't been a chance to see much of the town on the drive over. A few blocks from the station they'd turned onto a road heading into the mountains. A quick glance in the mirror gave Ashlyn a glimpse of a row of buildings that led to where a fire truck was still parked several blocks down the street, presumably at the site of the fire Tain and Nolan had referred to earlier.

In only a few minutes she felt like she was in the middle of nowhere. There were no houses or stores, not even power lines or hydro poles along the road. She was surprised by the patches of snow that clung to the earth in some places as they climbed up out of the town. The Isuzu Rodeo Nolan drove jolted as the front right tire dipped into one pothole, then another. The sport utility vehicle bumped along as they ascended the mountainside. When they reached a turn, Nolan went right, and Ashlyn soon found herself staring down a gorge with nothing but air between the vehicle and the edge of the cliff.

"That's why I didn't bring a company car."

They were the only words Nolan had said since they'd left the office, and she waited until they turned to the left and began driving on what seemed like a level path cut out from the middle of a large forest before she said, "I didn't realize we were that far up."

"You aren't from British Columbia?"

"No. Ontario."

He glanced at her. "The mountains can be deceptive."

"This is your vehicle?"

A quick nod was his only answer. Ahead, a few cars lined the side of the road, and Nolan pulled over and parked.

The ground crunched beneath Ashlyn's feet as she followed Nolan along the road. It was like thin ice, the pressure of each footfall cracking the early winter shell, except most of the road wasn't slick. She hadn't realized how much colder it could be after such a short drive up into the mountains, but she was glad it hadn't warmed up enough during the day for the ground to thaw completely because they would have been walking through mudholes. As it was, it had warmed up enough in some places for water to pool, and she guessed there'd been a fair bit of rain recently because the puddles looked deep.

A uniformed officer waited by the side of the road opposite from where they'd parked. "Nolan," he said. The man offered Ashlyn nothing more than a quick glance before he turned and led the way into the bush.

"I assume you told Rick there's no hunting in national parks," Nolan said.

"Yes."

"Was Rick surprised?"

"No, I was. He pulled out a map and argued over boundary lines with me. I didn't realize this part of the mountain wasn't part of the park."

"That makes two of us," Nolan said.

"He's got a permit."

"Guess that means he's got a legitimate reason to be wandering around in the woods in the middle of nowhere with a gun," Nolan said.

"Guess so." The first officer ducked under a tree that had fallen but remained elevated because its tip was caught in the crook of a branch on another tree. Ashlyn wondered how secure it was as she ducked underneath and glanced up at the tree providing support, a distraction that caused a split-second delay in her reaction as she turned and saw too late that a branch was swinging back toward her.

It caught her on the cheek and cut into the skin. Without reaching up she knew it was bleeding, because she could feel the trickle of blood racing toward her chin. Tears welled in her eyes from the sting, but she kept her focus on fishing through her pocket for a tissue so she could wipe her face.

Underfoot, the terrain wasn't what she'd describe as inviting. Although much of the ground appeared to be in the process of freezing, in some places where the earth dipped water had pooled. The ground on the sides of the small hills was soggy.

It was fall, and in the mountains that meant winter weather wasn't far away.

There were more patches of snow between some of the trees, but they were sporadically scattered, with no rhyme or reason that she could determine.

Nolan had said something to her, but she hadn't heard him.

"What?" she said, just as she put her right foot down and it began to sink into the earth.

Nolan turned and grabbed her arm, giving her enough leverage with her left foot to pull the right one free.

"I said to watch out for the hole."

"Sorry."

She looked down at her mud-caked shoe.

"You're going to need some boots," Nolan said.

She felt her face grow warm. "I have boots. I just haven't had a chance to unpack anything."

When she looked back up, she realized they were there. Three men were gathered in the woods at no place in particular, joined now by the uniformed officer who still hadn't introduced himself, herself and Nolan. She scanned the area. Nothing but trees and a gentle slope up the side of a hill before them, a slope down to the right. The area to the left looked as hilly as the ground they'd just covered.

It wasn't hard to tell who Rick was. He had a stocky Labrador by the collar with his left hand, and with his right he had a firm grip on his shotgun.

The other two men were park rangers. One had deep lines in his weather-worn skin and a weight in his gaze. The younger man had a wide-eyed look. While his partner carried a solemn burden in his bearing that made Ashlyn think if he'd had a hat he would have taken it off out of respect, the younger man bristled with an energy that reminded her of her nieces and nephews on Christmas morning. He was curious.

Neither spoke, but the older man nodded toward a hump of earth approximately half a dozen feet away,

Nolan walked toward the disturbed dirt and then stopped, still as a statue. From where Ashlyn stood, she couldn't see anything, and when she glanced at the rangers, the older man had turned his gaze toward the ground. The younger man glanced at her, then his partner, then looked away. The only one who didn't avert his gaze was Rick. His expression betrayed nothing, but his eyes were black as a moonless night and had a magnetic pull that kept her staring back for a moment before she looked away.

After a glance at the officer who'd escorted them to the scene, who was also focused on the ground, Ashlyn moved beside Nolan.

God.

She was glad she had her back to the men so that they couldn't see the look on her face.

Nolan turned back to the group. "Who else has seen this?"

Silence.

"Getz?"

After a tiny hesitation the voice of the officer who'd escorted them cut through the quiet. As far as he knew only the six of them had been to the site.

"Okay, first things first. Rick, you'll have to give a proper statement. Constable Getz can take you back to the station and get that down on paper. I want you to tell him everything. If you saw a scrap of fabric on a branch two miles from here, you be sure to mention it and draw me a map. I know you're capable."

Rick nodded.

"Did your dog have any contact with the corpse?"

"Yes." The voice was unexpectedly soft and soothing.

"Then we may need to take some samples. If we try to identify suspects based on animal fur found on the victims we want to be sure it's from the killer's dog and not yours."

"You saying this is a murder?" A different voice. Ashlyn could guess which of the men had spoken. The high-pitched tinge of excitement betrayed the younger one, but despite her desire to glare at him, she still didn't trust herself to turn around. She'd found a place on the ground, to the right and up from the open grave, where she could stare while she forced herself to take deep breaths.

"How good a look did you take, Gordy?"

"I . . . I didn't. I just saw the pit and was about to step forward, but he stopped—" Said with a tinge of defensiveness. As though he was trying to prove he was manly enough to handle it. That he hadn't held back out of fear.

"Good," Nolan said. "Walk over to that tree and stay there. Henry?"

The voice of the older ranger matched the deep lines in his skin that hinted at years of working in the sun. It had a weathered tone and was filled with the weight of experience. "I saw."

"Right. Go stand by that tree and wait for me."

What followed the sound of fading footsteps was an eerie silence, then a low growl from Rick's dog and a man's voice as he told it to behave.

Ashlyn turned as Nolan slid something into his pocket and walked away from Rick. He went to the older ranger, Henry, first. She could only see Nolan's back, and after a few minutes he slid something out of his pocket, but it was small enough to fit in the palm of his hand and she couldn't make out what it was.

Should she be doing something?

She glanced at the officer—Getz—and he quickly looked away. Whatever Nolan was doing, Ashlyn felt certain he'd resent any attempt on her part to get involved.

After a few minutes, Nolan turned and walked toward Gordy. He went through the same process of slipping something out of his pocket. Ashlyn still couldn't make out what it was, but she had a better view and this time saw Gordy step back for a moment and bend down before straightening up. Nolan seemed to stare at the ground before looking up at Gordy and nodding as he slipped the object back into his pocket.

Gordy bent down again, then stood. They appeared to talk in low voices for a few more minutes before Nolan turned and led Gordy back to where Officer Getz stood.

He turned to Henry. "You'll both have to go with Getz as well, and wait at the station. We'll need to take shoe impressions." He looked at the uniformed officer. "Getz, get photos and make a list of everything they're wearing. And if I find out that any of you said anything about what you've seen here, I'll make sure you're charged for interfering with a criminal investigation. Don't even whisper it over your mother's grave or tell a priest at confession. You tell no one. Clear?"

There were murmurs, followed by the sound of a twig snapping and bush pulling against fabric as the men moved away.

Ashlyn glanced at the grave and turned back as the

last man—Rick—disappeared under the fallen tree, his dog following faithfully.

She took a breath. "Are you sure it's a good idea to send them back?"

Nolan glared at her. "Take a look around. You think we're just a few miles from the nearest CSI lab and Grissom's going to show up with his little kit and get everything we need to find the killer? We aren't equipped for this. The closest coroner's office is a two-and-a-half-hour drive away."

"We haven't even identified her as one of our missing girls."

"Which is hardly important at the moment," Nolan snapped. "You think the press will care about that when they hear we're starting to recover bodies only a few miles from where the task force is based? By this time tomorrow, we'll need security just to get in and out of the station without being mobbed by reporters."

"But if none of them talk . . ."

"Are you really that green? You think one of them has to talk for a reporter to break this story? Rick called the park rangers. They called the RCMP. The way the press has been all over this case lately, Sullivan isn't taking any chances. He already called for a coroner to come to the scene. By this time tomorrow, the reporters may not know all the details, but they'll know that there was a report of a body found in the woods." Nolan glanced toward the unearthed grave. "I can live with that. I have to. But that's what I want them to keep reporting. The longer we can keep the truth a secret, the better."

"We've already been criticized for failure to act. When the press finds out what we're holding back—"

He pointed at her. "You disagree with me, Hart, you feel free to take it up with the sergeant, but until then you keep your damn mouth shut. You've been on this case less than a day. Of all the people involved with this investigation, you should be the last to question what's being done or what isn't being done. What do you think the press will do to you when they find out an inexperienced officer was put on her first plainclothes assignment to work on this task force? Have you even worked a murder before?"

A branch snapped a few feet down the trail they'd come up on. Ashlyn turned to see Tain approaching. He didn't say anything but continued walking until he stood close to Ashlyn, his gaze fixed on Nolan.

She decided not to point out the technicality, that she had done some work in plainclothes before. Asserting that her previous work was a legitimate claim would convince him she wasn't just green, she was an idiot. Deep down, she knew she'd been assigned over her head, but that wasn't her fault. She wanted to work the case and to learn, but in a moment of frustration, her partner's attitude had come shining through, and she knew she'd have to work twice as hard as anyone else assigned to the team just to hold her own.

Tain glanced at her before looking back at Nolan, his face was unreadable.

"Coroner's on the way?" he asked.

Nolan nodded. "Sullivan called." He looked at his watch. "About an hour ago now."

"Right. You two can head back to the station."

"We'll handle it. If you think we don't need all three of us here, you go back to the station."

"I have my reasons for staying. You two can go."

"So you can screw this up and make a mess of the scene?" Nolan said.

"How could I screw this up any more than you already have, Nolan? What happened to holding the witnesses here, taking the statements and getting the physical evidence? You sent them back. Getz had Rick and the dog, but those park rangers had to take their own vehicle. Plenty of time to get their stories straight, make a call on their cell phone, maybe even change their shoes. What the hell were you thinking?"

"Oh, yeah, you're going to lecture me about following procedure. You be glad you didn't do worse to Kurdy or you'd be facing charges for assault right now."

"So that makes your laziness okay?"

"It's not me who's lazy, Tain. I'm doing the best I can with a rookie for a partner, and every time I turn around you're AWOL or up to some bullshit like this morning."

Confirmation of what Ashlyn had suspected. Nolan had ditched her to keep an eye on Tain.

"You're fighting the good fight against affirmative action," Nolan said. "Deadweight in a uniform."

Tain's hands balled up into fists as he took a step forward. "You better watch your mouth, Nolan. You have no idea what you're dealing with here."

"And you do? Enlighten me. This ought to be good. You can't be bothered reading the files, following up on leads, attending meetings or filing reports, but you've got some keen insight into the case." It was Nolan's turn to take a step toward Tain. "You're useless."

"Back off, Nolan. I'm warning you."

"Or what?" Nolan's mouth curled into a snarl. "You're going to pin me up against a wall and give me a good talking to?"

"For once you have a good idea."

"Stop it!" Ashlyn stepped between the two men. "This is a crime scene. What the hell is wrong with you two?"

For a moment the only sound she could hear was her heart hammering in her ears. Then the low whistle of soft wind cutting through the trees. Nolan's jaw unclenched, and some of the color in his face faded.

Tain still bristled with anger, but he took a step back and turned away. That was when he took his first look at the grave and what was inside. The hostile posture gave way to a stoic stance.

Nolan was staring at Ashlyn with a look she couldn't quite read, and as she glanced away from him she thought about what she'd seen in the grave and everything that had happened since she'd arrived at the station that morning and felt her stomach twist into a knot and pull tight.

She wasn't sure she was ready for this.

CHAPTER ELEVEN

Eighteen months ago

Sullivan stood not far from where Ashlyn had been when she'd stopped beside Nolan. He remained silent as he looked down at the grave.

When he turned to look at them, there was a weight in his face coupled with a wide-eyed stare. The horror of what they'd all seen was going to haunt them, and if Ashlyn had thought otherwise even for a second, the look on her sergeant's face erased any doubt.

"The coroner's on the way," Sullivan said in a hushed tone, and glanced at Tain, then Nolan. "Where are we on this?"

"Getz is taking statements from Rick, Gordy and Henry. I also told him to get shoe prints and to photograph their clothes and take samples from Rick's dog because there was contact with the victims."

Sullivan frowned. "You trust him to handle that?"

"I—" Nolan began.

Tain cut him off. "I think he should go back to the station and handle it himself. This should be looked after by the task force."

"She hasn't been identified yet," Nolan said.

"Hardly the fucking point. Once the press hears about bodies in the woods—"

Nolan took a step toward Tain. "They aren't going to hear about bodies. At least, not from me. I already warned those men to keep their mouths shut, and I told them if they said anything, anything at all, I'd have them charged with jeopardizing a criminal investigation."

"Shame we can't do the same to you." Tain turned to Sullivan. "He sent them from the scene. Three men and a dog, with one uniformed officer. Nolan didn't follow procedure—"

Sullivan stopped him. "Sometimes we have to make the best out of the situation, Tain. These are hardly normal circumstances."

"And not every constable is the son of a sergeant. Some of us have to do our jobs, not just show up."

Nolan's face reddened. "You've got some nerve, especially considering—"

Sullivan held up his hands. "If you've got a legitimate complaint, I'll hear it, but it better be good."

"Fresh reactions. No time to overthink the story or the details or start drawing conclusions. Procedure's there for a reason. They should have been questioned by a member of the team, and considering the distance from the station, they should have been questioned here."

Ashlyn looked away for a moment as she tapped her notebook against her hand. When she turned back, Nolan was looking at her.

She thought back and replayed what had happened before the witnesses left.

"They were."

Sullivan looked up, and Tain spun around to face her.

"Nolan questioned them all, individually."

Tain scowled. "And what did you do, take notes?"

Her chin jutted out. "Don't make me the issue. The point is, they were questioned before they were sent back. Nolan also took a sample from the dog."

Sullivan turned to look at Nolan. "Is that true?"

Nolan reached into his pocket and pulled out a bag and a small digital camera. "I also took photos." He put the camera and plastic bag back. "Gordy didn't see the bodies. Rick keeps to himself, has no love for the press, and Henry knows the job. He won't talk."

"Well, gee, I feel so much better now that you've vouched for him."

Nolan stiffened. "It's no secret we have a leak in the department—"

"Which is exactly why someone from the task force should have handled formal statements and collecting physical evidence. Every person outside the team who's involved makes it harder to figure out who's leaking what."

"We know someone's been feeding information to the Native leaders, Tain."

"You better have some evidence to back that up before you make that kind of an accusation, Nolan."

"Nobody can cover their tracks forever."

"You sonofa—"

"Enough." Sullivan's voice carried the weight of authority, and both men fell silent.

The copied documents, the way Tain had reacted that morning . . .

Ashlyn hadn't known someone was leaking information.

She glanced at Nolan, who was turning away, but as he did he saw her looking at him and stopped. For a few seconds they stared at each other until a shadow flickered across his face. His eyes hardened as he turned to look at Tain, but he said nothing.

If Nolan was thinking about the papers and her silence, it looked like he was going to keep it to himself.

"We have enough problems to deal with. What we don't need is reckless accusations." Sullivan glanced at Nolan. "Or renegade cops." He glanced at Tain. "Put your personal differences aside, stop the bickering and bullshit, and get to work. Both of you. Understood?"

There was silence, neither man wanting to be the first to speak. Ashlyn hated pissing contests.

She stepped forward. "Yes, sir."

Sullivan's head snapped as he turned to look at her. His expression changed subtly, just for a second, but she was certain she'd seen a softening around the eyes.

He nodded at her. "Good. We're going to have to do a search of the woods—"

"I'll organize that," she said, aware Tain and Nolan were still staring at her.

Sullivan shook his head. "No. Tain will. I want you and Nolan to start working on identifying the girl."

"We may have to wait for more information from the coroner," Nolan said.

Ashlyn walked right up to the grave and crouched down. She took a deep breath as she thought back to the photographs she'd seen in the files, and she studied the girl in front of her.

She was wearing an old-fashioned white nightgown that appeared to go down to her ankles. Her legs had been wrapped in plastic, but her arms were lying out from her sides so that her body formed the shape of a cross.

Why wrap the lower part of the body and then stop? Inside the wrappings, Ashlyn could see a dark stain. Had her killer or killers put plastic underneath her to help dispose of the evidence? Ashlyn looked at the girl's chest. The wound that had apparently caused her death was partially concealed, but that part of the body hadn't been wrapped, and as far as Ashlyn could tell, there wasn't plastic underneath the rest of the body either.

Just under the legs.

There was a gap between the nightgown and the plastic where the body of the baby lay across the girl. Ashlyn tilted her head and leaned down.

Blood was running along the side of the plastic.

"Is it possible she was kept frozen and dumped here recently?"

Tain said nothing as he walked over to her.

Ashlyn moved out of his way so he could get a better look.

When Tain stood and turned around all he said was, "You may not be completely useless."

Ashlyn thought she saw Nolan smirk before he lowered his gaze and stepped around Tain so that he could get a closer look at the body as well.

She wasn't sure if it was her discomfort or the comment that had amused him.

Sullivan frowned as he looked from the victim to Tain, who offered one curt nod, and then Ashlyn. "We'll have to wait for the coroner to be sure about that. You think of anything else that might be useful?"

"It's Mary Donard."

"You're sure?" Sullivan asked as Tain turned around again and looked at the girl.

Ashlyn nodded. "Pretty sure. I was looking at file photos just before we came out here. She's got a small scar on her chin and a tattoo on the right side of her neck, and looks to be the right height."

"Okay. Then we get the evidence we need to confirm her identity, and we say nothing about the second victim."

"Will you brief the other team, or should I?" Nolan asked the sergeant.

Sullivan paused. "I haven't decided yet."

"Aiken opened the file on Donard," Ashlyn said.

Sullivan turned to her partner. "Nolan, you've done an excellent job bringing Hart up to speed."

Tain's turn to smirk, but he was standing behind the sergeant, so only Ashlyn saw him.

"I'll go speak to Aiken myself, just in case." Sullivan glanced at Nolan. "Any questions?"

"Why would you keep them frozen only to dump them in the woods later?" Ashlyn asked, almost without thinking. It was what had been going through her mind since she'd stepped away from the body.

"That's easy," Nolan said. "You've run out of room and have more victims to store."

An awkward silence followed. Ashlyn could only guess that each one of them, like she, was thinking about the very real possibility that all their missing girls might be dead.

Only a matter of hours ago they'd just been missing.

What Nolan's response didn't explain was the one thing none of them seemed ready to talk about yet.

The second body.

CHAPTER TWELVE

Eighteen months ago

Nolan drove with a void face and appeared solely focused on the road. The night was as black as molasses with a heaviness in the air that made it feel almost as thick. There was tension in the atmosphere, as though a storm was coming, but other than the blanket of nightfall, the sky didn't look threatening. There wasn't even a breeze.

On the walk back through the woods, Ashlyn had felt so tired she could barely hold her head up, but once she'd shut the car door and they'd begun the drive back to town, a nervous energy had prickled at her, some inexplicable sixth sense kicking in, insisting something wasn't right. She scanned the road ahead of them and the ditches. The movement of a rabbit doing a one-eighty made her heart leap into her throat, and no sooner had she caught her breath than she'd been forced to brace herself against the door as Nolan slammed the brakes and swerved to avoid a deer darting across the road.

Behind them she could see the headlights from Tain's truck.

The tension in her body began to ebb as more of the trip passed uneventfully, and once the mountainside and forest gave way to sporadic buildings and paved streets with dim lights pushing back the darkness, she breathed deeper.

She straightened up a bit. The streetlights were dim, but the town had a bright glow to it, the shimmering haze of light over buildings that you expected when house after house was adorned with Christmas lights.

"What the—"

Nolan had turned a corner and slowed the vehicle. Ahead of them, a bonfire had been set in a vacant lot, right across from the RCMP station, and the crowd of people that had gathered spilled out onto the road.

The air was blanketed by stillness, and not even the crackle of the fire completely disrupted the uneasy quiet. Ashlyn scanned the crowd as she tried to guess how many people were gathered around the fire.

Nolan turned the vehicle toward the station.

She looked at him. "Aren't we going to respond?"

"Take a look, Constable. What do you see?"

Ashlyn indulged him with a quick glance out the window. "A group of people gathered around a bonfire."

"Look again."

She did, this time not skimming the crowd to gauge its size but looking at the individuals, the solemn faces that had turned to watch their vehicles as they approached.

"I thought things had calmed down with the creation of the task force."

Nolan glanced at her. "They only heated up. Our bosses have done the bare minimum to win the public-relations war elsewhere in the province, where people don't have to walk the streets in fear or worry about their daughters disappearing. The tribes, they never really have figured out how to win the PR game."

"So that makes it okay?" she asked as he parked the

Rodeo in front of the station. Uniformed officers were making their way across the street now, addressing the crowd with a bullhorn.

Ordering them to leave the area immediately.

They got out of the vehicle, and for a moment she wasn't sure what Nolan intended to do, but he walked around the Rodeo toward the group on the street. Ashlyn glanced to her right, confirming that Tain had already parked his truck and was walking out toward the officers as well. Nolan was on an intercept course.

She followed.

From the bullhorn: "You are trespassing on private property. You must leave the premises immediately, in an orderly fashion, or face prosecution."

"Yeah, because a trespassing charge is a real threat to these people." Nolan muttered the words under his breath, but she still heard them.

The man standing at the front of the group facing the officers was almost a stereotype. Long hair, a weathered face with deep lines, dark eyes that carried the pain of sins borne by generation after generation of his people. He crossed his arms and turned around.

So much for meaningful negotiations.

The crowd followed his cue and one by one they all turned, arms folded, standing still as stone, staring at the fire.

"What do they want?" she asked Nolan.

Before he could answer, Tain interjected. "Answers."

The officers conferred with Sullivan, but she couldn't hear what they were saying. As she surveyed the group, she noticed a woman to her right. The woman pulled her coat tight around her body and wrapped her arms around herself as she looked down at the ground, her long, dark hair falling down to cover the side of her face. When she raised her head, it wasn't to look at the fire. She turned toward the officers, watching Nolan, then Tain.

Their gaze met, and the woman's look had the force of

a blow, as if she'd just crossed the distance between them and physically pushed him. There was something about the face that seemed familiar, but Ashlyn couldn't place it.

Sullivan walked over to them. "You could try talking to them," he said to Tain.

"You think we Injuns all speak the same language, that because of the color of my skin they'll listen to me?" Tain replied.

The woman who'd been watching started walking toward them as other vehicles approached. Ashlyn glanced at the vans, then at Nolan, whose eyes widened. More trouble they didn't need.

"We won't leave until we get answers," she said. Her comment was directed at Tain, not Sullivan.

"Then you'll be here for a long time, because we don't have anything to tell you," Tain said.

"Fine. We'll stay."

"Look." Sullivan glared at Tain as he reached for the woman's arm. "Can't we go somewhere more comfortable and talk? I'm sure that we can come to a reasonable—"

"Talk?" The woman practically spat the word into Sullivan's face. "For years, we've talked. Whole generations of our people have lived in poverty, driven from their lands, their children taken from them so that they could be raised by your people, and always your answer is the same. Talk. This isn't about land, and it isn't about what your ancestors stole from mine. This is about finding these missing girls. It's about finding my sister. I don't want talk. I want action."

It clicked into place, and Ashlyn realized why the woman looked familiar. Summer Young. Her sister had been the first to disappear.

"I assure you, we've brought in more manpower, and we're working around the clock," Sullivan said. He kept looking to Summer's right, where the reporters were taking positions, cameras already rolling. Sullivan had a wild look in his eye, that of a desperate man who might do anything to stop the situation from spiraling any further out of control. Through the cameras, the eyes of the world could now focus on Nighthawk Crossing, a small community close to several reserves where First Nations peoples resided and a stone's throw from the US border. The Native communities felt more kinship with the tribes in Washington State than they did with Canadians, and the difficulty of monitoring a border that stretched thousands of miles was a tangible reality the police grappled with on a daily basis. Drug trafficking, human smuggling . . . no one wanted to know what was being smuggled across the border on any given day.

Much of it coming through Native lands.

Summer looked at Tain. "You've found a body."

It wasn't a question. Nolan had been right—it hadn't taken the public long to find out.

Tain's face betrayed nothing. "This isn't the way, Summer. You have to leave."

"Or what? You'll arrest me?" She stepped toward him, her head held high, barely an inch between them.

"If that's what it takes," Tain said.

Nolan used the gap that had opened when Tain reached back for his cuffs to worm his way between him. "You're right. We found a body."

For a moment there was an uneasy silence as Summer looked from Tain to Nolan. "You'll give me answers?"

"What I can," he said.

"I've heard that before." Summer glanced at Tain. Ashlyn noticed his fist was clenched at his side, the other hand still on his cuffs.

"You've got no reason to trust me," Nolan said. "The only thing you can be sure of is that I haven't lied to you before."

She paused. "Not exactly reassuring."

"Would you be more likely to believe me if I fed you a line? Made you some promise that things would get better, that your people will be afforded the same justice every citizen of this country deserves? Maybe I should tell you they brought the best and brightest to work the cases, instead of covering every politically correct base they could think of—bringing in community cops who'd want to keep the local people happy, a woman, and someone who has the same skin color as you."

"You aren't much of a diplomat, are you?" Said without the sarcasm one might have expected. Summer relaxed, shrinking down a few noticeable millimeters.

Nolan smiled, stepped back and extended an arm toward the RCMP station. "Let's find you some answers."

Summer glanced at the reporters, then nodded and allowed Nolan to lead her across the street.

Ashlyn walked to her desk and plopped down in the chair. It felt good to sit after all the hours on her feet. She reached up and rubbed her temples and started to laugh.

"What's so funny?" Tain barked. She stifled a groan. When she'd returned to the office, she hadn't realized he'd walked in behind her.

"I smell about as good as you did this morning," she said.

It had taken the better part of an hour to get the crowd to leave. Sullivan had calmed down after Nolan left with Summer. She was the first domino. After that, the sergeant was able to persuade the leaders that they were doing everything in their power, and wouldn't their time be better spent investigating the murder of the girl they believed was Mary Donard instead of handling crowd control outside the RCMP station?

The fire department had paced anxiously throughout the negotiations, eager to put out the fire, not willing to take any chances of it spreading to nearby buildings after the blaze they'd had to contend with the night before.

Reasonable men had eventually conceded, although they'd also promised they would not remain reasonable for long. They wanted answers, and they weren't prepared to wait another year to get them.

"You should go home and get some sleep, Hart, while you still can."

He had his back to her and was standing still. It looked like he was staring at the blank wall in front of him.

She wondered if he realized how creepy it was that he'd just stop and stare off at nothing for minutes at a time.

"I don't even know where home is."

Tain remained in his fixed position. Whatever was on his mind, it seemed to have prevented him from processing her words. Part of her wanted to remain in her chair, which seemed much more comfortable than it had that morning, but if she did, she'd lack the willpower to track Sullivan down and find out where she was supposed to be staying.

As she forced herself out of her chair, Tain turned and held up a hand.

"Wait."

It was all he said before disappearing out the door and down the hallway.

Ashlyn started to sink back down, then stopped herself. It would be even harder to get up the second time. Instead, she interlocked her fingers and reached up to the ceiling, then to her left and finally to her right.

Too many days like this and she might be tempted to start drinking coffee.

She glanced at her watch. He'd been gone several minutes, and it was getting late. The other shift had arrived, but they weren't in the office. Ashlyn started walking back and forth, swinging her arms in an effort to keep the circulation flowing. She glanced at her watch again.

Ten minutes.

When Tain returned a few moments later, he stopped beside his desk and stared straight at her. "In a day or two there's a cabin available at Similkameen Valley. That's where they've got Nolan staying. I'm in one of the rental houses on the same property. Until then, Sullivan had a room for you at the Blind Creek Inn."

She groaned. Obviously she wouldn't be staying there. "I can try the motel I—"

Tain shook his head. "It's full. Every motel in town or on the outskirts has been filled with people who were staying at the inn." He grabbed something off his desk and was halfway out the door before he turned back toward her. "Well?"

"Well what?"

"I have a spare room."

She gaped at him for a moment. "You're kidding, right?"

"Look, suit yourself. I'm not begging. If you want to curl up with a bit of floor in the storage room and a blanket or sleep in a holding cell, that's up to you."

"Well, since you put it that way," she muttered. "You aren't at the same cabins?"

Tain shook his head. "One lane over. I had to get something with a fenced yard. I have a dog."

He turned down the hall toward the front door, and she followed him. He marched with purpose and didn't even look back to see if she was keeping pace.

It wasn't until they passed a small room with windows that allowed a clear view of the occupants that he even broke stride. He paused and turned long enough for her to see the twist of his jaw, the way his hand balled up into a fist.

She opened her mouth to ask what was wrong but stopped when she saw Nolan and Summer sitting in the room.

Summer tucked her hair behind her ears. Her lips

were mashed together, and she pulled her coat around her body and held it tightly with her arms.

Trying to hold herself together.

The first tear fell. Her lower lip quivered, and her head dropped forward. Trying to be brave. Strong.

To hide the pain.

Nolan had his arm around her and after a halfhearted resistance, Summer rested her head on his shoulder as she cried.

Tain's hesitation had allowed her to close the distance between them, and for a moment he was so focused on what was happening with Nolan and Summer that he didn't notice she'd caught up to him. But as soon as he realized she was there, he turned away and marched down the hall, silent as he continued through to the front of the station and out the door. He didn't pause to hold the door for Ashlyn or check to see if she was still right behind him.

It wasn't until they were almost at his truck that she realized her things were in her car. "I need my bag," she said. "Or do you want me to follow you?"

Tain shook his head. "Just get your stuff." He climbed inside the vehicle and slammed the door shut.

Ashlyn walked to the back of the station, where she'd moved her car to, and quickly removed a small suitcase from the back, along with her overnight bag. As she closed the trunk, she realized she could hear voices coming from the alley behind the station, by the Dumpster.

She moved toward the sound, straining to hear what they were saying.

"If I get caught . . ." The voice was trying to be quiet, but had a higher pitch to it that resonated with fear.

The voice that responded was lower and softer. Ashlyn took another step forward, which enabled her to see around the side of the Dumpster, but the hum of an engine behind her and the sudden flash of brightness caused her to turn around. From the corner of her eye, she could see movement in the alley, shadows being absorbed by the darkness as they withdrew from the light.

She walked to the truck and got in.

"What were you doing?" Tain asked.

Ashlyn looked back down the alley as he backed his truck into a stall and then turned to drive around to the road. "There were two men back there."

Tain looked at her, his scowl softening to a frown as he hesitated. "Hardly illegal."

She turned and looked out the window. He was right, and whatever she'd thought she'd heard, Tain wasn't the first person she'd choose to confide in.

For now, she was keeping what she'd heard to herself.

The next morning, Ashlyn followed Tain into the office. Nolan was already there, and when he turned to look at them, Tain's gaze locked with his and Nolan's face clouded.

All the muscles in Tain's arms and back were tensed, evidenced by his rigidity and the way he got taller as he glared back at Nolan, but he hesitated only a few seconds before marching over to his desk.

Nolan turned his glare toward Ashlyn.

She tried to ignore him and walked to her desk as she pulled off her jacket.

"Any word from the coroner?" she asked as she looked at the mounting pile of messages in front of her.

"I'm on my way over there."

Ashlyn looked up as Nolan slipped into his coat. He nodded at her. "Keep working on chasing down leads."

He turned and was out the door before she could think of an appropriate response.

Tain waited a moment, then marched out of the office. Ashlyn heard the back door slam shut and sat down in her chair.

The youngest member of the other shift stalked into the room, stopping short when he saw Ashlyn.

"Morning," she said.

He muttered a response under his breath and walked past her. She heard him rummaging through his desk, and then a door slammed shut. Ashlyn held her breath as she listened to what sounded like the faint sound of metal scraping against metal, and then Campbell marched out of the office without so much as another word.

Sullivan stormed into the office a moment later. "Where is everyone?" He didn't wait for an answer. "Get your coat, Hart."

She was on her feet with her arms already worming their way into the sleeves. "What is it, sir?"

"They've found a body in the rubble from the fire yesterday."

"At the inn?"

"Actually, the old house the inn connected to, across the street. It used to house hotel staff, but a couple boys from the shipping company were living there."

"Why?"

"Why? Blind Creek Inn was owned by the same people who run Blind Creek Shipping."

"And the house burned as well as the inn?"

"It's too soon to say for sure, but they think the fire may have started there." Sullivan held up his hand. "You keep that to yourself for now, though. We need to go check out this body."

Ashlyn reached for her notebook. "One of ours?"

He hesitated, then turned and started speed walking down the hall. "Too soon to say."

Something in his tone suggested that wasn't what he was thinking, but she didn't push it. Ashlyn followed him to the car and spent the few minutes driving over in silence. She'd seen so little of the town, this was an opportunity for her to start piecing it together.

It was her first real awareness of how large the First Nations population was. The bonfire didn't really count because it was a staged gathering. It was where the day-to-day routines of normal people collided that you got a sense of the local population. She'd grown up in a town where it wasn't uncommon to venture down the main street day after day after day, to go to school your whole life and live and work for more than twenty years and rarely see someone from the Reserves.

She thought about her question regarding the tribal police. In other parts of the country, the RCMP were working with tribal police to try to address the growing crime that accompanied the gambling trade that thrived on tribal lands.

Why couldn't they work together here?

About half a block before the charred remains of the hotel there was a small green space with a fountain and a few park benches. A woman was bending down by the fountain, placing flowers on the sidewalk. She stood and tucked her hair back behind her ears, then stilled for a moment. When she turned, Ashlyn recognized her.

Summer Young.

"It's the latest development," Sullivan said. "They're having some candlelight vigil or prayer service or something there later. To remember the girls the rest of us have forgotten."

When Sullivan parked the car, she got out and followed him in silence. The coroner was already there, waiting outside a small makeshift tent.

"I may as well set up a field office here," he muttered as he led them inside. As soon as Ashlyn stepped into the small space, she felt the bile push up into her throat. The charred remains of a woman were lying on a plastic sheet on the ground. The victim was curled up in the fetal position, arms hugging her knees. What looked like the remnants of a gag were in her mouth.

"Let's hope you won't be needed here much longer," Sullivan said. "What can you tell us?"

"There are a few identifiers I can work with. A tattoo still visible on her right ankle, and if there are dental records we should be able to ID her."

"Just one body?" Ashlyn asked.

The coroner looked at her. "Yes. I'll know for sure once I get her on the table, but it looks like she died in the fire. There is head trauma, so it's possible she died before the fire started."

Sullivan looked at Ashlyn. "What do you think, Hart?"

"Sir?"

"We can cut this case loose and let someone else work it, or we can keep the folder as part of the investigation until we've identified her."

She could see the arguments both ways. If they passed the case off now and found out later there was a connection, they'd have to be brought up to speed. And if they took it on and it didn't connect, whoever was left with the investigation would be behind.

As she opened her mouth to answer, the flap of the tent was pulled back and Tain stepped inside. He surveyed the body wordlessly before kneeling beside her and looking closely at her shoes and pant legs.

"This is ours," he said as he stood. "I'm taking it."

"I think Constable Hart should—"

"I want this case, Sergeant."

"And I want you at the rally this afternoon."

"I'm not your token Aboriginal officer."

Tain had spoken with so much force everyone in the tent and anyone standing within a few feet of it outside fell silent.

Sullivan sighed. "Look, I know that shipping company owns this hotel, and I know you still want to find a way to get to them. And we will, when the time's right. But we're stretched pretty thin right now, and we need to stay focused. If this is going to be a problem—"

"It isn't. Look, you brought Hart out here yourself. You were already thinking about giving this one to the task force, just in case. Don't change your mind just because I want it."

Sullivan paused. He glanced at Ashlyn. Tain's eyes almost begged for her cooperation, while a muddled uncertainty lingered on Sullivan's face. Ashlyn took a breath, then gave one quick nod of her head.

"This is a team effort, Tain. You're working it, but so is everybody else. It isn't all yours, and I expect you to let Hart, Nolan, or whoever else is available back you up."

Sullivan turned and left the canvas structure that had been erected to keep their victim concealed from curious onlookers. As soon as he was gone Tain turned to Ashlyn.

"How much progress have you made going over all the missing-persons records?"

This was the first time anyone had mentioned them to Ashlyn. "I—"

"Get back to the office and dig through them. We need to make sure there aren't any other girls out there we should be looking for as part of this investigation."

"But Sullivan—"

"Do you see him getting in Nolan's face for leaving you in the office? You aren't even my partner, Hart. I don't have time to give you a tour and hold your hand while you figure out what it means to work a real case."

Ashlyn looked at the coroner, who'd suddenly developed a fascination with his own paperwork. Tain was still staring at her. There hadn't been any discussion the night before when they'd arrived at his house. He'd simply pointed her to the spare bathroom and bedroom and marched upstairs, his husky following him. That morning, he'd made breakfast wordlessly, which had been a bit of a surprise, because she'd expected some sexist jibe about performing her womanly duties. The only thing he'd said was that she could leave her stuff if she wanted, in case her cabin wasn't ready until the next day. She was staying at his house and he still wasn't ready to give her a chance or hear her out.

For a moment, she wondered who annoyed her more, Nolan or Tain. Then she realized it didn't matter, turned and left the tent without another word.

CHAPTER THIRTEEN

Eighteen months ago

"Mrs. Bird? My name is—"

"Are you trying to sell me something? You aren't trying to sell me something, are you? I don't like to be bothered at home by people telling me what they think I need to spend my money on."

Ashlyn rubbed her forehead. "No, Mrs. Bird. This is Constable Hart calling, from the RCMP."

"Who?"

"The police, Mrs. Bird. I'm calling about those missing girls."

There was a small pause. "I can't imagine why."

"Why what?"

"Why would you call me about those missing girls." The high-pitched voice cracked. "I don't have them!"

"Mrs. Bird . . ." Ashlyn looked at the slip of paper in front of her. Another dead end she'd wasted time on. Not that it mattered much. She was stuck in the office and not going anywhere. Not if Nolan had his way, and Tain wasn't about to let her off the leash either.

"If you call again, I'm going to phone the police!"

The click was followed by the dial tone. Ashlyn squeezed her eyes shut for a moment, the top of the handset resting against her chin as she rubbed her ear. She'd made so many phone calls the side of her head hurt from having the handset pressed against it, usually balanced on her shoulder as she tried to take notes or catch up on reading reports while she returned phone call after phone call.

She'd been able to move into her cabin. Although Tain had barely said a hundred words to her outside of the office in the two days she'd spent at his house, she'd developed a fondness for his husky and was missing the companionship of a pet.

An explanation about why they weren't working with tribal police had never been forthcoming. In fact, since the morning she'd walked in with Tain, Nolan had barely said a hundred words to her in office.

To make matters worse, she couldn't find the missing-persons folders she was supposed to be combing through. She'd asked Constable Keith, one of the officers who worked patrol in the area and knew where things were supposed to be, to search the filing cabinets in the rest of the station for her and had gone over every inch of community space in the task force office, but hadn't turned up anything.

When she opened her eyes, she glanced at the locked drawer in Tain's desk and thought of the scraping metal sound she'd heard when Campbell had been behind her. Too many secrets and too many male egos in conflict, marking their territory, fighting over what was still unclaimed. She made a note on the message from Mrs. Bird that confirmed she'd called back, the date and time, and included Mrs. Bird's address before adding it to the mounting pile of useless tips.

She was on her last one.

It took a few seconds to dial the ten-digit phone number. It took longer for someone to answer. As Ashlyn waited on the line she found half of her hoping nobody would pick up so she wouldn't have to deal with another bogus tip, and the other half just wanted to get it over and done with, crossed off the list so that she could move on.

Hopefully, move on to something more productive.

"What?"

The demanding tone was so unexpected Ashlyn wondered for a split second if the phone had been answered already and she hadn't heard.

"Mrs. Wilson?"

A pause. "Who's this?"

"Constable Ashlyn Hart, from the RCMP." Ashlyn drew a breath. "You placed a call, something to do with the investigation into the disappearance of those girls."

Silence.

"Mrs. Wilson, I'm calling because you left a message that said you knew something about the missing girls that could help our investigation."

Ashlyn paused. Since the day she'd been transferred to Nighthawk Crossing, she'd made at least three hundred phone calls. Most had been useless, but the process of determining whether the would-be tipster was crazy or confused was unpredictable. Some proved unreliable from the moment they answered the phone, like Mrs. Bird, and others prolonged the ordeal by seeming lucid and serious for several minutes before their stories unraveled.

A few had called because they knew one of the girls and just wanted to talk.

Those were the hardest ones. Ashlyn never knew what to say. There had been one phone call from someone who knew Mary Donard, and all Ashlyn could do was agree when the girl had said they hoped Mary had just run off and would come home soon.

They'd succeeded in limiting the press coverage of the discovery of the bodies in the woods, and that included concealing the identity of the older victim. The press didn't know about the baby, and they wanted to keep it that way. The advantage they had was that they still controlled the details that went public.

Despite that, the problem they faced was that the phone calls had tripled in the past few days. They'd seen an increase across the board, with families phoning for updates, friends calling because they didn't know what else to do, and a few possible legitimate sightings interspersed in the nuisance calls.

"Mrs. Wilson, do you have some information for us?"

"That girl in the fire. The body. It was Jenny Johnson."

Ashlyn straightened up. "Which fire?"

"The inn. The house across the street. The body inside."

"The fire at the Blind Creek Inn?"

"It was Jenny Johnson's body."

"How do you—"

The click was followed by the familiar sound of dial tone.

Ashlyn stood. Adding the bogus calls to the thick file of useless tips was instinctive, and she placed the calls from family and friends in another folder. The few slips of paper that might contain helpful information had been placed on her notebook.

She grabbed the small pile with her left hand and picked up the message from Mrs. Wilson with her right, then marched down the hall to the small room where they'd previously met for shift changes.

Now, they met there when summoned, the shift lines blurred as they worked as long as they could to follow up on any possible leads. In the three days since discovering Mary Donard's body, they hadn't done much more than annoy the media.

The long table had been removed so they could try to comfortably seat a group of people who functioned as a team in name only. A handful of scattered chairs took up a fraction of the floor space, and a small table had been placed in the corner. A coffee urn sat on top.

Sullivan paced back and forth along the far wall.

As she slid into a chair in the back left corner she wondered if that meant there'd been a significant development. Nolan had been leading the meetings, and Sullivan had rarely been present for the regular rundown of their standard checklists.

It seemed Nolan was being groomed for leadership. The older officers appeared indifferent to that fact, while Tain made no effort to conceal his contempt for the constable.

Oliver entered the room, walked over to the urn and poured himself a cup of coffee. As he turned he took a sip, his face scrunched into a look of disgust and he spit the liquid on the floor.

"Tastes like lukewarm piss," he said.

"Time for the little lady to prove herself useful. Make them some coffee."

The all-too-familiar voice came from behind her, to her right side. She turned and glanced at Tain as he leaned back against the wall on the other side of the door, then realized it was a mistake.

She'd acknowledged the comment was meant for her.

The three older men didn't seem to know whether they were supposed to laugh at Tain or lecture him. Oliver turned and set his cup down, his face a crimson shade. Campbell and Aiken glanced at Sullivan, who'd turned to stare at Tain.

Nolan walked to the front of the room.

"Hart's been doing an excellent job—"

"On clerical duty."

Tain's voice again, eliciting a snort from Aiken that was quickly stifled when he looked up to see the sergeant glaring at him.

"She follows orders, which is more than I can say for you." Nolan didn't give Tain a chance to respond. "Hart's followed up on all the calls that have come in. Unfortunately, we don't have many leads to work with, and I've done the follow-up with the legitimate tips that did come in. We've hit a roadblock. There are a few other potential witnesses we can track down, but we're talking about people who may or may not have seen someone who looked like one of our victims months ago. Memories are hazy, and the information is getting thin, but we have two witnesses who believe they saw Kacey Young getting into a semi at a truck stop just outside Osoyoos around the time she was reported missing."

Ashlyn sat up in her chair. A trucker would make sense. It explained the size of the region the girls had disappeared from. Truckers knew the roads, knew the areas, and their presence didn't automatically arouse suspicions. It was a promising lead.

"Hitches a lift with a trucker eighteen, nineteen months ago," Campbell said. "That's a whole lot of help."

"It's a place to start," Nolan said.

"Thousands of hitchhikers get in semis every year. She could be on the other side of the country. It's a waste of time."

"This is what we do, Campbell. We follow the leads we have until we either exhaust them or turn up some useful information."

Campbell shook his head. "What you've got is nothing. It's a dead end."

"No. It's a beginning." Ashlyn had surprised herself by saying the words out loud, and apparently everyone else in the room had been caught off guard as well. They were all looking at her, so she tried to explain.

"There would be shipping records, weight scale information from the highways. If we can get someone out to the truck stop and talk to other truckers we might find some guys who work regular routes in the area."

"Which would tell us what?" Campbell said. "Who delivers produce and who's hauling livestock? We've got no probable cause. You can't send us out there to start questioning truckers and requesting shipping manifests without a damn good reason."

"Actually, in the wake of 9-11, you'd be amazed at what

we can do without a warrant," Ashlyn said. "The proximity to the border—"

Campbell jumped out of his chair. "You've got no idea what you're dealing with here."

"Then why don't you enlighten me?" she snapped back, sick of Campbell's attitude and unable to conceal her frustration.

Campbell looked at Sullivan, and some of the color drained out of his face. His breathing steadied, and he sat back down. "Look, so what if one of them got a ride near here a few months ago? It makes sense since they all went missing from this area. There's nothing suspicious about that."

"Except the fact that the trucker hasn't come forward," Ashlyn said. "I'd like to know why."

"Then you follow up on it. I'm sure if you could find some tight jeans and park yourself outside a truck stop you'll have no problem getting the guys to talk to you." Campbell almost smiled. "They'll probably tell you anything you want to hear."

"You know what, Campbell? I think she's got a point," Tain said.

"Oh, well, aren't you suddenly the knight in shining armor." Campbell's sneer didn't fade when he looked at Ashlyn. "Don't worry, hon, it's not all about you. Tain's got a hard-on for a couple of local punks he hasn't been able to bust, and since they work for a shipping company, I'm sure he figures this is a good chance to try to find something he can use on them. Isn't it, Tain? Only problem is, you tried that already, and you came up empty-handed because there's nothing to find."

"Yeah? Maybe I came up empty-handed because you shot off your mouth."

Campbell was on his feet, quickly followed by Sullivan, Aiken and Oliver. The accusations and insults were lost in the chorus of shouting, and Ashlyn looked at Nolan, who'd stayed out of it.

Sullivan's voice rose above the others. "That's enough! Sit down, now."

Tain slithered back to his spot against the wall, and the others found their seats. Campbell's face was as red as a ripe tomato.

"Look, this is a tough investigation. We don't have the resources city departments have, and we don't have enough manpower," Sullivan said. "I understand that everyone's tired and we'd all like to see some progress, but we can't start pointing fingers at one another, especially without facts."

The speech was followed by silence, but Ashlyn noted that the color didn't fade from Campbell's face. He also hadn't looked up since he'd been ordered back to his chair.

"You don't actually think it's somebody local who's killing these girls, do you?" Oliver said. "Those of us who've worked here for a while, who've put down roots, we know these people. Sure, you've got your drunks, you've got your bullies who use their wives as punching bags, and there's the odd bit of petty theft, occasional drug use, but most people in this town are good folks."

"We have to look at every possibility," Sullivan said. "Until we've made an arrest, that means chasing down every possible lead. Okay, before we get to assignments, anybody have anything else?"

"Actually, I have something I want to chase down," Ashlyn said.

"Oh really? What's that?" Tain asked.

Ashlyn ignored him and kept her focus on the men at the front of the room. "It might be nothing, but we had a call about the body in the fire. I have reason to believe she could be one of our missing girls."

"You mean the body found at Blind Creek Inn? We don't have an ID yet that I'm aware of, and there's been nothing to tie that victim to our investigation," Sullivan said. "What have you got that suggests a connection?"

"Women's intuition," Tain muttered, but not softly enough to prevent her from hearing.

Ashlyn held up the slip of paper in her right hand. "A tip that says it was one of our girls."

"Credible?" Nolan asked.

She nodded. "I think so. At least worth following up on." She almost held her breath. Sullivan had every right to pass the tip over to Tain, and she knew it.

"Which victim?"

Tain's voice cut through, but his tone had changed. The attitude and arrogance were gone, replaced by something bordering on concern. There was a look in his eyes, as though he was going back over some information in his mind, trying to piece something together.

"Jenny Johnson."

"Okay, Hart. You and Nolan can track it down."

"Sir—" Tain said. Sullivan cut him off.

"Tain, you have other things to deal with, and I told you before, it's the team's case. Not just yours." The sergeant glared at him for a moment, then turned back to Hart. "Let Tain know if it's credible. We can't afford to ignore anything that hasn't been called in by a crazy. Oliver can start tracking down shipping records and weight scale information," Sullivan said. "Campbell, you and Aiken will deal with the truck stop."

"Hang on. They found three bodies in Surrey this week, all young girls who'd been sexually assaulted. Each one had been stabbed through the chest," Campbell said. "Why aren't we looking to see if there's a connection?"

"Were the girls held? Were they impregnated?" Tain asked. "Dressed in an old-fashioned white gown, partially wrapped in plastic and frozen before their body was disposed of?"

"Maybe they were," Campbell said. "It's not like we're releasing all the details."

He had a point, acknowledged by the fact that not

even Tain challenged him. Ashlyn watched Tain lean back against the wall again, fold his arms and give the slightest shake of his head.

She looked at Sullivan.

"We'll be following up on that investigation, to see if there's a connection. Campbell, you and Aiken start co-ordinating with Surrey, but if it turns out to be a dead end, I want you to follow up with Nolan's lead right away. And, Campbell, that's an order. Understood?"

Campbell glared at Nolan as he swallowed. "Yes, sir."

Ashlyn stood, aware of Tain watching her with a solemn gaze. She wasn't sure if he intended to intercept her, but she hoped she could exit the room quickly and avoid any other confrontations.

"Hart?" Sullivan gestured to her and pointed at Nolan as he walked toward the front of the room. When he passed Tain he said, "I would have thought this would make you happy." Tain only glared at Ashlyn and Nolan before marching out of the room.

Sullivan shook his head. When he reached Ashlyn and Nolan he started to talk about her valuable contributions and that he hoped she felt settled and like part of the team. Placating her because of Campbell's comments, compounded by Tain's sexist jabs and his own inability to quash them or discipline his men. That's what she suspected. The fact that Sullivan hadn't even tried to give Tain instructions hadn't gone unnoticed.

Whatever Tain was working on, it trumped the body from the fire, and it seemed he was getting his instructions privately.

A voice from the back of the room cut through her thoughts.

"Sergeant Sullivan? There's a man here to see you and Constable Nolan." Ashlyn turned to see the same uniformed officer who had escorted her and Nolan through the woods only a few days earlier, the one Nolan called Getz.

Sullivan muttered an apology as he marched from the room, Nolan right behind him. Ashlyn let out a breath.

It only took a moment for her to get back to her desk. She folded the slip of paper with Mrs. Wilson's information on it and stuck it in her pocket and took a look at the new messages that had come in, skimming them one by one.

Mrs. Wilson hadn't called back, but as she flipped to the last message in the new stack she saw that Mrs. Bird had. Mrs. Bird had even conveyed her address, which had been written down on the slip of paper.

If Ashlyn waited, she'd be having her second conversation with Mrs. Bird in a matter of minutes, while Nolan left her behind. She grabbed her coat and made a decision, but she was too late. As she turned around and looked up, she saw Nolan walking toward her.

"Thanks for backing me up on the tip about the trucker," he said.

"Sure." She resisted the urge to add that she'd just been doing her job. "Did . . . whoever it was have something for you?"

"Oh, not really." Nolan waved his hand dismissively. "Nothing pressing anyway. You know, it's a shame you got transferred in just as this case exploded. There really hasn't been a chance to show you around." He sat down on the edge of his desk. "We'll have to find some time to do that."

"That would be good."

Nolan had a charming smile, an intensity in his eyes that hadn't gone unnoticed but had been overshadowed by his attitude. He was also smart and calculated, and there was no doubt in her mind that his decision to sit instead of looking down at her was part of his new strategy. She had information he wanted, and he knew that trying to finesse it out of her by making her feel like part of the team, like she was working with him instead of for him, was best.

With Sullivan under pressure for results and Tain looking for any way to upstage Nolan, she guessed Nolan felt he needed to keep Ashlyn happy and cooperative. He had his hands full and didn't need any more problems.

Ashlyn knew what he was doing, but she found herself fighting the urge to talk to him about the case. The naïve side of her clung to the idea that if she could just get him to see her as an asset instead of a liability, he'd work with her willingly.

"Campbell's a bit of a loose cannon," she said.

"It's his job to coordinate with tribal police, and in the past year reports of criminal activity on the Reserves have nearly doubled. There have been several murders, and Washington State Police have been calling, trying to get us to work with them to crack down on cross-border smuggling. Everything from cheap cigarettes to pure cocaine is finding its way back and forth, and most of it that's headed our way ends up on Native lands. That's what Campbell was dealing with when they threw the task force together."

"Shouldn't he be happy to have a chance to look at shipping information then?"

"He's not too happy about a rookie officer making him look inept."

Ashlyn flushed. "That wasn't what I was trying to do."

Nolan waved his hand. "I know. Don't worry about it." He smiled. "So, what's this lead?"

"I—" She paused, forced a smile of her own. "I know you're busy and have so many things to follow up on. I can handle it for you."

Nolan lifted his hands in mock surrender. "Nobody's disputing that, but I need you to look after something else for me."

"The sergeant said—"

"Divide and conquer." He smiled. "It's not like we've got a first-class team to rely on, filled with the best and brightest. Tain's a bit of an ass, Oliver and Aiken have focused on community policing and an investigation like this is new terrain for them. Campbell's taking it personally. I need someone here who I know will get the job done."

She knew where this was going. "And that's me?"

"Look, I admit I was a bit of a jerk when you started. It's only been a few days, but I know I can count on you. You're catching on quick. There's no doubt in my mind that you were given this assignment because you could measure up, and that's exactly why I need you here. You understand, right?"

"Sure." Baiting her with false praise. "You want me to keep chasing down the calls that have come through."

"Exactly. There have to be some flakes of gold amidst the dross, and you're the only person I can think of who will be thorough enough to find them."

She forced a smile. Let him believe she took his crap seriously.

"So, where's the message?"

Ashlyn had a half second to think about what she was about to do as she grabbed her pen, scribbled an address on the slip of paper in front of her and passed it to Nolan.

"Thanks, Hart. Oh, and good work."

She dug her nails into her palms as he turned and walked away.

The car crawled along as she swerved to avoid potholes and braked for the dip. Part of the road had no shoulder, and it was barely wide enough for two vehicles, which she found out when an oncoming truck clipped her mirror.

She glanced at the slip of paper she'd taped to the dash. It was the right road, but she hadn't passed a house for at least a mile. As far as she could tell, Mrs. Wilson's place was the last on the road. Ahead, she could see a small truck had pulled over to the practically non-existent shoulder, but she couldn't see a driver in it, and there weren't any brake lights on.

To her right, the foliage gave way to a dirt driveway, marked by a faded mailbox leaning at an awkward angle. The *W*, *I* and *S* were most clearly visible, with the stem of the *N* and half of the *O* just barely legible.

She turned down the driveway, and the curtain of leaves that had blocked the property from view from the road gave way to a small yard that led up to a sagging bungalow. Ashlyn parked her car and got out.

The steps moaned as she walked up to the porch and knocked on the door. After a moment she knocked again.

"Mrs. Wilson? It's Constable Hart from the RCMP."

A call answered with silence. Ashlyn knocked again, then checked the address on the slip of paper she'd pulled from her pocket, although she didn't need to. It was the right house.

She took a step back from the door and turned around.

There was a stillness to the house that told her it was empty. For a moment she tapped the slip of paper and considered her options.

Hurry back to the station and hope Nolan didn't find out she'd left? Play dumb when he asked about the information she'd given him? Ashlyn wondered if she could lie that convincingly.

The other obvious choice was to wait and hope that Mrs. Wilson returned before Nolan figured out the information she'd given him was wrong and figured out where she really went. There were call records. And there were files of slips. He'd have to spend the time cross-referencing them, but it wouldn't take long before he found the number that was missing and traced it.

Nolan may not like chasing paperwork in the office, but he was smart, and Ashlyn was sure he was capable.

Especially if he was motivated, a fact proven by how he responded when goaded by Tain.

The steps groaned as she walked down them and stuck the slip of paper in her pocket. From the front of the house, she had a clear view of the mountain slope where they'd recovered Mary Donard's body. A sea of green was all that was really visible between the road and the tree line of the mountain, but although Ashlyn hadn't had much time out of the office to orient herself, she was confident she knew approximately where they'd found their first official victim.

Ashlyn started to walk around the side of the house. The paint was peeling off the wood in some places, and below the eaves a hornet's nest hung among the tattered cobwebs. Gravel crunched beneath her feet, and by a basement window a faucet dripped.

She thought about the small truck she'd seen pulled over on the road. If it was Mrs. Wilson's vehicle, why wouldn't she just park in her driveway?

Behind the house there was a small shed beside a garage, which looked like it had been painted recently. It stood out in stark contrast to the dingy appearance of the house, but she realized structurally the house was solid. Most of the repairs it needed were cosmetic.

The backyard stretched out from the house with a gentle downward slope to the point where it overlooked a hill. Ashlyn was getting used to the deception of the mountains. They'd look like they went straight up, without a break in the trees, but once you started driving up them you'd find they had hills and cliffs in different places, that you could be heading up a mountain and actually driving down for periods of time.

On the far side of the house was a separate area that contained an overgrown garden. The grass was creeping in under the fence and had infiltrated some rows, and in other places there were weeds almost as tall as the plants that had been ignored.

"She'd sneak into the garden and steal the strawberries."

Ashlyn spun around at the sound of the voice she recognized as the one from the phone earlier. Mrs. Wilson wasn't a tall woman, and she couldn't have been accused of being slim either, but she wasn't chubby. She was solid, with stocky legs and arms that matched her body, short white curls that framed a round, weathered face.

"Mrs. Wilson, I'm Ash—"

"I know who you are. You called your name at the front door. Ain't nothing wrong with my eyes, my ears, or my head, and I may be old but that doesn't make me forgetful or confused." Mrs. Wilson nodded toward the garden. "She was a little thief and on track to be a good-for-nothin' two-bit whore like her mother, but she was murdered all the same."

"Mrs. Wilson, I have to ask how you know that."

The woman's face looked like it was twisted in a scowl most of the time, but she found a way to make the creases deepen. "Problem with you young folk these days is you don't sit still long enough to know anybody. Move from one place to another and think we're all just the same, just swap out the names. You want to know this town, you have to be in this town. Then you wouldn't have to ask."

"Then why not call one of the other officers, the ones who've worked locally for a long time? Why not talk to them?"

Mrs. Wilson's dark eyes narrowed. "They're why I'm talking to you. I hear you got problems down at the station."

"You hear a lot. Especially considering nobody's identified the body from the inn. I'm trying to work out how you'd know who it was . . ." Ashlyn let her voice trail off at the end.

The old woman cackled. "What? You think I put her there? Missy, if you aren't gonna take this seriously, you're wasting my time, and that of the taxpayers, come to think of it." Her face hardened. "Jenny Johnson's mother lives about a mile down the road, that way." She nodded again, out past the garden. "You'll find she's got one sorry man after another goin' in and out of the house. Been that way since before the girl was born. Everybody 'round here knows it and ignores it. 'Bout half a mile back toward town there's a dirt road. First turn off's for the house, the driveway. The road narrows up some then, but snakes its way out to this hut where Jenny stayed. You can see the shack from the road, easy. The road dead-ends not far past it. By the time she was a teenager, she'd all but moved into that little shack. It's right near the property line. My fences run right up to the road."

"Did she still live there?" Ashlyn was trying to remember the last known address listed in Jenny Johnson's file. She couldn't remember the specifics, but she knew it wasn't her mother's address.

Was it possible Jenny had just run off from problems and been mistakenly reported as missing? Jenny was the last girl who'd had a file opened, and her disappearance had ultimately prompted the creation of the task force.

"She lived there most of the time for a few years. And then she was gone, into all sorts of trouble, and would only show up out here from time to time."

"You know a lot about her."

"When you got a neighbor kid who steals things off your property, you pay attention. Wouldn't be surprised if it was her mother who put her up to it. Stealing carrots and potatoes and tomatoes. And strawberries. Mostly, she liked her strawberries. I always thought she'd start comin' after the TV and the stereo someday, maybe try for the truck. Never did, though."

Mrs. Wilson started walking past Ashlyn, toward the garden. Ashlyn turned, but didn't follow her. "You have to give me more than that if you want me to take you seriously."

The old woman stopped walking. "I had the greenhouse built two years back. Let the garden go a bit in time. Too hard on the back at my age." She was silent for a moment and still didn't turn back to face Ashlyn. "Your bunch is sayin' she hasn't been seen in a few months now, but I saw her not three weeks ago at the little shack. I'd only gone for a short walk, to check on the signs I got posted at the far end of the property. You think it's bad to have a kid stealin' from your garden, but what's worse is havin' them damn hunters turn up on your property, shootin' at deer."

Ashlyn paused. "Mrs. Wilson, if you saw Jenny three weeks ago, why didn't you report it?"

The old woman turned. "She was out there with one of the men you work with. They were arguing." Mrs. Wilson held up her hand. "All I know is it was something about a delivery truck and Blind Creek Inn."

"I don't understand."

Mrs. Wilson shook her head. "That fool of a girl had been running with Bobby Hobbs from the time she was a child. Him and that friend of his, Eddie, they're no good. Bobby was always the leader, but there was something in Eddie's eyes, 'specially since his mother died. Something was wrong with that boy. No surprise to me that they got her into some trouble. That cop, he was beggin' her to keep her distance, to stay at the shack. Just a few more weeks, maybe a month, he said."

"What did Jenny say?"

"That if they found her, they'd kill her."

"Who? Bobby and Eddie?"

"Well, that cop, he should know, shouldn't he? Talk to him." Mrs. Wilson shook her head. "You go out there, see the shack yourself. Then you'll understand."

"Mrs. Wilson, I—"

"I got nothin' more to say to ya."

For a moment Ashlyn stood and watched the old woman walk away. She'd taken a gamble coming out there alone, and now she wasn't sure if Mrs. Wilson was credible. The wizened old woman certainly seemed lucid, but she'd given Ashlyn nothing to back up her claims about the identity of the body recovered from the arson scene.

Ashlyn returned to her car and drove back the way she'd come, watching the odometer closely until she found the dirt road Mrs. Wilson had mentioned. She turned.

It wasn't long before she passed the entrance of the driveway, which curved to the right shortly after the turnoff. Ashlyn couldn't see the house from the road, but the driveway was marked by a faded sign with nothing but the Johnson name.

The road narrowed, and some of the branches hung low enough to brush the roof of her vehicle. When the trees thinned a bit, she could see the small shack, which seemed to be made of tin and wood and sat on a small hill nestled between three trees that seemed to serve as support beams.

How could anyone live there?

Ashlyn parked her car and slowly approached the shack. A quick survey of the woods revealed nothing out of the ordinary, and behind her she could see the gap in the brush that revealed the fence marking Mrs. Wilson's property.

Instead of approaching the makeshift door, which appeared to be made from a sheet of tin somehow secured over an opening in the wood behind it, Ashlyn walked around behind the structure. Near the ground there were some holes that had been dug out by small animals but no evidence of pipes or plumbing. Around the back there appeared to be an outhouse. Beyond that, there was the start of a path heading through the forest, back toward the house where Jenny's mother lived.

The only other thing of note from the back was the dingy window covered by plastic. As she circled around, she also saw a metal vent that looked like it might be for a wood stove.

Ashlyn paused in front of the shack. There was no doubt that she was trespassing. Did Mrs. Wilson's statement give her probable cause to enter and search the building?

A quick glance at her watch told her that she'd been gone from the station for long enough now that somebody must have noticed. If she returned empty-handed, it would cost her.

Still, she felt uneasy as she stepped toward the door. All the lectures about calling for backup, following procedure, not overstepping your boundaries . . . Everything her mentor had drilled into her for months ran through her head. It was all good in theory, but what could you do when you had an uncooperative partner and were stuck on a dysfunctional team?

She took a deep breath, reached forward and pulled at the door. The hinges groaned as light spilled into the small space. A rat scurried across the makeshift floor as she coughed, and it disappeared in the dark corner behind the wood stove. On the far side of the room was a small stove, but Ashlyn could tell it hadn't been used in days. A layer of dust had settled on the scattered furnishings, including the hammock strung between two of the trees the shack had been built around.

In a gap between one of the trees and the back wall of the hut a small patch of sky was visible.

Ashlyn surveyed the small space. There wasn't much of anything inside worth noting. A sleeping bag was slung over the hammock. A metal cart sat near a pile of wood stacked loosely by the far wall. A small backpack was on top of the cart, one shoulder strap dangling in front of the door.

She looked at the tin roof and noted no light fixtures

of any kind. Along the near wall, to her left between the door and one end of the hammock, a lantern, a poker, some metal barbecuing utensils and a couple of dirty dishcloths hung on large nails protruding from the wood.

Ashlyn had seen children's forts that had better construction.

The door clanked and quivered as it struck the wood planks that made up the wall as Ashlyn turned back to the car. Nothing in the shack was going to tell her that Jenny Johnson had been killed in the fire.

She got into the car, turned around and began driving. How had Mrs. Wilson known Jenny was arguing with an RCMP officer? She should have pressed the old woman, made her back up her claims, threatened to charge her for impeding an investigation unless she talked. Was that what Nolan would have done?

More importantly, why did she even care?

As she rounded a bend in the road she saw a familiar vehicle turning down the driveway, to the Johnson residence.

Nolan's Rodeo.

She held her breath as she pushed the brake down. Had he seen her? What was he doing out there anyway? It wouldn't take long to cross-reference the processed messages from the call records at the station, but that would lead to Mrs. Wilson's, and she hadn't passed any vehicles before turning off to go to the shack.

Even if Nolan had enough time to go to Mrs. Wilson's and had talked to her before heading to the Johnson property, why talk to Jenny's mother first, instead of heading out to the shack? Had he somehow identified Jenny's body and gone to notify her mother?

What if Nolan had been the officer Mrs. Wilson had heard arguing with Jenny?

Ashlyn released the brake and hit the gas, accelerating faster than she'd planned. Gravel sprayed into the air behind her as the tires found purchase. A quick glance down the driveway as she passed told her Nolan wasn't waiting there, so he must have gone to the house.

But why?

That was the secondary question. As soon as she hit the main road, she turned back toward Mrs. Wilson's house.

Ashlyn hadn't processed how dark it was getting until she saw the oncoming headlights of another vehicle. She switched her own lights on, then flashed the high beams, but the other driver didn't turn their high beams off. Ashlyn raised her left hand to partially block the intense lights shining at her, lowering it only after the truck had flown by.

She hadn't caught a glimpse of the other driver, only a blur of darkness against the growing night sky, but there was something familiar about the vehicle. As she glanced into the rearview mirror, she saw a flash out of the corner of her right eye, followed by a loud *thwack*.

The rear passenger side window cracked, and a burning line was drawn across her right arm. As she hit the brake hard and swerved to the left, she thought she saw the glow of brake lights in the rearview mirror. The tires squealed and then a thud shook the car. Ashlyn raised her arms in front of her face instinctively as the windshield smashed. She was aware that somehow, her body was turning upside down while being pulled back against the seat and then jerked forward until she hit the steering wheel. Pain shot down her spine and into her shoulders. She could feel a warm dampness on her forehead and hear the sound of a horn, but it seemed distant, and the sound faded, as though it was coming from a car that was moving away, as though it was coming from something that had been muffled by the darkness that swallowed her.

PART THREE

CHAPTER FOURTEEN

When Tain arrived at the station Ashlyn was already there, poring over papers at her desk.

"Did you sleep?" he asked her.

She shook her head as she glanced up at him. "Doesn't look like you did either."

For a moment he stood still, staring down at her while she processed the information on the pages in front of her. Only twenty-four hours earlier he would have expected her to be offended by the question, to resent the idea of him checking up on her.

The early hours of an intense murder investigation had allowed them to shift back to normal.

When she glanced up at him again, he realized he hadn't sat down, and quickly pulled out his chair and skimmed his desk.

No messages.

He looked across the desk, at his partner.

"Not a single call," she said.

"Nothing?"

She shook her head and looked back down at the open folder.

"What are you working on?"

Ashlyn didn't lift her gaze and didn't answer right away. Then she picked up the folder and passed it to Tain.

He started to skim the contents, realizing he was reading over a transcription of the full autopsy. Burke had made good on his promise. Tain set the report down on his desk as he read. He felt Ashlyn watching him as he turned the pages. Burke was a talker, which was a blessing because it provided them with a blow by blow of the entire procedure. It wasn't uncommon for official autopsy reports to take a month or more to be completed, a truth shows like CSI made it hard to convince the public of. They pressured for immediate answers and expected quick results, unaware of the time it took to have all the tests done. Short of a gunshot wound or something equally obvious, it could be days before a cause of death was conclusively determined.

Especially if drugs had been involved. They could be kept waiting for the toxicology report while they worked with a partially educated hunch.

There was something in the report that had caught Ashlyn's attention, and he didn't doubt what it was when he found it.

Millie had given birth.

Had this stood out because it seemed significant to the case, or was it personal? Tain resisted the urge to pinch his eyes shut. This case was tough enough already, but this . . .

Could she handle this? Steve might have been right. Staying on this case could be a mistake.

When he looked up, her face was blank, as though she hadn't seen the truth hit home, the subtle change in his expression that had exposed his thoughts.

"What are you thinking?" he asked.

Putting it back on her. Not making an accusation or jumping to conclusions.

"Maybe she was involved with someone."

"It's been quite a while since we saw her. It's possible she had relationships during that time."

Ashlyn shook her head. "I mean, what if she was currently involved with someone, or just had a recent breakup?"

"I'm not sure I follow, given the cause of death . . ."

"I think that if anyone would know about Millie's past, if there was anyone she might have told about what happened to those other girls, it would have been someone she was involved with. I know it's just a theory, but it explains the similarities."

Tain thought about what it would mean if Millie's death wasn't connected to the case they'd worked before. They could leave those skeletons in the closet, possibly wrap up this investigation without asking the one question nobody wanted to consider.

Especially after what had happened months before between Craig and Steve over one of Steve's old cases that was now fresh in everyone's mind. The questions of whether the investigation had been thorough, whether an innocent man had gone to jail . . . Mistakes had been made that had been outside Steve's control, and though his name had been cleared, Craig hadn't been able to let it go.

It seemed to Tain that Craig was the only one unable to accept that he had his own mistakes to account for, that he held his father to a higher standard than he expected to be held to himself, but that was incidental. What he couldn't forgive Craig for was what he'd done to Ashlyn.

He pushed that from his mind and nodded. "Good thinking. The question now is, how do we start piecing together Millie's life?"

Ashlyn tapped a pile of papers stacked to her right. "Missing-persons reports. Nothing matches the description."

"Provincewide?"

"National for the last four days."

"Which means she's either been missing longer or doesn't have someone waiting for her at home."

Ashlyn opened her mouth, hesitated. "Not necessarily. Remember that family last year, the ones who never reported their daughter was missing because they were illegals?"

It wasn't really a question because she knew he remembered, as much as part of him wished he could forget. From time to time he wondered how those girls were doing, then realized he probably didn't want to know the answer.

"If they were involved in anything illegal, a partner might not come forward." Tain sighed. "Which leaves us with what?"

"Birth records."

Tain groaned. "Do I even want to know?"

"Over 42,000 births recorded between July 1, 2006 and June 30, 2007 in British Columbia alone, and it's holding steady for the current reporting year."

"And we're assuming she actually reported the birth." Tain leaned back in his chair. "If she's involved with someone currently, someone who wouldn't want to report her missing, would she name him on the child's birth certificate?"

"And there's different protocol for First Nations children, depending on where they're born."

"You think . . . ?" He frowned. "Isn't that a bit of a long shot?"

"I'm just pointing out that a search won't be conclusive. For all we know, she left the province for a period of time, but if we could turn up a birth record, it would give us a place to work from."

Tain reached for his phone.

"What are you doing?"

"Asking for Sims to follow up on the paperwork."

"You have something else in mind for us?"

He nodded and covered the mouthpiece with his hand. "Get your coat."

Tain was vaguely aware of the cold metal of the car he was leaning against as he watched Ashlyn reach up, rub her shoulder and twist her neck back and forth. Through the growing darkness, he could still make out her movements as she walked down the pavement to the street where they'd parked.

He even believed he could see her eyes turn toward the Dumpster where Millie Harper's body had been found, but as she drew closer and the glow of the streetlight enveloped her, all he could see was her steady gaze at him and she sighed.

"Nothing," she said.

"Damn it."

She leaned against the car beside him for a second before straightening up. "There were six apartments in the building on the corner where nobody answered." Ashlyn flipped some pages in her notebook. "Nine in the building across the street." She glanced at her watch. "Maybe more people are home now. We should—"

"Be realistic. Most of those apartments don't overlook the alley."

"That doesn't mean they couldn't have seen something. People could have been outside, driving home, walking the dog. You're the one who didn't want to settle for the canvas done yesterday, who wanted to talk to people firsthand, make sure everything was done properly."

"We've done that. We left a card on every door that went unanswered. Now it's time to let it go."

She tapped the notebook against her other hand for a moment, an old mannerism he suddenly realized she'd outgrown in the time they'd worked together in the Lower Mainland. When they'd worked together the first time she'd done that a lot.

Her hands dropped to her sides. "What did Sims say?"

"Nothing so far."

"How hard can it be to track down birth records?"

"Ash, you said it yourself. There's different protocol,

depending on where a child is born, and there's a hell of a lot of records to sort through. It could have happened in any town, district, city. For all we know, Millie was married and had a different name."

"I—" She looked away as she took a deep breath and let it out slowly. "I know. I just want to make some headway on this."

"From the amount of blood loss, they're pretty sure Millie didn't die here. We aren't looking for someone who had prolonged exposure. Just enough time to dump the body."

Ashlyn glanced at him. "One of the things that makes this different."

Tain paused. "It is different, Ash. But we can't pretend it isn't connected."

She yanked the passenger door open without looking at him and got in. He stood up and walked to the driver's side door. Once inside, he reached for the keys and realized they weren't in the ignition.

He held out his hand. Ashlyn fished them out of her pocket and dropped them in his palm, then faced the window.

The turns were instinctive as he wove through the streets toward the station and as he thought back over all that had happened since he'd been paired with Ashlyn the summer before, Tain realized he'd worked in the Lower Mainland for the better part of a year.

More than enough time to see through some of the façade. Proximity to the ocean and the close embrace of the mountains that hugged the Tri-Cities from the north facilitated regular escape from the concrete and stainless steel, the malls and the condos and an endless stream of traffic flowing to and from Vancouver. Many who lived in the area genuinely loved nature and took advantage of every opportunity to escape the constructs of the city, but the illusion of nature served as rose-colored glasses for others who couldn't admit they'd succumbed to the urban lifestyle, unable to give up the shortened commutes, mass transit and the ebb and flow of thousands of motorists churning out fumes as they polluted the neighborhoods of others if it meant they could get home twenty minutes faster at night and have more time to watch TV. Why did it matter to anyone if the city was pretty if they never went outside?

The Greater Vancouver Regional District—commonly dubbed the GVA, or Greater Vancouver Area—was comprised of twelve cities, six municipalities, an unincorporated area and three villages. The Lower Mainland did not include Bowen Island, which was part of the GVA, but encompassed cities farther east in the Fraser Valley, such as Abbotsford and Chilliwack. When Tain thought of the Lower Mainland, he didn't think of the valley. He thought of the mess of high-rises and high-priced condos crowding the sky where the land pushed up against the Pacific. It was an illusion. Thousands lived there, convinced that being able to walk where they could see mountains in the distance made them environmentalists. They wore their MEC sports gear as they drove their gas-guzzling sport utility vehicles to the parks so they could hike trails that were cut through the woods, and then they complained about paths being closed because of bears and cougars. They wanted nature as long as they could control it. Along the coast, residents had been known to shoot otters. It was one thing to kill an animal for survival, but to Tain it reeked of hypocrisy to move closer to nature only to cull the wildlife because you find it a nuisance.

It wasn't that he disliked the area, though, and given the choice he'd take the false embrace of nature over the sprawl and smog of Toronto any day.

One of the reasons he chose the RCMP over the Ontario Provincial Police.

Instead of making the turn to go to the station he continued straight past it, prompting Ashlyn to lift her head off her hand and look at him.

"It's been a long day. I'll drop you off at home."

She dropped her head back against her hand, and they continued as they'd been, the silence in the car offset by the sound of the motor and occasional horn and squeal of tires as someone misjudged the time left before the light turned red, but those sounds faded as he went deeper into the residential area near the mall.

He'd forgotten that she'd gone to work so early that morning that she'd taken the car. Instinct still had him turning toward Craig's house in Port Moody from time to time, but he was getting used to Ashlyn's new residence, although he hadn't been inside, other than to help her move. When he approached the duplex he pulled up by the curb.

"Do you want me to pick you up in the morning?"

She shook her head. "I'll walk." Her hand was already on the handle. A burst of cool air rushed in as she pushed the door open and started to get out of the vehicle. Ashlyn turned back. "Are you going back?"

"Just to drop off the car." He returned her gaze steadily. "We'll go at it fresh tomorrow."

After a moment she nodded and started to walk toward the door. "Good night," she said as she lifted her hand, but she didn't look back.

He climbed back in the car as she disappeared inside the house without so much as a final glance in his direction.

Once he returned to the station and signed the car back in, he left. Traffic was thinning along the major thoroughfares and he had the advantage of close proximity to work, but he didn't head home. At the start of every major case that had the feel of an investigation that would run all hours of the day and night, he had the breeder he'd bought Chinook from look after him. There was nothing waiting but an empty house that would offer the silence his ghosts needed to come out and play.

He followed the road to the Barnett Highway to where it merged with Hastings Street in Burnaby, then turned onto the Trans-Canada Highway and drove into North Vancouver. Less familiar streets wound through the hills and buildings that filled the city, forcing him to pay attention to the road signs so that he wouldn't miss a turn while *Five Dollar Bill*, a Corb Lund CD, worked its way through songs about cross-border smuggling and settlers discovering the desolate prairies decades ago.

The Lion's Gate Bridge brought him back across the Burrard Inlet, this time at the mouth, and to the west he could look out over the ocean and see lights in the distance moving across the water. He followed the road into Stanley Park and took the outer loop until he found a quiet place to park.

Noelle had loved the ocean. He'd brought her to the shore once, convinced she'd be scared to death of the endless blue water. Instead, she'd scared him with her eager dash into the waves, one crashing over her head and pushing her just beyond his grasp for a split second.

Long enough for fear to consume him.

The CD changer flipped the disc, and scruffy country gave way to the smooth sound of the Inuktitut and English blends Susan Aglukark was known for. The image of Noelle dancing madly around the house, not long before her death, flashed through his mind. He hit the button to change the disc as he wondered how that one had ended up in rotation again, his pulse slowing as "Til I Am Myself Again" started.

Ironic, considering the doubts that plagued him about his future, about the futility and frustration that had weighed on him for months. In the past, the first hint of unhappiness would cause him to move on, to avoid the questions he didn't have answers for, to keep him from facing his own uncertainty about his career and where he wanted to be.

Tain started the engine and pulled back out onto the road, soon losing himself in the bustle of Vancouver, a city that seldom slept. The barrage of lights from businesses and cars kept the darkness at bay on the main streets, but down the alleys the shadows swallowed the homeless people he knew were there. British Columbia's Lower Mainland had a mild climate when compared to the rest of the country, and even in January Vancouver rarely saw more than a centimeter of snow or temperatures that fell far below freezing. The Vancouver area and Vancouver Island served as beacons for would-be snowbirds who didn't want to travel to Florida or face the cold of a typical Canadian winter, and those of no fixed address who had to sleep rough when the shelters were full.

As he circled back toward his own beat, he followed East Hastings. If the Vancouver area was eye candy for nature lovers, East Hastings was eye candy of another kind, and not for anyone Tain would describe as having normal tastes. Various vices were bought and sold on street corners, and on one block uniformed officers were trying to separate two groups of people shouting at each other.

A headlight shimmered on a blade one of the men held. Tain thought about pulling over, aware that he was out of uniform, but the flash of lights in the rearview mirror signaled the arrival of help as the two groups the officers had worked their way between were pushed apart, dispute already dispersing.

He kept driving, back toward the Tri-Cities.

Somehow, after all this time, Millie had found her way to the city where Ashlyn and Tain—and normally Craig—worked. He'd said himself that she didn't look street hard, but given her history, it would have made more sense for Millie Harper to up plying one trade or another on East Hastings than murdered and left in a Dumpster in Coquitlam.

He parked and unlocked the door. The house smelled of stale air and sour milk. Tain dropped his coat on the table, walked to the kitchen counter and dumped the contents of the jug down the sink. He'd forgotten to put it back in the fridge the night before.

In his bedroom a half-empty mug sat on the nightstand by his bed. Tain grabbed it, as well as the few items of clothes stacked on the lone chair against the wall by the closet and went to start the laundry before rinsing out the mug and putting it in the dishwasher.

The simple act of doing could be a welcome distraction from so many demons.

CHAPTER FIFTEEN

It wasn't until Craig reached the station that he remembered he didn't even have a desk to work from.

This assignment was supposed to be just another in a string of temporary assignments. Most of the time he'd been filling in for an injured officer on leave or someone on holidays, and had used their desk or an empty one. He'd been sent to Kelowna for the manhunt as extra personnel, not a substitute. As he entered the station he saw one of the other men he recognized from the gravesite the day before, the one with the gravelly voice.

The man nodded at him.

"Make any progress yesterday?" Craig asked.

The man just shook his head and kept walking.

Craig searched the station and saw a handful of men he recognized who'd been assigned to the manhunt, but he hadn't worked directly with them himself. They were in the midst of packing up supplies, so he only stopped to ask if any had seen Mac.

Nobody had.

That was when a uniformed officer approached him with a message. He took the slip of paper.

Yeager had given them a room to work from.

When Nolan found the small room near the back of the station, it was empty. Only a long table, a small filing cabinet and a couple of chairs filled the space. Someone had placed a phone on top of the table that was strung over from the wall with an extended cord. It was beside a file, a few pads of paper and a couple of pens. A laptop sat on top of the filing cabinet.

He walked around the table, to the far side where he could keep his back to the wall, sat down and reached for the file.

It was the one he'd started the day before, after they'd been officially assigned the case, and it didn't hold more than a few scraps of paper. They didn't have anything official from the coroner at this point, and his own notes from the excavation were in his notebook.

He didn't need them to tell him what they'd found in the woods. It was all fresh in his mind, an image he couldn't shake even if he wanted to. The body had been partially wrapped in some sort of sack. They'd managed to extricate the body from the woods by early evening, but Dr. Winters had insisted they wait until the body was transported back to the lab to remove the bindings.

She'd also decided to call it a day. He knew Mac wasn't going to back him up if he insisted they keep going, and he also knew the coroner was right. The autopsy could take hours, especially if the bindings were difficult to remove, so he hadn't offered much protest.

The sack bindings were one of the things that made him think this case didn't connect, but his mind kept going back to the one other apparent difference between the scene and the other decomps he'd investigated. Without an estimation of how long the victim had been deceased, he didn't even have a timeline to work from, and until the body was unwrapped, he wouldn't know for sure. But it appeared there was only one victim this time, and the cause of death was different.

Those girls from that old case had been impregnated

and after they'd given birth they'd been murdered with their newborn babies. Craig didn't want to jump to any conclusions, but he couldn't deny he hoped that this case wasn't connected to the others, despite the knot that had settled in the bottom of his stomach. Part of him would like to close the book completely, to find the victims they'd never recovered, but it would mean opening old wounds.

Craig had enough things to deal with, without reliving that part of his past. He wasn't ready to pull missing-persons files just yet. Craig stood, grabbed his coat and the file, and left the station. He saw no sign of Mac on his way out, and he opted against drawing attention to his partner's truancy, so he didn't leave a message. After he got in his vehicle, he punched in the number.

After six rings the voicemail kicked in. "It's Nolan. Call me when you get in."

It didn't make sense to drive the few blocks to the coroner's office, so he walked. It was a cold, clear day, almost like you'd expect to have in February instead of April.

Dr. Winters hadn't wasted any time. She'd begun the delicate process of extricating the remains from the wrappings and was so engrossed in her task Craig had been watching her for a full minute before she looked up and saw him.

"I called you an hour ago," she said.

He thought back over the scant contents of his makeshift office. "I didn't get the message. Have you . . . found anything?"

Her dark eyes studied him for a moment. "What is it about this body that you aren't telling me?"

"You were at the scene yesterday. You know as much as I do."

The slight pinch of her eyes suggested she didn't believe him, but she turned her attention back to the examination table. "It will be hours before I make some progress with this. There's no point in you wasting your time here."

"But you called . . ."

"To tell you not to come over."

Craig blew out a breath. "That's it?"

She looked up at him. "Don't you have something else to do, Constable?"

"This is a decomp from the forest. Right now all the physical evidence I've got is lying right in front of you. Without knowing how long she's been deceased there isn't a whole lot I can do."

"Well, I can tell you one thing. This wrapping? It's made from some sort of canvas bag that was date-stamped. This one's from 2007."

"2007? You're sure?"

"Quite sure, which is a good thing since it seems to make you happy." Her eyes narrowed again. "For reasons you apparently don't feel the need to share with me."

He ignored that. "Any chance she may have been wrapped in this material after she'd been deceased for some time?"

Dr. Winters hesitated. "We're theorizing she was moved because of the lack of animal activity with the body, and she wasn't properly buried."

Craig shook his head. "We know she was moved because the body isn't fresh and we've been searching the woods for days. That part of the woods was covered thirty-six hours ago. She wasn't there."

"I can tell you that you're looking at a female victim, at a guess between five-six and five-nine. It's hard to tell if there is extra cushioning around the feet that's making her appear longer than she is. As for whether she was moved, you're convinced. The lack of animal activity is a factor, but for all I know, someone's been watching over the body night and day and protecting it. I don't base my findings on external variables alone. I base them on what I see in front of me, and I don't have enough to make a conclusion yet about time of death. She was frozen, but that could be the result of being outside in these temperatures. Just because men searched the area doesn't mean they weren't sloppy."

Dr. Winters straightened up. "As for whether she was rewrapped, it would be pure speculation at this point. I like to deal in facts, Constable. Not guesswork."

He felt the heat creeping up from the back of his neck. "Sorry. It's just . . ." He couldn't tell her what he was really thinking, just how important the timeline on this case was. "The date will be critical in helping us narrow down the investigation, that's all."

"At this point, the only other thing I can tell you is that the tip of a carving knife or sword is protruding from her back."

A rush of cold crept up his spine and spread through his skin. "I . . . I don't remember seeing that yesterday." Fumbling for the words as he scrambled to recall the exact moment the body had been lifted from the ground.

"It wasn't noted until we got her back here and moved her onto the table. We theorized the pressure from the weight of the body must have made it break through while we were transporting her, because I saw no indication of a protrusion when I did my survey of the body at the gravesite either."

Craig nodded. "Shouldn't there be evidence of a handle then? Is there any sign—"

Winters held up her hand. "It could be a small knife that was absorbed into the body, which would mean the handle might be inside the rib cage. It all depends on the force with which she was stabbed, and if someone threw the knife at her that would also affect the depth of penetration." She paused for a moment, her mouth twisting into a small frown. "In fact, it could even be the tip of an arrow if someone fashioned one from the right kind of metal. We simply don't have enough details right now to form a conclusion."

"But it's definitely a murder."

"How often do you find bodies lying in the middle of the woods that have been frozen and partially wrapped and got there by natural causes?"

If he'd wanted to be flippant, he would have pointed out her conclusion was based on circumstantial variables, not facts, but he kept that to himself, and he didn't try to explain what he'd meant.

"Are you working this alone?" Dr. Winters asked.

He started to shake his head, then shrugged. "I may as well be."

"Mac's worked here for long enough to have friends and a reputation," Dr. Winters said. "My advice? You're better off on your own."

"I still have to answer for him when the sergeant calls me in."

Dr. Winters looked at him for a moment, then walked to the counter, wrote something on a slip of paper and passed it to him. "He always parks in the alley."

He thanked her, handed her a card with his cell number on it and asked that she call him directly as soon as she had something.

As he walked back to the station to get his vehicle he looked at the address she'd given him one last time before folding the slip and putting it in his pocket. Forty-seven Old Main.

It didn't take him long to find it, and a short drive down the alley confirmed that what Dr. Winters had told him was true. Mac's car was parked behind the bar.

Craig turned around and went back to the street, found a spot a few blocks down and got out to walk. There was a chill in the air that justified him keeping his head down, hands burrowed in his pockets. As he walked by the bar, he risked a glance through the dark windows.

A group of men he recognized from work were gathered, most holding bottles of Kokanee and looking relaxed, but not over the line. In the center of them, Mac held court. He was a storyteller, a social drinker, the life of the party.

Craig kept walking. His partner was a liability and there was nobody he could trust. He was on his own.

CHAPTER SIXTEEN

The room was all stainless steel and white walls. Johnson was perched at a sterile counter in a room that actually had more personality than he did.

He looked up as they entered, his gaze already shifting back to the file in front of him before he processed what his eyes had seen and did a double take.

It gave them enough time to reach the other side of the counter before Johnson had even straightened up. The way his hand fell on the scattered photos hinted at Johnson's desire to slap the folder shut and conceal its contents from their eyes, but he hadn't been quick enough.

Not quick enough to hide the split-second deer-in-the-headlights look in his eyes either.

Johnson compounded the issue with a wide smile that was as phony as a three-dollar bill. "You won't believe this, but I was just about to head over to your office."

"I guess that makes you the lucky one," Ashlyn said. "We saved you a trip."

Johnson's smile dimmed. "Sometimes it's nice to get out of the office."

"Sometimes you get out and you get called back," Tain said.

"I had nothing to do with that crank report," Johnson said.

Tain glanced at Ashlyn, who arched an eyebrow. He set his hands down on the side of the counter and nodded toward the file.

"What do you have for us?"

"Well, not as much as you'd like. The team is still sifting through the contents of the Dumpster, and we've identified a few items we think could be connected to the victim, but we haven't had a chance to chase anything down."

"That's okay," Tain said. "That's part of our job."

For a split second, Tain thought he saw Johnson's eyes narrow, and then the hard lines that had surfaced in his expression were smoothed over again. Still perched on the stool, hand resting on the photos, he looked like a man who'd been caught off guard, one who knew he was supposed to be handling the case more than investigating and felt uneasy that the officers he was supposed to manage were pressing him.

"Is this the report?" Ashlyn asked as she reached for the folder.

Johnson hesitated.

"Well?" Ashlyn said. "You don't mind, do you?"

He sighed and pushed the folder across the counter.

It took Tain only a few seconds to realize it was a condensed version of the real report. Ashlyn went through the pretense of flipping pages, then riffled through the pile of photos and double-checked a few things against the papers before looking up. "There seem to be a few things missing."

Johnson blinked.

Ashlyn held up a photo. "No details for this item or"—she flipped to another picture—"this one. The report's missing the distance from the body, suspected source, fingerprints. There's no information at all."

As she'd flipped the photos, Tain had noticed some seemed to have duplicates.

Johnson swallowed. "I know. That's why I got held up.

I was going through the photos, trying to sort out which ones didn't match the file."

"What do you mean?" Ashlyn said.

"It's possible these photos are from another crime scene . . ."

Ashlyn flipped one over, then another and another. "Funny, the time and date stamp seem to put these together. Unless you were working multiple Dumpsters yesterday." She turned the pictures over. "See, there's information for the contents of this photo." She turned it around and slid it toward Johnson, "And in the corner you can see the things that are in this photo, which haven't been detailed."

"I'm . . . sorry. This is very sloppy. We've had some turnover lately . . ."

"No real harm done. Maybe we can track down the missing pages, or help compile the information ourselves." Ashlyn tapped the folder. "Ah, it says right here there should be eighteen pages, but I only counted seven."

Tain had to admire the way she kept her tone light, nonthreatening. As though she might truly be that naïve, and if not naïve then forgiving, willing to overlook a deliberate attempt to limit the information they had to work with.

He doubted Johnson was fooled by her act, but he also knew that Ashlyn had given Johnson no excuse to refuse them. She hadn't made accusations, hadn't provoked him so he had a reason to take a defensive posture. Any inferences of blame or neglect had been conveniently left at someone else's door by Johnson himself. As Johnson flipped through the folder, pretending to note which pages were missing from the file, he said nothing.

The man was backed into a corner, and he knew it. He slid off the stool. "If you can wait a moment, I'll see if I can get to the bottom of this."

As soon as he'd closed the door, Ashlyn spoke. "The look on his face sometimes. It's only ever there for a split second before he suppresses it, but the way his mouth twists and his eyes narrow . . . I've seen that look before."

He knew she was thinking of the first case they'd worked together, the way he and Craig had been at each other's throats.

"I've gotten used to ignoring the contempt. Besides, it's usually directed at me by some guy who wants to hit on you."

Her eyes narrowed. "I don't think that's the case here. I don't know. I could be wrong, but for a split second I thought he hated both of us."

"He can't be too happy about the situation he's in, especially if he was ordered to hold information from us. We just made his life difficult." Tain paused. "Did I see right?"

She nodded. "Two sets of photos for all the pictures they included information for. Single copies of the pictures that were detailed on the missing pages." She shook her head. "Did they really think we'd be fooled by that?"

"No." He felt her turn toward him, felt her gaze as she tried to read his face. Tain looked at her. "They just wanted to stall us," he said. "Johnson comes to our office. Information is missing. He leaves, swearing he'll track it down. There'd be a call, some excuse about mustard leaking from a corned-beef sandwich or an eager analyst pulling out sheets to make calls and confirm data. Or the classic standby, about new staff who weren't up to speed with procedure, or just didn't know the report was being sent out yet and hadn't pulled it all together. Whatever the explanation, it would have been plausible. We would have had no grounds to accuse them of stalling, but it would set us back."

"No way of even knowing if it was someone else pulling the strings or Johnson's idea."

She pulled out her notebook, wrote down eleven numbers and flashed it at him before she stuck it in her pocket.

He nodded. Whatever they wanted to see, it was on the pages Johnson's people had removed from the copy of the file.

In the pictures they'd never intended to give Tain and Ashlyn copies of.

Johnson returned, a sheaf of papers in hand and a look of defeat on his face. "Here you go."

He dropped them on the table and walked away.

Tain noticed Ashlyn looking at him. "What should I do with the duplicate photos?" she asked.

He shrugged. "For the moment, that's the least of my concerns."

She'd driven, so when they returned to the vehicle she passed him the folder and told him to go ahead.

"Looks like the main item of interest on the first page is a newspaper article," he said slowly. "About the task force." He saw Ashlyn glance at him, her face clouded. "About forming the task force in Nighthawk Crossing to investigate the disappearances of all those girls."

Was it his imagination, or had her grip on the steering wheel tightened?

"What else?" she asked. Her voice was unwavering.

Practiced control.

"Another newspaper clipping."

"About the Missing Killer case?"

Tain shook his head. "About the recovery of a body from a burned-out building last summer."

A horn blared and tires screeched as Tain's body was snapped back by the seat belt. Beside him, Ashlyn was drawing a deep breath as she wiped the sheen of sweat from her brow.

"Light changed faster than I expected," she said.

He knew the truth, but he didn't challenge her with it.

"What's next?" she asked as she looked at him.

The light turned green, and he nodded toward the

road. Ashlyn's hands had steadied again, but he could see the shadows under her eyes, the paleness of her skin.

He flipped to the third page Johnson had tried to hold back from them.

"Another news story?"

Tain looked at her. "About Jeffrey Reimer."

Ashlyn was silent for a moment. Tain could only guess at her thoughts while he tried to keep from jumping to conclusions himself.

"There are stories about all the major cases we've worked together?"

Tain flipped through the pages, one by one. "Not just us. There's an article about Lisa Harrington's suspected involvement in the murder of her daughter. Another about Donny Lockridge's murder."

"The one that laid the blame for Lisa's escape at Craig's feet." She spoke softly, and it wasn't a question.

He continued skimming the pages. "Yes, that's here too. Another about the arson investigation, one about . . ."

She kept her focus on the road straight ahead of her and sat a little straighter. "Don't hold anything back, Tain. I'll find out soon enough."

"Lori's shooting. Dennis Hawkins and his suspension." He closed the folder, wished he could find a way to soften the final blow, but accepted that he couldn't shield her from the truth.

She seemed to sense his hesitation and glanced at him. "It's like a scrapbook of our history. Ours and Craig's. Even if Millie hadn't been identified . . ."

"Even if the bosses hadn't called us out there, we would have ended up involved. Whoever put Millie's body in that Dumpster made sure of it."

That truth settled into her face with a look of stone

He nodded, unable to tell her one more story that had been included. She'd find out soon enough, but he couldn't bring himself to tell her whoever had planted the stories hadn't missed the ones from when she was attacked.

The first rays of the morning sun warmed his skin, and he felt the fogginess of his dreams slipping away as he pried his eyes open, then blinked as he sat up. A blanket was haphazardly draped across his legs. *Salt River* lay on the floor under the coffee table and as he lifted himself off the couch, he felt a kink in his right shoulder protest.

It was later than he'd planned on sleeping and by the time he made it to the office it was almost eight a.m., but Ashlyn's desk was empty.

He looked around for her jacket before he stopped short. She would be walking, but she did that most days now, ever since she'd moved out of Craig's place.

A quick scan of the desks revealed a couple of new messages that had been tossed down. He picked them up and skimmed them.

Nothing more from Johnson. No callbacks from the second canvas. They'd left their cards on every unanswered door, but it seemed they'd have to go back out before they could cross the remaining addresses off the list. A reminder about court prep for a trial that would start the next month was followed by a note about a call from the internal board reviewing the circumstances surrounding the death of Christopher Reimer.

He flipped to the last message and read it twice before his hand fell to his side.

The phone on his desk rang.

"Constable Tain."

"It's Sims."

"Ashlyn must really not be in yet if you're calling me."

Sims hesitated, and Tain almost smiled. He knew he'd struck a nerve, although in the aftermath of Ashlyn's assault and assumed breakup with Craig Nolan, Sims had kept a respectable distance. "I have two things for you. One, a record of Millie Harper being admitted to the hospital in Kelowna nine weeks ago."

"What for?"

"Not sure. When I couldn't find any birth records that connected to Millie I widened the search and just started looking for any hospital records. That's all I've come up with so far."

"You looked out of province at all?"

"I'm starting with Alberta. Nothing yet, but there's a lot to go through."

"Good, thanks. This is a place to start."

"I've also got an address."

"Really?"

"Millie Harper was receiving orphan's benefits. I've got a mailing address for you."

"It's current?"

"It's where her last check was mailed ten days ago." He rattled off the address. "It's a small community in the—"

Tain cut him off. "I know where it is, Sims."

There was a pause before Sims spoke again. "I'll keep looking for medical records and let you know—"

"Great. Thanks." Tain was already on his feet but stopped himself. "Good work, Sims. We really appreciate it."

He hung up the phone. It took only a matter of seconds to walk down the hall and raise his hand to knock on Sergeant Daly's door, but it felt longer.

The door opened before he touched the wood.

Steve nodded and gestured for Tain to come in. "I was expecting you." He closed the door as Tain sat down.

"Because of this?" Tain held out the slip of paper. Steve took it and skimmed it before he passed it back, walked around his desk and sat down.

"I can talk to her."

"Too formal."

"I mentored her, Tain."

"And now you're her commanding officer and the father of her ex-boyfriend. I think it should be me."

Steve leaned back, scratched his head, then nodded. "Fine. Just let me know if you change your mind." He looked at the piles of paperwork on his desk as the tick-tick of the clock marked off the seconds. "How's the case going?"

"We haven't made much progress."

Steve nodded again, but it was automatic, coupled with a vacuous gaze that suggested he'd expected that answer. Then he looked up at Tain and stared him straight in the eye. "You know there are some obvious avenues of investigation you might have to go down."

"I know."

"You're ready for that?"

"We have to go to the Interior."

Steve didn't blink. "You found a connection?"

"No. Nine weeks ago Millie was admitted to the hospital in Kelowna, but she was receiving government benefit checks at a post office in Nighthawk Crossing."

Steve was silent for a moment before asking, "How's Ashlyn taking it?"

Tain shook his head as he stood and put the slip of paper in his pocket. "She doesn't know yet."

For a moment there was no sound other than the constant tick-tick of the clock. Tain had found it annoying at first, but it didn't seem to bother him as much now.

"It's a reminder, you know. No second is faster or slower than any other. I was reading about how we make arbitrary conclusions about time, about how it's been spent, about how it's treated us and how we've used it, but it's a constant."

"It's also a judge."

A shadow settled over Steve's face. "I made my mistakes, Tain, but I own them. You can blame me for not being here for Craig after what happened—"

Tain held up his hands, then turned and opened the door. "Whatever's going on with you and him is your problem. Just don't take it out on Ash."

"I've known Ashlyn longer than Craig has, longer than you. You think I'd take sides?"

The wood of the frame was smooth, and Tain gripped it for a moment instead of walking through the open doorway. So much that wouldn't have happened if Steve had been there . . .

No. That wasn't fair. There was no way to know how things would have unfolded if Steve had stood his ground and not taken temporary reassignment.

Steve's way of owning one of his mistakes. No wonder Craig had left. Apples and trees.

He wasn't much better himself. Staying in the Tri-Cities and partnering with Ashlyn was as much consistency as he'd had in his life since he'd lost Noelle, and he could feel it now, the itch, the part of him that feared his past catching up with his present and forcing him to confront his pain and process it. The Reimer case had brought it all back, and he'd tried hard in its wake to push it away but couldn't. His worry about his partner was his necessary distraction, the thing he could focus on outside himself to ease the hurt he carried, but it wasn't enough anymore.

Tain shook his head. "No. But we've got to trust she's strong enough to face this and get through it." He thought about the note, the one he'd shown Steve when he arrived at his office. "We can't protect her forever, and we shouldn't. If what happened to Lori taught me anything, it's that."

He let go of the doorframe and turned to look over his shoulder. All the color had drained from Steve's face, and the lines around his eyes made him look as though he'd aged ten years in the past ten seconds.

Steve closed his eyes for a second and let out a breath. "Sh-she's like family. No matter what." He looked at Tain.

"With your kids you'd do anything to take their pain away. You'd carry it for them if you could," Steve said as he leaned back in his chair, his hands covering his face.

"You think I don't know that? This is . . . There is . . . I've carried this for years." Tain shook his head. "She isn't struggling with her past; she's mourning the loss of the future she won't have. Not just Craig but the baby."

"What are you talking about?"

Tain turned. "You didn't know?"

"Know what? What aren't you telling me?"

"I—" Tain held up his hand. "It's not my place to say." He turned and walked away. Time was compounding Steve's guilt, every tick of the clock one more second of alienation from his son, making it harder to bridge the gulf between them. He knew the guilt could eat Steve alive from the inside and that what he'd just let slip could serve as fuel to the fire, hastening an inevitable confrontation with the pain Ashlyn carried, but Steve could still find a way to mend fences with Craig if he could swallow his pride. Steve and Craig had time to make things right.

Tain thought of Noelle. He'd give anything to have that second chance.

CHAPTER SEVENTEEN

When Craig was called to come back to the coroner's office, he'd hoped for more concrete evidence. Instead, Dr. Winters greeted him with a question.

"We never located dental records for Kacey Young?"

"No. There'd been water damage. The most recent records had been destroyed."

Dr. Winters arched an eyebrow.

"Something about the heat being out, causing the pipes to burst overnight. By the time they found the mess the next morning, a number of files being stored in the basement during renovations to part of the building were destroyed."

"Impressive memory."

"I reviewed my notes," Craig said as he consciously avoided taking another look at the image he was holding. "Just in case."

Dr. Winters nodded. "Well, as you can see, she'd started to decompose. The deterioration was compounded by freezer burn. I'm willing to say that this was an aboriginal female. Teenager. Based on the wear and tear of the joints, I'd guess early teens, maybe fourteen or fifteen. Five feet, eight inches."

"That helps. What else can you tell me?"

Dr. Winters hesitated. "I wish I had more concrete evidence."

"What about the wrappings?"

"They were misleading."

"How so?"

"The date? It was partially concealed. All I could see was the end. Turns out it was a tagline for the business, which had been founded in 1992. What it actually says is, '1992-2007: Celebrating fifteen years of serving our community.' The strips had been cut apart, stitched together in a different order. I'm still trying to piece them all together. We'll need more time to analyze dyes and the fabric to try to narrow down when the canvas was produced, but—"

"But it doesn't make sense that they'd produce the bags a year or more before their business anniversary." Maybe the body wasn't connected. "What about a company name?"

"Blind Creek Shipping Co. Based in—"

Craig fought the urge to close his eyes. "Nighthawk Crossing."

Dr. Winters was silent as she stared at him, her dark eyes filled with a sympathy that suggested she understood the significance of this fact, that she could know the questions he was wrestling with and the conclusions he had to fight to keep his mind from jumping to.

"You weren't surprised," he said slowly, "when I said I'd reviewed my notes."

"And you haven't exactly been straight with me." She looked away. "I was pursuing a career in medicine when my father was injured on the job. I came back to look after him, eventually started doing this." Dr. Winters turned to face him. "I believe you know what happened to my dad."

"I . . ." All the tired expressions, the common apologies and standard sentiments went through his mind. None seemed appropriate. He shook his head. "I didn't know Tim was your dad."

"No reason you would."

For a moment he stared at her. It seemed too trite, too conventional, to say he was sorry, but what else could he say?

She didn't look away. "I don't blame you," she said.

The feeling wasn't mutual.

"Sometimes," she said softly, "a bag is just a bag. And sometimes a knife is just a knife. If I looked at this body and just tried to find all the things that were similar, I'd miss the other things that might be just as important."

"Such as?"

"Newspaper clippings in the layers of bags she'd been wrapped in."

"What kind of clippings?"

Dr. Winters reached for a folder on the counter behind her but didn't pass it to him right away. The lines on her face and dark smudges beneath her eyes betrayed how tired she was, but the way her brow wrinkled emphasized her concern. "These are copies you can take with you." She handed him the folder.

He took it, but didn't open it. Whatever was inside, it was personal, and Dr. Winters had offered him copies prior to making her report available so that he could digest the contents alone.

Craig looked at the body. She'd been wearing an old-fashioned white nightgown. Cause of death appeared to be blood loss from a wound in her chest, caused by the knife they'd removed.

And the similarities didn't end there.

"We, uh . . ." He cleared his throat. "We still need an approximate time of death," he said.

"I'll keep working on it. Whoever did this had no idea what they were doing, and there's been extensive cellular damage."

"I don't think they were concerned about preserving her appearance."

"Probably not. She was stored until she could be disposed of."

Craig paused. He thought back over what Dr. Winters had told him. "You said you wished you had more concrete evidence to give me. What about circumstantial evidence? A hunch? Is it just what's in here?" He held up the unopened folder. "Or is there something else you aren't telling me?"

She sighed and closed her eyes as she rubbed her forehead, the corners of her mouth weighed down as though he'd just dropped a heavy burden on her. "I was hoping you wouldn't ask."

"Damn it, Nolan, I thought I told you to keep this quiet." Sergeant Yeager slammed the door to her office and spun around. "Did I not make it crystal clear? Two days ago when you were in this office didn't I tell you that you were to keep the fact that only you and your partner were working the body in the woods under wraps?"

"Yes . . . Sergeant."

Her nostrils flared, and then she let out a breath. "Where the hell is your partner?"

A good question, and he could guess the answer, but he doubted that was what Yeager wanted to hear.

"Nolan, I asked you a question."

"I . . . I don't know."

"You don't know?"

"No."

She straightened up and folded her arms across her chest. "You've had a bit of trouble with partners, Nolan. Not much of a team player."

As he thought back over the past year of his career, he realized he couldn't argue. "I haven't spoken to Mac since you reassigned us to this case. He wasn't here when I came in yesterday morning. I asked around. Nobody had seen him."

"You mean to tell me that your partner was MIA for a whole day and you didn't report him?" Yeager's nostrils flared. "Have you tried calling him?"

Nolan felt the heat spreading up his neck and into his face. "Yes. Once. I got called to the coroner's office—"

Yeager stomped around to her side of the desk, busying herself with the task of looking through notes and riffling folders before she gave up and put her hands on the work space. For a moment she stood still, resting her weight against her arms, before she looked up at him. "I would expect you, of all people, to understand how important it is that we don't screw this up."

He did. All too well.

"So help me, Nolan, if I find out it was you who went to that damn reporter . . ."

Yeager didn't need to finish the statement, and she knew it.

"The coroner hasn't finished with the body," he said. "We don't have much to work with. More men won't make much difference without an estimated time of death."

"She hasn't got anything for you to go on?"

Craig paused. "The victim was wrapped in strips cut from bags that have a date on them from 2007."

Yeager's eyes widened. "I've only had time to go over some of the newspaper reports, but from what I've read, there seem to be a few other differences from the Missing Killer's signature. I was thinking about putting in a request to pull the other officers who worked that case, make sure we did a thorough review, but maybe that would be premature."

Craig remained silent. Considering what had happened during the original investigation, he couldn't imagine that any member of the team who was still alive would want to deal with revisiting the Missing Killer case.

There were some members of the team who wouldn't be happy to hear from him either. And there were other members of the team he wasn't ready to see.

People who'd know the one truth that had haunted him when he'd been reassigned to this manhunt. A truth he'd assumed had led to his transfer. It wasn't until they'd found the body that he realized the one obvious connection nobody was mentioning, which meant they hadn't connected the dots.

And he hadn't drawn those lines for them either. A truth he was unable to share.

"Do you agree, Nolan? Is there enough to suggest there isn't a connection?"

"I—" He paused. Craig didn't want the case linked prematurely, but Yeager would learn the facts soon enough, and if she found out he'd held back, there'd be hell to pay. "There's something protruding from the back of the victim."

He watched the truth hit home as Yeager's eyes sagged and her mouth curled into a frown. Yeager nodded, and Craig left the office before she could say another word.

As he marched down the hall, his hands balled into fists. Just outside the side door, in the parking lot, was his partner, laughing as he smacked another officer on the shoulder.

•

Craig barreled his way through the door.

"Nolan! Where ya been? Bill here's got a hell of a story to—"

"You sonofabitch." Craig grabbed him by the collar and pushed him back against the squad car. "Out here with your shit-eating grin while Yeager reads me the riot act."

The smile was gone from Mac's face in a heartbeat. "I did the best thing for you."

"Bullshit. Yeager gave you an order."

Mac pulled his arms up under Craig's and shoved him hard. Craig loosened his grip as he stepped back.

His partner was off the car and bearing down on him. "I did you a favor."

"Yeah? By showing up to work this case this morning, or by shooting off your mouth to the press?"

"Me?" Mac laughed, breath heavy with the smell of beer. "Who's gonna believe that when the reporter's a woman you're known to be tight with, Nolan? Feisty little thing too." The shit-eating grin was back. "I mean, from what I hear."

Craig was aware of someone grabbing him from behind and pulling him back almost before he realized he'd raised his arm to take a swing at Mac.

His partner was staring at him, eyes smoldering, betraying the rage that had been building inside him. Mac took a step forward as Craig pulled against the arms that held him from behind.

He couldn't loosen their hold.

"Just remember, Nolan, I've got friends here." Mac looked past Craig and nodded. Whoever had grabbed Craig let him go. "We've all heard about you. It's one thing to be at odds with assholes, but to go after your old man? You're on your own."

Mac walked around him and as he tried to catch his breath, Craig was aware of footsteps, a voice saying, "Later," car doors slamming, the hum of the engine and sound of vehicles moving away and the door behind him opening and closing.

He squeezed his eyes shut, ran a hand across his face.

The door behind him creaked open again but didn't close.

"Constable Nolan?"

Craig dropped his hand from his face and nodded.

"There's someone here looking for you."

He still didn't turn around. "Okay." No response or retreat from the voice behind him. "I'll be right there."

"She's in the lobby." The door fell shut as Craig counted to ten in his head. He turned and walked to the door, right hand shaking as he reached for the handle.

He'd been so focused on clearing his head he'd reached the lobby before he wondered who was looking for him. A quick scan of the area didn't produce anyone who stood out or seemed to be interested in his arrival.

Craig glanced outside and saw the dark hair blowing in the soft breeze, the slim body wrapped in a long coat. Even with her back turned and with all the months that had passed, his breath caught in his throat.

He walked outside and took a few steps toward her, then stopped. What had happened during the Missing Killer investigation was buried so deep he hadn't thought about all the people who'd be affected if the body in the woods did connect to that old case. Until Yeager had raised the possibility of assembling the remnants of the original team, he'd even been able to push Ash, Tain, Sullivan . . . He'd pushed everyone from his thoughts, to prevent his mind from posing questions he didn't want to consider the answers to.

He realized now he hadn't been able to let himself think about that because he hadn't been able to face the possibility of this.

She turned to face him, her dark eyes weighed with a sadness that could break your heart. He remembered that penetrating gaze all too well.

"I'm sorry," he said.

"You find her." There was a quiver in her voice. "After all this time you find her, and you can't pick up the phone?"

Craig shook his head. "We don't know it's her."

"It's in the newspaper."

"That doesn't mean it's true. We just don't know yet."

"You say you don't know, but it's possible."

Craig swallowed, then nodded.

"Did you even stop for a moment to think about how I'd feel?"

"I—" He stopped himself. Every feeble excuse he could think of would ring hollow, because it was. "I'm sorry, Summer."

"Don't tell me what you know in your head. Tell me what you know in your heart. Can you look me in the eye and tell me you know it isn't her?"

Words with the force of a punch to the gut, able to knock the wind out of him. He stood with his mouth open, unable to respond.

Unchecked tears trickled down her cheeks. "Where is she? Have your people cut her into a million pieces to learn nothing they didn't know before they put her on that table? Tell me, Nolan. Where's my sister?"

"Summer, we really don't know—"

His skin smarted from the force of the blow, and he felt the blood rush out of his nose as he reached for her arms.

"We don't know if it's her. Whatever I think . . . it doesn't matter. We just don't know." Summer pulled against him, but he managed to keep hold of her. "They aren't done yet."

"And he's killed again. You got the wrong man and you hide behind your procedure and your lies and you don't tell me you might have found my sister."

He'd killed again? Craig didn't know what Summer was talking about, but he needed to find a newspaper and figure out what the hell was going on. Had Mac leaked the apparent link to the Missing Killer cases, casting doubt on Hobbs's guilt?

As far as he knew, Mac hadn't even reviewed the files, and Craig hadn't left his notes in the office, so how would he know about what Craig had learned from the coroner?

When Yeager had told him to keep it quiet, he'd been relieved but hadn't been able to put his finger on why until now. All the families of the victims, the families of the girls who'd never been found—even the ones they'd told they were certain hadn't been taken by the Missing Killer—they'd all want answers.

Answers he didn't have yet. Answers he might not ever have for them.

Summer's body shook with the sobs and she lowered her head, her dark hair falling in front of her face. Craig let go of her, put his arms around her and held her while she cried.

For a moment Craig stared at the copies of clippings in the folder, then squeezed his eyes shut. Was he really looking at what he thought he was looking at?

He opened his eyes, sat down on the bed and skimmed the first article, then the second.

Every case he'd worked on since the Missing Killer investigation was chronicled, as well as when he'd been shot and the story about the death of his partner, Lori.

The articles also told the fragmented story of Tain and Ashlyn and all the cases they'd worked since leaving Nighthawk Crossing. As Craig flipped through the clippings, skimming the headlines, he stopped at one article.

RCMP Constable Assaulted.

He knew the words by heart, but he read it again, and when he neared the end he picked it up, as though through the slip of paper he could reach out and offer the comfort he'd never given Ashlyn after she was attacked.

There was something stuck to the back of the paper. A note above stated, *This is how we found it*, and below there was a smaller clipping.

Assaulted constable released from hospital with undisclosed injuries.

The paper slipped from his hand, back into the stack, and he closed the folder.

Craig stepped into the bathroom as he peeled off his shirt and tossed it on the floor. He ran the water and ignored the glimpse of his reflection in the mirror as he reached for a washcloth. When he was finished, he turned the tap off and braced his arms against the vanity, gaze lowered.

"You've looked better."

He turned before his brain connected the voice with a name, and when he saw her standing in his motel room, door open behind her, he groaned. "What the hell are you doing here, Emma?"

"Is that any way to greet an old friend?"

He thought back to the last time he'd seen her, before she'd disappeared to print the exclusive he'd handed her. She'd called a few times, but he hadn't answered.

"Friends don't lay blame for failed manhunts without facts."

"If you hadn't had blinders on from the beginning, maybe you would have seen the bigger picture."

He took a step toward her. "You've got some nerve, showing up after all these months, throwing that in my face. You wanted something and you used me to get it, and the minute you had what you wanted you were gone."

"Don't tell me you missed me, Craig."

He clenched his teeth as he walked around her and crossed the room to the side of the bed near the door. Craig grabbed the shirt he'd draped over the chair.

"You forgot this."

As he slid his arms into the shirt and reached for the

buttons he turned around. His coat was dangling from her hand.

The coat he'd left in his office, after he'd talked to Summer.

Summer had told him she'd hung up the phone after the reporter had called, and then picked it up again to book the first flight she could get.

Somehow, he'd reassured Summer, persuaded her that he'd let her know as soon as they had any information. Summer had put her trust in Craig Nolan a year and a half before, believing he'd find her sister, and this time she had no one else to turn to for answers. She had to take the risk that he'd let her down for a second time in as many years.

He'd given her his card and taken down her number, never once thinking to ask for the name of the journalist who'd tracked her down to her home in Nanaimo and asked how she felt about the police finding her sister after all this time.

"How the hell did you get in my office?"

"It's not like you keep it locked."

"The same can't be said for my motel room."

Emma sighed and tossed his coat down on the bed. "Look, Craig, I know you're upset—"

"Don't you stop to think for a second about what you're doing? You call up the family of a missing woman, and I have to tell her we haven't even ID'd the body yet. She comes all this way thinking we have answers, and she could end up leaving with nothing."

"So you don't have an ID?"

"I'm done talking to you."

Emma straightened up. "You need more than one half-assed partner who climbs inside a bottle every night of the week. I can hurt you or help you. That's your call. I'll get my story one way or another."

Craig spun around and grabbed the back of the chair, squeezing his eyes shut as he yelled, "What the hell is wrong with you? You can't stop long enough to imagine what it's like to get a call from some reporter asking how you feel about the cops finding your sister's body after all this time?" He turned to face her. "Or because you lost your sister it's okay for you to put everyone else through hell?"

Emma's mouth dropped open. "You sonofabitch." She turned and started marching toward the door.

"Get out! Just get the hell out," he shouted as she slammed the door shut behind her.

Craig pressed his hands against his temples for a moment as he took in the sight of his coat on the bed, next to the opened folder, the clippings scattering haphazardly, not like he'd left them.

When Yeager found out about this . . .

He grabbed the book off the nightstand and flung it across the room.

Fuck.

CHAPTER EIGHTEEN

The tires squealed as Craig wove around the car blocking the intersection. A look in his rearview mirror revealed the one-finger salute the driver was giving him.

Guy was lucky Craig had better things to do than turn around.

Every time the rage reached out from behind his eyes he saw red, then black. He tightened his grip on the steering wheel.

Think, think, think. If he wasn't at work, where would . . .

Of course. He smacked the steering wheel, glanced in his side mirror, then turned down the next street.

Despite the risks he took drinking when he should be on duty, Mac was smart enough to park in the back alley behind the bars he frequented.

He turned down the alley. If he hadn't been seeing blind when he'd sped away from the motel he might have had the presence of mind to figure out where Mac would be sooner, but the timing couldn't have been better. As he pulled over and stopped the Rodeo he watched Mac saunter through the parking lot, fumbling with his keys.

Mac leaned more than the tower of Pisa.

"You bastard." Craig spat the words as he walked up behind him.

Mac turned slowly, stumbling as he moved and reaching out to balance himself as he wobbled.

Craig grabbed him by the collar and shoved Mac against his car, then let go of him. "You goddamn sonofabitch!" He swung with his right fist, then his left.

The hazy sheen of alcohol burned off Mac's eyes after the blows and he shoved Craig. His movements were still sloppy, but he hit hard in the stomach, enough to knock Craig back. Mac didn't wait for him to catch his breath or find his footing; he plunged at Craig headfirst.

Craig jumped to the side, and Mac tried to pull up too late. He cracked his head against the Dumpster and staggered back, blood oozing down his face.

There were shouts in the distance, followed by the sound of a heavy door slamming shut.

Mac roared as he came after Craig and jumped on top of him. Craig felt the jarring blow of the hood of the car impacting with his back, between his shoulders, and raised his arms to shield his head as Mac swore at him and swung wildly. Some of the blows hit the car and others hit Craig.

A door creaked. Pounding against metal. Footsteps on pavement.

He pulled his leg to the side and braced himself as he swung his foot down against Mac's back. Mac yelped as he fell forward, into Craig, and then slid down onto his knees.

Craig felt hands on him then, pulling him away from the car, away from Mac. Their words were muffled, their faces a blur.

Nothing coming into focus until the sound of a siren, followed by the feeling of being pushed face-first against a car and the officer calling out, "Gun."

CHAPTER NINETEEN

Yeager had always looked rigid before, but when Craig saw her talking to the uniformed officers on scene, she looked like someone had stuck a metal rod up her backside, her no-nonsense expression coupled with raised shoulders and a back so straight she was a chiropractor's nightmare.

The more they talked, the taller she got.

They'd left him sitting in his Rodeo, on the front passenger seat with the door open and an ice pack pressed against his jaw.

The ice was doing more to help his hands at the moment. He lowered the pack and switched it to his left hand, already bruised and swollen. The dried blood on his knuckles worked like a glue on the gashes and he felt the protest when he tried to straighten his fingers.

Someone shut the back door to the ambulance and knocked on it before walking around to the passenger side door. The officers who'd been getting the third degree from Yeager were getting into their cars. One cast a glance in Craig's direction and shook his head. The ambulance parked on the other side of them was crawling along the alley, lights flashing off the buildings silently.

On cue the crowds began to disperse, one group heading into the back door of the bar, another cluster walking behind the ambulance toward the apartment building that shared the alley, a few others coming toward Craig, down the other alley that led to the nearby shops.

Yeager marched across the parking lot and overtook the stragglers walking down the alley. They slowed, staring openly at Yeager and Craig until she turned and glared at them. Their pace quickened, and once they'd passed, Yeager turned back to Craig.

"When I reassigned you, you took it well."

Craig shifted the ice back to his right hand.

"I knew you wouldn't want the case, but I gave it to you anyway. And you never complained."

He risked a glance at her face. Anger etched in stone was what he expected, but there was a softness in her eyes he didn't anticipate, as though she was begging him to cooperate.

"MacDougall was a pain in the ass. Openly arguing. I know he wasn't showing up, and I know you covered for him." She glanced to her left—the bar Mac had come out of—and sighed. "And I know he'd been drinking on shift."

There was silence for a moment, but he didn't look back up. "What I don't know is why you assaulted him."

Mac's words: *Who's gonna believe that when the reporter's a woman you're known to be tight with, Nolan?*

The look on Emma Fenton's face when he'd kicked her out of his motel room flashed through his mind.

Mac: *Feisty little thing too. I mean, from what I hear.*

Craig lifted the ice pack back up to his jaw and looked at Yeager, returning her steady stare. Tough as she was he thought he saw a flicker in her eyes—disappointment, sadness, maybe regret—but as soon as he thought he saw it, it was gone, perhaps nothing more than the trickery of sunlight as the clouds broke for a moment, then closed in over them again.

The softness, if it had ever really been there, was gone.

"Have it your way, Nolan. You're suspended, pending an investigation into this incident." She paused. "And if MacDougall decides to file charges this silent tough-guy crap won't help you."

Yeager turned around and started to walk to her car, the one lone police vehicle that remained in the alley, before she stopped and looked back.

"And Nolan? Don't leave town."

He sat, half in and half out of the vehicle, and watched her get in her car and drive away.

CHAPTER TWENTY

"I used to think I'd like to spend some time here in the summer. With the mountains and the lake it's so pretty, and there's waterskiing, tubing, Jet Skiing . . ."

"Looking for Ogopogo."

"Said with the scorn of a disbeliever."

Tain shook his head. "Just a gimmick to sell key chains and stuffed monsters to tourists."

"Wait." Ashlyn held up her hands, her mouth wide with the feigned look of sudden revelation. "Isn't that what some people say about the RCMP?"

"It's obviously not the same thing. We're for selling stuffed moose and bears in little red serge coats."

For what seemed like the first time in days, a smile lit Ashlyn's face, one that seemed to reach her eyes. She'd been quiet ever since he'd told her what Sims had learned, and they'd spent the drive into the mountains in silence.

"So what changed your mind?" Tain asked.

"Hmmm?" She glanced at him as she stopped the car for a red light, brow furrowed.

"About spending time here in the summer?"

The lines vanished as her face lengthened. "Too close."

He nodded. It wasn't an explanation that needed more words for him to understand.

She followed the directions to the hospital. Ashlyn had parked the car and was halfway out of the vehicle before she stopped.

"We haven't checked in," he said.

Ashlyn climbed back into her seat and groaned. "They've got a big case, the manhunt. I haven't been reading the papers and I know we've missed the briefings, but I still overheard something about it at the station."

"Ever since we found Millie in the Dumpster, I've been avoiding the news."

"This could take a while."

"It's the right thing to do."

She looked at him with her eyebrows raised into an *Are you kidding me?* expression but didn't argue with him.

He pulled out the map and guided her through the turns, somehow managing to muddle up a detour around an accident that had one road closed. It wasn't until they were a few blocks and one last turn away that Tain set the book down.

"Oh my God."

Just as quickly as Ashlyn had said the words, she'd clamped her hand over her mouth but it was too late. Tain looked past her and followed her gaze to the woman walking out of the coroner's office, toward the sidewalk.

First Millie, followed by the newspaper clippings—something he realized he hadn't even told Steve about—then the link to Nighthawk Crossing.

And now Summer Young.

Tain closed his eyes for what felt like a second, and when he opened them they were parked outside the RCMP station.

Checking in should have been a formality, perhaps more time-consuming than usual because of the manhunt, but straightforward nonetheless. When Tain had checked in with Steve to tell him they were leaving, Steve had assured him he'd call ahead to let Kelowna know they were coming.

"Yeah, someone called about that." The reception area was in chaos and the person behind the counter mumbled the words while changing extensions on the phone as they riffled through a stack of message slips that was thicker than a paperback novel. "Kelowna R . . . They haven't answered yet? . . . I can try . . . Just a moment." Identified only as 'Joe' by his nametag, the man glanced at them. "Sergeant said to go ahead, but come back before you leave town. She wants to talk to you, but she's in the middle of something right now . . ."

Joe shrugged as he punched another button and started talking.

Tain and Ashlyn left the station in silence and returned to the hospital.

"What was Sims able to tell us?" Ashlyn asked.

"Just that she'd been admitted here about nine weeks ago."

They found the reception area and went through the formalities of presenting ID and explaining what they were after, first to one woman, then another, then a shift supervisor, then someone from management who didn't look like a doctor.

After explaining who they were and what they wanted for the fourth time, they were left in a small room with a few armchairs, a couch, a poster about STDs and another poster about the benefits of getting the flu shot.

When the door opened, the woman from management accompanied a female doctor, who had dark hair pulled back in a bun and glasses with thick, black frames. "I'm Dr. Waters," was all she said as she sat down.

Both women carried folders.

Tain glanced at Ashlyn, who held up her ID. "Constables Tain and Hart. We have a few questions about a patient you treated just over two months ago. Millie Harper."

The doctor glanced at the bureaucrat, who nodded.

"Ms. Harper was treated for a sprained ankle and a sprained wrist, as well as a concussion."

"Did she provide a local address?"

The manager opened her manila folder and cleared her throat. "Nighthawk Crossing." She extended a sheet to Tain. "You can keep this copy."

"Do you know why she came to this hospital?" Tain asked the doctor as he took the offered paper.

Dr. Waters hesitated. "No."

"But you have a theory."

"She only wanted me to look at her ankle and wrist, but the moment I touched her, she winced and pulled back. That was to be expected with her injuries, but I moved my hand up her arm and she cried out. When Ms. Harper changed into a gown there were faded bruises visible upon examination, as well as bruises that were purple and black on her arms, legs and back."

"You're saying she was abused," Ashlyn said.

Dr. Waters paused and glanced at the manager, who looked down as she smoothed her skirt. "She claimed she fell down the stairs."

Tain looked at the sheet in his hand. The reason they'd been forced to jump through hoops and the reason the doctor was being supervised as she answered questions was clear: there was reason to suspect abuse, but the hospital hadn't reported it. "I understand it was her right foot that was injured."

The doctor flipped through the pages in the folder. "That's correct."

"Did she drive herself?"

"No," Dr. Waters said. "She was dropped off by an RCMP officer."

"He left his card," the manager said smoothly. "I have a copy for you."

Tain took the sheet and stared at it for a moment. He looked up to see Ashlyn watching him, her forehead pinched.

The hospital had assumed the RCMP officer brought her in after she'd filed charges.

"Did you speak to this officer?"

Dr. Waters shook her head. "I didn't see him when she was admitted. According to the file, he picked her up when she was released."

"How did you get his card?"

"He left it with the nurse who admitted Ms. Harper," the manager said.

"And he never questioned you about her injuries, requested a medical report?" Ashlyn asked.

The doctor shook her head.

"Can I get the name of the nurse who admitted Ms. Harper?"

The doctor and the bureaucrat exchanged a glance, and the manager cleared her throat. "Shelly Brown. She was a temp, and hasn't worked here since."

"Do you have her address?"

The bureaucrat offered a thin smile. "I'm sure you understand we have to follow protocol when it comes to releasing confidential information. As it is, we've volunteered information to you about Ms. Harper's case willingly, in an effort to demonstrate our willingness to cooperate with the authorities—"

"You mean cover your ass because you didn't report suspected abuse to the police when you saw the nature of Ms. Harper's injuries," Ashlyn said.

There was silence for a moment. Dr. Waters looked at her lap while the bureaucrat stared back at Ashlyn. Tain cleared his throat.

"Okay, we'll need a copy of her medical file from when she was treated."

"We're correct in believing that Ms. Harper has filed assault charges?" the manager asked as she turned to look at him.

"No, she never filed charges," Tain said as he stood.

The manager rose to her feet. "Then why—?"

"She was murdered."

When they returned to the station, they were intercepted before they even had a chance to approach someone and show their ID. They were directed to an office assigned to a Sergeant Yeager, where they were left to wait.

The woman who entered the room a few minutes later was the no-nonsense type and didn't ask them to be seated.

"Did you fail to catch the real killer?"

Tain was aware of Ashlyn's sideways glance at his face, but he didn't look at her. He kept his focus straight ahead, on Yeager's unyielding stare.

"The Missing Killer case. Did you"—the woman took care to enunciate every syllable slowly—"make a mistake?"

"No, Sergeant."

She had piercing green eyes that seemed to be trying to bore a hole through his skull. "Yet here you are, investigating the murder of one of the original abductees. You'll forgive me for being a little sidetracked with this search for a multiple murderer that I'm dealing with, but from what I understand, there are similarities between how she was killed and the murders in Nighthawk Crossing."

Tain swallowed. "Yes."

"Why is it I seem to be the only person who thinks maybe you made a mistake and that there's someone out there who's finishing what they started a few years ago?"

"With all due respect—" Ashlyn began.

Tain cut her off. "It would be rash to form such a conclusion based on the facts available at present. If we find any evidence that suggests that there was another participant in the murders, who was not apprehended, you'll be the first to know."

"Then you're maintaining that your victim doesn't have anything to do with the body we recovered in the woods here, a few days ago?"

He hesitated. "It's too soon to say. We haven't had a chance to review this new case."

Yeager maintained her stare. Tain had seen fish that blinked more often.

"We will pursue every lead until exhausted," he told her. "That's why we're here."

She shifted her glance to Ashlyn, who remained silent, and then Yeager nodded. "I expect you to."

"We're going to need access to the files. Who's working the case?" Tain asked. He ignored the sharp glance Ashlyn gave him.

Yeager sighed. "Nolan was pretty much handling this on his own."

"Craig Nolan?"

She nodded.

"Is he here?" Tain asked.

Yeager's mouth formed a hard line. "He's been suspended."

From the corner of his eye, Tain could see the color drain out of Ashlyn's face. He didn't know what to say.

He wasn't sure he wanted the answers Yeager might have for him.

"I can give you his local number."

"And an address for where he's staying. We'll need to talk to him."

Tain watched her nod as she picked up the phone, dialed an extension, requested the phone number and jotted it down before hanging up without so much as a quick thank-you. She passed the slip of paper to Tain.

"Keep me informed" was all she said before she dismissed them.

Once they were back in the car, Ashlyn turned to look at Tain. "What the hell is going on?"

"I have no idea," he told her as he handed her the second piece of paper with the photocopied image of Craig's business card. He'd only needed a quick glance to confirm the number for the cell phone was the same number Yeager had given him moments before. "But we need to find out. Fast."

CHAPTER TWENTY-ONE

Whatever had happened between Craig and Ashlyn in the aftermath of her assault, Tain had never asked.

She'd stayed with him during her medical leave. For hours at a time he was at the station and he'd never questioned her about how she'd spent her days. One afternoon when he'd returned home, he'd found her sorting through some boxes.

More things she'd brought from the house she'd shared with Craig.

Whatever had happened between them, he'd told himself it wasn't any of his business. He'd told himself he didn't need to know. He'd told himself Ashlyn was one of the strongest people he'd ever met, and that in time, she'd come to terms with her grief over the loss of her unborn child.

He'd never concerned himself with whether she'd come to terms with the end of her relationship with Craig. Craig, so hell-bent on questioning whether his father was infallible that he wasn't there for Ashlyn when she'd needed him most.

There were days he found himself wishing Craig would rot in hell. Usually, they were the days he saw the shadow of pain in Ashlyn's eyes as she walked by Craig's empty desk, the paleness of her skin when someone mentioned his name. The act of walking into her sergeant's office served as a daily reminder.

He would have throttled Craig himself if he could be certain that every ounce of pain he inflicted would be less pain Ashlyn would need to carry, but it didn't work that way. He knew that. His own scars ran too deep, and in the years since the death of his daughter, he'd come to terms with the hollow realization that no amount of punishment Noelle's mother faced was enough. The woman who'd given Noelle life and then ultimately took it from her had faced justice from the courts, but the judgment against her had only compounded the grief he still carried within him. The years of Noelle's life that she would never have had been measured against the time her mother had served when they released her on parole after only a few years behind bars.

Thinking about the injustice of it made him wonder why he'd stayed with the RCMP when the system he served had failed him so completely, first with Noelle's death, then with the hand slap they'd measured out to punish the woman who'd killed her.

As Tain looked around the motel room at the liquor bottles scattered across the floor, the picture dangling above the bed by a thread of wire, the phone book lying open near the doorway, some of the pages bent beneath it like it had been hurled across the room and left where it landed, the blood on the sheets left in a heap on the bed, he realized the justice he would have measured out against Craig was being served.

If his wish had the power to inflict this upon Craig, he would have retracted it the moment he saw the look on Ashlyn's face. She moved for the first time since Tain had opened the door and crossed to the nightstand beside the bed, where a torn photo lay. He walked over and stopped beside her and looked down.

A photo of Ashlyn, in black and white. She was in a dark skirt with a matching jacket, one that always caused more men than usual to give her a second glance, talking to Liam Kincaid, the detective constable from the New Westminster Police Department who'd assisted with the Reimer case.

He knew it must have been taken only a few weeks earlier, when they'd been called to answer questions relating to the pending charges against Officer Parker.

Parker. The kind of cop who liked the uniform because of the power it brought the person, not because of how it enabled the person to serve the public. Tain doubted he'd met a more egotistical sonofabitch in all his years on the job, and Parker's recklessness had jeopardized Tain and Ashlyn's investigation of the murder of Jeffrey Reimer from day one.

Parker had ultimately been responsible for at least one more murder.

Some would argue Parker was partly to blame for four deaths. Tain included.

He remembered the day they'd been summoned to answer questions. Parker remained a suspect in Ashlyn's assault, and Tain had worried about how Ashlyn would handle the proceedings, but Officer Parker hadn't even appeared to hear the testimony given.

At the time he'd been relieved, but now he found himself wondering why.

Craig hadn't been there, so what was he doing with a photo of Ashlyn and Liam Kincaid? Had he been stalking Ashlyn, having her followed?

Tain walked around the bed to the dresser and pulled the drawers open one by one, then checked the bathroom, returned to the main room and looked under the bed.

Nothing but carpet and one single slip of paper. He picked it up.

Forty-seven Old Main.

He looked around the room again, and this time, instead of focusing on the mess his eyes took in what wasn't there.

No clothes.

CHAPTER TWENTY-TWO

Craig stared down at the photo in his hand. They'd rushed to get it done.

"They're going to keep working," Dr. Winters had told him when he'd stopped by the coroner's office twenty minutes earlier.

He'd told her not to worry, that he understood it took time to generate an image from remains. What he held in his hand was the baseline, like a picture that was slightly out of focus. The more time the team had to scrutinize the measurements and factor in the state of the body and damage to the corpse, the closer the image would be to the actual girl it portrayed.

Craig pried his gaze away from the ghost that stared up at him and slipped the photo back into the folder.

The body they'd found was the right height and ethnicity, but one thing that didn't fit was the image they'd come up with after scanning her face and trying to generate a reasonable likeness.

Kacey Young had been a slender girl. The victim had been heavy, and her jawbone had been poorly set after a blow, which caused it to twist to the left side permanently.

Jane Doe's eyes were dull, not at all like the vibrant eyes that had sparkled in all the photos he'd seen of Kacey Young, but he had to remind himself that Jane Doe's eyes weren't real eyes.

They were just part of a generated image. Placeholders. What dreams, what experiences, what happiness and hope all combined to make Kacey Young the energetic, lively girl she'd appeared to be was something no doctor or artist looking at a corpse could detect. Dr. Winters had said it herself; she preferred to deal in facts. She had to.

He glanced at his watch. Summer's hotel was on the other side of the city, but he'd been careful to pick an inconspicuous diner that had a narrow entrance beside a gas station on the outskirts of town. This was the type of place that picked up a fair bit of passerby revenue from highway traffic, and made its bread and butter off local residents who liked a certain kind of atmosphere. For those who wanted privacy, there were more booths in the back, where the décor changed to dark paneled walls. Near the entrance there were smaller booths to the one side, a long counter area with stools to his left, which spoke to the type of trade the diner specialized in. Customers who usually came in alone, on their way to work, looking for a friendly face to chat with and quick, cheap food that was made to order.

It wasn't where the tourists or upper middle class thought to stop for coffee.

Craig opened the door and went inside, careful to keep his face tilted so that the swelling wouldn't be so obvious. It was a diner filled with shadows, which was exactly what he wanted.

He picked a booth in the back and took the far side so that he could watch the door, then pulled out his cell phone and sent her a text confirming he was there.

A few minutes later, the string of bells on the door clanged as it opened. Summer paused as she scanned the room, then let the door fall shut behind her when she saw Craig. She'd started to sit down across from him before she got a good look at his face.

"What happened to you?"

"Don't worry about me." His jaw still hurt like hell.

"What can I get for yas?"

"A Coke," Craig said. "Egg-salad sandwich and fries." He wasn't taking chances trying to chew a burger, and once he left he didn't want to stop anywhere else before leaving town.

"Toasted?"

"No. Thanks." He looked at Summer.

She ordered tea.

Craig waited until the waitress was out of earshot. "Like I said on the phone—"

"I know. It's a pretty basic image."

He slid the folder across the table and watched the battle on Summer's face. She blinked and reached for it, but then paused as she looked up at Craig, her eyes wide with the fear. Summer would tell herself Craig's caution was part of the job, to make sure he didn't say anything that would cloud her judgment. Summer would tell herself whatever she needed to, so long as she could hold on to the hope that there might be a break in the case. Once she looked inside, she might have the answers she'd sought for so long, but part of her was starting to realize that the answers might hold truths she wasn't ready to face.

To have a sister disappear was hard enough. Craig knew that. Hope hovered like an angel of light, while despair lurked like a creature of darkness. Every phone call, every knock at the door threatened to confirm your deepest fears, to bring answers that could serve as wounds that would scar the soul forever. The initial pain of suffering a loss could be compounded by the awareness that your sister had suffered, that her final days were spent in agony, that she'd died at the hands of a madman before you had a chance to tell her you loved her one last time.

The things left unsaid between loved ones often cut the deepest.

Ashlyn's face flashed through his mind.

"You'll have to try to imagine how she might have changed in the months since you last saw her."

Summer lifted a trembling hand to tuck her dark hair behind her ear. A mechanical motion, one Craig remembered from before. She came off strong and confident, ready to fight anyone who dared to stand in her way, but beneath the tough exterior there was a tender heart. This was the woman who'd talked to the press before the task force had been created, the person who'd first accused them of racism.

The person who'd made the task force happen.

She was also the woman who'd created a makeshift memorial for the girls listed as The Missing.

The waitress came and set down their drinks and left again.

"There are no answers in that folder," Craig said as he placed his hand over hers and squeezed it gently. "Only possibilities."

Craig drew his hand back and fought the urge to press his fingers against the glass of Coke. He looked past her, down the aisle. The chain of bells jingled again as a man in a lumber jacket entered, making a great fuss as he greeted the waitress, and sauntered over to the counter. He was talking past the waitress too, and laughing. Craig guessed he must know the cook, who was occasionally visible through the opening in the wall where orders were set when ready.

From the corner of his eye he could see Summer's shoulders lift and fall, and then she opened the folder.

The man in the lumber jacket took off his cap and unbuttoned his coat while he sat down at the counter and talked to the waitress. There was the faint ding of a bell, and he stood, buttoned up his coat and put his cap back on. The waitress grabbed a bag and started packing wrapped items in it before she poured a coffee, passed it to him along with the bag of food and rang up the order on the till. He fished out his wallet and handed the waitress some money, argued with her over his refusal to take his change, and then turned and stood beside a booth, gabbing with a couple men who'd come in shortly after Craig had.

As he waited for some sign to tell him Summer was ready to talk, he wondered how he expected to know she'd processed the image and was able to discuss it. He'd been doing this long enough to know that you could never predict the way a person would respond. The man in the lumber jacket waved and went to the door, the bells clanging as it slammed shut behind him. From the pass-through he realized how much time had passed.

The waitress came with his food and he nodded his thanks, her service providing a natural opening for him to shift his focus back to the table he sat at and the person across from him. He didn't push it, instead taking the time to eat slowly, which was necessary because of the pain when he moved his jaw.

Summer hadn't moved or said anything. Craig glanced at her as he pushed his plate aside. The image the lab had generated was in her hand, her dark eyes staring at the face, probably trying to find some point of likeness between the picture before her and the face she remembered from more than three years earlier.

She set the picture down and whispered, "I don't know."

Craig nodded. "I'm sorry to have to ask you this—"

"You need a blood sample."

"We don't have dental records. It's the best way." The echo of déjà vu was in his words. He'd said them to Summer before, told her they might have to ask for a sample, just in case. Something they'd need to do if they found Kacey's body.

He'd never imagined the request would come eighteen months later, more than three years after her sister had gone missing.

"I understand. I already went to the coroner's office, earlier."

Craig watched her as she shut the folder and pulled her coat on. "I'm sorry."

Summer stood and offered him a smile that didn't reach her eyes. "It's been more than three years, Constable Nolan. I'll just have to wait a little longer."

She hoped.

"I have to go out of town for a few days, to follow up on a lead," he said. "I just wanted you to know that you can call my cell if you need me. Don't try to reach me at the station." He passed her a business card with his phone number on it. "Do you want—"

"The only thing I want you to do is find out if this is my sister."

She turned and walked away, her coat wrapped tightly around her small frame, the way it had been the night he'd first seen her standing outside the station.

Another one of her tells. Something she did when her whole world was falling apart and she needed to find a way to hold it together.

He looked at his knuckles and straightened his fingers, pushing past the pain as the dried blood glue cracked and bled again.

He knew how she felt.

CHAPTER TWENTY-THREE

Tain held up his ID. "I need you to put a call through to Summer Young's room," he said.

The hotel wasn't ostentatious, but it was a neat and tidy establishment with a large foyer, a marble floor and a vaulted ceiling. Words had a way of reverberating around the room.

Sam, the hotel clerk, smiled politely, discretely keyed some information into a computer, then picked up the handset of the guest phone and dialed a number. Tain had watched closely, the man's practiced fingers moving too fast for Tain to make out the extension number.

"I'm sorry, sir." Sam's smile hadn't wavered since they'd approached the counter. "There's no answer."

Tain turned and started walking to the door.

"We can leave a message," Ashlyn said.

"We need to find her." He turned around. "What was Craig doing, bringing Summer here?"

"It wasn't him."

A voice from his past, behind him. He didn't hear her footsteps but felt her move around him, closer to where Ashlyn stood.

"Craig never asked me to come here." Her voice was as calm as her face. There were no lines hinting at anxiety or tension, confusion or concern. She looked unaffected, as though Tain had just asked her if she liked the hotel instead of asserting she'd been asked to come to the city to ID her sister's body.

"But you have spoken to him?" Tain asked.

Summer nodded.

"When?"

The first lines crept into Summer's brow as she looked at Ashlyn, gave a tiny shake of her head and turned away.

Tain reached out for her before she could leave. "Please, Summer. It's important."

She didn't pull away from him, but she didn't turn around either. "Let me go, Elim."

He walked around in front of her. "This isn't personal, Summer." The look on her face as she met his gaze was like a knife in the heart, but he couldn't undo what had been done. For a few moments they stood, looking at each other, and then she turned away.

"I just met with him."

"Where?" He reached for her face and turned it so that she couldn't avoid his gaze. "Summer, is the girl—"

She pulled back from his hold as she shook her head. "We don't know."

He let go of her and she wrapped her arms around her body and blinked as she looked from Ashlyn to him. "I've given blood so that they can check the DNA."

"Is that where you saw Craig? At the coroner's office?" Tain thought back to when they'd driven by the office earlier, when he'd seen Summer. That had been hours ago.

"No. It doesn't matter. He was leaving town."

"Did he say where he was going?"

"No. He only said that if I needed him, to call on his cell, because he'd be out of town following a lead."

Ashlyn stepped forward then, reached between Tain and Summer and put her hand on the other woman's arm. "Can you tell me how he is?"

Summer's dark eyes were wide as she looked at Ashlyn. "What do you mean?"

"Is he okay?"

"He was bruised. There were cuts on his hands. They weren't . . . He wasn't like that when I saw him earlier. I don't know what happened to him."

She walked around Tain, and he let her go. The look in her eyes had been raw, and in her words he'd found more answers than he could have hoped for.

Craig was still working on the case. He hadn't told Summer he'd been suspended, but it sounded as though he'd been in a fight.

The clippings found around Millie's body hadn't just contained information about cases Tain and Ashlyn had worked. They'd covered Craig's major cases, until he'd left the Lower Mainland on temporary reassignment.

He marched outside and down the street to the car and kicked the door. It hurt like hell, but it reminded him he could still feel.

Tain leaned against the car drawing deep breaths. After a moment he looked up. Ashlyn was lowering her cell phone and closing it.

"Sims," she said. "I asked him to follow up on the apartments we missed in the second canvas."

It was a good idea and made him think Ashlyn was handling this better than he was. She'd had the presence of mind to follow up on tangible leads, to leave no stone unturned, no matter what the circumstantial evidence suggested.

"Where now?" Ashlyn asked.

Tain turned and leaned back against the car for a moment before he straightened up again. "The coroner's office."

PART FOUR
THE PAST

CHAPTER TWENTY-FOUR

Twenty-one months ago

Jenny paced back and forth in the dark at the far end of the diner. They were concealed by shadows that would keep her from being easily identified at that distance, but she was unwilling to risk moving into the light and taking the chance that there might be someone inside who'd recognize her.

"We've gone a long way," he said.

"They're truckers. You think this is far to them?" She stared at him. Maybe it had been a mistake. Maybe she should have found some other way, just ran as far as she could . . .

Bobby would find her.

He'd always told her he would. Promised he'd never let her go.

"Look, do you want to do this or not?" he asked. "I'm not going to push you . . ."

She paced back and forth a few more times, then spit out an order. "Bacon cheeseburger and fries. No pickles or onions. And a strawberry shake. I'll wait in the car."

Jenny stomped back over to the vehicle and yanked the door open. After she slammed it shut, she slid down in the seat, fingers tapping the door frame as she peered out over the dashboard, scouring the parking lot.

Keeping watch.

She looked at the man who'd brought her there, the

one who'd driven with her in silence for more than two hours before he'd insisted they stop and get something to eat and talk. His patience was wearing thin. She could tell.

He wanted the answers she'd promised him when she'd called.

After a few minutes, he walked down the sidewalk that ran the length of the building, to the entrance at the far end. She glanced in the side mirror, then at the door of the diner and saw him hesitate, looking back in her direction before he turned and went inside.

No vehicles arrived or departed during the twenty minutes she waited for him to return. He scurried back with a paper bag in hand, was quick to shut the door and extinguish the interior light of the car, fumbling in the trickle of light from the building to read the labels on the food and make sure she got what she'd asked for.

She fought to keep from cramming the food in too fast. Bobby had been in a mood lately. Complaining about girls who get fat.

He hadn't been giving her much to eat, and now that she was throwing up every morning, she was even scrawnier than usual.

If Bobby suspected, she didn't have much time. That's what she'd figured when she turned it all over in her mind, again and again.

Jenny turned to the RCMP officer beside her. It was the only way out she could see, the only hope she had. Get Bobby cornered on the drugs and the smuggling. She knew enough about the operation. There had to be a way to catch him.

And if it all went bad, it would go straight to hell, but she couldn't think about that now. She'd made one deal with the devil, and it had cost her. Now, she was making a deal with a different devil, in the hopes that it would save her.

Jenny took a deep breath and started to explain how she'd gotten involved with Bobby Hobbs.

CHAPTER TWENTY-FIVE

Eighteen months ago

It took a moment to realize that the groan she heard was coming from her own body. The first attempt to sit up was met with a searing pain that shot up through her back, into her neck and shoulders, and kicked her in the head.

"Mrs. Wilson?"

She opened her eyes and blinked at the brightness.

"Maybe she hit her head harder than we thought."

Ashlyn turned toward the sound of the voice. Nolan, feigning humor, a tinge of genuine concern not fully masked by the look of casual indifference he'd adopted.

"She remembers where she was going. That's a good sign," Sullivan said as he appeared beside Nolan. "How are you feeling?"

"Fine, sir," she said as she forced herself upright. A wave of black rose up within her and for a second she felt her body wobble, but she refused to reach out and steady herself with her hand. "A little stiff, touch of a headache. Nothing a couple of Tylenol won't cure."

"Or a night in the hospital."

A nurse appeared on the other side of the bed and began nudging Ashlyn back down against the pillow.

"Sir—"

"Don't argue with me, Hart. You can barely sit up without falling over. You'd be no good to us back at the office right now."

"But Mrs. Wilson—"

"Nolan's already filled me in. I'm just glad you two didn't run that errand together, or you might both be on a morphine drip tonight, and lucky for you he wasn't far behind when you hit that deer. You did a number on that car when it flipped into the ditch. Mrs. Wilson can wait until tomorrow. Nolan can head out there and talk to her in the morning."

"I-I hit a deer?" She blinked.

"You don't remember?" Sullivan asked.

She thought back over the flashes that were clear. Talking to Mrs. Wilson, going to the shack, seeing Nolan's Rodeo turn onto the Johnson property . . .

"It's not surprising it would be a bit hazy." Sullivan glanced at Nolan. "We'll get a full report from you when you've had a chance to rest."

They were moving away from the bed. She glared at Nolan, but he didn't look at her.

"Doctor says you should be back on your feet within a day. Two at the most. Don't worry. If you aren't up to it, we'll keep you in office tomorrow. Just get some rest."

In office. All this time Nolan had been finding reasons to leave her behind and now she'd handed him one she couldn't argue against.

Sullivan was already out the door. Nolan paused and turned to look at her.

He'd told their sergeant that they were going to meet at Mrs. Wilson's . . .

The blur of the truck going past her and the sense that something about it was vaguely familiar was hazy. She knew she saw it just before she hit the deer, and there'd been a noise . . . She remembered seeing Nolan's Rodeo turning on to the Johnson property before that. He must have been headed to Mrs. Wilson's if he'd found Ashlyn's overturned car, but he'd gone to the Johnson residence first.

Had he already known what Mrs. Wilson had to say?

She felt her eyes widen. Nolan stared back, unblinking, and his expression didn't soften as he said, "Get some rest. I'll talk to you tomorrow."

Something about his tone suggested it wasn't a conversation to look forward to.

Ashlyn didn't respond as he walked away.

"Ashlyn. I'm surprised."

That wasn't what she'd expected to hear Sergeant Steve Daly say. He'd been her mentor from The Depot— the RCMP academy where all cadets did their training— and had been transferred back to the Lower Mainland only a few weeks earlier. She'd been on one of her temporary assignments then, and the last time she'd talked to him was by phone before she'd left for Nighthawk Crossing. "Sis too soon ta call?"

"No. It's just that in the past, you've always been in touch within twenty-four hours. I didn't expect you to wait this long."

There was a projected lightness in his tone that was trying to conceal the concern she detected. She smiled, then winced. Ashlyn may not have hit her head as hard as they thought, but her face had struck the steering wheel. When the nurse had helped her to the bathroom she'd seen the purplish-blue patches expanding on the right side.

"Mmmm sahry."

"Don't worry about it."

"Reawy, Sssteve. I—"

"Ashlyn, it's okay." He paused. "You sound . . . a little out of it."

"Ssss jes . . ." She rubbed her forehead, took a breath and focused on enunciating every word. "It's been busy."

"How are you settling in?"

A fire, a confrontation, a partner who dumped her every chance he got, a body, a lie . . .

"Ashlyn?"

She exhaled. "SSSSs all sech a mess."

"What happened?"

"Uh hit a deer."

"You hit a . . . Please tell me there isn't a bad joke about women drivers somewhere in this."

"No, it's not thahht. I jess . . . it's juss . . ." Her head was starting to clear a bit, and she focused on every word to get it right. "We've been working pretty much nonstop since we found a body."

"You couldn't tell me where you were going before you left. Are you sure you can talk about it now?"

Ashlyn rubbed her forehead. "Yeah. I don't know why they wanted it kept quiet. This task force, the case, it's a real mess."

"Wait. You're on the task force, the Missing Killer?"

"The what?"

"It's what the press are calling it now. The girls go missing for a long time and are murdered months after they disappeared. Some reporter must have thought it was clever."

"Good thing the press doesn't know the holdbacks. I can just imagine what they'd come up with then."

"So you're in Nighthawk Crossing."

"Um hmm."

"And?"

"I'm in de hawshpital." She felt the clouds coming back to cover her brain and tried to keep her eyes open, but they pushed shut despite her efforts.

That was met with silence.

"I'll be awwite."

"Well, good. You want to talk to me about what's going on?"

She glanced at the cup on the portable tray table beside her. "I jest took some . . . sumthin for de pain."

"Which explains why you're fading in and out. We can talk tomorrow. Whenever you're up to it."

The blur of the truck, something about it familiar, Nolan's Rodeo turning onto the Johnson property, her giving Nolan the wrong information, Nolan lying to Sullivan about why they were out there in two vehicles. . . .

"Sis a mess."

He paused. "You said that."

"Sahwy." She yawned. "But it's twoo."

There was another pause. "What's eating at you, Ashlyn?"

She closed her eyes, pinched the bridge of her nose and tried to focus. At least in her own mind, her next sentence came out crystal clear. "Did you ever have a partner you couldn't trust?"

Silence. In her mind's eye she could imagine Steve's face, the look of shock as he sat down in his chair. He wouldn't want to answer the question, he'd want to advise her. That was what he did. Her mentor, not really her friend.

"Yes."

Her eyes opened. "How'd you deal with it?"

"I . . . I don't know. It didn't last long. I guess that means I didn't really have to deal with it."

"This case."

"What about it?"

Close her eyes and she could see herself standing outside the station the first day, knocking on the door, nobody answering. Like a symbol of the whole case to date. Her trying to find a way in, the boys shutting her out.

"Ashlyn?"

"I . . . I found these copies of the files someone was sneaking out. People are lying. I don't know what's going on." Her brain was starting to feel foggy, and she pushed herself upright with her left arm so that she could try to stay awake.

"Papers haven't said much. They named three or four men with more experience, guys who've worked in the communities in the area for a while."

"Makes no sense," she murmured.

"What?"

"Small-town men. Ahwl togeddah. This . . . not . . . not used to dis." Her brain was fogging up again.

"You aren't on the same shift with them?"

She started to shake her head, then felt the protest of her neck and remembered she was holding a phone. "Nah."

"Who are you working with?"

"I godda young . . ." She pinched the bridge of her nose. "Tain. Jerk."

"He's your partner?"

"No." She squeezed her eyes shut and rubbed her forehead.

"Ashlyn, are you sure you're okay?"

"T-tiwed. Dwugs. Call . . . latah."

Whatever he said back to her, she couldn't make sense of it as she leaned back against the pillows and dropped the phone.

When Ashlyn opened her eyes, she blinked at the brightness, which was somehow different from how she remembered it from earlier when she'd woken to find herself in a hospital bed. Strange. Wouldn't they have turned the lights off or down during the night?

Against the far wall, the light filled in the gaps. Sunshine was filtering in through the window.

"Damn." It was morning, and not first thing in the morning either. She glanced around the room until she remembered her watch on stand by the bed.

8:57.

"Argh." It wasn't a shooting pain that soared through her as she sat up this time, but a dull ache that spread into her arms but didn't hit her in the back of the head.

The door had been closed. She hadn't processed the fact that she was in a private room the night before. It seemed odd, especially since her injuries weren't supposed to be that severe.

A quick glance over her hands and arms told her she

wasn't attached to any monitors or IVs or anything. The tray table had been moved over, closer to the wall, and the cup she'd used the night before was gone.

She looked to the other side of the bed and saw that the handset had been replaced. Ashlyn had a vague recollection of dropping it before she'd passed out.

The one thing her scan of the room hadn't revealed was clothes. As she thought back over the night before she tried to remember if she'd seen her clothes in the bathroom, but couldn't recall.

Ashlyn swung her legs over the side of the bed and slid off. The jolt of hitting the floor caused a small ripple of pain to spread up her back but it passed quickly and she made it to the bathroom without reaching for anything to steady her balance.

Other than the standard hospital bathroom essentials, it was empty.

Breaking out of the hospital in a thin gown that was loosely tied in the back didn't strike her as a good idea, and it suddenly occurred to her that she hadn't seen her keys or coat either. All she'd been left with was her watch, wallet and cell phone.

And she'd crashed her car. It wouldn't be waiting for her outside.

Ashlyn hobbled back to the bed and eased herself down. Until a doctor released her or someone from the department showed up, she was trapped.

She reached for her cell phone and flipped it open. As she pulled up the number she grabbed her wallet and took out her calling card, then set it on the table beside the bed. The pain trail deepened as she lifted her feet and twisted her body to lie down on the bed, and she reached for the mattress with her hands to take some of the pressure off her lower back.

Another day of desk duty.

Ashlyn grabbed the handset of the hospital phone and made her call.

"Good morning."

"You sound better."

"Sorry about that." She glanced at her watch again. 9:31. Had it really taken that long to walk to the bathroom and back? She'd have to count herself lucky to get desk duty instead of a day of sick leave. "You busy?"

"I made a few calls after you dropped the phone last night."

She felt her cheeks burn but noticed it didn't hurt as much when she smiled this time. "Sorry."

"Have you noticed how many times you've apologized to me?"

"I'm—" She stopped herself.

"Last night you sounded hesitant. Unsure. I thought maybe it was the painkillers." He was silent for a moment. "What's eating at you?"

Same wording he'd used the night before. She was starting to realize just how appropriate it was.

"You said something about finding copies last night. This is strictly between you and me," Steve said, "but from what I hear, someone's leaked information about the investigation. That's why the newspapers got involved."

"But . . . that doesn't make sense. The task force was formed in response to the media pressure. How would somebody leak information about an investigation before they were assigned to it?" She closed her eyes, the answer hitting her just as she finished asking the question. "Okay, someone who was involved before the task force was created has a big mouth."

"Well, someone's been talking, because it's been splashed all over the front page of the *Sun* today that the task force believes there's a connection to some recent murders in Surrey."

She groaned. "We're pursuing that as a possibility."

"I think you're looking for someone closer to home. One of the officers named Winters was following up on the most promising lead. He'd questioned a trucker who'd been seen talking to Millie Harper just before she disappeared. Turned out the trucker's name had come up when he questioned witnesses who'd reported seeing one of the other girls just before she went missing."

Ashlyn frowned. "That's not in the files."

"Winters was originally partnered with a constable named . . . Tain. For some reason, Sullivan didn't want Tain on the task force. Something about a tip Tain had, about a cross-border smuggling operation. A bust went bad, but Tain didn't want to give it up. This is where it gets hazy. All I know is, Winters was assaulted, and that's when Sullivan finally made Tain part of the team. Winters is on medical leave. And I didn't get that through proper channels, Ashlyn. I made some calls."

Nobody had told Ashlyn what had happened to the man she'd replaced. Now she understood why. She groaned. "All this time he kept leaving me in the office. I thought I was being brushed off."

"Who, Tain?"

"No. He's on my shift, but he's not my partner."

"Now you're wondering if you were being protected."

"Honestly, I . . . I'm so confused. My partner lied to our sergeant."

"And now you have to decide if you're going to get his back or rat him out."

"Thing is, I . . . I tricked him."

There was silence for a moment before Steve asked, "Why would you do that?"

"To get out of the office. To prove I can do more than dial phone numbers and take messages."

"Ashlyn, you can't let these guys rattle you."

"That's easy for you to say."

"If you start off thinking they're against you because you're a woman, you'll be trying so hard to prove yourself you won't have any time left to do your job. And they'll sense it, and only make things harder for you. If you let them know they've got your number they'll keep dialing the phone." Steve paused. "Look, I don't have much time now. What are you going to do about Sullivan?"

Ashlyn bit her lip. "I don't know. All I know is someone's leaking info. You confirmed that yourself. All these guys were involved with at least one of the cases before the task force was started. Even Sullivan. I don't know who to trust."

"Listen to your gut. What's one thing you're certain of?"

"That Nolan's going to take my head off first chance he gets."

"Nolan?"

"Craig Nolan. My partner."

Silence. After a moment, she heard Steve release a deep breath. "He lied to your sergeant?"

She sighed. "I gave him the wrong address for this lead. Sullivan had ordered us to chase it down together, but as soon as the sergeant was gone Nolan told me to stay at the office. I had the info, I'd brought it up at the meeting, and I'd just backed Nolan up on a lead he was following . . ."

"So you felt he owed you, and you were mad that he was leaving you behind."

"Something like that."

"Why'd he lie to your sergeant?"

"I was following up on this tip I got when I hit the deer. Nolan was . . ."—she paused, unsure of whether to mention her doubts about what Nolan was really doing—". . . tracking me down. He found me after I hit the deer."

"And he had to come up with an explanation about why you were in separate vehicles when Sullivan had ordered you to go together."

Ashlyn rubbed her forehead. "When you put it that way, I sound worse."

"Yes, you do."

She squeezed her eyes shut as she groaned. "This is a mess."

"Look, Ashlyn, I can't say much about the rest of your team." He paused. "But I'm glad you're partnered with Nolan."

"There's some stuff I haven't told you."

"It doesn't matter."

Her eyes opened. "You know him."

There was a tiny hesitation. "Yes."

"How well do you know him?"

"I trust him, Ashlyn. I trust him to watch your back."

Ashlyn was silent. She opened her mouth, then thought about what Steve was saying. He was a fair person, and he believed in second chances. Trusting someone, and not just to do the job but to look after an officer you'd mentored, wasn't a small thing.

"Look, I know it's probably been harder than you've let on. You've just got to trust yourself, Ashlyn. If you don't trust yourself to do the job, how can you expect them to trust you on the street?"

She looked up as the door opened. "My partner's here," she said. "I have to get back to the office."

"Okay. Take care of yourself."

"Thank you, Sergeant."

She would have sworn she could hear Steve smiling at her words as he said good-bye. Knowing she was trying to make it sound like she'd been on an important call.

Making it sound like she had connections to people who outranked her partner.

Nolan stopped right inside the door. "You aren't dressed."

"I couldn't find my clothes."

"I figured if we left them in sight, you'd be out of here at the crack of dawn. They're under the bed."

Ashlyn felt her cheeks burn as she got up and bent over. Everything had been folded into a neat pile and set in a plastic bag, except her jacket and shirt. There was another bag with a T-shirt and a sweater inside, tags attached. She grabbed it and straightened.

Nolan had turned to face the door. When she returned

from the bathroom she said, "It's okay. I'm decent." As he turned she added, "Or at least as decent as I can be in this thing."

She held out her arms and winced. The sweater someone had purchased was about three sizes too big.

"They had to, uh, cut your coat and shirt. I didn't know your size."

Ashlyn thought back to the night before, the feeling of a line of fire being drawn across her arm. There was a bandage, so she guessed it had been cut, but nobody had said anything about stitches. About the need for surgery.

Nolan turned and opened the door and she grabbed her wallet, watch and cell phone off the nightstand and walked to the door.

For a second she wasn't sure if she should let him hold it for her, then decided not to argue. Nolan stepped into the hallway after her, but when she continued down the hall she realized he wasn't behind her. He'd turned the other way.

She could make out the sound of words, but they were muffled by the footsteps and rumble of cart wheels as orderlies brought food to some of the rooms. Ashlyn tried to filter out the sounds as she turned and focused on Nolan's back.

Beyond him, she could see enough to recognize Constable Getz and one of the uniformed officers she had only a little bit of contact with when she was searching for files, Getz's partner, Melissa Keith. Another recent transfer, Keith was a platinum blonde who looked to be about the same age as Ashlyn. Something about the way the woman stood, her expression as she responded to Nolan, and the look Getz gave her told Ashlyn that Keith was in charge.

Not wholly surprising, as Getz had deferred to Nolan without question at the scene in the woods.

She thought about what Steve had said, that if she

didn't trust herself the team would pick up on it, and they wouldn't be able to trust her. Somewhere between being manhandled by Tain and being ditched by Nolan she'd let them get to her, and she'd lost sight of her strengths, and nobody she didn't know already was going to express a confidence in her that she didn't have herself.

Worse than that, nobody would risk their life working with someone who lacked confidence but felt they had something to prove.

Nolan was walking back toward her with a bag in his hand when he looked up and saw her watching him. She looked past him, to the backs of the officers retreating down the hall. "Has something happened?"

"What makes you think that?"

She straightened up to her full height. "Why were there two uniformed officers outside my hospital room?"

Nolan paused. "I was just passing on a message from Sergeant Sullivan. Here." He passed her the new bag. "Sullivan sent you a jacket." Nolan walked down the hall at a brisk pace, forcing her to keep up with him. "I'm surprised he didn't mention it when you were on the phone."

"I wasn't talking to Sullivan," Ashlyn said. She dropped her wallet and keys and phone into the bag and pulled out the jacket, cringing as she slipped her arms into it.

She looked down. Big enough to conceal the sweater.

Nolan slowed as he turned to look at her. "Is there another sergeant involved with this team that I don't know about?"

She felt her chin stick out as she stared straight ahead and kept walking. Nolan grabbed her arm and she stopped and turned and looked at his hand. He let go and held it up apologetically.

"My phone call is none of your business." Ashlyn turned on her heel and started walking again.

"The hell it isn't. If you know something about this case, I expect you to tell me."

"You aren't my boss, Nolan. Just because you have control issues doesn't mean I have to run when you snap your fingers. I'm not your servant."

"You're my partner."

"A fact that's finally convenient for you." Ashlyn pushed the door open and walked outside. She realized she had no idea where she was going, so she turned to face him. "You've been shutting me out since day one. You want me to treat you like a partner, fine. You first."

Nolan stared at her for a moment, then nodded toward the parking lot. "This way."

They walked to his Rodeo in silence. It wasn't until she recognized the turn for the station and he drove past it that she spoke.

"Where are we going?"

"Mrs. Wilson's."

The exchange with Nolan and Sullivan in her hospital room was still blurred around the edges, but she remembered most of it. "I figured you'd go out there last night."

"I told Sullivan I'd like to wait so you could go with me, if possible." He flipped the signal light on and slowed as he approached the intersection, then turned left. "That was before you regained consciousness."

They drifted back to silence. Nolan's attitude, his willingness to play nice when he wanted something, his presence at the Johnson property, his lie to Sergeant Sullivan . . . All of it collided with Steve's words on the phone.

Nolan was finally taking her out on the street, but it occurred to her that the move came after she'd gone off on her own. You keep your friends close and your enemies closer.

She realized she'd wanted to trust Nolan from the beginning. She wanted to trust someone, and Tain wasn't easy to warm up to. He was a sexist jerk in public and a thousand miles removed in private. Steve had given her an excuse to make the leap with Nolan, but it had come after there were enough factors in play to muddy the waters.

When they got to Mrs. Wilson's property, Nolan reached in front of her and opened the glove compartment. "Your gun. I didn't want to risk leaving it in the hospital. Sullivan told me to lock it up back at the station . . ." He let the words hang as she took the holster wordlessly.

Should she feel better or worse about the fact that he'd ignored an order but wanted her to be armed before going to talk to a potential witness?

She reached for the door handle, then stopped. Nolan was already out of the vehicle but hadn't closed the door.

"Ashlyn?"

She lifted her head and looked at him. "Was Tain out here yesterday?"

Nolan frowned. "No. At least, not that I saw."

Ashlyn pushed the door open and stepped out. Mrs. Wilson's house looked much the same as it had the day before, a sense of quiet lingering over it as they approached the front door. There was a cooler breeze blowing and as Ashlyn turned to look back at the road, she realized one thing that was different.

No truck.

In the distance she heard a thud followed by another thud. They weren't at regular intervals, and she couldn't place the sound, but it wasn't coming from inside the house.

"It doesn't sound like anyone's home," Nolan said.

She put her finger on what she'd noticed the day before when she'd stood there. The total absence of a hum. Like there wasn't a single appliance wasting electricity in the whole house.

"What do you think?" Nolan asked her.

"The house was this quiet when I was here yesterday, but I talked to Mrs. Wilson out back." She started to walk toward the side of the building.

"You were here?"

She stopped and glanced over her shoulder. "Yes."

"You already talked to Mrs. Wilson? Then what were you doing coming back?"

She turned to fully face him. "I had a few more questions."

Nolan closed the gap between them and stood right in front of her. "Why did you ask if Tain had been here? What did she tell you?"

The flash of the truck going past her on the road, something about it familiar . . .

"Look, Nolan, I don't remember everything. Some of it's jumbled. She didn't really give me a lot to go on, and I . . . I remember thinking you were going to kick my ass if I had to admit I'd misled you about the tip so that I could get to the witness first, especially if I came back to the station empty-handed." She felt the warmth in her cheeks and wasn't sure if he believed her or not, but she didn't lift her gaze from the ground. No matter what Steve said, Ashlyn wasn't ready to confront Nolan about being at the Johnson property the day before.

"You know where you're going. Lead the way."

Ashlyn glanced at his face as she turned around, but he wasn't looking at her, and she couldn't read his expression. She walked around the side of the house to the back. There was no sign of Mrs. Wilson, but the screen door for the rear entrance was clapping against the side of the house, so Ashlyn walked up onto the porch to latch it properly. The door to the house wasn't fully closed, so she pulled it shut first.

Nolan was scanning the overgrown garden, fields and woods.

"She's got about a half mile in that direction alone, and you can see how far back the property line is. I'm not sure how far it goes in that direction." Ashlyn pointed to the other side of the Wilson property, in the opposite direction of the Johnson home.

"So she could be anywhere." Nolan looked at her. "What does your gut tell you?"

A trick question? A test? Ashlyn shook those thoughts off. "The greenhouse."

"Is that where you found her yesterday?"

Ashlyn shook her head. "No. Truth is, she found me. I was looking around. One minute the yard was empty, next thing I knew she was standing there"—she nodded at the spot where Mrs. Wilson had appeared the day before—"watching me."

The left side of Nolan's mouth curved up in a half smile. "Not exactly a comforting thought, is it?"

"If you're going to follow that with a lecture about why we take backup with us, you just remember you were headed out here alone too."

"Hey, I've seen Mrs. Wilson. I just meant she's not exactly the cuddly grandma-baking-cookies type, is she?"

Ashlyn flushed. "No, she isn't."

They walked around the other side of the house. The greenhouse was at the end of the garden, and the open door banged against the side of the structure.

"You know, Mrs. Wilson never struck me as careless," Nolan said as he glanced at her. Ashlyn shook her head and found herself reaching around behind her for her gun at the same moment Nolan started reaching for his.

They approached the doorway, him on the left side, her on the right. The view into the structure told her nobody was standing. It was still possible someone was crouched down beside one of the tables. Through the building she could see an open doorway on the other side.

It was one of the worst possible structures to deal with. Go through it, and be an exposed target for anyone outside. Go around it and risk anyone inside getting out the other exit.

Ashlyn scanned the property, thought again about

the truck she'd seen the day before, possibly the same truck that had gone past her on the road later that night, then stepped inside the greenhouse. She moved forward in slow steps, cautiously surveying the floor to her left and then to her right. Mrs. Wilson was nothing if not meticulous. Although her garden outside was somewhat overgrown, all the plants inside the structure were in neat rows, carefully marked. There was no evidence of disarray. The tools hung on hooks mounted on the tables, and underneath the work areas there were plastic totes, all stacked in neat rows. Ashlyn was aware of Nolan moving behind her but not relying on him to cover any of the ground for her. If someone had been at the property looking for Mrs. Wilson, there was one thing Ashlyn was already certain of.

They weren't there now.

A plant had been dropped on the floor about two-thirds of the way through the greenhouse, just to Ashlyn's right. Dirt was scattered over the side of the table above, and spilled onto the ground below, the planter half empty and the small green sprout lying on its side, half buried by the soil. She nodded in its direction.

As she approached the rear exit with Nolan right behind her, she exhaled. "It's clear."

"Bit premature to say that, don't you think?"

Ashlyn turned to glance at him. "There was a truck parked outside the property yesterday."

"You think someone was here while you were questioning Mrs. Wilson?"

She considered that. "No. She didn't give me much, but it wasn't like someone was telling her to get rid of me or trying to keep her quiet. It was more like being difficult just came naturally to her."

Nolan smirked as he turned to look out the door, and the grin slipped from his face. Ashlyn turned. She couldn't see anything because the open door was blocking her view so she stepped outside.

The way Mrs. Wilson's short hair blew in the cold wind was what stood out. Mrs. Wilson must have set her hair in rollers every night, because when Ashlyn had seen her the day before the white locks had been in tight curls. Now, they were wisps of strawlike hair that fluttered against the grass around her body. She was facedown, one hand reaching above her head as though she'd tried to crawl away.

Nolan took another look around before he crouched down. "Shot in the back."

One minute Mrs. Wilson had been working in her greenhouse, tending to her plants. The next she'd been fleeing out the back door, running for her life.

Only to trip and fall and be shot in the back and left to die in the dirt.

The murmur of words seemed distant, like it was coming from far away and it wasn't until she looked up that she realized Nolan was talking on his cell phone. His gaze was fixed on her.

She walked over and crouched down on the other side of Mrs. Wilson's body as he closed the phone.

"A team's on its way."

She nodded. They lapsed into silence, neither proceeding with an examination of the body or search of the area. If Nolan was tempted to have answers ready for the team when they arrived, he didn't let on. Every second of the approaching hum of vehicles, engines turning off, doors opening and closing, gravel crunching beneath the feet of the officers approaching—it all imprinted itself on her brain as she squatted beside the body of a woman she'd spoken to the day before.

Ashlyn looked up as Nolan stood. Sullivan was approaching them. He paused as he surveyed the body, then looked at Nolan. "Is this connected?"

Nolan looked at Ashlyn, then turned back to the sergeant. "Hart was here yesterday. She'd already talked to Mrs. Wilson. She left"—he glanced at her again—"to follow up on something, and was on her way back with more questions."

Sullivan's eyes narrowed. "And where were you?"

A bit of color crept into Nolan's cheeks. "Following up on another lead."

"You let a . . ." Sullivan looked at Ashlyn and stopped himself. He turned back to Nolan. "Get her back to the station and take her statement."

"But, sir, don't you think we'd be more useful here?"

"In case you didn't notice when you first joined the RCMP, this isn't a debate club."

"I'm sorry sir, it's just . . ." Nolan paused, but didn't look down at her, although she noticed his shoulders drop just a touch. "She doesn't remember everything."

Sullivan's eyes widened, and he spoke with a forcefulness Ashlyn hadn't witnessed from him since her transfer. "Then let's at least try not to contaminate her memory with anything we turn up here during the search."

She followed Nolan to the Rodeo without argument, and they drove back to the station. It wasn't until they walked into the office that someone spoke.

"Well, well. If you'd stuck to answering phones and filing papers, you wouldn't have had the chance to try the local hospital cuisine."

Nolan stepped in front of her. "Shut up, Tain."

"Touchy, Nolan. You getting a bit fond of your new partner? Must have been really hard to spend the night without her."

Ashlyn caught Nolan's arm as he pulled it back. It took all her strength to hold it until some of the rage faded and the force of his pull waned, and she felt the strain on her muscles, the burning bite in her own arm beneath the bandages that remained. "He's not worth it," she said as she let go of Nolan and walked to her desk. As she sat down, she caught Tain watching her.

He grinned and walked out.

Nolan's face was still red as he yanked his chair out from his desk and sat down. He pulled his coat off, reached for papers on his desk, then slammed his hand down instead. "Don't you ever get tired of it?"

"What? Being harassed by him or excluded by you?" Nolan's face cooled a touch at her words, and she almost regretted them. She drew a breath. "Look, if you let them know they've got your number they'll keep dialing the phone."

"Sounds like something my father said once."

"Well, it's something my mentor reminded me of when we talked this morning."

"Ah, so that's who you were talking to." Nolan nodded. "Makes sense."

Part of her wished she'd held that back. "And I told him more about what I remember than I've told you."

Nolan wasn't settling down to look through his messages. An energy was still coursing through him, evident since he'd exchanged words with Tain, and his head snapped up at her words. "Constable Hart, a woman has been murdered."

She sat locked in a stare with him, willing herself to show that she wouldn't be pushed around. He blinked and his eyes softened for a second, a small enough measurement of time to make her doubt what she thought she'd seen but long enough for her to falter in her own stance. Part of her felt guilty for not taking the leap and trusting him, but there was a spark of anger still smoldering within her over how Nolan had treated her and tried to play her just the day before.

He had to yield something first.

Tain marched into the room, his pace slowing when he glanced at Ashlyn and then Nolan. Ashlyn broke the stare with Nolan and looked down at the desk as Tain muttered, "Get a room already."

Nolan was on his feet before Ashlyn had fully lifted her head, his chair clanging to the floor as he shoved

Tain against the wall. "If you were anyone else, you'd never get away with your bullshit."

"But I'm not anyone else." Tain smirked. "Must be hittin' pretty close to the truth to get you so worked up, Nolan. Your daddy may be a sergeant, but that rank isn't high enough to protect you from an assault charge."

"You sonofa—"

Ashlyn was on her feet and between them before Nolan could finish. She held his arm back again, her muscles burning in protest of the strain. "What the hell is wrong with you?"

Nolan blinked as he squeezed his fists, his mouth drawn into a hard line. He took a step back, turned on his heel and marched out of the room.

"It's really so sweet that you've got his back," Tain said as Ashlyn turned around. "Or is it that he's got yours?"

Ashlyn felt the sting of skin against skin when her hand struck his face. She stepped back and glared at Tain, and thought of the look she'd seen in Nolan's eyes. It was a rage that didn't just border on hatred but sailed right across the line. Nolan was convinced Tain had been bumped in because of the color of his skin, and Tain believed Nolan was being carried by his sergeant father. Ashlyn thought about what Steve Daly had said to her hours before. Of course, it made sense. Steve would trust the son of a sergeant, especially if he knew him. She thought of how Steve had reacted when she'd said Nolan's name and almost couldn't blame Tain for his assumptions.

None of it excused the level of animosity that had been allowed to build between them, but the blame for that lay at Sullivan's feet. She'd seen enough herself to know that he seemed to give Tain a lot of latitude, despite not appearing to like him, and Sullivan worked closely with Nolan and gave him leadership opportunities.

A fact that probably only served to reinforce Tain's

dislike of Nolan, but none of it excused Tain's behavior. She looked Tain straight in the eye. "You're supposed to be an RCMP officer. Show up and do your job, and leave your attitude, your cheap shots and your inferiority complex at the door."

Tain had a way of looking stone cold and immovable at times, with a depth to his gaze that could make you feel like he could read your mind. She'd felt uncomfortable when he stared at her that way before, but he was sporting a grin that he seemed to be trying to rein in, a grin that was suppressing a laugh. His eyes twinkled with an almost good-natured amusement.

"What's so funny?"

"You slapped me."

"If I'd known you'd find it so funny I would have smacked you a long time ago."

"You found your backbone." The smile on his face disappeared, replaced by a solemn look. "Maybe almost getting killed was a good thing for you. It didn't work out so well for Winters." He straightened up to his full height and looked down at her. "I heard you found Mrs. Wilson's body today."

She looked up at him but didn't speak. He took a step closer, drew a breath as he glanced over his shoulder toward the door and then turned back to her. "You better watch your back, Hart. The only person on this team you know you can trust is yourself."

"Like I hadn't figured that out already," she muttered. She walked over to her desk and stood looking down at messages and paperwork, trying to find something to focus on.

He moved toward her and touched her arm softly. "I mean it."

She stared up at him. He hadn't even appeared to respect her as a person, hadn't given her a chance to prove herself as an officer and didn't seem to give a second thought to making crass comments and alienating everyone around him, and yet there he was, reaching out to her, cautioning her.

Acting like he cared.

"You almost sound concerned, Tain. I'm touched."

The sarcasm saturated every syllable, and for a split second she thought she saw the same look in Tain's eyes that she'd seen in Nolan's, a softening that hinted at a crack in the armor, at a heart that pumped blood instead of ice water.

Was it possible they blamed each other for what had happened to Winters and that they'd both thought that by pushing her away and leaving her behind she'd be safe? Or was it what Steve had suggested, that they didn't trust her because she didn't fully trust herself?

The approaching footsteps stopped abruptly and they both turned to see Nolan standing just inside the room. His jaw muscles tightened as he looked at Tain first, then Ashlyn, then focused on returning to his desk and grabbing his jacket.

"They've found another body."

"She stays," Tain said. All the edge was gone from his voice. "I'll go with you."

Nolan's head jerked up as he leveled Tain with a look. "She's my partner. She's going."

"Would you two stop talking about me like I'm not even here?" Ashlyn grabbed her jacket. "We'll all go," she said as she reached behind her head to straighten her collar. Tain hadn't moved, and neither had Nolan. "Is that a problem?" she asked him.

His only response was to snatch his keys off his desk, turn and walk out the door.

Nolan's hands gripped the steering wheel with visible force, and he stared straight ahead, not uttering a word, his face as dark as the thick clouds gathering in the sky.

Ashlyn didn't need to ask. The weather could turn fast in the mountains, and it was late enough in the year that clouds could just as easily mean snow as rain.

Snow that could hamper their efforts to search the woods for more bodies. Tain had organized search parties, and they'd been out every day, but so far hadn't turned up anything.

Tain was silent as well, a stillness about him that stood out in stark contrast to how he'd carried himself since she'd met him. He wasn't relaxed, but he was controlled, his hand resting on the door handle, his eyes focused ahead of him. Waves of hostility rippled off Nolan, but it was as though the surge rebounded off Tain and swept back to the point of origin, Nolan's grip on the steering wheel tightening, the color in the back of his neck darkening as the drive progressed.

Whatever tension Tain carried, he was in control of it. Nolan's anger owned him.

Ashlyn sat in the back, at her own insistence, feeling every second of the drive.

The gaps between buildings grew, and then Nolan turned off down a road that seemed to head straight into the woods.

"I thought the body was found in a Dumpster."

"That's right." Nolan sounded like his teeth were clenched.

"I'm not doubting you." Except she was. Nolan's inability to control his emotions, his obvious anger and frustration about things she'd been kept in the dark on, since day one.

When Nolan made another right turn she understood. The town dump, obviously, the landfill consuming the gaps where the trees had been cleared. The reduce, reuse, recycle mantra hadn't eliminated these eyesores or prevented their expansion, and wherever possible large communities shipped their trash north to the wilderness. Out of sight, out of mind.

"How'd this come in?" Ashlyn asked.

"Anonymous 911 call."

She felt an eyebrow rise. This was a dump where locals could still drop bags unchecked, something Ashlyn hadn't thought existed anymore. Nolan drove up a hill until they were level with the tops of three Dumpsters, a sign between the farthest one and the middle one detailing what people were and were not allowed to dispose of, the "No Appliances" line sprayed through with red, an old fridge left teetering on the edge of the hill above the Dumpster behind the sign.

As soon as Nolan put the Rodeo in park, Ashlyn got out and surveyed the Dumpsters.

The body lay facedown in the garbage in the middle one. The tip of a blade protruded from the middle of her back, a circle of red surrounding the metal. An old-fashioned white nightgown stretched down to her ankles and her arms were spread out from her sides, so that her body formed the shape of a cross. There was a rigidity to the limbs, something artificial about the way they lay on the refuse, the sharp right angles betraying the fact that the body had not simply been shoved over the side or tossed in with the trash. She had been placed in the partially filled Dumpster deliberately.

Carefully.

The manner of display as important as the method of death.

"She's been posed," Ashlyn said.

Tain was beside her. "Like Mary Donard."

"But Donard was partially wrapped, wasn't she?"

"Other than the fact that Donard was faceup, it's the same pose, and Donard had a similar nightgown on under the wrappings."

"That's not the only thing that was different with Donard," Ashlyn said.

Tain looked at her. "The scene has to be processed before we'll know what's different, and what isn't."

"Almost everyone we have is tied up with Mrs. Wilson," Nolan said. "This case snowballed so fast we're stretched thin. Sullivan might need to bring in more help."

Tain glared at him. "Let's hope not."

"Come off it, Tain. With Winters gone, it's down to five men."

"Not counting Sullivan, or any man in uniform."

"Or any woman," Ashlyn said. "Look, this isn't helping. We need to process this scene before the weather turns. That's what we brought our own gear for, right?" Ashlyn turned back to the Rodeo and walked around to the back of the vehicle. Nolan followed and helped her remove the supplies she'd insisted they take the time to pack before leaving the station.

They eased themselves into the Dumpster. Tain and Ashlyn started from the corners and worked their way in, bagging and tagging as they went, photographing items of interest. Nolan worked from the center. When a body lay on the ground it was often easy to start with the victim and work out from there, but in a Dumpster, making a move for the center where the body lay could mean disrupting crucial evidence. Someone had disposed of this girl's body. They'd taken the time to lay her in a very specific way.

Whoever it was, they'd been inside that Dumpster, only hours before, and with a little luck and careful processing, the constables would discover that a body wasn't the only thing the killer had left behind.

"We aren't going to make it," Nolan said after an hour of slow wading through trash. "I just felt a raindrop."

"Was that a tent in the back of your Rodeo?" Ashlyn asked as she rolled her left shoulder and fought the urge to reach behind her and rub her neck. She couldn't risk removing the work gloves that protected her hands, and considering what she'd been forced to sift through, she didn't want to touch her skin with the gloves still on. "Can we use a canopy to cover the scene?"

Nolan turned back to the edge of the bin and gripped it with his hands, then pushed himself up. When he got to the top he removed the coveralls and disappeared.

She could make out the sound of the spare-tire holder clicking into place, the window opening, the back tailgate dropping down, and a thud that could be Nolan partially climbing into the back to reach something. Then the tailgate slammed shut, followed by the window, and the tire holder clanked as it snapped back into its other locked position.

Instead of Nolan reappearing at the side of the Dumpster, the sound of another door opening and closing and hum of an engine filled the silence.

"I just felt a drop," Ashlyn said as gravel crunched with the Rodeo moving away from them.

Tain frowned. "What the hell is he do—"

More gravel crunched as the hum grew louder, and where Ashlyn had originally expected to see Nolan brake lights appeared instead.

The lights faded, and the hum of the engine died. Another door slam and Nolan appeared at the side of the Rodeo.

"Use the signpost for one end, and we can tether the other corner to the vehicle. Turns out I had a tarp in there I hadn't opened yet."

Nolan worked the upper corners while he tossed rope and the other ends of the canvas to Tain and Ashlyn. They both inched their way through the Dumpster, trying to avoid sharp metal or glass or a puncture from a discarded needle or God knew what that had been discarded there.

Ashlyn was just glad the Dumpster wasn't completely full. Not only did it mean she wasn't up to her neck in trash, it meant she could work her way along the edge without disrupting all the potential evidence she had yet to look through.

Not to mention the obvious fact that it was making the process of sifting refuse less time consuming than it might otherwise have been.

Ashlyn had just finished tethering the rope to the corner of the Dumpster when the tap-tap of rain began beating against the tarp. The first few tentative drops gave way to the rhythmic drumming of the rain falling against the covering.

Nolan had replaced his coveralls and returned to the Dumpster, and Ashlyn turned to find him approximately where she'd been before moving to secure the covering.

"I've worked my way through everything up to the body from that side," he said.

"Should we call Sullivan?" she asked.

"Done. When I was moving the vehicle."

Ashlyn nodded. Across the Dumpster she could see Tain's furrowed brow, and even in the growing darkness she could tell there was a shadow behind his eyes.

Nolan didn't want to be the first to assess the body.

The distant hum of engines broke the stillness and she listened as she opened the next bag of trash and began going through the contents. Within a few minutes she'd tossed the bag behind her and moved on to the next one, just as the sound of crunching gravel grew closer and a flash of lights cut through the thick gray that shrouded them.

A door slammed shut and the silhouette of a man appeared in the headlights beside Nolan's Rodeo.

"Jesus."

Ashlyn glanced at Nolan as the figure above the Dumpster disappeared. More doors slammed, but the hum of that engine and glow of the lights remained.

Sullivan returned wearing coveralls and the steel-toe work boots that were best for Dumpster diving. He slid in along the edge near the center, where Nolan had already cataloged potential evidence.

"We've covered that area already," Nolan said. "We haven't touched the body."

Their sergeant looked at them for a moment. Since he was backlit, Ashlyn wasn't sure if she could really see his eyes narrow, or if she imagined the reaction.

"I called the coroner's office earlier. They already sent someone down because of Mrs. Wilson." He remained near the side of the Dumpster, still as stone, staring at the body.

"I didn't realize they'd gone back after the first bodies were found."

"It's not like they've got a field office here," Sullivan said. "The back and forth is slowing things down."

In the time since their arrival, there had been many questions going through Ashlyn's mind. As much as she'd tried to focus on the tasks in front of her and not consider what they might still find, she'd felt the anticipation building.

She didn't want to know, but she needed to know.

Something about the whole case didn't sit right. What was it Tain had said earlier, about Winters?

Why had he tried to leave her behind?

Why had he warned her not to trust anyone?

The longer she stood in the Dumpster, the more she felt the stiffness in her neck, the pinch in her shoulders protesting prolonged use.

She pushed her way through the trash bags that had already been sifted, which were stacked behind Nolan, and waded through the scattered debris that remained between Sullivan and the girl. Nolan had said he'd already processed everything, and she remembered seeing him right beside the body.

He hadn't removed the last few bags when he'd finished, but left them in place. Ashlyn might have believed that he wanted to help clear the Dumpster as quickly as possible in the hopes that the coroner would be present to assess the body before they had to move her, but his unwillingness to move those bags suggested that wasn't the reason he hadn't started assessing their victim.

Nolan was unable to face what they all feared they'd find.

Ashlyn pushed the questions from the forefront of

her thoughts and reached for the bags. She pulled one out of the way, followed by another and another, and after a fourth bag was moved, only the extended left arm remained propped up by piles of rubbish.

She had a clear view of their victim's body from the side, and with the garbage removed, a second body was exposed. Ashlyn fought the urge to wrap her arms around herself, her spine quivering as though a bucket of ice water had been poured down her back. Despite the chill, it was a sharp intake of breath beside her that made her jump. As she blinked, she looked up at Tain, his gaze fixed on the body of the baby that had originally been concealed by its mother.

CHAPTER TWENTY-SIX

Eighteen months ago

As Ashlyn watched Constable Melissa Keith, she felt like slipping back into the hallway and waiting until later to approach her. Keith's easy banter with Getz and the other uniformed officers and her infectious laugh had a way of making Ashlyn feel like she was back in junior high, in her awkward ugly duckling phase, when she had feet three sizes too big for her body, felt like everyone was staring at her, and second-guessed her every word.

A few weeks earlier, Ashlyn couldn't have imagined feeling so insecure, but she'd let the indifference of Oliver and Aiken, the resentment of Campbell and the tension with Tain and Nolan get the better of her.

She took a deep breath, drew herself up to her full height and approached the group of officers.

"Constable Keith, do you have a moment?" she asked.

Keith's wide smile didn't fade as she nodded and started walking out of the room, into the hall. Ashlyn offered Getz and the others a small smile before following Keith.

"I've been trying to track down the missing-persons reports—" Ashlyn began.

"All we can find are reports for younger children, men, and women over thirty. The other ones are missing," Keith said.

"Like someone went through the folders and took out all the teenage girls and younger women who could be considered potential victims." Ashlyn frowned. "I can't even get a handle on how they came up with the list of eleven we're investigating."

"That I can help you with," Keith said. "A few weeks before the task force was assembled, Constable Tain compiled a list."

Ashlyn felt her eyes widen. "You mean, Tain's the last person we know of who had access to all the files?"

Keith hesitated, her smile now completely gone. "No, I know the task force started going through them, and Tain wasn't even originally assigned to the group. Tain had been partnered with Winters, but when Winters was put on the team, Tain was left on regular rotation. Nolan was part of the task force before he was." She stopped talking abruptly.

"What aren't you telling me?"

"The day Winters got attacked? It was Nolan's first day. Sullivan reassigned Tain after Winters was hospitalized, and then Tain started looking for those files. It seems that between the time he made the list and the time he was reassigned, they went missing."

Ashlyn considered that. "Why did Tain make the list if he wasn't originally part of the task force?"

Keith shrugged. "All I know is that Tain had a tip, something about cross-border smuggling. He was trying to find a break in the case. They tried for a bust, and it went bad. Before that, he'd asked me to gather the missing-persons files for him, but that was before there was a task force. I just assumed Sullivan had him do it. Nobody really knew what he was working on, except Winters."

"So Tain took the list to Sullivan?"

Keith shook her head. "The names came from the local paper. An anonymous tip from someone close to the investigation."

"Did you tell Sullivan that Tain had made the list?"

She glanced over her shoulder, then leaned closer and lowered her voice. "Look . . . maybe I shouldn't have said he made the list. I think he did. But he never told me why he wanted the files or what he was doing with them."

"You sounded pretty confident a minute ago."

"I went by his desk and he had them stacked with a piece of paper on top. Ten names. When he came in, I asked if he wanted me to put the files back or if he wanted to see the new ones that had come in. He told me to get lost." Keith hesitated. "I'm sure it's the same list, but if you ask me, it's not Tain's style to talk to reporters."

Which raised the question of how someone had taken Tain's list and fed it to the press.

"Look, I know you're pretty new to the area, but you've been on the streets more than I have. What can you tell me about Bobby Hobbs and Eddie Campbell?"

Melissa Keith gave her an *Oh my God* look and her upper lip curled. "Hobbs thinks the world of himself. Most nights of the week you can find him out at The Goldmine. Find a pair of tight jeans and a low-cut shirt and you'll have the displeasure of meeting him inside of five minutes."

"What about Eddie?"

"He's there sometimes, too. If Bobby gets lucky, he ditches Eddie."

"Eddie not much of a ladies' man?"

"When I first came to town, I thought it would be good

to get to know people, know who hung out where. I wanted to have a feel for the place."

Ashlyn nodded. It made sense. It was something she hadn't had a chance to do herself.

"Bobby and Eddie were sitting together, drinking. Bobby started hitting on me, and he wouldn't take no for an answer. I was about to pull out my badge when Eddie came over and told him to lay off.

"It didn't really fit with what I'd heard. Everyone had always told me that Bobby was the leader and Eddie did whatever he was told."

"Maybe they had it backwards."

"No." Melissa shook her head. "I've had my share of run-ins with the two of them since, and it wasn't the first time I'd seen them together. Bobby usually calls the shots, but that night, Eddie stepped up."

"Why?"

"It wasn't chivalry, if that's what you're thinking. Bobby had a few choice words for me and took off. For a minute, Eddie stood there, staring at me. I said thanks, and he still didn't say anything. You know the look a guy gives you, when he's undressing you with your eyes? It was like that, only creepier."

"So Eddie's lacking social skills?"

"Which fits with what everyone says, about Bobby being the leader and Eddie just following him around and doing what he's told." Melissa frowned. "But that night? Eddie just stood there, staring at me. Eddie sat down, uninvited. And he told me a story that put chills down my spine.

"According to some old Native legend, there was a woman stealing children from the tribes. She would make them eat from her food, and once they did, they grew a root that went into the ground and chained them there forever."

"Was it a white woman?" Ashlyn asked.

"Funny, I thought that might be the punch line too.

Some way for Eddie to tell me I'm evil or to remind me of all the bad things that we've done to his people for hundreds of years. Don't get me wrong. Our ancestors left us with a lot of things to answer for."

Ashlyn nodded. She didn't want to get sidetracked with a discussion about the history of the mistreatment of the First Nations population. The problem was, there was no way to really make restitution for all the sins committed, and the crimes that were on her mind were current ones. Land claims and reparations were for the lawyers and politicians. She wanted to find out who was abducting and murdering these young girls.

"One of the children cut off the root, and when she did she was able to run home and lead the people to the old woman's home. They rescued the children, but when they cut their roots, they got sick. They were in terrible pain and cried and begged for their lives to end, and after several days they died.

"The only one who didn't get sick and die was the girl who'd cut her own root."

Ashlyn had heard the legend about the stolen children and the roots, but she'd never heard that ending. "Are you sure he wasn't making up a crazy story just to have some fun at your expense?"

Melissa shrugged. "Anything's possible. It wasn't what he said. It was how he said it." She let out a breath and folded her arms across her chest. "When he'd finished telling me that part of the story he leaned in real close to me and didn't blink. All he said was that it would have been better if their mothers had stabbed them through the heart themselves."

Ashlyn felt a chill run down her spine. Melissa didn't know all of the crime-scene details from the bodies they'd recovered, so she had no way of realizing just how creepy Eddie's comment was. "Is there a psych file on this guy?"

"If there isn't, there should be, but if you want more

info, you should talk to Tain. The smuggling operation he was going after? Word was Hobbs was at the center of it."

"Really?" Ashlyn started to turn, then stopped. "Any chance you can follow up on that 911 call that came in?"

"The one that reported your accident?" Keith asked.

"No, the one about the body . . ." Ashlyn stopped. "What do you mean, reported my accident?"

"The call came in after Nolan had found you, so we were already on our way. A 911 call reporting that someone had shot at a vehicle being driven by an RCMP officer, and she was injured." Keith frowned. "You mean you didn't know?"

Ashlyn shook her head. "Nobody told me."

Keith leaned closer and lowered her voice. "Well, you didn't hear it from me, but they pulled a bullet out of your dashboard. I can't believe they didn't tell you. I mean, after what happened to Winters . . ."

Ashlyn nodded, but it was an automatic action, and she went through the motions of thanking Constable Keith and walking back down the hall. She stopped at her desk long enough to perform a few quick web searches. After Mrs. Wilson's murder, she'd looked up photos of Bobby Hobbs and Eddie Campbell, and made a note that at some point they should be questioned about Jenny Johnson.

After all, if they'd hung out with her all the time, wasn't it possible they knew something about her disappearance? Jenny's mother hadn't been too attentive. The fact that she'd waited several weeks to report her daughter missing proved that.

What Ashlyn didn't understand was why none of the local cops had talked to Bobby or Eddie. If they knew everybody, they knew who Jenny's friends were, but there was no evidence that anyone other than Winters had tried to follow up.

And as she'd learned from Steve already, some of what Winters had reportedly learned had been left out of the files.

Why?

The answers would have to wait. At some point adrenaline alone wasn't enough to fend off the fatigue, and over the past few days the entire team had hit the wall. The Surrey lead had stalled, and with the discovery of more bodies, they'd been unable to follow up on Nolan's lead. Campbell had been surlier than usual, and everyone was on edge.

It was only seven o'clock, but Sullivan had all but thrown her from the building himself. Everyone had been ordered to take time off. She wasn't expected back for thirty-six hours.

Since they'd discovered the body in the Dumpster and identified her as Wendy George, Ashlyn had been combing through the autopsy reports and information collected from the coroner while trying to stay on top of the tips that continued to pour in.

Tain had spent the past few days searching the woods.

With Tain and Nolan out of the office most of the time and the second shift investigating the murder of Mrs. Wilson, Ashlyn hadn't been confronted with the tension within the team for a few days. For all the hours they'd put in, they didn't seem to be making any headway with the investigation.

The day before Nolan had sat at his desk and started asking her about the reports and the tips.

"I can make some calls, split things up so we can get through them faster," he offered.

She'd accepted the olive branch readily and handed him a stack of slips, but Sullivan had entered the room two minutes later. Nolan had held up a finger while he was on the phone, and kept the sergeant waiting until he'd finished writing down the details of his call.

"My office. I have something you need to handle," Sullivan had said as soon as Nolan had hung up.

Nolan had flashed her an apologetic smile, set the messages on his desk and told her to leave them. Before he left he'd said, "If I get back before you're done, I'll go through them."

He hadn't. She wasn't surprised, but she wasn't annoyed either. Just the act of offering to work with her helped dispel any doubts that had surfaced in the few days since he'd argued to take her to the Dumpster. She didn't question that it wasn't his choice to leave her in office this time, but rather Sullivan's.

When Nolan had returned, he'd been apologetic. "Sorry. Where are we at?"

"A few more tips about truck stops." The open folder she'd passed to him had a map taped inside, with the truck stop sighting locations marked in red, and the girls' homes marked in green. "One guy said he'd seen Millie Harper talking to a dark-skinned man before getting into his truck."

"So the purple line connects the girl's home to the truck stop she was reportedly seen at?"

Ashlyn nodded. "They're all within a few miles. I wrote the distance down in the margins."

"Maybe when we regroup we can follow up on this."

What she didn't tell him was what was missing from her map. An unconfirmed sighting of Jenny Johnson at a diner two months earlier, right around the time she went missing, with a man who sounded a lot like Constable Tain. She'd leaned back in her chair, unaware she was tapping her notebook against her fingers until Campbell had walked in and glared at her, wondering if she might be able to make it to the diner herself.

Whatever she decided, first she had to go to the store and as she drove, she turned over everything that she'd learned from Constable Keith as she picked out enough groceries to carry her over for a few more days, paid,

loaded them into the car and drove to the cabin the department had provided for her. As she turned down the
now-familiar roads, she thought about what Melissa had
told her, about Eddie's strange story that was one part
legend to two parts pure fiction.

Or was it fantasy?

Was that why Tain had been so edgy? Had he seen the
bodies and thought of some twisted version of an old
Native tale and feared the killer was living on the Reserves? Most serial killers were white males, but the
particulars of this case, the fact that the killer had kept
the girls alive for an extended period of time . . .

They'd done preliminary tests. The infants recovered
with the women shared the same father.

Technically, this wasn't a serial-killer case. Not yet.
The problem with serial-killer cases wasn't just the
strain on the department as they tried to find enough
manpower to investigate, and it wasn't the public's
panic. The real problem was that the individual victims
got lost in the crowd. They just became a number. It was
too easy to lose sight of the fact that every girl was an
individual, who'd had hopes and dreams, and their lives
had been cut short brutally and senselessly.

It was almost necessary to lose sight of those facts to
stay sane. Out of eleven missing girls, they'd recovered
three of their bodies, counting the one found in the
burned-out building. That meant there were eight more
girls out there, somewhere, and the pile of tips that
needed to be investigated was mounting.

She loaded her groceries in her left arm as she slipped
her shoes off outside before entering and picked them
up with her right hand after unlocking the door. Although she barely took notice of her surroundings, she
was vaguely aware of the sound of Nolan's Rodeo pulling up to his cabin as she closed the door behind her.

Ashlyn bent down to set her shoes on the shelf in the
bottom of the closet, then walked down the short hall

and set the bags, and her coat on the counter. It took less than a minute to put the cheese, milk and yogurt in the refrigerator and then she turned around and looked at the Spartan cabin, and wondered how she was going to keep her mind off work for a few hours, never mind a full day.

Melissa had given her an idea, and she took less than half a second to debate it before she went to the bedroom, dug out a pair of black jeans, a purple shirt with a scooped neck that had sleeves long enough to conceal her bandages, and got changed.

By the time she arrived at The Goldmine she felt transformed, no longer a new cop in the area, trying to fit in with a team of men who didn't want to work with her, but just a new girl in town trying to get a feel for the place.

She asked for a table that appeared to be in the center of the action on the bar side.

"Menu?" asked the gum-chewing waitress with bleach-blonde hair that had grown out long enough to show the dark roots asked.

"Please." Ashlyn slid her jacket off and set it on the chair behind her. She tried to lean back and look relaxed as she scanned the menu and occasionally glanced around the room.

Bobby Hobbs and Eddie Campbell were at a table in the corner.

She looked back at her menu.

"What can I get ya ta drink?" A different waitress. Slim and pretty in a wearing-too-much-make-up kind of way. She would have looked better if she'd gone easy with the face paint.

"A Coke, thanks."

The menu was as generic as they came, with burgers and fries, sandwiches and fries, steaks, ribs and more alcoholic beverages than dessert options. She'd finally settled on what to order and closed her menu when the chair beside her slid out.

Bobby Hobbs sat down and put his hand on her shoulder as he leaned over and whispered in her ear, "I bet a girl like you knows how to have a good time." Said as he worked his hand over, to the back of her neck.

The waitress returned with Ashlyn's drink and was setting it down.

Ashlyn reached up and grabbed his wrist and twisted it hard, suppressing the wince from the strain on her own arm as the stitches pulled. The fact that Bobby had titled the chair back helped, and he crashed to the floor before her arm gave.

The waitress grinned and gave her a wink. "I'll be back to take your order in a minute."

Bobby Hobbs had picked himself up. "That wasn't very nice."

"Leave 'er be, Bobby."

Eddie had joined the party.

"Look, I'm jest tryin' to have a good time here," Bobby said. He scowled. "Ya used to be more fun." Bobby stood and leaned over as he whispered in Ashlyn's ear, "Be seein' ya." Within seconds he'd found another girl to drape his arm around.

"Thanks," Ashlyn said as she extended her hand. "I'm Ashlyn."

Eddie looked at her hand for a moment, then reached out and shook it for a second before letting go.

"I'm new in town," she said. He stood staring at her with huge black eyes. No wonder he'd creeped Melissa out.

"Best take care then," Eddie said.

"I'll be fine."

"You ever hear the story about the Native kids who were stolen from their parents?"

Didn't he ever blink? Ashlyn reached for her drink and took a slow sip before she responded. "I'm not sure." She couldn't believe he'd gone straight for the jugular within seconds of meeting her. Definitely lacking social skills.

"Did you start without me?"

A different voice. Ashlyn turned as Nolan sat down beside her. When she turned back, Eddie was gone. She looked at Nolan. "What are you doing here?"

"What was that all about?" Nolan asked her.

"Just getting acquainted with the locals."

"Yeah? Interesting that the ones you picked happen to work for a shipping company and drive trucks."

Ashlyn ignored that. "You haven't answered my question. What are you doing here?"

He held up his hands. Before he could answer the waitress returned. They both placed simple orders. She left and returned within a minute with Nolan's drink. When the waitress disappeared again, Nolan shrugged. "Thought it was time we acted like partners."

"You followed me here?"

"Look, Hart, I was going to ask you if you wanted to have dinner when I saw you leave. After what happened to you before, I'm not going to let you start asking questions without backup."

"Eddie and Bobby were both friends of Jenny Johnson's. What I can't figure out is why they weren't questioned when she disappeared."

He leaned back in his chair. "All this time here, and you're immune to the local charm? Nobody wants to believe it's someone from here who'd do this. They need it to be a monster from somewhere else so that they don't have to start locking their doors and living in fear."

"These girls were lured somehow. If there is a connection with the truck stops—"

Nolan held up his hand. "It's pure speculation at this point."

"Why haven't Hobbs and Campbell been questioned?"

"Tain's been after those two for a while now. We get too close to them, we risk being accused of harassment." He reached for his drink and after he'd taken a sip set the glass back down. "People think if you know someone's dirty, you should just be able to arrest them, like it doesn't take time or evidence. The shipping company's been edgy ever since the failed bust in the summer, and they don't want their employees held up crossing the border, so they don't mess around." He nodded in the direction of Hobbs, who still had his arm draped around the girl he'd found after Ashlyn had sent him sprawling across the floor. She was starting to look uncomfortable, a shadow flashing across her face as she brought her arm up between his body and hers and pushed back, trying to work in some distance. He held on tight and pulled her back closer. "They find out you're a cop, and you'll be in hot water just for talking to them."

"You'd think their employer would just cut them loose, save themselves the hassle."

"Not when the company's owned by Hobbs's family. Word around these parts is they built the family fortune during Prohibition and have maintained their bank balance off one form of illegal trade or another for years."

Ashlyn reached for her Coke. "And yet the locals don't want to think about their neighbors being criminals."

"No, monsters. There's a difference. Bootlegging was one way of sticking it to the man when he tried to keep people down, and smuggling is all about robbing the government of money for taxes."

"But drugs—"

"They don't see it that way. You're from Ontario, right?"

She nodded.

"In Western Canada, there are plenty of people who want less government in their lives. Mostly in Alberta, but some places in BC too. Bringing cheap cigarettes over the border means they save money, so everybody wins, right?"

"But it doesn't stop there."

Nolan shook his head. "I know that. You know that.

But people have a way of seeing what they want to see. They don't just turn a blind eye to the cigarette trade; they encourage it. And if the cigarette smuggling becomes drugs and weapons and girls, it makes them part of it. They might have to answer to themselves for letting this happen."

"I think you give them too much credit. Most people have a remarkable ability for dismissing personal responsibility."

"Maybe so, Hart, but you've seen how edgy even our own team is. Remember how Campbell reacted when you asked about coordinating with the tribal police?" Nolan shook his head. "From the beginning, with the task force, there were people it was obvious we should be questioning, leads we should have been following. And that's exactly what we've been stopped from doing."

"I don't believe the RCMP would create a task force and then try to keep us from solving the case," Ashlyn said.

"And what if it is Hobbs and Campbell? What do you think they'll say when it comes out that we've had tips about illegal activity involving these two going back several years?"

"I think we're a lot better off answering for any mistakes now and putting a stop to it before someone else gets hurt than pretending girls aren't being murdered."

"You're an idealist, Hart." Nolan reached over and squeezed her hand for a second before letting go of it. "Thing is, there isn't much in this world that is ideal."

"So if Tain's been after these two and you suspect they're involved, why are you two at each other's throats all the time?"

"Some reports came in this afternoon."

She frowned. "I was at the office—"

Nolan shook his head. "I was out with the canine team, searching the woods. Sullivan called and told me.

The fire at Blind Creek Inn? It started in the old staff house across the street. Looks like the insurance company will be on the hook for the inn, because even if the house was set on fire deliberately, it doesn't look like they planned for it to spread."

"I'm sure they're happy," she said, not commenting on the fact that Sullivan had taken information straight to Nolan without informing the rest of the team.

"Something else turned up in the autopsy. The victim in the fire? She was pregnant."

She felt her eyes widen. "That supports the idea of a connection, although it doesn't explain—"

Nolan held up his hand. "Enough talk about work." He reached for his drink. The waitress was coming toward them, plates of hot food in hand.

"Can I get yas anythin' else?"

"We're good, thanks," Nolan said.

Ashlyn smiled as the waitress left, then turned to her partner and opened her mouth.

He glared at her for a moment, a look in his eyes that told her he was done talking about Tain or the investigation. So much for her attempts at snooping around. Finding out more about Bobby Hobbs and Eddie Campbell and the source of the tension between Nolan and Tain would have to wait.

CHAPTER TWENTY-SEVEN

Eighteen months ago

Ashlyn gently set the bag on the floor and fumbled through the darkness, hand searching for the shape of the small light Tain kept on his desk. When she hit the base of the lamp, she felt her way along the cord until she found the switch and turned it on.

It would have to do.

Picking locks wasn't her specialty, but she pulled the lamp toward the edge of the desk, got down on her knees and started on Tain's top desk drawer. Within a minute it was open. The stacks of papers she'd found the day she'd arrived in Nighthawk Crossing were still inside.

Ashlyn stood and looked at the documents. She pulled them up.

There wasn't anything else in the drawer.

Once the papers were returned and the drawer closed, she opened the next drawer and riffled through the contents, then sank to her knees and opened the bottom drawer. Her initial skim of the papers inside revealed nothing about her unanswered questions regarding the case.

Ashlyn pushed the drawer shut. As she reached up to the edge of the desk, it was the shape of the shadows under the desktop that made her pause.

A legal-sized envelope, taped underneath the work surface.

Ashlyn ran her fingers under the edge until she removed all the tape. The flap wasn't closed. As she glanced at the door she slid the papers out, skimmed them, then pushed them back in.

She turned Nolan's desk light on before shutting Tain's off, and on her way back to Nolan's desk she grabbed the bag she'd brought with her and put the envelope inside.

Nolan had three drawers, all locked. She started at the top.

Inside, she found a filled notebook from prior casework. She leafed through the pages, checking dates. None of it seemed to connect to the current investigation.

Ashlyn slid the drawer shut and moved on to the next one.

There was a stack of papers inside that was thicker than the one in Tain's desk, but it wasn't copies of case files she was looking at. She flipped through the first few pages, then a few more.

The missing-persons files she'd been looking for.

She picked them up, put them inside the bag and riffled through the rest of the drawer. It contained nothing more than blank notepads and a few pens.

Ashlyn pushed it shut and looked at the bottom drawer.

She had what she'd been looking for. One discovery offered reassurance. It didn't cross every *t* or dot every *i*, but it was enough to dispel her doubts, while the other revelation raised more questions than answers.

A quick look at the doorway confirmed she was still alone. Ashlyn picked the last lock and slid the drawer open.

It took her a moment to realize what she was looking at. A glance at her watch told her she had about twenty-five hours. What were the chances that she'd get through all the material before their shift the next day?

Slim, but she could copy it if she had to, and if she found a way to zero in on what she needed . . . Ashlyn picked up the files and put them in the bag. She zippered the bag, pushed the drawer shut and stood.

There were a few messages on her desk and she walked around to that side to skim through them.

Most were the usual reports of sightings and tips that would need to be followed up. Nothing stood out, so she set them down. They could wait. Two were from Constable Keith, and after she skimmed them, she folded the slips of paper and put them in her pocket. She walked around to Nolan's desk and turned the light off. One final glance around the office confirmed she was leaving it as she'd found it. She bent down, picked up the bag, and after a quick check stepped out into the hall and walked to the back door.

At the back of the station she took a deep breath before opening the door.

It didn't look like anyone had arrived while she'd been inside, and she released a breath of air as she hurried to her car. She slid the key in the lock and within seconds had tossed the bag inside and shut the trunk.

Ashlyn walked to the driver's side door. A couple of quick clicks of a button and that door was unlocked. As she extended her hand she heard a voice behind her and jumped.

"Sullivan said to take the day off."

She forced herself to take steady breaths as she turned. "So what are you doing here?"

"Believe it or not, looking for you."

Tain's face had the solemn expression she'd come to associate with him from time to time, when he'd been intently focused on the details of the case.

When he'd been less interested in hurling insults than in assessing the information they had to work with.

"Why?"

Tain looked to his right, then left. "There are some things I think you need to know."

"Wow. That's the understatement of the year."

The sound of a trash can lid clattering to the ground made them both look toward the alley. As the noise subsided, Ashlyn looked back at Tain, but he remained turned to the side, his hand resting on his still-holstered gun.

She'd yanked the car door open and was halfway inside before she glanced up at him. "I'm sure you mean well—"

Tain looked at her, looked back at the alley, then walked around behind her car and pulled on the passenger door.

She'd flicked the lock as soon as she had her door closed.

"We need to talk," he said.

"Fine. Give me your cell number."

"What?"

"Give me your number. I'll call you when I'm ready and tell you where to meet me."

"Ashlyn—"

"Take it or leave it, Tain."

She watched the conflict on his face and then he spat out the number. Ashlyn keyed it into her cell phone and then put the car in reverse.

"I'll call you."

He stepped back and she backed out of the spot and drove away.

Ashlyn checked her side mirrors and rearview mirrors. It was so early that attempting to follow her would be obvious, and there wasn't a moving vehicle anywhere in sight.

Once she was a comfortable distance out of town, she pulled over to the side of the road. The first place they'd look for her would be the cabin. A rented room would connect to a credit card that could be traced.

We know someone's been feeding information to the Native leaders, Tain.

Nolan's words from several days before. Meant to deflect suspicion from himself?

Steve's word should have earned him at least the benefit of doubt, but despite the nuggets Nolan had shared with her during their impromptu dinner the night before, he'd also lied to her and to Sullivan, and lingering questions about why he was hiding the missing-persons files and why he'd gone to see Jenny Johnson's mother remained unanswered.

Ashlyn got out of the car and opened the trunk. The woods were quiet, but not uncomfortably so. A glance to her right caught the flash of a squirrel's tail as it jumped onto a different branch, and she could hear the faint chirps of birds.

The woods weren't holding their breath in fear.

She returned to the car with the bag. The backseat offered the lure of more space, but the front seat offered the use of mirrors and a chance to leave quickly if she felt the need.

Tain had spooked her. The promise she'd made to call him may have been a mistake. She'd be putting herself in the open, at a scheduled time.

Despite the risk, she intended to go through with it. Tain had been on her list for the day before he'd surprised her.

She'd gone in search of answers, and the missing-persons files that had disappeared. What she'd found was more than she'd imagined. The unexpected file from Nolan's desk was on top, and she pulled it out and flipped through it again.

Jenny Johnson. Blind Creek Shipping. Constable Tain and a failed bust, followed by a series of arrests that hadn't held up in court. Drug trafficking, prostitution, illegal firearms possessions . . .

Bobby Hobbs and Eddie Campbell were suspected of being in the middle of a highly profitable cross-border enterprise, smuggling everything from cheap cigarettes to live girls and raw cocaine into and out of the United States.

Jenny Johnson.

The envelope she'd retrieved from under Tain's desk was on the bottom of the bag, and it took a minute of shifting other files before she could remove it without ripping it.

She slid the papers out again, confirming they were what she'd thought they were before counting them. Ten papers in all, each removed from a different file. She mentally checked off the list. The only missing person involved in their investigation who didn't have a sheet in the envelope was Jenny Johnson.

As soon as those papers were replaced, she started skimming through the names on the missing-persons files. Nothing stood out. She exhaled. If she didn't find a way to narrow it down, she might have to read all of them.

Where had Nolan worked before, when he'd handled the report on the missing girl that was part of their case? She pulled her notebook out of the glove box and flipped through the pages.

Penticton.

Ashlyn started skimming every file to see if Nolan had originally handled it. She was halfway through, and a glance at the clock told her she'd spent a few hours going over what she had so far. None of the girls had lived in Penticton or been reported missing there, and none of the officers who opened the files she'd looked over so far connected to their investigation.

How could she narrow it down?

Ashlyn picked up her phone and started to dial. When the voice mail answered she hung up without leaving a message.

She flipped through the folders again and skimmed the contents one file at a time. When she reached the file labeled KAITLIN COLLINS it clicked into place. As soon as she saw the name in the file, she went back to the top and read it line by line.

Kaitlin had been reported missing from a small town in the interior Ashlyn vaguely recognized. Her date of birth made her . . .

Fifteen years old.

Ashlyn continued to skim the file. It read like many of the others, the tale of a small-town girl who'd disappeared without much evidence of where she'd gone or why. As she skimmed the folder, she realized that there wasn't one single thing that readily stood out to make the file any different than the ones officially connected to the investigation, or the ones locked in Nolan's desk. She slowed down and covered the information line by line until she found it.

Reported missing by Craig Nolan. Brother.

She picked up her phone and dialed again. This time, he answered.

"I found something interesting in these files, Steve."

"Ashlyn—"

"She's still missing?"

Steve hesitated. "What does the file say?"

"Look, these files have been missing for weeks. If there was an update for any of them, it wouldn't be in here because Nolan's had them locked in his desk."

"Then how did you get them?"

"Don't ask questions you don't want answers to."

"Ashlyn, is this what it's come to? Sneaking around, going through people's desks? Why didn't you go to Craig?"

"I—" She glanced around, suddenly aware that her volume had increased while they'd been talking, then leaned back for a second and closed her eyes. "I know you trust him, but there are things he's hiding. Things that, as far as I can tell, have nothing to do with his sister."

"At some point you'll have to decide who to trust, Ashlyn."

She opened her eyes and looked in the rearview mirror as the hum of a truck engine faded. The occupant of the truck got out and shut the door, his empty hands raised as he approached her car.

"I've almost worked that out," she told Steve. "I have to go."

"Okay. Be careful."

Ashlyn flipped the phone shut, opened the car door and got out. "Dare I ask?"

"You used your cell phone."

"Does anyone on this team work within the law?"

Tain glanced at the bag on the front passenger seat of her car. "Not anymore."

She almost smiled.

"Can we talk?" he asked her.

"Where?"

"Drive. It's safer."

For him or for her? She was beginning to wonder, but didn't argue. She got in the car and it only took a moment to stuff the files back in the bag and put it in the backseat. As she backed out of the parking spot she glanced at Tain. "You have fifteen minutes to persuade me this is worth my time."

"In that case, I'd better start talking now."

CHAPTER TWENTY-EIGHT

Twenty months ago

"All I know is, they're planning for Saturday."

"They aren't saying what the shipment is?"

Jenny shook her head. "Not exactly. We hafta do diff'rent things, dependin'. They don't have me doin' clothes, so I don't think it's girls."

"Doing clothes?"

"They burn whatever they come over in, get rid of it. Make sure the last clothes they were seen in are never seen again."

Tain nodded. It made sense. "So you're thinking drugs."

"Eddie said somethin' about snow." Jenny made a face at him. "Eddie never was too smart."

She was fidgeting with a stir stick, the fourth she'd cracked apart since they'd sat down. Her strawberry-blonde hair had an oily sheen and a few fresh pimples dotted her pale skin. She was wearing those gloves, the kind that had the tips of the fingers cut out.

Tain never could make sense of that particular fashion trend. Why wear gloves in the summer at all? Unless they were work gloves or gardening gloves . . .

That was when he realized there must be marks on her hands, wounds that were reopened before they could properly mend. For Jenny the gloves weren't about fashion. They were about function.

He sat back as the waitress approached their table and slid two plates of food and two glasses of orange juice in front of them. Jenny always picked the booth in the very back, where she could curl into the corner and keep an eye on everything around her. They were in a roadside diner not far off the highway, but far enough off to not be a truck stop. It was the kind of place that had clung to its faded green and dusky white décor not out of nostalgia but because of budgetary restraints. The uniforms the staff wore were so faded Tain wouldn't have been surprised if they were hand-me-downs from the original staff. He'd met Jenny on the outskirts of Nighthawk Crossing and driven more than a hundred kilometers from her hometown, to a place she'd never been to, and still she glanced around the restaurant as she wolfed down the eggs and toast, keeping watch for any familiar faces.

"Okay, look. You need to go, just like normal. Do whatever they ask you to do. You'll be arrested along with them."

"I don't know if I can do it this time."

"If you aren't there it'll look suspicious. They'll start wondering if someone talked to the cops, and if you're the only one missing they'll know it was you."

She sat still for a moment, then reached for the orange juice. "What about the other thing?"

"The girls?"

"Yeah."

"You told me about the ones they smuggle across the border, in both directions. Runaways recruited for prostitution. Once we get these guys we'll try to track down all the victims."

She shook her head. "No. I mean the other girls. The ones I gave you dates for."

Tain hesitated. "There are girls who've gone missing around those times. You mean they aren't part of this other thing?"

She fidgeted with the empty orange juice glass and shrugged her right shoulder. "How many did I give you days for?"

"Nine. Is that how many there are?"

Jenny shrugged and shook her head. "I've never seen them all together."

"But you have seen them?"

Jenny's wide eyes searched the room before she looked at Tain again. "Once. Some of them."

"But you said—"

"Look, I overheard them talkin'. Sayin' these ones weren't for the other stuff. There's a cellar at the inn and it connects with tunnels, over across the street to where the inn staff used to stay. That's where my room is, part of the cellar. I saw two of them there once. The girl they'd had for a while, she wasn't too skinny, not like the ones they use for the other stuff. She was out to here." She made an arc with her hand that indicated a swollen belly.

Pregnant.

"The other one, they'd just gotten her. She was tied up. They always kept them tied at first."

As far as he could tell, Bobby and Eddie were pretty small-time criminals who'd stumbled upon an easy trade. Eddie was a trucker and didn't get much hassle at the border because he lived on the Reserve. Bobby's family had owned the shipping company for years, and they'd been plying one form of illegal trade or another for as long as Blind Creek Shipping Co. had been in business.

Tain knew that could happen when Reserves bordered each other. There were different rules, and Aboriginal policing was nothing short of a nightmare. Some might say it was a joke, but he wouldn't go that far. He understood the politics, the conflicts, the inherent distrust passed down from one generation to another.

There were reasons he didn't want to work on Reserves.

"Where are they keeping them?"

Jenny took another glance around as she reached for the fork and twirled it in her fingers. "I don't know. The pregnant one, I'd seen her when she first came, when she was tied up and skinny. Eddie stays at the staff house."

"What about Bobby?"

She shrugged. "Sometimes, sure. But not all the time."

Why keep a group of missing girls at an inn downtown? Tain understood that the same person who ran the shipping company owned the inn, but it still didn't make much sense. There were too many risks . . .

He looked up. Jenny was watching him. Light never danced in her eyes. She looked like she'd lived a lifetime and a half already, instead of just the meager handful of years she'd spent in the Interior.

Since their first meeting, he'd done some checking. Her mother was a known prostitute. She'd forced Jenny into the trade as soon as she developed, but Jenny had left the house to live in a small shack, working odd jobs and stealing what she couldn't afford to survive.

It was no surprise she'd ended up working for Hobbs. She was small and wiry and had the ability to get into a lot of tight spots, and she was already a thief. Despite her appearance at the moment, she had the looks to survive by moving from one bad relationship to another if she needed to. The odd time Tain had seen her when she'd been cleaned up he'd hardly recognized her.

"And they're all involved with this? Bobby? Eddie? Kurdy?"

She hesitated, then shook her head. "I don't know

about Kurdy. That day I saw the two girls, they'd sent me down for some cleaner. As soon as I saw them I grabbed what I needed and got out of there, but I dropped a jar on the stairs. Kurdy started comin' down and Eddie lost it. I think he mighta beat him half to death, but Bobby stopped him."

"You think Eddie didn't want him to see the girls."

"Not those ones. Kurdy, he's got a thing for young girls."

Tain had heard. "But you figure Bobby knows."

Jenny shrugged. "Eddie does whatever Bobby tells him to. It's always been that way, since they were kids. Thing is, seeing Eddie go at Kurdy like that, that was scary. Eddie was the kind of kid who tried to be cool but wasn't, you know what I mean?" Her eyes had a faraway look for a moment. "I used to think he was a nerd, a real loser, but he coulda been real sweet. If it weren't for Bobby. He wasn't mean the way Bobby was."

"Any chance you can find out more? Where they're keeping them?"

She shrugged again. "I-I don't know. I've only seen a few of them."

"But the dates?"

"Eddie'd get real funny when they had one of the girls there. I guess 'cos I work with the other ones sometimes, they weren't worried about me. Probably just didn't want Kurdy touchin' them, you know? But Eddie'd get edgy. I just kinda knew when they had a girl there."

The waitress returned with the bill, and Tain reached for his wallet. As he put the money on the table, he looked at Jenny, still sneaking glances around the room, unable to let her guard down long enough to eat a simple breakfast.

"If it's too much for you, Jenny, we can pull you out now."

"What do you mean?"

"We'll get you out. See what we can do to set you up

with a place. Vancouver. Victoria. Give you a fresh start."

"But those girls . . ."

Tain looked her straight in the eye. "Jenny, you've done a brave thing. The crimes on Reserves are a huge problem, and we want to do anything we can to stop the drug trade. What you've told me should be enough to put a major trafficker out of business permanently. You deserve a second chance."

The hard lines on her face softened and her eyes glistened with unshed tears. "But you said yourself, if I'm not there, they'll work it out."

Tain nodded.

"So I need to be there for at least a few more days."

"Okay. But then we'll talk about a new home, job training. Maybe college."

Jenny offered him a wry smile. "Sometimes, you just gotta accept that not everyone's meant for an easy life."

He was tempted to say few were, but kept the comment to himself. "I know you've been trying to help us put a stop to this for a while now, and we've let you down. You never did say why you decided to talk. What was it, Jenny?"

She stood and paused a moment, then reached down and patted her stomach, then started walking toward the door. As Tain got up and followed her out, he wondered if Jenny would be strong enough to make a fresh start, strong enough to make a better life for herself and her child, or if she'd find herself caught in the cycle of prostitution and poverty that she'd been raised in forever.

CHAPTER TWENTY-NINE

Eighteen months ago

"The night of the raid, it all went bad."

Tain's voice drifted off. They'd been in the car for almost an hour, his story interspersed with long silences, but Ashlyn didn't push him. She kept driving, waiting for him to tell her the rest.

"The trucks were by the book. Instead of pulling them off the road or holding off on the shipment, they dumped every bit of contraband they had and scheduled a clean load.

"Jenny wanted out after that, and at first, I worried about pulling her. We could guess they knew they had a leak, but we didn't know if they knew who it was. If I did pull her out, they'd know it was her and they'd be out on the streets, free to try to track her down. And leaving her where she was had risks because I couldn't figure out how they found out about the bust." Tain shook his head. "I finally pulled her out."

Ashlyn glanced in her side mirrors. They were all alone on a logging road that wove into the mountains a few miles out of town. She pulled the car over. "You did the right thing."

Tain looked over at her. "Jenny jumped at the sound of someone sneezing three apartments over from hers. She couldn't shake the fear. She didn't know anybody. She'd spent so long thinking she'd never amount to anything, hearing her mother tell her she was useless." He turned to look out the window. "She believed it. And she thought she'd spend the rest of her life waiting for them to show up."

"So why not get it over with."

"Yeah. I guess that's what she thought."

Ashlyn thought about what he'd told her. "It was Jenny's tip that connected a group of missing girls. The bust went bad, but you pulled together the files and persuaded Sullivan to listen to you."

Tain shook his head. His mouth opened, but then he closed it and didn't speak.

"What happened?"

"I went to Summer. She talked to the press."

"You mean, you told her you thought you knew where her sister was and nobody was investigating?"

He looked at her. "I let it slip. I had a lead. A lot of girls had gone missing, but now that there were a few white girls, we stood a chance of getting the funding for a proper investigation."

Ashlyn closed her eyes. He'd poked the racial hornets' nest himself.

"And ever since then you've been distancing yourself from the Native groups lobbying for answers."

Tain stared straight ahead. "It's an explanation, not an apology."

She felt the corner of her mouth tug into a smile and looked down until she could straighten her face. What she'd come to expect from Tain was just that, and here he was, giving her more answers than she'd asked for, but she still didn't know why. He wasn't seeking her approval.

"I know you didn't leak the information to the Native leaders."

"How?"

"It's still in your desk drawer."

He turned to face her. "That's what you were doing at

the office this morning. How do you know I wasn't waiting for things to cool down, or I didn't make a new set of copies because you'd seen those ones?"

She paused. "Because I know who's been leaking information to the Native leaders."

Tain's eyes widened. "Who? How?"

Ashlyn held up her hand. "You first. You fabricated the report of Jenny's disappearance?"

"It was the only chance we had to protect her. If the men she'd been working with thought we believed she'd been abducted, maybe they wouldn't try to track her down."

"Or maybe they'd be more determined than ever to silence her. They'd know they didn't have her."

Tain leaned back in the seat, staring straight ahead. "I guess that's what happened. It was a mistake."

"But you thought it might throw them off. Make them think you were looking in the wrong direction."

He didn't respond. He didn't have to.

He'd tried to find a way to protect Jenny Johnson, whose disappearance was used to finally launch the task force. Winters had been following up, investigating. Tain's former partner.

"What did Winters have to do with it?"

"He didn't know."

"But something happened?"

Tain was quiet for a few minutes. The entire time she'd been listening to him he hadn't raised his voice, he hadn't asked for forgiveness. He'd simply told his story.

What he didn't know was that she, thanks to the file she'd found in Nolan's desk, already had most of the facts. What Tain was telling her merely hung the meat on the bones, connected the dots. She'd seen the pieces of the puzzle, but Tain had put them together in a way that made it all make sense.

"Winters was good. Nolan's good too, not that I'll admit it to him. I hid the information that connected the cases because Winters started to piece it together. He was reading up on the failed bust, and he started digging on the shipping company.

"One morning, he called and said he had something on Bobby Hobbs and he wanted to see how tough he was. It was the day I'd found out Jenny was back in town, and I was on my way to talk to her.

"At first, he was angry. He said it was just like me to never be there to back him up, while I left him to do God knows what.

"Then he blew it off and said not to worry about it, that Nolan was supposed to be starting that day and he'd take him instead." Tain paused. "I should have talked him out of it. When I was on my way back to town, I saw Nolan outside the station, talking to Sullivan. I'd never even met him before, but I knew it was him, because of"—Tain's face twisted for a second—"something I'd seen once. Different case. The way my gut twisted, I headed straight out for the shipping company.

"I found Winters's car partway back to town. Someone had taken a shot at it, and when the bullet hit him he'd lost control."

"Was there a search?" She didn't remember hearing about the incident, and the attempted murder of a fellow officer was something every RCMP officer would know about.

Tain shook his head. "I called for an ambulance. Winters, he was in and out. All he said was they'd roughed him up. He passed out again before he could tell me who. It wasn't until we got his car back to town and started going over it that we found the bullet, and by then it was too late to search the woods. I was worried about a neck injury, and I thought the blood was from hitting his head, so I didn't move him, and I didn't realize . . .

"The doctor confirmed that some of the injuries were from the car accident, but that there was pre-existing head trauma and indications he'd been kicked in the chest. Whatever happened out there, Winters barely got out alive."

"And that still wasn't enough to go after them?"

Tain shook his head. "When he came to, he didn't remember what had happened. Sullivan thought Winters had been following up on a lead for my case, but Winters hadn't told me anything. He didn't have anything solid. Sure, Sullivan sent Campbell and Aiken out there. They asked if anyone had seen Winters, and they said no. They let them take a look around."

"So it all looked clean, there was no proof, and Sullivan didn't realize it connected to the task force investigation." Ashlyn thought about that. "You can't blame yourself for what happened."

"No? You mean, like I can't blame myself for what happened to Jenny?"

"We don't know what happened to her."

"You talked to Mrs. Wilson yourself."

"She told me about Jenny in the cabin a few weeks ago, but she wouldn't even tell me which of you Jenny had been talking to. I have no idea why she thought the body at the inn was Jenny's. She didn't give me any evidence, Tain."

"She didn't have to," Tain said. "I saw the tattoo on the ankle. It wasn't all burned off."

Ashlyn frowned. "But there was no record of a tattoo in the file."

Tain leaned back against the seat. "She'd gotten it a few months earlier. Only people who would have likely known would be Bobby and Eddie, and nobody questioned them. I saw it when I talked to her at the shack. A butterfly. 'Something beautiful and free.' That's what she said."

And short-lived.

"But . . . you didn't ID her to Sullivan."

"Somehow, they found out about the bust. The Native leaders started talking, and they knew things I hadn't told Summer. There was a leak in the department, and we didn't know who it was. The best chance we had of finding the leak was by withholding information and planting false leads and seeing what happened."

"And the search warrants you were trying to get . . ."

"Blind Creek Inn and the staff building where Jenny lived."

"But you had nothing more than an anonymous tip."

"Nolan wouldn't budge."

"You've been working with Sullivan, still trying to find a way to take down the smuggling operation?"

Tain paused. "Yes. But that's it. Just because it was my lead."

"Does Sullivan know about Jenny?"

"Not that she wasn't really missing."

"Tain—"

"I went to Native groups to get funding to hide Jenny. I kept it all off the books."

God, what a mess. He'd done everything he could think of to make sure nobody found out that Jenny had talked, and it had still gone horribly wrong.

"You never told Sullivan there was a link between the smuggling operation and the missing girls?"

"How could I? I didn't have any proof."

"What I don't understand is, why did you tell me to go through the missing-persons files," Ashlyn said.

"I couldn't find them. You were spending most of your time in office, and it was the one place you were probably safe."

"Did you know Nolan had them?"

Tain shook his head. "All I knew was that Nolan was suspicious about the task force, and after Winters got hurt on the job he started digging."

"He found out you'd put together the names of the girls, and that someone was leaking information to Native leaders, put two and two together but came up with six." Ashlyn thought about her first night in town, remembered the look on Tain's face when he'd seen Nolan talking to Summer. "What I don't understand is why you didn't trust him. Nolan was brought in after the investigation started. He doesn't live here. He couldn't have tipped anyone off about the failed bust."

"I just thought it was better if people thought I was difficult, that I didn't have any idea who was involved."

"You didn't want them to think you were getting close."

He held up his hands and said, "Huh. Thing is, I'm still not close." Tain looked at her. "I know Nolan's not involved, but he's still hiding something."

Tain had put a lot of cards on the table, but she hadn't offered him the answers she'd found. To his credit, he hadn't pressed her. At a guess, he was feeling vulnerable and had reached out to the one person he knew was clean, who had nothing to hide.

When she looked up, he was watching her. She reached for the bag she'd tossed in the backseat and pulled out the files that she'd set on top.

After she found the one marked KAITLIN COLLINS she passed it to him and watched as he flipped it open and read it wordlessly. When he was finished he looked up at her.

"It doesn't explain everything."

Ashlyn reached into her pocket and removed the messages Constable Melissa Keith had left on her desk. "You called 911 the night of my accident. You know Nolan went to the Johnson house."

"He'd been suspicious for a while and he'd started asking questions. If he'd been looking for the abductors instead of looking for the leak, he might have solved this already."

"Not without the missing pieces," Ashlyn said. "That day in the woods, when we found the first bodies. You tried to get rid of us."

"To make sure you didn't find anything that would lead you to Bobby Hobbs and Eddie Campbell."

"But why, Tain? If we had the evidence we could have gone after them."

"We still don't know who leaked the information. If someone at the station heard, and they were involved . . ."

It could jeopardize everything.

"Hell, for all I know they got spooked and that's why they've been dumping bodies."

She thought about what Keith had told her, about Nolan transferring to the task force before Tain.

"Nolan started after the main group, but before you did. Was he part of the team, or was he investigating the team?"

Tain paused. "I don't know."

"But you thought it was possible." Ashlyn stared out the window for a moment. Tain hadn't just tested the limb; he'd crawled all the way out onto it. His fate was in her hands. No matter what his reasons, he'd contributed to filing a false report and withheld pertinent information about an ongoing investigation from his supervising officer. "If he was investigating the team, it was Aiken, Campbell and Oliver he was looking at."

Tain nodded. "He probably stirred it up with me so nobody would be suspicious."

"You'd be the one they'd watch. You had the original lead on the smuggling." She thought about what he'd said. Everything fit. It all made sense, except one thing. "Why tell me this now?"

Tain looked down at his lap and remained silent.

Ashlyn reached over and touched his arm. "The bullet in my dashboard. It wasn't meant for me, was it?"

"I don't think so."

She reached over the seat and removed the other file she'd found in Nolan's desk, the one she'd never dreamed of finding, and passed it to Tain.

"You need to read this."

He took it from her silently and she watched as he opened the folder and started reading.

CHAPTER THIRTY

Eighteen months ago

Ashlyn parked in the driveway next to the cabin she was staying in and walked to the door, where she performed the automatic tasks of inserting key in lock, twisting the doorknob and entering the house. As she pulled off her shoes she heard a vehicle nearby and glanced out the window. Nolan had parked his Rodeo and was heading inside. Ashlyn left her shoes in the hallway, then walked down the short hall, tossed her coat on the kitchen counter and returned to the entrance. It wasn't until she bent down to put her shoes on the shelf in the closet that she noticed the floor.

There were faint prints on the beech tile, obviously smudged by her movements when she entered. A glance at her socks confirmed her suspicions.

All the tired muscles were at attention then, and she felt the tension coursing through her veins as she reached for her gun. Whoever it was had entered like a pro. She hadn't noticed anything when she'd unlocked the door.

The thudding of her heart echoed in her ears as she moved forward, to the hallway.

Thu-thump thu-thump thu-thump. The speed increased as she tilted her head, first enough to see into the bedroom, then so that she could see the opening to the bathroom. The stairs were on the opposite side of the wall she was against, and she felt fear give way to doubt.

It was a short walk along a path through a wooded area to the small house where Tain was staying. Woods that could conceal. She thought about the loft of her own cabin. Weren't there two windows on the back side that overlooked the path?

And the time it would take to get in the car and start it would leave her vulnerable. She'd be a sitting duck.

The fact that nobody had tried to shoot her already was the counterargument, but if someone was lying in wait they were probably hoping to flee undetected, that like Mrs. Wilson's remains, Ashlyn's body would have enough time to grow cold before someone even discovered it. Shooting her in the car or in the woods would be a last resort, but if they realized she suspected their presence they'd probably take the chance.

She wondered if she'd be thinking about someone trying to kill her if she didn't know about the bullet in her dashboard, and thought of the gash on her arm.

She thought of the sound of Nolan's Rodeo pulling up only moments before. It took only a split second for her to make up her mind and she eased herself back from the wall, moving carefully toward the door while keeping her eyes on the corner ahead of her.

When she felt the door behind her Ashlyn reached back with her left hand, grabbed the knob and twisted it. She moved forward as she pulled the door open and kept her eyes on the hallway, ears straining to hear any sound of movement from within the cabin, gun ready in her right hand.

She bent down and grabbed the shoes, twisted her left foot around the door and pushed it open a little wider, and backed out onto the step.

Damn. Her cell phone had been in her coat pocket.

A glance at his cabin revealed the trickle of smoke rising from the chimney, the faint shadow against the curtains of the living room. When she'd found out where he was staying, she'd been glad of the extra distance, but now she silently cursed the fact that she'd been given a cabin across from him, instead of beside him.

Ashlyn slipped her shoes on and started backing down the steps as she scanned the windows of the cabin. There was no sign of movement, no evidence of disruption, no indication someone had even been inside.

She saw nothing out of the ordinary, but that wasn't reassuring.

The gravel crunched softly under her feet as she backed away from her cabin, her eyes turning from side to side, scanning the trees between the little cabins. She was in the open, exposed.

When she reached the driveway she paused. The door to her place was in the front, but the door to Nolan's was around the side. If she went to the door she'd break visual contact with her cabin, and that meant that if someone was inside they'd have a chance to leave without being seen.

Ashlyn winced as her foot hit an exposed tree root and risked a glance at the ground so that she could try to avoid tripping again. Step by step she inched closer to the building until she could reach up and rap on the living room window with her fist.

After she counted to five, she reached up to knock again, but the curtain pulled back from the edge and she felt her breath catch as she saw Nolan's face. As soon as he saw her he glanced at her cabin.

As though he knew.

He held up his hand. The curtain shut out the light from inside again, and she took a deep breath and exhaled.

As she drew a second deep breath, she could hear movement from the side of his cabin, the door closing, footsteps, the crunch of gravel as he followed the driveway.

"You okay?" Nolan asked. He had his gun in his hand, but his arm wasn't raised.

She nodded. "Someone's been in my place."

Nolan paused. "You're sure?"

"Shoeprints on my landing."

"Did you call the station?"

"My cell phone is inside."

He started walking toward her cabin and she followed.

"No sign of forced entry," he said as he walked up the steps and surveyed the door.

"I never noticed anything until I'd already gone in."

He pushed the door open, and she pointed to the spot on the floor where she'd seen the prints as she kept her eyes on the hallway in front of them. Nolan bent down and looked at the floor. When he stood and entered, he kept to the far side so he wouldn't smudge the prints any more than she already had.

Near the landing was a mirror with a ledge and a few small hooks for hanging keys. Nolan eased it off the wall.

From the corner at the far end of the hall, where Ashlyn had entered the kitchen earlier, it was possible to see almost all of the main living area. It didn't take more than a look the length of two heartbeats before Nolan nodded to her.

She was following and had eased the door closed behind them.

Nolan inched his way along the wall that bordered the stairs, unknowingly retracing her steps from earlier. He reached out with the mirror in one hand and tilted it toward the stairs.

A nod was the only confirmation she got that the stairs were clear.

Checking the rest of the bedroom and bathroom felt like a formality. The bed lacked a spread that reached to the floor, so with the use of the mirror Nolan could see underneath easily, and the closet was on the far side of the room, with the door open. Ashlyn hadn't fully unpacked, so it took no more than a quick glance to see that all the space contained was a handful of clothes and a couple of unpacked suitcases stacked on the floor.

The shower curtain was drawn back fully and the design of the bathroom meant there was no place for anyone to hide.

Nolan nodded toward the stairs. He tilted his head back to scan the area above them as he climbed one step at a time toward the second level. She followed, easing herself up the stairs slowly, gun ready, ears straining for the tiniest sound. But the only thing that threatened to break the silence was their movements.

When Nolan reached the turn in the stairs he held out the mirror. Ashlyn finished climbing the first section of the staircase with her gaze fixed at the railing on the upper level.

If anyone was up there, that's where they'd appear.

Nolan turned the corner and she followed. He was about halfway up the stairs when he lay down against them instead of climbing the rest of the way to the second floor.

Ashlyn followed his head. From that position they could see out over the top of the landing, through the doorway to the room. It was a long, narrow attic loft. The space to the left and right of the top of the stairs was storage, filled with shelves built into the walls.

There was only a few feet of floor space on either side of the stairway to hide.

Nolan held up three fingers, put one down, and then only one finger remained. When he lowered it they both jumped up the stairs and he swung to the left while she swung to the right.

The landing was clear.

They positioned themselves beside the door. Nolan reached out with the mirror again, first tilting it to the far side of the room, then turning it slowly back toward himself. He looked at her as he set the mirror down on the floor behind his feet and nodded.

He entered the room first and she followed, scanning

from the wall on her left all the way to the wall on her right. This room had no closet, which meant the only place left was under the bed. Nolan approached it and she bent down as he pulled up the bed skirt.

"Clear," she said.

For a split second her eyes closed as she drew a deep breath.

When she opened her eyes, she saw Nolan holster his gun. He led the way down the stairs in silence, but as soon as they reached the landing at the bottom of the stairs, he turned to her.

"I think you should call Sullivan."

She holstered her gun. "I was wrong. I overreacted. Is that what you want to hear?"

He walked through the living area, scrutinizing it more closely than he had when they'd been clearing rooms. She watched him scan the end tables and the bookshelves and the small dining table between the oversized chair and the kitchen.

"You're a good cop, Ashlyn."

He brushed past her, into her bedroom. She was on the verge of asking what the hell he was doing when he turned to her.

"What's this?"

He gestured at the small nightstand beside the bed.

Ashlyn at the beach with her arms wrapped around a smiling two-year-old who looked just like her, give or take twenty-plus years.

"My niece," she said. "The photo sits on my night-stand, but it's been knocked over. I didn't leave it like that."

"Do you have a plastic bag it can fit in?"

She left the room and went to the kitchen to find one and when she returned passed it to him.

"We'll see if we can get a print off it." Nolan bagged it, then looked at her. "Did you see anything else that looked like it had been moved?"

Ashlyn finished scanning the room and shook her head.

"Pack a bag," Nolan said.

"But—"

He reached out and touched her arm, the same way Tain had only days before. "I'm not taking no for an answer. If you won't call Sullivan you can't stay here."

Nolan walked out of the room without another word. Although there were still doubts in her mind about him, one thing she was certain of was that he wouldn't give in on this. Silently cursing the fact that she hadn't tried to reach Tain instead, she turned toward the closet and grabbed a small bag.

From the corner of his eye, Craig could see Ashlyn's head in her hands, her elbow propped against the arm of the couch. He could guess at the debate raging in her mind, part of her convinced she'd overreacted, still looking for some logical explanation for the prints and the picture.

Another part scared and a different part altogether furious that she'd been put in a position where she'd had to reach out for help.

No matter how much training an officer had, cops, especially female cops, felt the pressure to act like they could handle things on their own. How could a woman who chased down drug dealers or armed robbers on the streets, who stood over dead bodies in Dumpsters, be afraid of a bump in the night, the creak of the stairs, the sound of a strong wind thudding against the wall? No, a cop should be tough. Fearless.

Invincible.

It was a fallacy Craig knew only too well, but he carried his own fears deep inside, nothing on the job scaring him like the rage he knew burned within. Too many years spent pulling himself through the darkness. What scared him was the thought of losing sight of what he'd gained while the bitterness over what he'd been denied overtook him.

What he feared more than anything was losing control.

"You can have the downstairs bedroom. It has its own bathroom, and I sleep upstairs," he said. "Pasta? Salad? Anything you don't like?"

She shook her head. "Can I take a shower?" she asked. Not really asking permission, since he'd already suggested it when they'd arrived.

He nodded and within seconds she'd taken her bag into the downstairs bedroom. As he walked back to the kitchen he heard the click of the door.

The evening's events turned over in his mind as he went through the motions of cooking strips of chicken, boiling the pasta, grating cheese and mixing a sauce. He took the time to bake buns as he chopped fresh vegetables and finished the salad.

Once he'd finished with the food, he took out plates and cups, trying to keep his hands busy. From behind the closed bedroom door the faint sound of running water had stopped, but Ashlyn hadn't emerged yet, and he didn't want her to think he was keeping an eye on her.

He glanced at the clock, determined to wait fifteen minutes before he knocked to tell her dinner was ready.

Ashlyn's car had been gone most of the day. He'd finally driven through town, past the station, and down some of the back roads, but he hadn't seen her car anywhere.

Now that he thought about it, he hadn't seen Tain's truck either.

There was no doubt that someone had broken into her place. At least, none in his mind. Whoever it was, they were good. Very good. Two small slips that most other people wouldn't even have noticed, or could have been easily persuaded to dismiss. The mind could rationalize a single item out of place without much prodding.

After all, how many times did a person ask themselves if they'd remembered to turn off the oven, or turn down the heat, or unplug a space heater when they left the house?

Even a strong mind was susceptible to the power of suggestion. He'd seen the conflict in Ashlyn's eyes as she'd walked into his cottage, felt it in her prolonged silence as she'd sat on the couch. She could have persuaded herself she must have picked up the picture in the morning and set it down in a hurry, and she could even persuade herself she'd been thinking about other things, so distracted that she'd reentered the house that morning and left the footprints herself.

He trusted her instincts. Ashlyn had backed out of her house, gun in hand, and come to him for help. She'd had plenty of time along the way to talk herself out of it. If she hadn't been certain, she would have stopped herself before knocking on his window.

Craig glanced at the clock again. Ten minutes had passed. He sat down and waited.

No matter how hard she tried to find an alternate explanation, Ashlyn kept coming back to the same conclusion. The problem was, she had no idea who would have been in her house. Was it the same person who'd put a bullet in her dashboard only days before?

Maybe she'd been wrong. Maybe the bullet had been meant for her.

Why hadn't anyone told her about the 911 call? She thought about Getz and Keith outside her room when she'd left the hospital.

There to ensure her safety, while nobody told her they thought she was in danger.

Whoever had been in the house hadn't done anything, other than take away her peace of mind. Robbed of her sense of security, she'd been forced to turn to Nolan for help.

Nolan. Ashlyn hung the towel on the bar in the bathroom and stepped into the bedroom. Here she was, in his cabin, trembling like a tattered leaf on a chilly autumn day, ready to fall with the first strong breeze. She felt a mix of self-reproach and grateful appreciation at Nolan's insistence that she stay with him. The more she admitted to herself that she was glad he'd refused to take no for an answer, the more she loathed her own fears and weaknesses.

She pulled on her pajama pants, zipped up a sweater over the tank top she was wearing, tucked her chin-length hair back behind her ears and opened the bedroom door.

As she walked into the living area, she pledged to stop beating herself up. A quick glance showed that Nolan had the table set and was heading back into the kitchen to get the food.

That was when she realized whatever she smelled, it smelled good. Her tummy rumbled as he turned toward her, bowl in hand. "Coffee, tea, milk, juice?"

"Tea would be great, thanks."

Nolan walked over to the table and set the bowl down. "It'll take a minute. I need to boil some water.

The phone on the small table at the closest end of the couch rang.

"Can you grab that?" Nolan asked as he reached up into a cupboard.

She answered. Her greeting was followed by a split-second hesitation before the caller asked, "Is this Craig Nolan's residence?"

The voice was familiar. "Yes." What was he doing calling here? "I didn't expect it to be you."

"And I didn't expect you to be answering Craig's phone." Steve Daly paused. "Have you fully recovered?"

For a few seconds she felt dizzy from the blur of things running through her mind. Her heart had only returned to its normal rhythm partway through her shower, but her hand had shaken just a touch when she'd answered the phone.

Then she realized he didn't know about the break-in. He was asking about the car accident.

"Back to normal."

"The other day, it didn't sound like you and Craig had exactly hit it off."

She looked up into Craig's face as he stopped by the table. He was watching her, as though it had only now occurred to him that she was still talking to whoever was on the phone.

He'd probably assumed it was someone they worked with, someone from the task force.

"I'll get Nolan for you," she said. She passed the phone to her partner and watched him walk up the stairs.

"What the hell is going on, Craig?"

"Dad . . ."

"Is Ash okay?"

"How do you know her?" Craig asked. He heard his father sigh.

"I mentored her."

"So the other day . . ." Craig thought back to the conversation Ashlyn had been having at the hospital when he went to pick her up. "That was you on the phone?"

"She called after the accident. Craig, what's going on?"

"Someone broke into her place."

"But she's okay?"

"She wasn't home."

"That's not exactly an answer."

"She's rattled, but who wouldn't be?"

"You don't have to get defensive with me, Craig. I know Ashlyn's a good cop, and I trust her. She's got nothing to prove to me."

"This wasn't random. There was no sign of forced entry, and if it had been anyone else, I'm not even sure they would have noticed someone had broken in."

"But you're sure?"

"Yes."

"It couldn't have been kids breaking in for kicks?"

Craig sat down on the stairs. "Her cabin wasn't the only one broken into."

"Well, that should help her feel a bit better."

"I haven't told her yet."

There was silence for a moment before Steve asked, "Why not?"

"For one thing, she can feel safe here right now."

"Did she come crying to you, asking to stay at your house?"

"No, bu—"

"So she's an excuse. You can hide your own insecurity and blame it on chivalry."

Hundreds of miles away and his dad could still turn his face red. "If I tell her, it'll take away her peace of mind."

"And she'll just kick your ass and feel betrayed when she finds out later."

Craig rubbed his forehead. "Maybe."

Steve was silent for a moment before he asked, "What does Sullivan think?"

There was no response that wouldn't get him in more trouble, and he knew it.

"He doesn't know," Steve said.

"Before you put the lecture on autopilot, that was her call, not mine."

"About the break-in at her place. She doesn't even know about the one at yours, so don't throw that at her feet. That's on you."

"I . . ." Craig realized his father wasn't going to like what he was about to say, but stalling wouldn't make it any better. "I haven't exactly made this easy on Constable Hart."

"Let me guess. The team's welcomed her with open arms."

Craig thought about how many times Ashlyn had been left in office, alone. The few times they'd been out together at a scene she'd been more than capable. There really was no excuse. "No."

"And with all the men undermining her she doesn't want to look vulnerable."

"To be honest with you, I'm surprised she reached out to me."

"I told her she could trust you."

It made sense, but until that moment it hadn't even occurred to him that his name had come up before, when Steve had spoken to Ashlyn on the phone.

"There's something else she doesn't know." Craig paused. "The accident? Someone took a shot at her."

"I thought she hit a deer."

"So does she."

Craig listened to the silence on the other end of the line and the silence in the house and wondered where Ashlyn was, and whether she could hear him.

"Why wouldn't you tell her?"

"That was Sullivan's call."

"Craig, didn't you locate a murder victim the next day?"

"Three, and one of them was the woman Constable Hart was on her way to see that night."

It wasn't hard to picture Steve, his face long with the weight of the news, closing his eyes as he tried to digest what Craig had told him.

"I don't like this."

"Me either." Craig stood and started walking back downstairs. "Look, I know what you said, and I don't like asking—"

"I'll be in touch."

There was a click and the phone went dead. Craig returned to the main level and put it down on the small table where Ashlyn had found it.

She was standing by the fireplace and turned to face him.

"It sounds like we have a lot to talk about."

"How much did you hear?"

"Everything."

CHAPTER THIRTY-ONE

Eighteen months ago

After Nolan got off the phone with his dad, Ashlyn suggested they eat first, then talk. He seemed surprised, but agreed. They were halfway through the meal when there was a knock at the door.

That was when she told him she'd called Tain and asked him to come over.

The tension between the two men couldn't dissipate with the flip of a switch, and both had found themselves in the awkward position of putting their trust in her while she, in turn, had told them they needed to trust each other.

"Between the three of us, I think we have all the pieces," she said.

The problem was, they knew who. They even knew where. What they didn't know was why, and they had little in the way of evidence that would support a search warrant.

Lack of evidence had been the problem from the beginning.

"I say we call Sullivan," Nolan said. "We do this by—"

"Trying to do this by the book is what's had us going in circles. For all we know, there are girls out there who are still alive. We need to find them," Tain said.

"We've got no reason to search the shipping company property," Nolan countered.

Ashlyn returned Tain's gaze for a moment, and neither of them spoke. Nolan leaned back in his chair. "What aren't you telling me?"

"Eddie Campbell has a cabin. It was his mother's. She died almost two years ago."

"But Eddie stayed in town, at the old staff house for the inn. I thought you said that's where the girls had been kept."

Tain leaned forward. "Never for long, and we know they aren't there now. After Ashlyn and I talked this morning, she checked the land registries. Eddie's mother had a large property with some buildings on it. He took possession of the property at the beginning of 2005."

"Just before the first girl disappeared," Ashlyn added.

Nolan didn't meet her gaze. He kept his focus on the table, his face unreadable. After a few minutes he looked up. "Is the property on the Reserve? Don't we need to go through Campbell?"

"We can't. Campbell's been leaking information to the Native leaders about the investigation," Ashlyn said.

"Campbell's the leak? Tell me you aren't confused by the common surname, Hart. Constable Campbell's the wrong color."

"I know they aren't related," she said, fighting to keep the irritation out of her voice. "You were there when I was talking to Eddie at The Goldmine. I know Eddie's Native."

"It was Ashlyn who worked it out, in part because of something she found in your desk," Tain said. "Campbell's financial records. We could tell he was in debt, so he'd be the most obvious member of the team to try to bribe."

Nolan stared at Ashlyn. Whatever questions he had about her searching his desk, he didn't let them distract him from the issue at hand. "Yeah, that's what I'd figured, but I couldn't get any further. I was supposed to investigate the team, but I was also supposed to work the case. We'd never planned on what happened to Winters or the investigation snowballing the way it did."

"I followed up on Ashlyn's hunch," Tain said. "Campbell had a gambling problem. He'd been smart enough to keep it out of town, but he was in deep to some casinos on other Reserves. We think that when they found out he was the liaison officer from Nighthawk Crossing, they found a way he could pay it back."

"That's why he didn't want anyone talking to the Reserve police," Ashlyn said.

"Do you think they were part of it?"

Tain held up a hand. "All we know is, Campbell owed them. There's a serious problem with illegal trade on Reserves."

"And someone from inside the department tipped them off about the raid on Blind Creek Shipping a few months ago," Nolan said. "Campbell had access."

"He wasn't the only one, but he's the one who's got motive."

"And he wasn't too happy when we came up with the tip about truckers. Considering how difficult you were," Nolan nodded at Tain, "Campbell's complaining didn't seem unusual." He was quiet for a moment before he looked at Ashlyn.

"You think they're at the cabin?"

She nodded. Tain pulled a map out of his pocket.

"It's actually not on Reserve land. Not entirely. This little piece here"—Tain pointed—"is, but it's nothing but woods. Over here there's a house, and then out here there are a couple cabins. I asked around, quietly. Mrs. Campbell used to rent the cabins to fishermen in the summer and hunters in the fall. Had quite a business from what I hear, but the land was under dispute. She believed it was all part of the Reserve. When she died, the courts did an assessment and most of her land fell within town limits, so there were a lot of back taxes owing. There was an appeal, but Eddie lost."

"The ruling was made about a month ago," Ashlyn said.

"So they started taking girls out there, thinking it's Native land. When the courts decide it isn't, they appeal, and when they lose we start finding bodies."

"One other thing," Tain said. "The property had a walk-in refrigerator. Part of the services offered to the hunters, I guess. From the scale of this, I'd say there's about a mile between the house and the cabins, and there's another half a mile to the fridge, here." He tapped the paper. "It's partially underground, from what I was told. And a lot of people were pretty surprised Eddie didn't take up the business, because there was a lot of demand."

"If we'd been able to follow up on the leads about the truck stops days ago . . ."

"What's done is done," Ashlyn said. "We need to get out there, and if we call Sullivan, he's going to tell us we don't have enough for a warrant. We don't have anyone saying they saw the girls there, and with the Blind Creek Inn burned to the ground along with the staff house across the street, that's a dead end."

"That was probably the point," Nolan said.

Tain leaned forward, his hands folded in front of him, resting on the table. After a few seconds he looked up at Nolan. "Jenny came to me. She told me everything she knew. If it hadn't been for the leak in our department . . ."

For a moment they were silent. There could still be girls alive, but at the very least, they all knew that if Bobby and Eddie had been stopped months ago, Jenny wouldn't have died.

"She was pregnant. She wanted a second chance." Tain shook his head. "I thought we could give it to her."

Nolan nodded. "I understand that, but if we go out there, we risk any evidence we find being thrown out of court."

Ashlyn shrugged. "Then what if we go out there to

question them? Nobody's talked to Eddie or Bobby about Jenny Johnson, and she was on the payroll for the shipping company where they both work."

"Hoping for exigent circumstances?" Nolan reached for his phone. "First we talk to Sullivan."

Ashlyn slumped back in her chair and looked at Tain, who stared silently back, unreadable. They'd known this was the risk they were taking when they decided to talk to Nolan. Now they'd have to take Sullivan through it all again, and try to persuade him that the risks were worth it.

PART FIVE

PART FIVE

CHAPTER THIRTY-TWO

Despite the unpredictability of driving in the mountains in early spring with the dramatic shifts in weather that could make the roads treacherous, the drive should have been a refreshing change. The long gaps between towns, the trees and mountain peaks interspersed with valleys, the lakes and rivers all should have been a welcome break from the concrete and steel of the Lower Mainland. Cities hemmed you in, ensnared you in a man-made environment that showed off the best and worst of what man could create. Some thought the explanation for mass murderers and the senseless slayings that filled the news each night was too many people pressed in too close together, with no avenue for escape or natural release for the buildup of pressure.

There are cities that never sleep, and within them there were those who can't filter out the hum, unable to quiet the mind.

Tain knew that blaming any perceived rise in violence on urban sprawl was a fallacy. In the distance he could see more mountains. The one that drew his gaze was the one he was convinced they'd found Mary Donard's body on. From this distance, he knew he couldn't be sure if it was the right mountain, but it didn't matter.

All that mattered was that when he'd left Nighthawk Crossing, he'd been happy to put the experience behind him. He'd never planned to go back.

As he looked at the now-familiar roads and countryside as they approached the town he felt his chest tighten. Anyone, anywhere, was capable of the most horrific crimes. This small community that straddled the border between two countries was proof of that.

Beside him, Ashlyn sat in silence. She stared straight ahead with an unwavering gaze. He wasn't buying the calm demeanor, no matter how hard she tried to appear at ease. The coroner had confirmed his suspicions. Newspaper articles found with the body in the woods created a condensed history of their careers, carefully planted clues meant to ensure that even if the bodies had been found by someone else, Craig, Ashlyn and Tain would have been called in at some point, although whoever it was had clearly planned to dispose of the bodies where the three of them were working.

There had been loose ends with the original investigation, because they'd never recovered all of the suspected victims, but there was no doubt in Tain's mind that the guilty weren't running free. The only person they'd harbored doubts about who'd never been tried was Kurdy, and even Tain believed any involvement he had was peripheral, with the exception of Jenny Johnson's murder. Kurdy was a suspected arsonist with a long history of connections to fires, and he worked with Eddie and Bobby, but he was also experienced and arson was one of the hardest crimes to prove.

He'd never been charged.

Tain hadn't mentioned his suspicions about Kurdy to Ashlyn, and he was beginning to regret it. The body in the woods had been left with a neon sign that pointed to Craig, Ashlyn and himself, and Millie had been nothing more than a means to an end.

And that end involved getting their attention.

Who would do that? Why? As hard as he tried to shake the questions from his mind, his thoughts kept going back to Kurdy.

As they drove into town Ashlyn remained silent, but

Tain sensed the tension emanating off of her. She was striving too hard to look controlled, staring straight ahead instead of looking out the windows, trying to pinpoint what had changed and what had stayed the same in the small town they'd worked in months earlier.

Tain stopped in front of the station where they'd first met. "Ash—"

"I'm fine." She undid her seat belt and got out of the car.

He followed her to the front door and they stepped inside. The same beige carpeting lined the halls, the same receptionist sat behind the desk by the entrance, and waved them through without breaking her conversation on the phone.

The station was the way Tain remembered it, until they reached the sergeant's office. Sergeant Winters stood and waved them in.

Winters had never recovered the short-term memory loss he suffered about what had happened right before he'd been attacked, but otherwise he'd been given a clean bill of health after several months of physiotherapy for his injuries. When he'd returned to work they'd put him on desk duty, but he didn't stay there long.

Tim was one of the few officers originally involved in the Missing Killer case who hadn't focused exclusively on community policing. He'd spent time working in the Lower Mainland, had a lot of experience on the street, and hadn't been content to stay stuck in office. First he'd proven himself on the streets, and recently he'd earned a promotion.

"You must be my replacement," Winters said as he extended his hand to Ashlyn.

"Your stand-in, maybe. I was actually partnered with Craig Nolan."

Winters nodded as he waved at the chairs and returned to his own, behind his desk. He picked up a pencil that he twirled in his fingers and leaned back in his chair as he spoke. "Nolan's name lives on around here. Well, all your names still come up from time to time. I never did meet Nolan. Or you"—he gestured at Ashlyn with the pencil—"until now. Heard a few good stories about your current and former partners at each other's throats."

Tain saw Ashlyn glance at him. She hadn't sat back in her chair either. The small talk wasn't something she'd factored on, and he realized now she probably hadn't known it was the same Winters who had been promoted, if she'd even known the name of the new sergeant.

"Well, you might get a chance to meet Nolan for yourself," Tain said. "We believe he's here."

The first shadow crossed Winters's face. "What do you mean, believe?"

"He's been suspended," Ashlyn said. "We think he's heading out to the camp where . . ." Her voice broke, and she didn't try to finish the sentence.

All traces of the easy smile and casual demeanor Winters had displayed since their arrival disappeared. For a few minutes the pencil twirled in his hands, and then he tossed it down on the desk and leaned forward. "I know about Millie." Although he'd never met the girl, the way Winters said her name told Tain that the burden of that case still weighed on him.

"Hey!" A familiar voice cut in from the hall and Tain turned to see Constable Keith, hair a little longer but still blonde, nose piercing gone. "It's good to see you."

Whatever else Keith might have added, she quickly cut off the reunion when she glanced at Winters. As she backed away from the office she said she hoped to see them later.

"When I heard the news, I wondered how long it would take for you two to get up here," Winters said.

"The bosses were arguing over whether to have us work Millie's murder, and they were afraid the press would start pointing fingers," Ashlyn said. "I don't think they wanted us here unless it was absolutely necessary."

Winters nodded.

"And I know Nolan was working the manhunt. Christ, just the thought of Kurdy killing his wife and kids—"

"Wait, what do you mean, Kurdy?" Ashlyn asked.

"You didn't know? Hank Kurtis Jeffers. Otherwise known as Kurdy," Winters said. "I figured that was why they put Nolan on the manhunt."

"Yeager didn't say anything about the connection," Tain said. "And we didn't know."

"Come on. We all get briefings, and something as high profile as the manhunt . . . How could you not know?"

"We were both on leave," Ashlyn said.

"Our first day back we got called out to the Dumpster."

"Look, respectfully, we don't have time for this," Ashlyn said. "If Craig's out there, his life is in danger. Kurdy—"

Winters pointed at her. "I don't care if you think this is a simple courtesy, I'm not letting you run through the woods on a hunch with a loaded gun. Not after what happened last time. When they found that body in the woods, I wondered how long it would be before someone called, before the press started skinning us alive, saying we'd never caught the Missing Killer." He looked at them. "What aren't you telling me? You two may not have known about Kurdy, but Nolan had been assigned to the manhunt. He had to know."

And apparently, he hadn't said anything to anyone, his sergeant included.

"Kurdy wasn't in deep, not like the other two," Tain said. "We believe he was involved in the smuggling. He was known for doing odd jobs on contract, and he probably set the fire that burned Blind Creek Inn to the ground, but Hobbs never talked."

"You're sure he wasn't involved? He would have wanted in," Winters said. "He had a reputation."

"I know. But I think that's why they didn't want him involved. He'd been charged for statutory rape before and gotten a hand slap, but that was before he got married and had kids of his own." Tain paused. "My source said the one time Kurdy got close to those girls, Eddie Campbell went after him. She was pretty sure Kurdy didn't know about it."

"That wasn't what Craig thought, though," Ashlyn said. "He questioned Kurdy's wife during the investigation."

"What? When?" Tain asked.

"That day, the day you and I talked. The day we were off. It was something Craig told me about later. One last loose end he said he wanted to tie off, just to be sure."

Tain thought about that. He'd threatened to talk to Kurdy's wife and Kurdy had been enraged.

That was when Craig had interrupted their conversation. Kurdy had threatened Tain. If he actually knew Craig had followed through . . .

"We have to look for him. We need to find Nolan before Kurdy does."

"We will," Winters said as he got up and shut the door. "Just as soon as you tell me everything."

CHAPTER THIRTY-THREE

Inside, the station had remained much the same as it had been, but outside the station there was one noticeable difference. A semicircle path had been built on the lawn on the far side of the building, where a bench had been placed in front of a fountain.

A fountain of cherubs dancing around a cross, with a simple inscription beneath that read, "For he who sacrificed himself for the nameless."

Ashlyn turned to the bench, which had a single name inscribed on a metal plate against the back.

There was nowhere to escape. She was hundreds of miles from the city in a town where buildings were scattered throughout mountains and countryside, minutes from roads that wound their way through the forests and into the hills, away from homes and people, yet she felt as though it was all pressing in on her, that there was no place she could go where she could breathe.

Or where she could forget.

Months after her original assignment in Nighthawk Crossing and here she was again, waiting on a sergeant who had to consider the fact that they didn't have any physical evidence that justified searching the Campbell property.

The last time, Sullivan had been emphatic. There was no probable cause. They'd have to follow the leads they had and hope to find enough evidence to support a warrant. No shortcuts.

This time, Winters echoed those words. To make matters worse, Campbell was dead, Hobbs in prison. The property had recently been sold, and there wasn't one piece of physical evidence that tied it to the new cases.

Eighteen months earlier, when she'd come to terms with Sullivan's decision and went to see how Tain was handling it, he'd been gone. Unwilling to wait, he'd disregarded a direct order. They'd had no choice then; they had to go out on the pretense of questioning Eddie.

This time, Tain was inside, still pleading his case.

Her phone rang and she answered, half expecting it to be Tain, making sure she was okay.

"Ashlyn, it's Sims." There was a pause. "I did some checking on those addresses you gave me. From the original canvas."

"Oh, yeah, right." She remembered placing the call before they'd left Kelowna, not really expecting anything useful to come of it.

"Most of the residents have been cleared. There's

only two we haven't tracked down. Neighbors say Mrs. Thiessen likes to spend the winter in Arizona, and as far as they know she's still there."

"What about the people you did talk to?"

"Nothing useful. They'd either been out of town or at work." Sims paused. "The thing is, the more people I spoke to, the more interesting it got. Seems every single one of them was at something that was part of their regular schedule. They went skiing in Whistler the same weekend every month, or they always worked that shift on that day. There wasn't one person I spoke to who just happened to be out."

"Interesting." Except it wasn't. She turned from the bench only to be confronted with the fountain, and finally moved so that her back was to both of them. There were enough reminders without looking at permanent memorials. "Well, let me know if you find the last person."

"The last address? It's a rental. A new tenant moved in three months ago by the name of Parker."

It wasn't an uncommon name. No reason to think . . .

"I talked to the owner," Sims said. "His tenant's place of employment is listed as the Port Moody Police Department."

She closed her eyes, felt her body sway and opened her eyes again. "What are you saying, Sims?"

"It's the same Parker."

Lulu could have been telling them the truth, and they'd dismissed her out of hand. She might really have seen Parker, in uniform, moments after he'd disposed of Millie's body.

"Nobody I've talked to has seen him since Millie's body was found in the Dumpster. He didn't even show up in court last week when they dismissed the assault charges against him." His voice trailed off to a whisper. "But I'm sure you knew about that."

They hadn't been able to convict Parker for assaulting her. She wasn't surprised, because she'd never gotten a good look at her attacker.

What she was surprised about was the fact that nobody had told her the case had been dismissed. She looked down. Her hand had instinctively gone to her stomach.

She would have been showing by now.

" . . . I was thinking about heading back out there, canvassing the neighbors again to ask if any of them had seen Parker with a woman matching her description."

"Sounds good." She turned to look at the station. "One other thing. Can you check and see who purchased a property for me?" Ashlyn rattled off the address.

"After the canvas or before?"

"Before, if you don't mind."

"Sure thing."

"And Sims? Call me, okay? I'm just following a hunch."

"Speaking of hunches . . ."

"What is it?"

"Well, I called the prison where Hobbs is. He hasn't had any visitors, except one."

"Let me guess."

"Parker tried to get in to see him a month ago, but Hobbs refused. I'm not sure it means anything . . . After that, Hobbs started sending letters to a Hank Jeffers."

Who'd apparently gone off the deep end and murdered his wife and children and was out there somewhere.

With Craig.

"I did a few searches, dug a little deeper. Jeffers is wanted for the murder of his wife and children."

"I know. The manhunt."

"Thing is, Ash, the eyewitness who fingered Jeffers as the shooter? A vacationing Port Moody police officer who just happened to be in the area."

Parker. What the hell was going on?

"One other thing, Ashlyn. They did a search of

Hobbs's prison cell. He'd received letters from Parker. They're FedExing copies to us."

She thanked him, hung up the phone and took a short-cut across the grass to the parking lot behind the building. When she'd told Tain she wanted to get some fresh air he'd asked her to pick him up a drink. She hadn't done that yet, but she did have the car keys.

He'd have to wait for that drink a little longer.

PART SIX
THE PAST

CHAPTER THIRTY-FOUR

Eighteen months ago

Ashlyn stepped back inside Nolan's cabin. "He's gone."

"What do you mean he's gone?" Sullivan asked.

"I mean . . ." She looked at Nolan and saw his eyes widen. "I think he's gone out there."

There was silence for a moment, broken when Sullivan stood.

"Okay. We're going out there, to question Eddie about Jenny. That's it," Sullivan said.

"You mean, we're going out there to cover Tain's ass."

Sullivan turned to Nolan. "When this is over, I'll deal with Tain myself."

They drove out to the property in silence. A truck was parked at the main house. "Bobby's truck," Sullivan said.

Ashlyn walked up the door and pounded on it. "Mr. Campbell? Mr. Hobbs? It's the police." She lowered her hand. No answer.

She looked at Sullivan, who was scanning the property. Dusk was upon them, and she could make out the shape of shadows that she knew were trees, but soon it would be pitch black. "How far do you think it is to the cabins?"

"Tain said he thought about a mile." Nolan nodded toward a dirty road that cut off through the trees. "That way."

"Okay. Let's look there."

They returned to Nolan's Rodeo. He'd argued it would be the best vehicle to use, assuming the terrain was rough, and it was a good choice. They bumped and jostled as he tried to avoid the potholes on the old road.

"Guess once they stopped renting the cabins out, they really let it go," Sullivan muttered.

Ashlyn sat in the back. For a while, the only sound was the hum of the engine, the occasional spinning of wheels when they failed to find purchase and groan of the axel as the vehicle bounced over the uneven ground.

Her hands were clawing into the seat. Part of her wanted to be the first out so that she could kick Tain's ass herself, but there was a chill in the back of her neck that she couldn't shake, and another part of her prayed that whatever powers there might be that controlled the universe would make sure nothing happened to him.

She should have seen it coming. It had been so hard to persuade Tain to wait when she'd told him what she knew. Damn near impossible to convince him that they needed Nolan, at least, before they could check out the property.

It was too big and too risky, and even she had to admit that Sullivan had been right. They had circumstantial evidence, but nothing that would support a warrant to search the premises.

Nolan's headlights picked up a dark shape, and she leaned forward. "There. Tain's truck."

"It isn't much farther to the cabins," Nolan said. "About a quarter of a mile. Should I—"

Thwap. Ashlyn dove down as Nolan said, "Shit!" The headlights went out as he turned hard to the left.

He'd cut the engine and was yelling at her to call for backup. She pulled out her phone.

No signal.

"Do you have a radio?" she asked him.

"In the back," he barked as he tried to pull Sullivan free from his seat.

Shhhhwap. Another impact, but with something outside, near them. A tree. Ashlyn jumped over the back seats and started sorting through Nolan's gear in the back, hands fumbling in the dark, trying to find the radio.

The rectangular box shape felt familiar in her hands. Not exactly standard issue, but usable nonetheless.

"How is he?" she asked as she switched it on.

"Not good," Craig said as he pulled Sullivan across the driver's seat and out the door.

Glass cracked and shattered, covering Sullivan's legs. Nolan didn't stop pulling, and within seconds he was out of the vehicle.

She wasn't sure their chances would be much better there, and she felt her hands shake as she fumbled with the buttons and started calling for help.

Tain heard a gunshot in the distance. At a guess, it wasn't far from where he'd left his car.

Ashlyn. Shit.

After he'd parked the car, he'd gotten out and backtracked on foot, until he thought he'd gone a safe distance. Anyone who had heard the engine would come straight from the cabins.

They might go through the woods, just to give themselves cover, which was why he'd backtracked and circled around. It was more time-consuming, but it gave him a better chance of getting through without meeting up with unwanted company in the middle of the woods.

Go one way and reach the cabins, maybe put an end to this mess of a case once and for all. Go back and there was no telling what would happen.

A second shot was followed by a third. He cast one last glance in the direction of the cabins, cursed under his breath and turned around.

The closer he got to the sound of the bullets, the slower he moved. He could see through the road, and the thin slice of moon that had emerged through the blanket of clouds gave him enough light to make out the shape of a vehicle not far from where he'd left his own.

Nolan's Rodeo.

He saw the flash from behind the Rodeo and heard the shot. To his right there was the sound of returning fire, and he started to make his way through the trees in that direction.

More shots from the Rodeo, and a cry pierced the air. Whoever was shooting from the woods had been hit.

After that, things got quiet for what felt like a long time. He continued inching forward, looking for some visual clue so he could find the shooter hiding in the woods.

It wasn't until he heard the sirens approaching that a dark shape started running through the trees. He hurried forward and looked to his left, to where he'd first seen the shape move. Another shape, slumped against a tree.

Tain turned on the Maglite he had in his pocket. Eddie Campbell, empty-handed, clutching a gaping wound in his chest.

"Tried . . . tell . . . No . . . body . . . listen."

"Shhh. We're going to get you help, Eddie." He pulled out his cell phone. No signal.

A flash of light caught him in the eye and he raised his hands. "Constable Tain," he said.

The officer relaxed his hold on the gun and turned to look at the figure slumped against the tree. "Looks like a through and through. He needs help," Tain said. "There's another one who took off through the woods that way. I'm going after him."

He turned and started to run, barely aware of the voices that said, "Not alone, you aren't." Tain wasn't sure at what moment he realized Nolan and Hart were with him, but when they reached the edge of the woods and saw the shadow running up the steps into a cabin, the three of them moved instinctively, as though it wasn't their first time chasing an armed suspect on foot through the forest at night.

As soon as he was sure Nolan and Hart were in position, he ran up the stairs and kicked the door down, ducking just in time to avoid the shotgun blast that put a hole in the wall behind him.

PART SEVEN

CHAPTER THIRTY-FIVE

In the aftermath of Eddie Campbell's death and the arrest of Bobby Hobbs, they'd had plenty of time to search the old Campbell property.

In the woods, on the small slip of land that fell on Reserve boundaries, they found the graves. The search had yielded the bodies of five girls from the files. Five girls, ten victims in total.

Craig had spent days scouring the woods with a canine unit, and as his partner, she'd been there through it all. They'd covered every inch of ground.

They'd guessed that Hobbs and Campbell buried bodies when they ran out of room in the freezer, but when they found out that most of the land wasn't under Reserve protection, they'd gotten nervous. The tiny strip of land that did fall outside town boundaries bordered a steep gorge. They'd run out of room for more graves near the ledge, so they'd started dumping bodies in the woods and Dumpsters to make room for more victims in the freezer.

It was a theory, the best explanation they had. The only explanation. Hobbs had never talked, and part of Ashlyn didn't really want to know why they did what they did. Motives sometimes read like a criminal's excuse for unjustifiable acts of horror against other human beings, and there was nothing that could make sense of what Hobbs and Campbell had done.

She remembered one day at the station. They'd been

talking to Summer Young, letting her know about the status of the investigation.

Nolan had apologized. "They're starting with dental records, and if they can't identify the bodies that way, they'll ask you for a blood sample, but it could be some time before we know more."

He'd slumped down in the chair, looking a thousand miles away, skin pale, dark smudges under his eyes.

Tain was already gone by then. Sullivan's death had made it impossible for the RCMP to completely forgive his sins, and he'd been put on desk duty pending a full investigation.

Thinking back, she realized it was only a few hours after that conversation that she'd been reassigned. Whatever questions she didn't have answers for would remain unasked by her. The newspapers continued to speculate, but it all rang hollow, and she stopped reading. Who could grasp why someone would abduct girls, impregnate them, and then murder them and their newborn baby?

A nightmare case complicated by lies, secret agendas and abuse of power. Even Craig had been willing to risk disciplinary action by concealing the whereabouts of his sister when she ran away, a truth Steve had hinted at with his careful answers to her questions. *"What does the file say?"*

His way of answering her question without referencing whatever suspicions he had about Craig's sister should have been a neon warning sign then, but she'd assumed he was being an overprotective big brother.

After all, there were enough arrest records on file to paint Craig's stepfather—his sister's biological dad— in a very bad light. During the weeks she and Craig had spent searching the Campbell property Tucker Collins—Craig's stepfather—had been arrested for assault. It turned out it wasn't the first time he'd faced charges, and he had a history of hitting members of his family.

A few days later Kaitlin's file had been updated and closed.

She'd returned home, and despite Ashlyn's own subtle research, she knew little about what had actually happened to prompt Craig's sister to run away. Had Kaitlin's father hit her, or had it been something worse?

Funny that in his own way, Craig had been running for months.

CHAPTER THIRTY-SIX

The car bumped along the road to the old Campbell property, the wheels occasionally spinning as they sought purchase on the sides of deep, soft potholes.

Part of Ashlyn coaxed the vehicle through each dip in the road, as though sheer willpower could make it navigate the terrain, while the other part asked if she knew what she was doing.

At what point had Craig's opinion become so important to her? Or did she not even realize how she felt until she saw him again, months later?

And now? How did she feel now?

She pushed the doubts to the corner of her thoughts and focused on another question. Where would he be?

There were four options on the property, and arguments could be made for each, although she was ready to dismiss the house. It was the first thing you reached. You had to go past it to get to the cabins, and farther still to reach the walk-in freezer.

That's what they'd done with it. Turned it into a freezer, where they'd had enough room to store some of the girls.

The cabins were an obvious choice, and as brazen as Parker was, she expected more of a game from him.

Which left her with the freezer or the burial ground.

She turned a bend and could see the front of the old house. The roof was sagging, and the porch looked ready to give up. It had probably sat empty through the better part of two winters, hence the wear and tear.

Craig's vehicle was ahead of her, parked on the side of the road. No, not parked. The driver's door was hanging open.

Ashlyn got out of her car, pulled her gun out of its holster and walked toward the Rodeo.

She scanned the road and the edges of the woods. Nothing.

Her fingers tightened on the gun.

The sense of déjà vu as she looked inside Craig's Rodeo, shattered glass shards scattered all over the floor and the bloodstained seats, was overwhelming.

Process of elimination. If Parker had Craig and Craig was wounded, he'd pick the burial grounds. It was closer.

On the ground there were drops of blood, leading to the treed area that led to the burial grounds.

She followed the path. The woods had an eerie stillness to them. Not the kind of midday quiet that might be disrupted by the occasional chirp of birds or scuffle of leaves. It was the kind of quiet where everyone, or everything, holds its breath collectively.

The way her heart hammered in her ears, she was certain Parker could hear her coming. Ashlyn knew it was ridiculous, but she still couldn't shake the feeling.

Tain and Craig had been drawn into this, but the moment she'd heard it was Parker, she knew. He was there for her.

Craig was already out there, injured. Without knowing how long he'd been at the property, how bad his injuries were, it could be worse.

There was no way she could let Tain take the risk she was taking.

She moved slowly, trying to avoid crunching the

leaves and twigs scattered on the ground as she scanned the area in every direction, watching for any sign of movement.

To her right, something caught her attention. A large, dark splotch against a tree.

Ashlyn looked around as she knelt down and reached out with her free hand.

She touched the substance and lifted her fingers to her nose.

Blood.

If Craig had stopped to try to wrap his wound . . .

Or even to catch his breath . . .

She stood and scanned the ground in all directions. The blood trail was gone.

Ashlyn knew she was close to the burial grounds. Through the woods, she could see the small clearing where they'd found the girls. To the right, there were trees and rocks, but she found no sign of blood as she scanned the obvious gaps in the forest.

Craig could be hiding anywhere.

A flicker of movement to her left caught her attention and she spun around, gun ready, but there was nothing there.

Ashlyn took a step forward toward the clearing.

Snap.

She turned, looking for the source of the sound. Something—or someone—not far behind her had cracked a twig, but she couldn't see anything out of the ordinary.

It must have been her imagination.

The rocky outcropping that overlooked the gorge was where Parker sat. It was a ballsy place to be, out in the open, a rifle across his lap.

As though he had nothing to fear.

She crouched down and started inching her way around the woods on the edge of the clearing to get a better view.

Parker looked at his watch. "You know, I would've thought she'd be here by now. Noble guy that you are, I'm sure you'd rather bleed to death alone in the woods."

Silence. If Craig was still alive he wasn't taking the bait.

"You got a real martyr complex, Nolan. Let me tell you something, this guy Hobbs, he had it all worked out."

Ashlyn stopped behind a large tree.

"Women screw men to get what they want. And then they find other ways to screw 'em. The girls Hobbs brought here, they all failed him. All except one."

Ashlyn surveyed the woods to her left. She was running out of places where she could stay covered unless she worked her way to the right. There was a rock a few feet ahead of her, but she needed Parker to keep talking.

To be distracted.

"How'd you feel when you found out your little girl-friend lost the baby?"

Shit. She'd never had a chance to tell Craig . . .

"Or didn't you know?"

The time had never seemed right, not the few times they'd spoken on the phone when she was at work. He'd come back after the failed search for Lisa Harrington, packed a bag and taken a temporary transfer.

And another and another . . .

Parker laughed. "She gets herself pregnant, plans to screw you out of every cent, but she's not even telling you she's havin' your kid."

Nothing but the sound of a soft breeze rustling the trees.

Craig had walked away from their relationship, and for a time her grief had turned to rage, until she believed she hated him, but here she was, standing in the woods, gun in her hand, praying he was okay.

Worrying about how he was coping with what Parker had said.

"See, Hobbs knew the test of loyalty. Millie was the only one who passed." Parker shrugged. "She took it and strangled it herself right after it was born . . . That's why Hobbs let her live. Proof nothing was more important to her than him."

Parker was quiet for a moment. Just long enough to let his words sink in. Ashlyn felt a wave of nausea threaten to topple her, and a spine-chilling cold.

Sometimes, you hear something and know instantly it's true, despite the fact that you don't want to believe it.

"Millie, Millie, Millie. All that guilt. I did her a favor. Put her out of her misery," Parker said. " 'Course, it worked out much better for me that he didn't off Millie. She came in handy.

"So tell me, Nolan, if she really wanted you, why'd you two break up right after she lost the baby?"

Parker tightened his grip on the gun and picked it up. "Better you see her for the bitch she is."

"You think she doesn't care, why d'you think she'd come looking for me?"

The voice was labored and somewhere to Ashlyn's right. She started scanning the trees, looking for anything out of the ordinary.

Parker hopped down from where he sat, his actions revealing the bulk under his coat, and walked toward the trees and rocks on the other side of the clearing, moving slowly, carefully, as he scanned the woods.

Careful enough to wear a bulletproof vest, but too cocky to think of the risks of having a loud conversation in the woods. Too cocky to remember he might not hear her coming if he wasn't listening.

"Appearances. Can't have everyone else seeing what a cold-hearted bitch she really is."

"You . . . don't . . . know."

Ashlyn moved to another tree. Parker turned and for a moment his eyes narrowed as he scanned the woods a little to her left.

She thought she'd slipped up, but it wasn't her direction he was looking in. It was toward the area where she thought she'd heard noises before.

He turned back toward Craig's voice. "I ought to shoot you again, put you out of your misery. Hell, when I beat that bitch and she miscarried, I did you a favor. You should be thanking me."

Silence.

"No offense, Nolan, but I was kind of glad I didn't kill you in the woods before. It was risky sneaking out there to leave the body. But I had to make sure you got involved.

"I didn't even realize it was you I was shooting at until I heard it at the bar later. Went to all the work of tracking down those remains and planting the clues for nothing. Told ya, Millie was good for some things."

Parker looked at his watch. "You aren't provin' as useful as I thought you would, though."

"Sorry . . . let ya down."

"Sure you are. Don't worry, Nolan. She'll come. And this time, there might be better ways to show your old girlfriend who's boss before I deal with her, once and for all."

Something between a roar and a scream came from the woods, and the sound of movement. Ashlyn started to move out from behind the tree, but she felt something grab her from behind. She'd never had a lot of direct contact with Kurdy during the investigation, but in the aftermath he'd been brought in for questioning, and she'd seen him at the station. He'd cleaned up since then, hair a respectable length, clothes with a tidiness that defied the fact that he'd been on the run since allegedly murdering his wife and children.

He had a shotgun in his hand.

"Sorry," he whispered as he raised his gun and swung it down against her head. She staggered backward as the dots of color obscuring her vision grew until they

overlapped and blurred together before everything
went black.

CHAPTER THIRTY-SEVEN

She'd been gone too long.

The first three times he'd thought that, Tain had told
himself to relax, that she'd only been gone for a few minutes. Then it was ten minutes. Then fifteen.

Now, half an hour later, he couldn't wait any longer.
He marched down the hall to the back entrance and
pushed the door open.

The car was gone.

He turned and walked back down the hall, fighting
the urge to break into a run. His cell phone rang.

"Ashlyn—"

"Uh . . . sorry, Tain. It's Sims."

"What do you want?"

"Look, Constable Hart asked me to follow up on something—"

"I know. The second canvas."

"No, since then. I already told her about that. She
wanted me to check on who'd recently purchased a
property in Nighthawk Crossing."

Tain stopped walking and started listening to what
Sims was saying.

"—same Parker who rents the apartment near the
crime scene bought it."

"Wait, Sims. Is this the same Parker—"

"Used to be with the Port Moody police. I told Ash,
uh, Constable Hart that when I called before."

"How long since you called, Sims?"

"Forty, forty-five minutes."

Tain closed his eyes. "So why'd you call me this time, instead of Ashlyn?"

"I tried to call her, but I keep getting a message saying that the cellular customer is out of the service area."

Tain closed his phone without another word and ran into Winters's office. "She's gone out there."

Winters looked up. "You're sure?"

"Positive. The guy who bought Campbell's old property is a former cop with a grudge against us. Her. He was charged with assaulting Ashlyn a few months ago, but they didn't have enough to get a conviction."

"Christ, Tain, I thought you were the loose cannon," Winters said as he grabbed his coat. "We're not making the same mistakes again."

"Too late for that."

"What I mean is, we all get Kevlars, and we take enough backup."

Tain looked at the nameplate outside the sergeant's office and thought of the one that used to be there. Thought of the man who'd paid the price for his impulsiveness and nodded.

He'd take the risk for his partner, but it wasn't something he could ask of anyone else.

CHAPTER THIRTY-EIGHT

The return to consciousness was accompanied by a throbbing pain in her head. It screamed as she tried to open her eyes, and she lifted her fingers to her temple.

A goose egg was already growing where she'd been struck. And there was dampness, blood from the gash.

Ashlyn forced her eyes open. The dark blotches morphed into recognizable forms, and she realized she was on the ground, where she'd been standing when struck, looking up at the trees.

She sat up. Her gun lay in the dead leaves beside her. She grabbed it as she forced herself to her feet.

Why?

The last few moments before the blackness were hazy, but starting to come back.

Parker's taunting.

Craig taking the bait.

Kurdy . . .

Why hit her and leave her?

Why not kill her?

Why not take her to Parker?

She stood for a moment. There was nothing but an eerie silence. She took a step forward, swayed and reached out with her hand.

There was a body lying in the clearing and another on the ground not far away. Ashlyn staggered back as she processed what she was seeing. The stillness, the pool of blood oozing out over the ground . . .

It was too late for him. She forced herself forward, and when she stood over Parker she could see his blank eyes stared up at nothing.

Dead. No question, but she still kicked the gun away and bent down to check that he had no pulse. That was when she saw the other gun. Set on a rock.

The gun that had been in Kurdy's hands.

A faint moan from the other body to her left broke the silence. She knelt beside Craig and pulled his hand back from the wound, then gently unwrapped the shirt he'd tied around it and kept her focus on his injuries. It took less than a moment for her to rewrap the wound.

It wasn't until he lifted his hand again and touched her arm that she met his gaze.

It was one of those moments when no words were necessary.

She pulled out her cell phone and fumbled with it until she got it open. No service. As she flipped it shut, she looked up at him and fought the urge to reach for her forehead. The shooting pain mercifully settled to a dull ache. "Can you walk? We need—"

"Ash. . . ."

"Shhh. Save your strength," she said, vaguely aware of the sounds of footsteps in the forest. Someone shouted, "Over here," while someone else called in on a radio for an ambulance, and then she felt a presence behind her.

"What the hell happened?" Winters asked.

Tain knelt on the ground beside her.

"Kur—" Ashlyn turned, the dull ache turning to a roar again with the sudden movement. The clearing was empty. "Kurdy shot Parker."

"What?" Tain asked. "Why?"

Why. The question always asked.

The one they seldom could answer.

"How is he?" Tain asked.

She swallowed. "Clean shot through and through, but he's lost a lot of blood."

Craig lifted his bloody hand back up and put it over hers. For the first time since before her assault she looked him in the eyes and saw the ghost of a smile before his eyes flickered and closed.

In the aftermath of a police-involved shooting, there are a lot of questions to answer, and a lot of time is spent on paperwork and procedure, crossing every *t*, dotting every *i*. When the victim is a police officer who's been suspended everything triples.

At least, that's how it felt to Ashlyn. She'd been through it before, after she shot and killed Craig's partner.

This time, she had a weapon in her possession that she claimed she hadn't fired—gunshot residue tests had supported her claims, but that wasn't conclusive proof, and although none of her fingerprints were found on the gun, that was only more circumstantial evidence.

Emma Fenton had her exclusive and was only too happy to raise questions about Ashlyn's actions and whether she was responsible for Parker's death, but what was undeniable was the set of footprints found at the scene. Footprints that didn't match hers, Craig's or Parker's.

And the skin and blood they found on the butt of the shotgun. Skin and blood that matched Ashlyn's.

When the tests were completed, another unexpected detail emerged: the bullet that had torn through Craig's shoulder and lodged itself in his Rodeo had been fired from the same gun that had been used to kill Hank Jeffers's wife and children. Whatever Parker's game, he'd used Kurdy. Maybe to try to get them involved, maybe to draw them back to Nighthawk Crossing. Kurdy had been innocent of the crime he'd originally been suspected of, but that didn't change the fact that he'd killed Parker, and whatever he knew about the case would remain unknown until the day the police caught up with him.

Ashlyn was pretty sure it wouldn't be anytime soon.

Tain and Ashlyn walked toward the hospital doors.

"Everything okay?" Tain asked.

She knew he was wondering how she felt about going to visit Craig, but she avoided the subject. "That depends. Are you going to quit?"

"You know me too well."

"I think after what happened to your daughter, you thought being a cop would help you make sense of it all. That you'd be there to save other children from Noelle's fate. When we stood over that little boy's body last year, you looked down at Jeffrey Reimer and realized you couldn't save them. All you could do was deal with the fallout after it was already too late."

He didn't respond. He didn't have to.

"You know, Parker's mistake was that he thought you'd want an explanation. He didn't just want to win. He wanted you to know he'd won," Tain said as he opened the door to the hospital.

"Sometimes, we don't get answers, Tain," she said as she stepped inside. She turned around to face him. "Sometimes all we do is clean up a big mess."

He let the door fall shut behind him. "You're okay with that? What if we'd known the truth about Millie eighteen months ago?"

Eighteen months ago, when Tain had broken through the front door of the cabin, he'd ducked just in time to avoid having a shotgun blast rip his head apart. In the seconds it took for Bobby Hobbs to realize he'd missed, Tain had lunged forward and knocked Hobbs back onto the floor. Bobby had lost his grip on the shotgun, which had gone spinning across the floor toward the back door, which Ashlyn had just entered. Craig had been right behind her.

Tain had his hand wrapped around Hobbs's throat, and she pried him off the suspect. It wasn't until she'd pushed him back and Craig had cuffed Hobbs and removed him from the cabin that Ashlyn had looked up, still catching her breath, to see the petite blonde girl in the corner of the room, wearing an old-fashioned white nightgown.

"Millie? Millie Harper?"

Ashlyn had reached out toward her, but the girl slid down into the corner of the room, eyes wide with fright, hands rising to cover her face.

"It's okay, Millie. He'll never hurt you again. We've got you. You're going to be okay now."

"Please." The girl looked up, tears streaming down her face. "Please. Please let me die."

Millie had been put on a psych hold hours later, when she grabbed a pair of scissors and tried to stab herself in the chest.

It made sense. After what she'd been through, Millie would struggle with guilt, would wrestle with why she'd been rescued and the other girls had died.

Ashlyn had assumed Millie never got pregnant, which was why she'd survived. It had never occurred to her that Millie had murdered her baby, a sacrifice to prove her devotion to an abductor who believed the only way she could truly prove her worth was to give up the most important thing in the world.

Her own child.

Parker had learned her secret and exploited her vulnerability. The sacrifice Millie had made to save her own life had ultimately destroyed it.

Ashlyn was torn between the guilt she felt over Millie's death and the disgust she felt over what Millie had done. She knew she shouldn't blame Millie; the girl had been abducted, raped and held captive for months, but that didn't change the fact that every time Ashlyn thought about Millie murdering her own child she felt the rage boil up inside her, and when it passed she was left with nothing but her own emptiness.

She stopped outside Craig's hospital room.

"When Noelle's mother killed her, how'd you learn to forgive her?" she asked.

Tain pushed the door open and started to walk inside.

"Who says I have?"

"Ruttan has a spellbinding style."
—CLIVE CUSSLER

SANDRA RUTTAN

One year ago, a brutal case almost destroyed three cops. Since then they've lost touch with one another, avoiding painful memories, content to go their own ways. Now Nolan is after a serial rapist. Hart is working on a string of arsons. And Tain has been assigned a series of child abductions, a case all too similar to that one. But when the body of one of the abduction victims is found at the site of one of the arsons, it starts to look like maybe these cases are connected after all....

WHAT BURNS WITHIN

ISBN 13: 978-0-8439-6074-7

To order a book or to request a catalog call:
1-800-481-9191
This book is also available at your local bookstore, or you can check out our Web site www.dorchesterpub.com where you can look up your favorite authors, read excerpts, or glance at our discussion forum to see what people have to say about your favorite books.

SANDRA
RUTTAN

The police get the call: A four-year-old boy has been found beaten to death in the park. And almost as soon as Hart and Tain arrive at the scene, the case takes a strange turn.

They find the victim's brother hiding in the woods nearby. He says he saw the whole thing and claims his older sister is the killer. And she's missing....

When the boy's father is notified that his son is dead, his first response is to hire a high-powered attorney, who seems determined to create every legal roadblock he can for Hart and Tain. The search is on for the missing girl, and the case is about to get even stranger.

THE
FRAILTY
OF FLESH

ISBN 13: 978-0-8439-6075-4

To order a book or to request a catalog call:
1-800-481-9191
This book is also available at your local bookstore, or you can check out our Web site **www.dorchesterpub.com** where you can look up your favorite authors, read excerpts, or glance at our discussion forum to see what people have to say about your favorite books.

STOLEN
SEDUCTION

*The individual who collects all six statues and
deciphers the code locked within will be awarded
controlling interest in Roarke Resorts.*

YOUR PARTICIPATION IN THIS ENDEAVOR IS A
MATTER OF LIFE AND DEATH.

Hailey Roarke was never interested in her family's fortune.
That's why she became a cop. But with her father and now her
cousin dead, she's suddenly on the wrong side of a police inter-
rogation. The only way to clear her name is to solve the riddle
before the real killer. Without getting killed herself.

Detective Shane Maxwell can't deny the spark of lust he feels
every time Hailey is near. But the woman is clearly hiding
something. Trusting his gut — and the heat in her eyes — he
joins her on an elaborate global treasure hunt staged by her
late father. Caught between a sizzling seduction and a maniacal
murderer, for Hailey and Shane the biggest reward of all will
be making it out alive.

ELISABETH
NAUGHTON

ISBN 13: 978-0-505-52795-0

To order a book or to request a catalog call:
1-800-481-9191
Our books are also available at your local bookstore, or you
can check out our Web site **www.dorchesterpub.com**
where you can look up your favorite authors, read excerpts,
glance at our discussion forum, and check out our digital
content. Many of our books are now available as e-books!

☐ **YES!**

Sign me up for the Leisure Thriller Book Club and send my FREE BOOKS! If I choose to stay in the club, I will pay only $4.25* each month, a savings of $3.74!

NAME: _____

ADDRESS: _____

TELEPHONE: _____

EMAIL: _____

☐ I want to pay by credit card.

☐ **VISA**   ☐ **MasterCard**   ☐ **DISCOVER**

ACCOUNT #: _____

EXPIRATION DATE: _____

SIGNATURE: _____

Mail this page along with $2.00 shipping and handling to:
Leisure Thriller Book Club
PO Box 6640
Wayne, PA 19087
Or fax (must include credit card information) to:
610-995-9274

You can also sign up online at **www.dorchesterpub.com**.
*Plus $2.00 for shipping. Offer open to residents of the U.S. and Canada only.
Canadian residents please call 1-800-481-9191 for pricing information.
If under 18, a parent or guardian must sign. Terms, prices and conditions subject to
change. Subscription subject to acceptance. Dorchester Publishing reserves the right
to reject any order or cancel any subscription.

GET FREE BOOKS!

You can have the best fiction delivered to your door for less than what you'd pay in a bookstore or online. Sign up for one of our book clubs today, and we'll send you *FREE* BOOKS* just for trying it out...**with no obligation to buy, ever!**

If you love fast-paced page turners, you won't want to miss any of the books in Leisure's thriller line. Filled with gripping tension and edge-of-your-seat excitement, these titles feature everything from psychological suspense to legal thrillers to police procedurals and more!

As a book club member you also receive the following special benefits:

- **30% off all orders!**
- **Exclusive access to special discounts!**
- **Convenient home delivery and 10 days to return any books you don't want to keep.**

Visit **www.dorchesterpub.com** or call **1-800-481-9191**

There is no minimum number of books to buy, and you may cancel membership at any time.
*Please include $2.00 for shipping and handling.